Jennifer V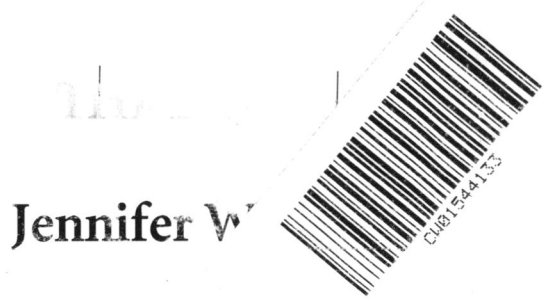

Suffolk Libraries	
ama2	08\18

30127085080559

About *The Liar*

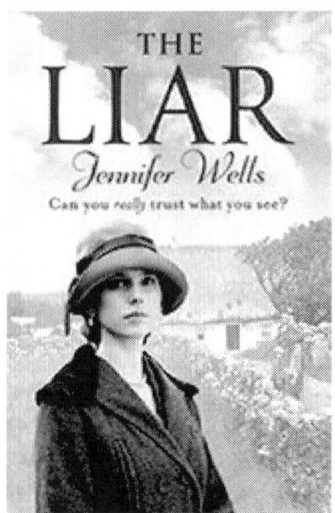

What would you do if you saw a girl in a crowd whose face had the same, identical birthmark as your only child? A child who, nearly ten years ago, you were told died?

It's 1935 and housewife Emma glimpses a face in a crowd – a little girl with a very unique birthmark.

Transfixed by the sight of a stranger; Emma becomes convinced that the girl is her long-lost daughter taken from her at birth.

There is only one problem: Emma's daughter is dead. So who is the stranger?

The Liar follows Emma's journey as she tries to find out what really happened to her daughter - a journey that unearths secrets from the past and ends in obsession...

For my family

Prologue

Emma: 1935

My name is Emma Marks and my life had been ordinary until the day I saw a girl at the lido. From then on everything changed, and the girl became my obsession.

It was on a hot day in August that I saw her. It had been nine years since we parted but I knew at once that the girl was Violet, my daughter. She had grown of course, so much that I would not have given her a second glance if it had not been for her face – her cheek stained with a birthmark like a rain of red tears. I had longed for her every day that we had been apart but, now that I saw her, I could not be happy.

How could this little girl be Violet, when I knew that my daughter was dead?

Nine years ago Violet had died. She was a baby, frail and ailing, but a fragile beauty, her cheek marked with red tears. Violet had never known a mother's warmth, only the dry heat of the incubator. She had touched only the coarse hospital linen, smelled only disinfectant and saw only the glare of the delivery room lamps.

She never had toys or gifts, merely a single sprig of violets from a well-wisher – intended for celebration or mourning, I did not know. Back in those days some people said that violets brought bad luck when they were taken indoors but, deep down, I knew that Violet's death could not be blamed on bad luck. Even from her conception, Violet had been caught up in my deceit – a string of lies and excuses to conceal the shame of her creation. I had brought this upon her. I had never deserved her.

I had returned home without her, back to my life as a dutiful doctor's wife in Missensham; a town where the Metropolitan Line trains glimpsed daylight through the leafy cuttings and brambles grew between the tracks. It was a place with a village green, a park, playing fields and a lido; the type of place where my husband and I could have given a child a perfect life, even if our own was not. Our house, Little Willow, was modern and warm, but its large garden would forever be empty of balls and skipping ropes. There was a nursery too, but the door remained closed.

Everything had been ready, everything had been waiting for Violet and, on that hot day in 1935, I was sure that she had returned to claim it. The girl I had seen at the lido was Violet. She was not dead, and right then I knew that I would do anything to bring her home.

Ruby

My name is Ruby Brown and my life had been ordinary until the day that I turned nine years old – a day meant for fond memories but one that I wish I could forget.

It had happened some time after my birthday celebration; a lunch of bread and butter, a card signed only with clumsy initials and a gift of a new polka-dot dress wrapped in brown paper and string. My brothers wore party hats made from old newspaper and there had been flowers too – a handful of violets that I had picked from the copse. Back then country people always said that violets brought bad luck if they were taken indoors, but it was my birthday and the petals had been so bright that, just that once, nobody had minded.

Maudy apologized for the lack of cake – she wished that she could have done more for the birthday of her only daughter but things would soon pick up, she said with a wink. Our home, Rose Cottage, was near to farms where my brothers could find work and only a short walk to the town of Missensham, where the new housing estates and smartly dressed people showed little concern for the Depression. Things were looking up for the Browns, she said, and I started to believe her and forgot about the cake.

But then Clarence had come home.

Things changed after that. The party was over, the jokes and the laughter stopped and Maudy turned to scolding us, urging silence out of respect for our father. As the clock chimed, the boys left for the orchards. I wanted to go too but Clarence put his arm across the doorway and stopped me.

That was when the Bad Thing happened.

When I woke, I saw the violets on the table again, their petals caught in the blur of light from the window. I saw the hardening crusts of buttered bread and the crumpled newspaper that had wrapped the dress. I saw a broken hinge on the stove and a gin bottle empty on the draining board.

From that day onwards I knew that Rose Cottage could never feel like home and I started to see Clarence everywhere – from the print of his boots in the dusty floor, to the dent worn in his chair. I could smell his ale and tobacco in every gust from the window and see his handprint on the door which could not keep him out. From that day, I always fancied that I could see a bunch of violets on the table, even though I knew there were none. Now I believed what people said about violets because I had known the bad luck that they bring.

1

Emma

Sometimes I wonder what would have happened if I had never seen her – the little girl with the birthmark on her face. I can recall her so clearly, standing by the pavilion in that spotted summer dress, her limbs striped by sunlight through the railings. Even after so much time has passed, I find that I can bring little details to mind – the dust on her shoes and the ribbon in her hair, the sugar cone in her hand and the beads of ice cream on her chin. But these are not the memories that come to me when I daydream or when I close my eyes to sleep. No, when my mind starts to wander, my memories of the girl are altered and I don't see any of this; I remember the droop in her smile as she saw me and the flinch of her muscle as I approached. I remember the jut of her collarbone as my hands tightened round her shoulders and the warp of my reflection in her pupils. I remember the shudder of her breath and the hiss of the scream caught in her throat. I remember her fear. I remember my love. She had returned and she would be mine again…

*

Until I saw her it had been a normal day, like any other Sunday that August. The summer of 1935 had been a hot one, the blue dome of cloudless sky offering no defence from a relentless sun. Back then, summers in the suburbs had a particular smell – an acrid stew of bitumen from the new roads, wilted stinging nettles and dog muck baking on the pavements. The heat had drawn people out of their houses and on to the streets. They came from the farms, the old town centre and the new housing estates, their bodies merging in the shimmer of air over tarmac as they jostled in the queue for the lido.

I had intended to stay at home, at Little Willow. I'm no good with crowds and I had plans for the garden; some gentle weeding round the pansies and a good lemonade to cool me down. Everything that was acceptable for a married lady to do. But that was all before Audrey arrived.

The doorbell rang as I was kneeling over the flowerbed but I pretended not to hear and lingered in the pantry as George answered.

There was a creak from the door and then a shriek: 'Doctor Marks!' Audrey always treated a visit to her neighbours with as much excitement as a chance encounter with long-lost relatives. I shrank back into the darkness of the pantry. Audrey and I had been friends once. But that was before… well, that was before everything.

'We can't have her indoors and miserable on a day like this!' cried Audrey.

Then came the mumble of George's voice. I imagined him stood in the hallway, one hand resting on the doorframe, his thin body stooped slightly, as he did when his back started to aggravate him. His starched collar would be hanging open, sweat sealing the shirt to his back and his balding scalp shiny with perspiration. Maybe he would send her away; I wouldn't stop him.

But Audrey called out: 'Emma! Emma!' And I had to step into the hallway in my gardening apron.

'Audrey. What a surprise.'

Audrey burst into the hallway, pushing a large black pram like a battering ram. She was a tall woman and upright, the kind who takes to motherhood like a strong, sturdy animal. Her features were too large to be pretty but she seemed oblivious to this, always dressing in the latest fashions, today a bright yellow skirt and jacket and a matching hat with a pleat on top that bellowed like a concertina when she moved. I felt small next to her, faded and grey. She fussed under the hood of the pram, trying to silence the grizzling baby with rattles and teddies, and glanced up for only a second to shoot me a polite smile, the season's red smeared on her lips like a life ring. Her three-year-old twins, Alan and Ethel, chased round the doormat, buckets and spades wielded like swords. And then, despite my protest and with little more than a goodbye nod to George, she grabbed my hat and bag from the stand and pulled me out of the door.

'It will do you good to get out,' said Audrey as she wheeled the pram down the driveway, gravel spitting from the wheels. 'You never go out these days, not since, well anyway, you know… well you just don't.' She span the pram in a wide circle, narrowly missing the shiny red paintwork on our newly washed Austin 12, and hurled herself into the throng of people on the pavement, a group of schoolboys stumbling off the curb to avoid being mangled by the pram's huge wheels. 'Oh no! buggering heel strap's gone.'

We crossed into the road and stood by the war memorial that marked the crossroads. I looked away, embarrassed, as Audrey leant her shoulder on the plinth and tightened the strap on her shoe. Back in those days, everybody respected the memorial but it did not just commemorate the fallen, it was the place where town met country and old met new – concrete and houses on one side of the road and the trees of the old orchard on the other. That day the stone cross was a meeting place for people, bringing them together from all directions to join the crowds that thronged to the lido. There were the well-to-do families who had not travelled far from the Sunningdale Estate, city dwellers hot from their walk from the Tube station and labourers coming from the dirt track that led up to the farms.

I pulled Alan away from a dirty-looking dog and kicked away a fallen apple that Ethel was grasping at. 'I'm not a recluse, Audrey,' I said, tightening my grip on Alan's hand, but my voice was caught up in the rumble of the pram wheels.

'Anyway,' she continued, 'it does one no good to be stuck indoors alone all day.'

I was about to point out that I had George so was not alone, but then realized that there was no point – I would have convinced neither her nor myself. Besides, I knew that Audrey's invitation was probably a last resort. Her other friends had their own families, yet she knew I would be free and easily bullied into watching Alan and Ethel as she basked in the sun.

The lido's lawns were packed with sunbathers; swimsuited walruses beached on the grass, their folds of white flesh turning an angry pink. Children dodged and weaved through the legs of chattering parents and a wet dog showered picnickers with droplets. We forced our way through the crowds on to a grassy bank overlooking the swimming pool. Most of the spaces were taken, but Audrey insisted that we could squeeze ourselves in.

'You just watch,' she said loudly, 'these city dwellers just aren't as fortunate as us Missensham residents. Just as soon as the two o'clock bus shows up they'll have to be home for dinner. There's not many buses on a Sunday and they won't want to wait until four. The place will be emptied, and then we will have plenty of room.'

People looked at us crossly as Audrey ploughed the pram through picnic blankets and towels. Oblivious to the stares, she shunted the wheels back and forth, the sunbathers grumbling as they shuffled to get out of the way. When she had cleared a large area, she wriggled out of her clothes, bumping her rump in the air to release her skirt. Underneath was a red swimsuit, striking against the dazzle of her white skin. The yellow concertina hat stayed firmly on her head – consciously, I thought, as if she was posing for a photograph in a magazine.

I lay back and tried to relax while Audrey screeched at the twins: 'No Alan, please, Darling, that's no way to behave… Oh Ethel… Don't do… oh no. Little bleeders!' Then she was up and fussing under the hood of the pram.

I turned my head to the pool and shielded my eyes, pretending to watch over the children as was expected of a loyal friend, but I soon found that my eyes were wandering. On the opposite bank a row of uniformed girls were on lunch break from the bus depot, their rigid hats and shoes discarded on the grass. One had taken her blouse off and was sunbathing in her slip and petticoat. An old couple lay hunched on their sides, the woman snoring gently and a child on a tricycle was cutting dusty rings into the grass. A girl sat on the edge of the pool, small breasts budding under the weave of her orange costume, her hair cascading over her face as she leaned forward to wave at two gangly youths. The boys swam over but she waited until they were close then kicked up her legs, spraying them with water.

The boys reminded me of the children from my old school, back when I had been the bathing beauty. We had gone on church picnics in Evesbridge and then there was a party at the end of the war, but those boys were dead now, dead or married, but either way they were gone. It all seemed like such a long time ago. I put my hand to my face, conscious of the heat of the sun. I had no wrinkles yet but my skin was slacker than it once was, a slither of fat under my jaw threatening a double chin and a couple of grey wisps in my hair. My youth had been kind, but it fades so quickly on the fair-skinned. And then, of course, there were the scars.

The orange-costumed girl stretched out on the bank, unaware a muscly youth was squatting beside her. She flinched when he pressed a cold bottle of lemonade onto her thigh but then laughed and lay back with him, holding hands as if permanently bound.

Suddenly my mind was wandering. A vague memory of when I had lain like this in the sun, many years ago. I remembered my skin stroked by a man, a gentle hand on my thigh, his fingers moving under my skirt. I was shocked at the memory and how easily it had returned. How long ago that day had been! But, in the daze of the heat, the days seemed to blend into one and I let myself dream, once more seeing my lover's face over me and once more feeling my body sink into the grass under the weight of his. I let the memory linger a little, my face warming, and my breaths becoming longer. Then I remembered how it had felt to open my eyes and see the violets in the hedgerows as our bodies moved together.

'You don't want to listen to George!' said Audrey suddenly. I lifted my head, shielding my face from the glare of the sun. Audrey's eyes were darting back and forth as Alan and Ethel ran along the poolside. 'I don't care about all that medical training. He's an old man now, just remember that – he's got fifteen years on you. He was born in Victorian times,' she continued, unaware that she had shattered my daydream, 'and that's where he should have stayed – the world has moved on. One just has to embrace the modern world. Embrace all things *la moderne*. But no, nothing for George that might sound a bit foreign. Heaven forbid, continental!'

In front of us, an old man shuffled in his deckchair, a tight vest straining round his belly. He coughed and took a knotted handkerchief from his head, wiping his nose with the yellowed cotton.

'Of course, there weren't any Missenshams back then,' continued Audrey, 'let alone any Sunningdale Estates, just a few run-down farms, but now look! Compared to how things were in George's day, this is paradise.' She swept her hand in a wide arc. As if it needed no more explanation; the paradise would speak for itself. The old man looked into the handkerchief and then replaced it on his head, patting it down so that the wetness hugged his scalp. He folded his thick arms and began snoring. On the other side of the pool a dog was flicking sods of lawn in the air with its back legs.

I nodded. 'Paradise.'

'Oh Emma, you should embrace it. She stopped to look me up and down. 'You do know that suntans have been fashionable for a good ten years now?' She laughed. 'Do you even own a bathing suit?'

'I'm fine,' I said, laying my hand protectively across my belly. 'Honestly, I'm fine.'

'Emma, really, at least brush the hair out of your eyes, get some sun on your face. You know that it's really not good to—'

'Look,' I said, standing up quickly, 'this heat is getting a bit much for me, how about I go to the pavilion and get us all ice creams?' That shut her up. Even though I had to buy her silence, and push my way through the crowds in front of the pavilion, just to get a moment away from her, it had to be worth the effort.

The pavilion was dark and cool inside, the chrome counter cold to the touch. I paid the money and stood in the doorway, four ice cream cones bunched in my hands like a bouquet. I tried to savour the last moments of shade, watching the reflections from the swimming pool dappling the whitewash.

It was then that I saw her – the little girl in a spotted dress. She stood in front of the swimming pool, her back to the railings, her mouth clamped round a dripping cone, trails of ice cream beading her dress. Her face was pale, an angry birthmark flaring red on her cheek and suddenly there was her and nothing but her as the world around her span away into a whirl of light and sound. She looked right at me, and I realized that I was stood, staring, molten ice cream cascading down my hands.

'Violet?' I whispered, the word catching in my throat. 'Violet!'

The girl started and her eyes widened. She looked round desperately and then started to back away.

I ran forward, the ice creams exploding on the concrete, and grabbed her shoulders. 'Thank you, God, thank you!'

The girl stared at me, shocked into stillness, our eyes locked together for the briefest moment, but it was a moment that connected us, a moment that told me that I had found her and the shock of seeing her faded as I became giddy with joy. But then she twisted her shoulders and ducked away, running along the pavement and into the crowd. I followed frantically. She was small and fast, slipping through the crowd like a knife as I barged and stumbled after her. An old woman tutted and put out her elbow and some youths whistled but my eyes were fixed on the girl – a little spotted dress flashing in and out of the crowd.

'Please... please let me through,' I gasped, but people were pushing all around me, the jostle of flesh getting tighter and tighter until I couldn't breathe.

At last I wrestled my way out of the crowd and fell onto the grass. There were a few cries of 'oh!' and a hand patting my back. Then concerned faces loomed and hands were offered but I batted them away, springing up to look over the heads in the crowd.

'The girl...' I wheezed. 'The girl in the spotted dress, with the birthmark?' But heads were shaken. Then I glimpsed a flash of polka dots and I was running again, hurtling past the pool and the sunbathers.

Audrey stared at me in astonishment – 'Emma what are you...' but she was just another face sailing past me as I ran.

Then came the blast of a horn from the road. Through the railings, I could see a bus pulling up to the stop and the girl swerved and disappeared into the throng of people heading towards the exit. The church bell chimed two. I was caught in the crush at the turnstile, faces closing in and bodies pushing all around me.

'Please, please. I have to—' but the mass of bodies did not move and I had to step back on to the grass, my chest heaving. I watched through the railings as the bus slowed, easing its way through the crowd on the road.

Then she appeared on the pavement looking around her wildly; she had found her escape and I was left trapped behind the iron bars, I ran back and forth as I tried to catch a glimpse of her face. 'Violet! Violet!' but she was gone again, my cries were swept up by the chatter of passengers pushing their way onto the bus. The conductor rang the bell and the engine clattered as the bus started to pull away. I clutched the railings, pressing my forehead into the metal as I searched for her face. There were still a lot of people left on the pavement, some waved fists at the conductor's shrugged shoulders, but the bus was already crammed with people hanging off the back deck or standing on the stairs. Bodies were jammed three to a seat and squeezed upright in the aisles.

Then I saw her face again. She was looking down from the top deck, the cheek with the birthmark pressed against the window and I was left standing helpless as the bus sped away down the road.

2

That was only the second time I had ever seen Violet. The first time had been nine years previously in the spring of 1926.

And there's not much more to say really. Of course, they did tell me not to talk about it, said that it would be bad for my nerves if I did. Let's be British about it and not get all sentimental, as George would say. Sentimentality was counterproductive and only for the feeble-minded and silly women. After all, having fought in the Great War, his generation had been through far worse and, as he liked to remind me, a stiff upper lip was the best way to get through these things. The thing is, I have to agree with him because, when all is said and done, it was a terribly brief meeting and I don't remember very much of it, only the odd snippet that I can bring to mind.

The location of the meeting is something that I do remember very well. It was a small sterile room in Oxworth General Hospital. The floor and walls were scrubbed a glaring white, electric globes of light mirrored in steel and glass, an unpleasant scour of carbolic in one's nostrils and the electrical hum of the incubator.

In 1926 the incubator was a new addition to the hospital. There had been a big to-do in the *Missensham Herald* about it; I remember that much. As a doctor seconded to the maternity ward and a prominent member of the hospital committee, George even had his picture on page seven, stood with a group of medical staff around the shiny new arrival. George had said that the contraption was particularly advanced for being electric. And I can remember thinking that he was right; it did look modern, but only because it was so clean and shiny. To me it looked more like a kitchen implement than something to nurture a baby, like something one would use to steam a ham, although I would not dare tell him this.

George had been on the ward when I had telephoned with crippling pain and blood loss. He had been at the birth, both as a doctor and a father, but neither of these obligations had endured after he saw Violet and, following the birth, he had swiftly left for other duties. No – when I met Violet, it was just her and me and, oh yes, a midwife – a moon-faced middle-aged woman. And I recall that she had her cape on, odd for indoors, I thought. Yes, I can see it now, for she must have been about to leave because she had her bag in her hand and was tapping her foot impatiently as she leant over the incubator, placing a small posy of blooms beside the steel box.

Of course Violet was just a baby back then – a newborn, though some might not even call her that - I'm not sure exactly how old, for she had been born five weeks before she was expected in this world; a terrible accident of nature which put her in that metal box. Forgive me but, as I said, I really don't remember her all that well. I will blame the fug in my head brought on by the morphine. After all, one cannot be expected to remember all of the fleeting minutes from their past. I seem to only recall a tiny little creature, shrunk by the swaddling that bound her. Her eyelids were still fused together, pulling a crease across her dome of a forehead. I don't remember much more about her. But for the marks on her face; she could have been any other baby but for those; birthmarks like tears of blood, an angry red against the greyness of her cheek.

And there was me, of course, Emma Marks. But Emma Marks was not the same person then as she is now. I was a twenty-five-year-old back then and practically still a newly-wed. And what was a person so young to do or say at such a meeting? Well, I'm sure that I was more concerned by the midwife's presence than Violet's. What would such a woman so neat and crisp in her starched uniform make of me hunched over in a wheelchair, my face pale and my hair dishevelled? I could sense her beside me as I stared into the incubator, her eyes on me and mine on Violet as I watched the irregular heave of the baby's tiny chest.

I do not recall how long I watched the infant but it cannot have been long, the midwife must have had her rounds to do, she would not have permitted any lingering. I remember that she seemed an impatient type. Eager to get to another appointment, I expect.

The next thing I remember is her kneeling next to me, her bag open on the floor as she rummaged around in it, frantically

I thought, as if whatever she was looking for could not wait another minute. But then she stopped and looked up. Her mouth was moving and I could hear the drone of her words but I could not focus on what she was saying. Her breath was stale and a single strand of hair had come loose from her cap, but it was her expression that I remember the most. The muscles of her face were tensed into a mask of blankness, her eyebrows raised slightly and her mouth pulled tight. Her eyes seemed distant as if she was staring at something far beyond me. It is a face that I have been unable to forget, if only for the fact that it wore that curious expression; one that I could not quite read.

Then her words came together in my head, something at last I could understand: 'Time to say goodbye to Violet.' Yes, that was it: 'Time to say goodbye to Violet,' is what she said.

'All right,' I said. 'Goodbye.' I could not have known how weak Violet really was and what would become of her after we parted, so I said Goodbye to her and just that. I did not know that I would not see her the next day, or the day or week after that and, over the months that I mourned her, I did not know that one day, nine years later, I would glimpse her face again.

3

Ruby

My name is Ruby Brown and I am the girl from the lido. Yes, I am the girl in the spotted dress that Emma saw standing by the railings and I am the girl that she chased through the crowds. But I expect you thought that my name was going to be Violet – Violet Marks even – but it is not Violet and this is not one of those stories. This is something different and I will tell it my way. I will start my story from the same day that Emma did; the day we met at the lido. It was the day that things began for me and Emma Marks…

The first thing I remember about that day is that it was hot, so hot that the sunshine stung my face like a slap and I had to shelter inside the cottage watching Maudy as she knelt half naked on the floor kneading cloth in a bucket, her arms dyed green up to the elbow.

'Done!' She sat back on her haunches and flicked the dye from her fingers, wiping a green smudge across her cheek. Just look at me: panting like an old woman,' she wheezed, but she was just fibbing because it didn't take her long to catch her breath: 'We need to get these ones hung on the line, Ruby. At least all this sun will mean that they dry by the time your cousin comes for them. I'm not losing my wages this week!'

I got up and trailed after her as she heaved the bucket into the yard and started draping the cloth over the washing line, trickles of green splattering the dust.

'We need to get out of here, you and me, don't matter about your brothers. Nor Clarence as it happens – your good-for-nothing father will be in the Red Lion until sundown – we ain't waiting for him.' She pegged out the last of the cloth and wiped her hands on her petticoat.

'Go and put on your best dress, Ruby, the one that you got for your birthday with the little spots. We're going on a trip to the lido, just my special girl and me.' She looked at me with her big gappy grin, like she was expecting me to be pleased but I just shrugged. I was only her special girl when she was going through one of her guilty moments. You see, something had happened to me a few months before – a Bad Thing. But I don't want to talk about that part of the story – I don't want to tell and, trust me; you don't want to know. All I will say is that there was a big to-do and the stove got broken. Nobody could fix it and months later the door was still hanging from just one hinge. Clarence blamed me, of course. Maudy knew that it wasn't my fault but she would never admit such a thing in front of Clarence, so instead I had become her 'special girl'.

Of course I should have been happy about a trip to the lido, but things were never straightforward with Maudy, so I bit my tongue and reminded her coolly that I had no bathing costume.

'Ain't you, Flower?' Maudy disappeared into the back room and I heard the grind of wood as she rummaged in the dresser. She reappeared holding up a pair of my old bloomers and a woollen vest stitched together and dyed green. 'Ta-da!' She held it against me, rubbing it flat over the curve of my belly. 'Your first swimming costume, Ruby. Now you won't feel out of place with those posh kids from the Sunningdale Estate. It looks the part, don't it? So who's to know?' She winked and pulled a pair of drawers with the legs stitched together on to my head. 'A bathing cap too, and look – green – it matches!'

I yanked the drawers off my head. I had been wondering what she had done with the leftover dye and just then I wished I had never found out.

Maudy stuffed the bloomer costume into a bag, together with a towel that was fluffy and white, with 'Property of the Grand Union Hotel' embroidered on it. Now, the towel I liked, it even had a crest on it, something that the king would have on his towels, and so I started to think that Maudy could be right – we wouldn't look out of place after all.

So a fluffy towel was all that it took to sweeten me and soon Maudy was striding off down the lane, with me trotting behind her, sweating in my spotty dress. Maudy shouted over her shoulder – I wasn't to dawdle, she said, or we would be late. I don't know what she thought we would be late for but I had the feeling that we already were. It was nearly lunchtime and we had left the house with no food. I thought about all those rich families sitting down together and sweating over a full roast and my mouth started to water just thinking about it. I felt a scouring in my stomach and started to drag the bag with the green bloomer costume, bouncing it over the wheel ruts in the hope it would fray.

At the end of the lane the trees stopped and we came out onto the crossing with the war memorial, where the dirt track joined the proper roads of Missensham town. There were grand houses lining the other side of the road. One even had a motorcar parked in a driveway, cherry-red paint winking in the sun and big round headlights like the eyes of an owl. I pointed at it and opened my mouth but Maudy already had other ideas.

'Oooh,' she cried, 'apples!' She was right; opposite the houses was an orchard, apple-laden branches hanging low over the road. She started picking the fruit, climbing up the bank and stretching over the fence, all the time looking round to see if anyone was watching, but there was nobody in the street so she kept on glancing over her shoulder to the grand houses, chuckling to herself.

'Now we will have a treat!' she said. The farmer wouldn't miss the apples of course, but I was still worried about looking like a thief if anyone saw her. The houses opposite the memorial had smart red bricks and big painted doors with four windows all neat around them, just how we had been shown to draw houses at school. The houses looked nice, like they would have nice people inside them, wearing nice clothes and sitting on nice chairs. I felt ashamed. The boughs hung ever so low over the road but none of the rich people from the houses had stolen the apples.

Then there was a rumbling sound and Maudy pocketed the apples quickly and stood up straight. There was a woman coming from town, a big woman pushing a pram, and little twin kids running behind her. She was tall and wide, like a farmhand in a posh dress, and there was a stupid hat on her head that flapped up and down like a big yellow pigeon caught under the wheels of a bus.

Maudy looked round like she was doing anything but picking apples. 'Good afternoon,' she said in her poshest voice. But the woman just gave a rude little nod, like she needn't bother talking to us, and passed right by. We watched her until she went into one of the houses across the road, the one with the red car and the owl eyes. Maudy turned back to the apples. 'Holler if anyone else comes,' she said. She managed to get a few more but suddenly there were people everywhere because the lido was about to open up again for afternoon tickets and she had to stop. We followed the crowds and I saw the farmhand lady with the yellow pigeon hat again, striding some way in front of us. I started to worry that someone had seen us picking the apples and I tried to dawdle, but Maudy was having none of it and kept pulling me along.

I had to lie about my age at the turnstiles, knock off a couple of years for a cheap ticket. I'm small for a girl of nine and Maudy always felt short-changed by this, as if God owed her free entry just because she had a scrawny child like me.

Inside the lido, lots of people were sunbathing on a lovely green hill, towels spread out on the grass. I pointed to them but Maudy said that the nice part of the lido was full and I had to put my Grand Hotel towel on the concrete, the white down getting all dusty.

Maudy told me to put on my bloomer costume but I was embarrassed to, so I lay back and pretended to sunbathe instead. She said that I would do no such thing and she quickly covered up my face with the bloomer hat, scolding that I mustn't get too much sun. I have a problem with my face, you see, with my skin. It's no good asking me about it though, because I won't talk about it, not with anybody. So I lay on the hard concrete in my sweaty dress with my drawers on my face, wondering why I was stupid enough to come.

My breath was hot under the woollen drawers, but I could watch the grassy bank of sunbathers through a crack of light out of the leg hole. The pigeon hat woman was there in the middle, bending over her pram, her bum like two medicine balls squeezed up inside her bright red costume. There was an old man coughing up into a hanky and a dog getting slapped with a newspaper as he tried to cock his leg up against a picnic basket. There was a little boy on a blue tricycle. It didn't matter to him that he could hardly ride it because of all the people. He was too busy showing it off – staring at the other kids, stopping by each of them and then riding off again, fast.

Maudy was watching people too. I fancied that she was scared of meeting someone who knew us and that Clarence would hear that she had been at the lido and not stayed at home dying cloth.

Then she sat up suddenly. 'How's about an ice cream for my special girl?'

I opened my mouth to remind her about the apples but then I realized that she might be trying to sweeten me about the Bad Thing that happened with Clarence, and that lidos and ice creams could just be the beginning. Of course she could never buy my forgiveness but there was no harm in letting her try. I closed my mouth just in time.

She pulled the green bloomer costume from my face and dragged me to the pavilion, hurrying all the way, but when we got there she said that she needed a piddle and that I could get the ice creams all by myself, like a good girl. I could meet her by the railings when I was done. I started to grumble but she gave me a whole shilling so I shut up and joined the queue.

The people behind me stared as a big peak of ice cream passed into my hands. I made sure that they all got a good look, but when the man at the counter served cones and flakes to the lady behind me, I realized that the people were still looking at me and I suddenly remembered that the green bloomer hat wasn't covering my face any more. When I got out, Maudy was gone and I had to wait for her by the railings all on my own, feeling stupid and looking it too.

I always hated moments like that, when people had time to stare. A little boy – the one on the blue tricycle – turned openmouthed, his head swivelling to stare at me as his mother pulled him away like I was diseased. I pulled a monkey face at him and he started crying. An old woman stopped and stared, pity on her face as if I was a cripple. I saluted her with my two fingers – and I don't mean like a girl guide.

That's when I saw her – the woman, the lunatic; mouth open and eyes wide, ice cream cones crumpling in her fists. She was saying something but it was gibberish: 'Violent! Violent!'

I looked behind me – maybe she was talking to someone else – but there was only the railings and the swimming pool. Then the ice creams slipped from her hands and splattered on the ground but she didn't even notice, just scuttled forward until she was right up close. I wanted to look away but I was scared that she would lunge at me.

She reached out like she wanted to touch me, her hands on my shoulders, fingers dripping ice cream. 'Thank you, God!

Thank you!'

So I ran. Of course I did. I ran as fast as I could. But this only made the woman run too, and she ran right after me! But I was quicker, I was just in my summer dress and she was all tied up in her long skirts and fancy shoes, I dropped my ice cream and tucked my skirts into my drawers and I was away. I was scared, of course I was, but I could nip between people's legs and be gone before they wanted an apology. So I ran into a big crowd, but when I heard whinges and whistles, I knew that she must be following. Then she fell and people were bending over her, trying to help, and I started to think that she might be out of breath or hurt but then she jumped right back to her feet and I saw her head above the crowd, swivelling this way and that. And then she saw me and we were both running again.

By then I was frantic. I ran back to the concrete but my towel was gone, and my bag, and so was Maudy and I charged through people's picnics, their rugs catching on the buckles of my shoes. I kicked over someone's lemonade. The dog started to chase after me and I ran into the boy on the tricycle, kicking him in the shin. Then everything was swirling around me – sunburnt faces, bathing costumes, deckchairs, hampers, towels, parasols – shouts and laughter ringing in my ears.

Then there was a loud beep from the road and, through the railings, I saw a bus slowing down for the stop. There was a big crowd by the turnstile so I shoved my way through. At last I was out of the lido. I was still scared, so I looked all around for the madwoman, but then I got trapped in a big jumble of people and couldn't see anything but elbows and bags.

Then I heard her shout again: 'Violent. Violent.' I panicked and pushed my way through the queue and squeezed myself on to the back of the bus as it started to pull away. The conductor yelled at me for the fare. I only had the change from the ice cream so I gave him that, and all I had left of the ice cream was down my dress anyway. I started to bawl; where was Maudy? How would I get home? How much trouble would I be in? but I did not think these things for long because, even from the window of the bus, I could see the woman grabbing at the railings, her eyes following me until she shrank into the distance.

Well you probably guessed that I saw the mad woman again, otherwise I wouldn't be telling this story, and you already know that the woman's name was Emma Marks and that she was a doctor's wife with a big house. And that she was a lady who liked to daydream and hide herself away, and I bet she has even prattled on about weeding her god-damn pansies by now. You see, you already know a bit about that woman, but back then I didn't know anything. And I did not know that, no matter how much I ran, Emma Marks would catch me in the end.

4

Emma

'Emma? Emma?' It was Audrey. She handed me a dainty cup. I tried to hold it but the china tinkled against the saucer and I put it down quickly and stared out the window. The throng of colourful people had dissolved with the daylight and I was left sitting on the window seat in my dim front room. Down the road a lone lamplighter raced to keep up with the retreating line of daylight, the war memorial at the junction throwing the long shadow of a cross on the road.

Ethel and Alan sat rigid on the sofa, shouted into silence as they pretended to read George's encyclopaedia, splayed open on their knees. The pram was wedged next to them, the quiet baby blunted from existence by the large black hood, the tick of the clock on the mantelpiece the only reminder that time was not frozen.

Audrey sighed deeply then hurried into the hallway, hushed voices as she spoke with George. I could imagine the scene: Audrey's head would be bowed, her hand on George's arm. The weak light from the yellow glass in the door would be mottling the floor tiles as it so often did at this time of day. The draught from under the door would be catching at the hem of Audrey's skirt. George would be nodding in silent agreement.

I couldn't remember how I had got home. I was told later that Audrey had dragged me through the crowds in the lido and out onto the street. I had been dumbstruck, following but not speaking, all the time Audrey hurrying, scared that I would pass out at any minute. But I don't remember any of that, only the face of the girl in the polka dot dress as she looked down at me from the window of the bus and the colour draining from George's face when he saw us.

'It's not something you get over easily,' I heard Audrey whisper.

Then a lower mumble from George: 'It's been over nine years.'

Audrey paused for a moment and I imagined her hand tighten round George's arm. 'Now and then there are going to be moments like this. It's to be expected. You should know that, you're a doctor after all.' Then silence – time for meaningful looks, pitying glances and shrugged shoulders.

Audrey's silhouette appeared in the doorway and she crossed the room quickly, as if returning to an abandoned child. She knelt by the chair and stared into my face as if I had been blinded and could not see her, stroking my hair and sighing dramatically.

'You can look after her, can't you, George?'

'Of course I can,' he snapped, 'as you keep saying, I am a doctor.'

Audrey hesitated, she opened her mouth – I thought she would start on the rant that I had heard so many a time before, something about how years poring over textbooks and slicing through cadavers taught one little about real life and empathy and just made one soulless – but she closed it quickly and focused back on me. For a moment, I thought she might stay.

But then Ethel let out a yelp. Her plait was stretched taught in Alan's fingers, her head craned towards him as he wound it round his fist.

Audrey stood up quickly. 'I have to go, George,' she whispered, bowing her head quickly as if offering condolences at a wake.

He nodded. 'Of course.'

She left hastily, with just a quick pat on my shoulder as a goodbye. I watched through the window as Audrey walked up the drive, pushing the big black pram, Ethel and Alan trailing behind her. They turned on to the pavement and the pram bucked on the curb, its wheels hissing on the tarmac. I watched them as they shrank into the distance, their footsteps fading into silence. The hood of the pram was the last thing that I could see: a big black sail; a signal to all about the passenger inside; a reminder of what I had for such a short time nine years ago; a reminder of what I had lost.

5

George left for work early the next morning, without saying goodbye. I told myself that he had wanted to let me sleep but deep down I knew that it was easier for him just to leave without waking me. I rolled onto my back and shielded my eyes from the chink of light between the curtains. George's side of the bed was cold, the dip in the mattress and the dent on the pillow outlining where he was not.

I had grown used to his little rituals and I knew exactly what he would have done that morning while I slept. He would have woken and reset the alarm clock, then sat on the edge of the bed and sighed, rubbing his eyes. Then he would have dressed quickly and put on his little round spectacles. Then to the kitchen – two slices of toast with marmalade and a cup of tea, milk first – the same every morning. Then he would return to the bedroom and stare at the hunch of my body under the blankets. He would stoop over me, silent for a few minutes, perhaps clearing his throat, as he wondered whether to wake me. Sometimes, long ago, I would have pretended to wake, perhaps kissed him on the cheek, but I hadn't done that for many years and now, as with every other morning, I lay still, not stirring until I heard the click of the front door closing behind him.

George had left a note in the study; he would be back the usual time, the hyacinths needed watering and could I write to the tailors in Bond Street and request the buttons that his dress suit was missing? I was to make it very clear that he would need them by October for the Hospital Ball. I was to watch that I didn't catch my skirts – the front gate had come off its hinges, 'miraculously' he had written, and then followed this with an exclamation mark which he obviously thought was all that was needed to convey his dissatisfaction with the hot weather and the hordes of undesirable gate-breakers that it brought into the road. I tore the page off the notepad, dipped the pen and started to write:

Mssrs Crooke of Bond Street,

Dear Sirs

but then I stopped and crossed it out, a blot of ink swelling onto the paper.

Outside, the hooves of the milkman's horse struck slowly down the road, the same way they always did at this time of day. Then came the predictable rumble of the morning bus. A blackbird sang from the orchard and there was the faint chatter of people going about their business in the road. George was determined for this to be a normal day but it was not – I could not forget what had happened at the lido. I tried to steady my shaking hand by gripping the pen and taking slow breaths as George always advised, but when I closed my eyes to contain the tears, I saw the girl again, the girl in the spotted dress, standing by the railings, the ice cream round her mouth and the sun-caught halo. She was the right age and had the same mark on her face – the red tears under the crimson smear on the cheekbone. She was Violet, my Violet, the girl that I had lost.

I took out my handkerchief and dabbed my eyes. Then I tore George's letter from the notepad and looked at the furred circle of ink which had bled through to the next sheet. I traced another circle next to it, elongating it and then peaking the ink at the top – a teardrop, then another two, staggered as if falling, then above them, a smear of ink. I encircled the marks with a large oval, adding eyes, nose and mouth so that the tear shapes rested on the left cheek. Then I added tresses of hair and shoulders, just enough to show the collar and some spotted fabric.

HAVE YOU SEEN THIS GIRL?

I printed at the top of the page. Then I stopped – Have you, Emma?

'Have I?' I said out loud. For the first time I hesitated. Maybe George was right; George, and Audrey too, and those people who pointed and laughed when I ran through the crowds at the lido. Maybe I was mad, seeing only what I wanted to see. Then the sunlight came through the blinds and the memory of yesterday became clearer. I saw the girl's face again, the brightness of the eyes and the expression of fear when I had startled her and I knew for certain that the girl I had seen was Violet.

I had used all the pages in the notepad by the time the hands on the desk clock said ten o'clock, and I had stuffed the papers into my bag and shut the door before the distant church bells had finished chiming the hour.

There was already a heat haze on the road as I turned out of Little Willow and struck out on to the street. I turned left, back to the lido, the road now empty but the sun still low enough for the apple trees to shade the road.

The main gates of the lido were closed, the signs covered over and a padlock on the turnstiles. I looked through the railings. The pool was deserted, the grass left pitted by the hurry of hundreds of shoes. A man in overalls stabbed at pieces of litter blowing all over the grass like chicken feathers after a fox attack. The pavilion shone cold with the first rays of sun, the walls of glass empty but for the blue light of morning. A child's sunhat was spiked on a railing.

'Can't you read? We're closed Monday mornings. You'll have to come back after twelve.' In the dark ticket office, eyes peered out from beneath a watchman's cap.

'I'm sorry,' I said. 'I just wondered if you had seen a little girl yesterday. If anybody had?'

'Were busiest day of the season yesterday. Seen hundreds of little girls.' Then he saw my face and softened: 'What like?'

I leant up against the turnstile and pushed one of my leaflets through the bars.

His lips moved slowly as he read. 'Poor little bleeder!' Then he checked himself. 'Well maybe something will come of having a face like that; should be easy to remember.'

'Please,' I said, thrusting more leaflets through the bars. 'Please could you hand these round to people coming in?'

'Well I ain't supposed to.' But then he wiped the sweat from beneath his cap and gave a brief nod. 'Will be difficult if it gets too busy.'

'I understand,' I said, my voice cracking, 'but—'

'I wouldn't worry yourself, Madam. I'm sure the police will do a good job.'

'I'm sure they will,' I said weakly.

There were no buses into town that morning so I walked down Willow Street and back past Little Willow. At the war memorial I took the route into town, following the road around the edge of the Sunningdale Estate. George always said that we were lucky – they had built the grandest houses on the edge of the estate, he said, the ones that could be seen from the road, the ones to be admired. I thought that it did not matter. It was true, Little Willow had three bedrooms instead of two, a garage and a study but, give or take the odd French windows, box rooms, weathervanes and potting sheds, all the houses on the estate were the same – pitched roofs and bay windows, porches and coloured glass. And while people moved out and new ones moved in, and children grew up and flowers bloomed and died, the houses always stayed the same year in, year out; I thought, just like me and George.

As I reached St Cuthbert's, I pinned one of my leaflets to the noticeboard on the gate. George and I had been married in that church. We had chosen it because of the honey-coloured sandstone and graceful spire and because we could hear the bells from Little Willow – bells that, whenever they chimed, would remind us of our marriage. I still thought of that when I heard them in the garden or indoors on a still day. But these days hearing their dull clank did not make me happy – each chime a reminder that time had stolen another hour of my life. Sometimes I wondered if George still heard the bells at all.

The sun was now high in the sky and children in school uniform were running down the road, eager to get home for lunch, their satchels flapping at their hips like wings. They took some of my leaflets as they passed, but I heard them chuckling in the distance, the discarded sheets fluttering away on the breeze.

At the old village green I saw George's car parked outside the doctor's surgery. After Violet's loss, George had resigned his place at the hospital – the humdrum life of general practice had suddenly become appealing to him and he said that driving that short distance to work every morning was the only excitement that he needed.

The green itself was deserted, the Red Lion and the general store all dark and lifeless. Shopkeepers hovered behind plate glass, peering longingly out onto the yellowed grass of the cricket pitch and the shady bench under the old oak tree.

When I came to the police station, I hesitated, my hand clutching a leaflet. I thought about what the watchman at the lido had said, that he was sure the police would do a good job of finding the little girl. But how could grown men look for a ghost? How could I explain what I had seen to a policeman? How could I explain it to anyone? I couldn't cause a fuss like that in Missensham! I dropped the leaflet back into my bag and walked on.

The teashop was closed for the morning, the chairs that usually accommodated the derrières of townsfolk as they sipped tea and nibbled scones now stood empty, a sign with opening hours hanging apologetically from the doorknob. My maiden name – Flanagan – was still faded into the brickwork on the wall. This building had been where my parents had served the ladies of the town with the latest fashions and fine tailoring, flattering them with the grandest silks and brocades, then working like drudges to get their alterations and creations finished on time. They had worked tirelessly in that shop and lived as well as died in the tiny flat above it. And I had spent half my life with them sewing seams and patching elbows.

But that was the old me and this was the old Missensham, the town as it once was. Even before my parents moved in with just a packing case between them, the town had started to grow, with each new development bringing more and more inhabitants. The canal came first, bringing navvies and workers' cottages. Then the main roads came, competing with the canal for the flat ground, the tarmac criss-crossing the water with humpbacked bridges. Then the Metropolitan Line had extended out of London, the track cutting deep into the earth and a new station had been built on the edge of town. The trains brought money and commuters, who moved into the new Sunningdale Estate. With each day the town was getting newer, but I was getting older.

The bells of St Cuthbert's rang out behind me as I walked. So many chimes! The day was passing quickly. But this time I heard the bells, I did not think about George for my head was crowded with other thoughts and, before I knew it, I had reached the far end of town. This was a place in limbo, where the fields were edged by billboards advertising the arrival of new housing estates – dual heating, tiled bathrooms, large sculleries and separate WCs. The new houses would be grander than those on the Sunningdale Estate, more modern and closer to the station.

I put my eye to a gap in the hoardings. The field behind it had been the place of my happiest memories. It was soon to be concreted over, but not just yet – for now at least the earth was still rich with grass and some memento of my time with my lover remained. For the first time that day I felt a burst of something close to happiness, the same feeling I'd had in my daydream at the lido. Beyond the hoardings, the violets in the field shone brightly.

6

The sun cast long shadows on the pavement as I hurried down the drive of Little Willow. George sat in the lounge, the glow of the low sun staining the room orange and casting his face in shade. He didn't look up when I entered, just held out a tattered piece of paper. I took it from him, but folded it into my pocket. I did not need to look at the bold letters or the inky teardrops folded into the crease to know that it was one of my hand drawn leaflets.

'I thought that yesterday was just a little setback,' said George, as if beginning one of his long speeches. 'A moment of hysteria – we can expect that from time to time. But I had hoped that a good night's sleep would do the trick, make you see that yesterday was just a delusion.'

I perched on the window seat, crumpling the paper between my fingers. Doctor's orders, I thought, doctor's orders to forget. 'How did you get it?' I said.

'How do you think? It's got our address on it. Emma, how could you? Can't you see that putting a Sunningdale Estate's address on something is just an invitation for any ne'er-do-well and charlatan to call round? This could just be the beginning.'

'Someone came?' I said, excitedly. 'Someone responded to one of my leaflets?'

'Yes…no! Not someone, just a boy, looked like a street kid. Dirty fingernails, a flat cap over his eyes – you know the type, probably the one who broke the gate. What if these people choose to exploit your fragile mental state – what then?'

'What did you do?'

'What do you think I did? I sent him packing of course.'

'Did he say anything?'

George pulled his spectacles down onto his nose and rubbed his eyes.

'Please, George, did he?'

'What do you mean?' Then he drew a long breath. 'You mean did he say anything about a dead baby?' he said slowly. 'A baby that was dead nine years ago and is still dead today—'

I gasped. George had never spoken of what had happened, not since the day we got back from the hospital.

'—Well no, Emma, he didn't. I didn't give him the chance!'

'George, please!' I whispered. 'How can we be sure of what happened all that time ago, I never saw the body, did I? Remember, they said it would be too—'

'No! I have to put an end to this stupidity right now. For God's sake, Emma, it's been nine years! Ten! I've given you plenty of time – don't you think it was hard for me too? I've been pussyfooting around, walking on eggshells and for what? A baby, a dead baby that wasn't even normal!'

'What do you mean by that?' I cried.

'You know what I mean,' he said wearily. Then he put his hand up to his face, his fingers stroking the air around his cheeks as if he couldn't bring himself to say it.

'The face,' he said quietly.

I felt my mouth open and close but no sound came out and he continued to stare at me, knowing just how to hold his head, his chin slightly down and to one side so that the thick lenses of his spectacles caught the light and his eyes faded away under the hard reflection.

'You think she was better off dead!' I said at last, my voice breaking. 'Better dead than disfigured?'

He said nothing, just continued to stare at me, hard glass shielding his eyes.

I sank down and started to cry. I could feel him staring at me, his eyes cold upon my back. Then I heard the rustle of the newspaper opening and the creak of the armchair as he crossed his legs. New tears came, silently this time. George sighed deeply and the pages rustled louder, as if he couldn't concentrate. Then I heard the pad of his footsteps and saw his slippers in front of me on the carpet. He put a hand on my shoulder, his touch so light that is rested on the fabric of my dress, as if he couldn't bear any closer contact.

'I'm sorry, darling,' he said, stiffly. 'Look, I think we both need to put all of this behind us. Make some changes. Think of it as a new start. Out with the old and in with the new and all that.' He laughed awkwardly, a strange little coughing laugh that he had when he thought he was about to say something clever. 'You know a fellow called round about the garden gate; noticed that it was broken and offered to fix it. A perfectly amiable chap, I found him to be rather pleasant and a decorator by trade. He offered some good prices for redecoration too. I thought that livening up the place might be a good place to start.'

'The house is only ten years old!' I heard myself say as if a new coat of paint in the lounge was a natural change of subject.

'Even so,' he said, 'I think some decorating would do us both good and give you a project to set your mind to. It is time you had a hobby outside that blasted garden. I think this could be just the thing – something trifling and domestic for you to manage. There's little to do in Missensham for a married woman – too much spare time for the mind to wander.'

I sniffed and rubbed my eyes on my sleeve.

'Good,' he said. 'I'll give the chap a call tomorrow. You can make a start immediately.'

I nodded weakly.

'All right then!' he said brightly as if everything was solved. He backed into the hall, smiling all the way and I heard the pad of his slippers and then the chink of the kettle on the hob as he hummed cheerfully, busying himself in the kitchen.

The bell of St. Cuthbert's struck eight. I put my hands over my ears and stared out of the window. Beyond the privet hedge was the war memorial and the crossroads, and somewhere beyond them was the sprawl of the Sunningdale Estate and the village green of the old town. There was the new main road, the canal and the Tube line cutting across the farmland until they reached other villages and towns and, beyond them, more roads, train tracks and waterways criss-crossing over hills and through valleys, counties and cities. Out there, somewhere, was my daughter, Violet – the girl with the birthmark on her face – and I realized then that I would be alone in searching for her.

7

The next morning George rang his perfectly amiable fellow, the master decorator. I listened to him on the phone – brief and businesslike, as if he was giving orders and expected to be obeyed as he reeled off a list of tasks that made it sound like the house was falling down around our ears. The decorator couldn't come for a few days – in fact he couldn't make it until Wednesday week – but that was all fine, George said to me, I mustn't worry because there was plenty to keep me occupied until then. The front garden was looking rather tired – there were dandelions pushing through the driveway and the privet hedge needed pruning. I found it easier to agree with him than to argue, so I made a start soon after he had left for work.

Ten years had not been enough to mellow the clay and rubble that had been dredged up from the construction of the estate. Everything I had tried to grow at the front of the house always wilted into little husks, yet the weeds seemed to thrive. I spent ages kneeling in the gravel that morning, jabbing my trowel into the hard soil and grasping the weeds with my bare hands until my fingers became sticky with dandelion sap. George's words from the previous evening's quarrel were still fresh in my mind and I worked my anger into the soil until the toll of the church bell informed me that I had missed lunch.

I sat up on my heels and took some deep breaths, wiping the sweat from my forehead with a gritty sleeve and glanced down the street towards the war memorial. A solitary spring of daisies rested on the low plinth, the stalks splayed over the granite. But today was not the anniversary of some battle or great defeat, it was someone's personal memory – the daisies marked a soldier's birthday or the day he fell.

The little tangle of daisies reminded me of the flowers at my parents' funeral, again just a solitary sprig. I had stood at the grave with my flowers, that little sprig, alone and barely twenty years old. Then another mourner had come, a stranger. She said her name was Audrey, drawing out the name in a breathy voice, her huge hand enclosing mine as she shook it. She wore a black cocktail dress shimmering with rhinestones. She had laughed apologetically – it was the only thing in black that she owned, after all, black was such a dreary colour. I had only just met her but she held my hand throughout the service. At the wake she talked about my parents, how they had served her in the shop – the ostrich feathers that my mother had delighted in fixing on to hats and headbands had been for her. I realized she was one of the glamorous ladies that I had imagined dancing in the dresses which I sewed until my fingers bled.

I worshipped her back then. She took my mind off what had happened in my life and soon I joined her, wearing ostrich feathers and sipping martinis as we danced together at the nightclubs in London. To me she was the height of sophistication. She was married to Walter, a psychiatrist, and seemed to have many glamorous friends. It was Audrey who introduced me to Doctor George Marks, a friend of her husband from the hospital. She said how lucky I was when he proposed – he was a respected doctor and, although a little older than me, he was still quite the eligible bachelor. He was good-looking too, she had said and I thought that, if I looked hard enough, I could see moments of handsomeness. But George was already in his late thirties by then, the last flush of youth draining from his body. I had told myself that Audrey must be right but I could not ignore the slackening skin under his jaw or the way his scalp reflected light from under his thinning hair. Audrey went ahead and arranged everything. There were flowers at the wedding of course, blooms and bouquets and petals everywhere. But as I looked at the war memorial, there was just one solitary sprig, and somehow, at that moment, those sorry little daisies seemed to be so much more meaningful to me.

The gate creaked loudly and I jumped to my feet. A little boy stood on the path, his eyes widening when he saw me. I dropped my trowel and trug, quickly forgetting my musings about martinis and flower-strewn weddings. The boy was small, his head barely level with the top of the gate. He was dressed in an oversized shirt, shorts that skimmed the bruises on his knees and a man's flat cap which he had to hold up so that he could peer from underneath the brim.

'It's you!' I gasped excitedly. 'You're the one who came yesterday.'

He didn't answer, but backed away slowly.

'It's all right,' I said. 'I won't shout at you like the man did. What's that you've got there in your hand?' It was a page from George's notepad, the ink furred through the paper where the clumsy oval of a face had been drawn. 'Yes!' I smiled. 'Yes, this is the place.'

He nodded.

'Do you know who she is? Wait there, I'll get a pen, you can write down the address. Have you come from there? How long did it take you to get here?'

He didn't say anything, just turned on his heel.

'Wait!' I shouted. Then, fearing that I'd startled him, added, 'I just need to get my hat. Can you take me to her?'

*

The boy walked quickly, sometimes trotting, I hurried behind, forced into long strides just to keep up.

'I wish you would say something,' I said, irritated, but he only quickened his pace.

At the war memorial he took the dirt track that led up into farmland. The orchards gave way to fields and copses, the slope of the path getting steeper where deep ridges of cart tracks scored into the hard earth. As the brambles grew higher I imagined George's ne'er-do-wells waiting for me behind the bushes, but the lane was empty, birds calling out in alarm and rabbits scattering as we passed. All the same, I wondered at the sense in following a stranger.

'Please,' I said, glancing at my wristwatch. 'We've been walking for over quarter of an hour, are we nearly there?' He started to run. I tried to grab his collar but it slipped through my fingers. Then he was gone. I went to hurry after him but my ankles buckled on the cart tracks, the back of my shoe slicing into my heel. My stockings caught on the brambles and laddered all the way to the knee, but I trudged on, the dust from the lane dulling my shoe leather.

I was about to turn back when I came to a sharp bend in the track where, behind an old, twisted oak was a small cottage, its front door opening out onto the lane. Its walls were bright but the thatch was low, darkening the windows. 'Rose Cottage' was stencilled on a tired sign above the door. Shouts came from inside, a woman's voice, loud and harsh, as if children were being scolded and I hoped that this was where the little boy had gone.

I knocked tentatively and the door swung open. A woman stood in front of me, her face furious: 'What?'

I hesitated. 'My name is Mrs Marks,' I said. Then, when I saw the wildness in her eyes, I drew myself up tall and added, 'I live on the Sunningdale Estate.'

The woman was silent, blinking her eyes quickly like a classroom dunce faced with a hard question. 'Well what are you doing out here then?' she growled. 'Don't go telling me that the Depression has hit the Sunningdale Estate!' Then her face suddenly softened in to a broad grin and her voice became low and gravelly. 'Come in, my dear.'

There was only one room at the front of the cottage and a door leading to what appeared to be a bedroom at the back. From what I could gather, the room was supposed to be a kitchen, but the random assortment of furniture suggested that it was used for anything and everything. At one end was a fireplace, and a couple of chairs round a dining table laden with mounds of green linen. At the other end was a large window, looking out over a dusty yard, a large stone sink and a draining board wedged under the sill. In a recess by the front door there was an old rocking chair and a pot-bellied stove with the grill hanging off at an angle, with a thin grey cat curled round its base in the hope of a fire. The sound of children's laughter drifted in through the back door, a small face sometimes peeping round the frame.

The woman squeezed behind the table and started to sort the linen. She had seemed large when her face was thrust up to mine but now I saw that she was slight, her collarbones jutting from beneath her tight brown dress.

'So, you've come about my advertisement,' she wheezed.

'Advertisement?' I echoed.

'Yes, but you don't look much of a seamstress to me – you'll have to prove yourself.' She picked what looked like a green chambermaid's apron from the pile of linen, holding it flat against her sunken chest so that I could see a large red monogram for the *Grand Union Hotel, Oxworth* stitched on the front. 'I can only pay you for one day a week: Thursdays. And

I've only got the one machine – I get to use that, but there's an embroidered part' – she pointed at one of the mounds on the table – 'needs doing by hand. Think you can cope with all those?' She gave me a hard look.

'I'm sorry,' I began, 'but there's been a mistake. I was following a little boy and I seem to have got myself lo—' Then I saw her – the little girl from the lido. She was lingering behind the doorframe, watching us through the gap. She wore a short grey pinafore, her exposed limbs twig-like, with no difference between calf and thigh. Her hair was fair and fine, the kind of custard yellow you only get in children, before it is muddied by age. Her eyes were bright, the birthmark on her left cheek like a rain of red tears.

I took a little step towards her but stopped myself quickly. What if she recognised me from the lido? What if she ran away again? I wanted to go to her. I wanted to speak to her. I wanted to touch her. I wanted to tell her everything. I--

'Are you all right, Mrs Marks?' said the woman. 'You seem to have gone pale. If you want to change your mind…'

'No!' I said quickly, breaking my gaze from the girl. 'Everything's fine.'

'Good!' The woman rubbed her hands. 'Seeing as you are here, you all right to start today?'

*

We stood together at one end of the dining table, a mound of green service aprons between us. The woman sat down heavily in an old basket chair, pushed aside the aprons to reveal a large Singer sewing machine and immediately started bunching swathes of green fabric behind the presser foot. I perched opposite and took up a needle and the top apron from the pile she had pointed to. Soon the room was filled with the clatter of the sewing machine.

The woman talked constantly, never breaking to look up from the machine, her words racing along with the rattle of the mechanism. Her voice was hoarse, peppered with screeches of laughter, as she amused herself with her own jokes. She said her name was Maud Brown. She took in work from a company called Walker's Fine Garments that had a big clothing factory in

Oxworth, right up in London, but had a lot of ladies working from home. She could do more than most because her nephew lived near the factory and owned a delivery van which meant he could deliver work all the way out to her in the country. She had five children, she said proudly; four boys and a girl. Andy was the eldest at fourteen down to Henry, almost eight years old, but a simpleton and practically a mute, she added, as if the punchline to a joke. I guessed Henry must have been the boy who had led me to the cottage, the one with the flat cap. She had a man – I noted that she did not say husband – called Clarence. One who she hardly ever saw because he held down several jobs – a bit of this and that, she said; helped up at the farm, fixed tractors, dug roads, that sort of thing.

I said very little about myself, relieved that I could get away with just nodding and smiling as I pulled the threads through the fabric. But as my needle shuttled up and down, my mind raced with thoughts of how to free myself from the situation and how to introduce a delicate subject into the conversation – the fact that I was a fraud, not an innocent seamstress who had answered her advertisement but a stranger in her home who wanted to take her daughter back.

Suddenly there was a pause. The fabric was still racing through the machine but Maud was looking at me. Her head cocked on one side and her eyebrows raised as if to say, And you?

I smiled, but of all the sentences I was forming in my mind, I could only manage to repeat my Sunningdale Estate address and that I was married to a doctor, but even then I left George nameless, imagining his fury at being mentioned in such company.

Then the clatter of the machine stopped and Maud looked at the apron bunched on my knee. 'You ain't doing badly for a doctor's wife from Sunningdale Estates.'

I laughed, glad that I could at last talk honestly about something. 'I'm not all that I seem.'

'Oh?'

'I used to be a seamstress before I married. My parents ran the dress shop; Flanagan's, on the green. Did you know it? It's a tearoom now.'

'I did,' she said, 'I did know it. And I remember the people in there too. A nice man with a moustache, I don't remember the woman so much though, she was a quiet little thing, always out the back.'

'That was them,' I said.

'I heard it was the Spanish flu that took them.'

'Yes.'

'I'm sorry.'

I shrugged, then continued, 'Worked my fingers to the bone since the age of ten, so I should know what I'm doing. It's been a while though.' Then I smiled. 'I'm surprised I ain't forgotten.' I felt myself blush slightly as I said the words. It had been too easy to slip back into my old parlance and I hoped that she wouldn't think that I was ridiculing her.

Maud smiled again, the same smile she had given me at the door but bigger this time. 'Once a grafter always a grafter,' she said. Then the smile spread across her face until her eyes were squeezed into little slits and her mouth became a deep gash, the gums stubbed with brown teeth. I was shocked by the sight of her teeth but her smile was so wide and genuine that I couldn't help smiling too. Then we laughed together – at what, I don't know, but a long and genuine laugh.

'You're a doctor's wife now though!' Maud said as she caught her breath. 'It's odd to see a married lady of your class working. Are your children grown?'

'No,' I said, 'I don't have…' but it was a sentence that I had never been able to finish, not even now, in front of a stranger.

But Maud didn't seem to notice my discomfort. 'I would have thought a well-to-do lady such as yourself wouldn't bother dirtying her hands for a few shillings – you lot are usually all about tea parties and bothering the vicar.'

'I need the money,' I said quickly. 'And nowhere in town would employ a lady who was married.'

Maud shook her head gently. 'Well, who'd have thought that after all that you'd be down on your luck again! I s 'pose business for a doctor out here ain't as good as in the city, with all the TB and measles that they get in them slums. The patients must pay better though, all the rich folk round this way. You only need a couple of bunions and the odd chilblain and a medical man could charge what he likes in Missensham. No need for you to turn your hand to this, surely.'

'He gambles,' I said and immediately felt guilty for saying it – it was unfair to George. He of all people didn't deserve that.

She opened her mouth but I changed the subject quickly: 'You have a lot of children, I don't know how you cope with five,' I said.

'Yes,' she said. 'It's all Clarence's fault – he's a randy old bugger, likes me in the family way.'

I blushed and immediately felt ridiculous, like a thirty-five-year-old schoolgirl. I lowered my head, wondering why she had spoken so openly, maybe she had mistaken my false confession about George's gambling as an offering of trust, or thought that her comment about always being a grafter had made us friends, but whatever had passed between us had put me in her confidence somehow.

'He blames me, of course,' she said. 'Says it's my desires.'

I looked down, pretending to pick at a thread, but she continued.

'I'd had plenty of lovers before him, mind you, but I'd never known a man like him before we met.' She waved a fist in front of her face. 'Dick like an oak truncheon.'

I wished I hadn't mentioned the children, but she was laughing raucously again and making wild gestures with her hands while the linen sailed through the hammering Singer as if it had a life of its own. 'Not that I mind, of course.' She leaned over and jabbed me in the ribs. 'About his dick, I mean!'

I smiled weakly, my cheeks burning. Honestly! George and I never spoke about such things and he'd even blushed on our honeymoon when I'd caught him looking at the naughty postcards on the seafront; grainy photographs of Edwardian women dressed in long bloomers, their breasts covered with little parasols. And of course, the act itself was performed in silence and never mentioned afterwards.

But then Maud smiled again, that ridiculous gape of a smile, and I couldn't help giggling along with her while she talked. Her foot was working furiously on the pedal and her mouth was just as active: children, babies, families, Clarence and dick – dick, dick, dick!

I nodded and smiled but my eyes drifted. The children had run into the yard, giggling, flashes of shadow in the window as they dodged past each other. There was the boy in the flat cap who had come to Little Willow, but others too – it seemed like hordes –running so fast that I wondered that it could just be the five she mentioned. I watched through the grubby glass, always looking out for the girl, but there were only glimpses to be had – a flash of pinafore, a trailing lock of hair and never a face.

'I wonder if I could trouble you for a glass of water, Mrs Brown?' I said, feigning an effort to get up from behind the laden table. 'Maybe one of your children could—'

'Ruby!' she yelled.

Ruby came in the back door her hair windswept and chest heaving. The sight of her was such a shock that I jabbed my needle into my thumb, a dome of blood swelling from the skin. Ruby! I had expected 'Violet', of course. But no, the little girl was called Ruby.

'Ruby, get the lady a glass of water.'

I suddenly started to worry, after all, this girl had fled my pursuit just days ago. I put my hand to my forehead, pretending to shield my eyes from the sun and searched her face for recognition but found none and she stared back at me, as she would a stranger.

'Ruby?' I said quickly. 'Is that your name?'

'You don't need to talk to her like that.' Maud laughed. 'She ain't five.'

'Of course,' I said, embarrassed. 'How old are you, Ruby?'

Ruby shuffled her feet and stared at the floor and I realized my question had sounded like a demand.

Mrs Brown looked at me weirdly out of the corner of her eye. 'Well go on then, Ruby, tell the lady!'

'Nine.'

'Say it nicely: "Nine, Mrs Marks"'

'Nine, Miss-us-Marks.'

The birthmark was brighter now that her face was flushed from the exercise. Four red marks, the highest one smudged under the eye. It was the same one I had seen on my frail baby daughter and it was the same one I had recognized nine years later among the crowds in the lido. It had to be the same. It just had to be.

'It ain't scabies,' said Ruby suddenly. 'No need to stare.'

'She'll stare if she wants to, you little shit!' growled Maud, taking a swing at the back of Ruby's head but only catching her hair.

'No!' I said quickly. 'I'm sorry, Ruby, I wasn't staring at anything. I just thought you had a lovely face.'

She looked awkward, but I thought I saw the flicker of a

smile.

'Don't you bother with all that, Mrs Marks, she don't like to talk about her face. Never does, you won't get nothing out of her about that. Now, what are you waiting for?' growled Maud to Ruby. 'Run and get the water!'

Ruby turned and ran out the room, the sound of an iron pump clanking from the yard.

'I'm sorry,' I said. 'I must have seemed so strange, you see, I had a daughter once—' I hesitated, trying to avoid saying what was so painful. 'She would have been exactly your daughter's age.'

Maud leaned over and patted my knee. 'I had a brother, Alphie, much older than me but just a young-un when he bought it. Passchendaele – blown up in the trenches, what was left of him trampled into the mud. Sometimes I look at fellas of that age and wonder what he would have looked like – whether he would have been like them.'

I nodded. 'Thank you for being so understanding.' I wanted to say more – to tell her about Violet, the birthmark and what had happened to her. I'm not sure why exactly, maybe I thought that it would encourage Maud to talk more about Ruby and that I might get an explanation, a confession even. I was about to open my mouth but then I remembered that, long ago, George had warned me not to talk of such things, because the details would upset me and, as I felt tears pricking my eyes, I feared that he had been right and, in the end, I said nothing more.

Ruby returned with the water, walking steadily and holding it aloft like a ring bearer at a wedding. The water was warm; a white cloud swirling under the rim of the glass. I moistened my lips on the glass and pretended to drink. I thanked her, smiling and trying to catch her eye, but she turned on her heel and soon she was running in the yard again, just the flash of her pinafore in the windowpanes.

'Now,' said Maud brightly, 'what was I talking about?'

I felt my face warm again and smiled blankly hoping she wouldn't remember.

'Ah, yes, with Clarence, how I got in the family way…'

*

I walked back home with my wages in my pocket – a couple of shiny florins. I would put them in the jar on the mantelpiece and would probably forget about them. But right now they meant everything: a memory of a strange but happy day, perhaps the beginning of many more; the warmth of the family; a new friendship; and time spent with Ruby, a girl who I was sure was my daughter. I had promised to return the following Thursday, and then all Thursdays after that, and suddenly a day that had been long and empty like any other became full of excitement and promise. I fingered the coins in my pocket. The sun was bright in the lane, the dust dappled with the shadows of birds flickering through the hedgerows and the fields were sunk with deep pools of violets.

8

Ruby

My name is Ruby Brown. That's right: Ruby like a gemstone, brown like mud. On the day that Emma came to the cottage, I was a ruby to her – her beautiful glittering jewel. But to Maudy I was mud…

'Ruby! Ruby! Just look at what you made me do!' she yelled.

I'd not even left my bed, so I ignored her, but it did me no good because she dragged me out of the warmth and sat me in the yard with a washtub and a big pile of the boys' undies. She gave Andy a book of sums and some threat about either learning numbers or mucking out chickens. Jim and John, Maudy decided, were beyond hope, so she just shooed them out the door.

I was stripped down to my drawers and covered in suds when I heard the rumble of the van in the lane.

'It's Fatkins!' I shouted. 'Fatkins is here!'

Maudy's head popped up over the sewing machine. 'No, blast it! What's the time?'

'I don't know, do I!' I said. 'You, you never showed me how.'

'No, no – it's too early. It can't be him.'

'It is,' I yelled. 'It's 'Fatkins and—'

But Maudy was already in a bad mood and she wasn't about to take any chat from me. 'Ruby! Don't you call him that, he's your cousin, show some respect and he ain't fat!' She was trying to sound all school-mistressy but it didn't work – she had never set foot in a school and her voice just sounded silly.

'I said "Atkins",' I said. 'I mean, what I meant to say was "Mr Atkins".'

'I heard what you said and it weren't that! Do you know what he'll do if he hears you call him that? He'll stop driving all this way and I'll lose all my jobs. How easy do you think it would be for him to get another worker up in Oxworth? He only drives all this way because we're family.'

'I'm sorry,' I said. 'You're right, Maudy; he doesn't look fat when he's stood next to Aunt Sadie.'

There was nothing school-mistressy about Maudy any more: 'Ruby!' she screamed. 'I've had enough of your lip! Get off your arse and get rid of that filthy water. And get yourself dressed while you are at it – you're an embarrassment you are.'

I couldn't get back inside quick enough and I ran into the backroom to do as she said, but my pinafore just wouldn't go on right, one arm got all twisted inside itself and I couldn't find my shoes.

I still wasn't ready by the time the van rumbled into the yard, and before I knew it Maudy was yelling at me to answer the door and I had to run back into the kitchen with, one arm still out of my pinafore.

'Hello, Ruby.' Fatkins filled the doorway, his head bowed. 'How's my favourite cousin?' he said it like I was a grown-up, a proper lady from Missensham. It didn't really bother me whether he meant it or not because he was nice like that and I knew he would say it whether my pinafore was twisted or even if I was a pig in a dress.

'Very well,' I said in my best church voice. Maudy always said that I should be polite to Fatkins and Aunt Sadie because they were proper people and would look out for us. 'Very well,' I said again, and then it just slipped out: 'Fatki—'

Henry shrieked and clapped his hands: 'Fat-kins-fat-kins-fat-kins-fat…'

Maudy jumped up quickly and I thought she would slap me but her hands went to her mouth. 'Oh shit!' she barked. 'The last ones ain't bagged yet!' Some aprons were still hanging on the washing line and she barged past Fatkins to get them.

Fatkins smiled politely, like he was trying to ignore a bad smell.

I ran at Henry but he was too quick and dodged past me out the door, still chanting, 'Fat-kins-fat-kins-fat-kins-fat…'

Fatkins looked relieved when Maudy shoved past him again, a pile of green aprons hanging from her arm. They had left a big damp mark on her chest but she smiled at him like everything was fine. Maudy had a good way of lying that didn't even show on her face – her smile said that the aprons were dry and pressed and smelling of roses.

Fatkins took the aprons from her, rubbing the damp between the tips of his fingers, then he sighed, folded them together neatly and put them carefully into one of the factory sacks. He wrote in his book, not looking up. His pencil moved quickly, not like Andy who had to concentrate hard on the letters, or Maudy who just pretended she could read and write. When he'd finished, he showed Maudy what he'd written.

'So this time it is twenty per sack, as agreed?' He pointed his pencil at a heap of bulging sacks, stabbing the air six times as he counted.

She nodded.

'That's five shillings then.' He tore the sheet out of his book and handed it to her.

She took it and held it close to her face, but her eyes didn't move over the numbers the way his did. 'Yes,' she said firmly. 'I can see that's what it says.' But I knew that the receipt would just go in the dresser with all the others without a second glance.

'I'll take this lot to the van and get you your money.' Fatkins grabbed a sack from the floor and lifted it high on his back as if the aprons inside had turned to feathers. Then he was out of the door and slamming it into the van.

Maudy gave me a wink and bent her arm up like a circus strongman. 'Told you, didn't I!' she whispered. 'It ain't fat, it's muscle – look how fast he moves them sacks, even with his limp. You know how Andy struggles with them.' Just as Maudy's nephew wasn't fat to her, he wasn't a cripple either, just a brave veteran, wounded doing his duty in some foreign hellhole.

Fatkins leant against the draining board. 'I've left next week's lot in the yard – five sacks. Andy can bring them in for you. Forty-odd aprons this time, dyed and hemmed, just as before, but these are for upstairs, so there's a monogram, must be embroidered. Like this.' He took a scrap of material from his pocket. 'Mr Walker wants quality, so use the thicker thread. We are nearly out of the red, so you will have to dye what you've got left over. It's a penny for each apron. Mr Walker says he can't afford to give any more'.

Maudy nodded grimly.

He made a note in his jotter. 'Right! So it was five shillings I owe you for last week.' He reached into his bag.

'Only five shillings,' said Maudy sadly.

'Aunt Maud, we agreed—'

'Oh, I know that, darling, it's just that this is a big job and it may take me longer than usual, you see, it takes an age for the stove to boil the water for the carmine now. I need money for a man to take a look at it or I'll still be dyeing that thread into next week.'

'I'll take a look for you, Aunt Maud,' Fatkins said, squatting down beside the stove. He opened the little door and swung it back and forth on the hinge.

I felt my face go all hot. I didn't like it when the stove got mentioned. I didn't like the way Clarence blamed me and I didn't like thinking about the Bad Thing again.

'Sorry, Aunt Maud,' he said. 'I'm not up to fixing that kind of damage. It must have taken a fair whack from something. There's a man you can ask for at the ironmongers behind Partridges. He would come out here for five shillings.'

I think that Fatkins realized what he had said as soon as the words left his lips. He drove the van away that afternoon with a load of damp aprons and a wallet that was ten shillings light.

As soon as Fatkins was gone, Maudy clouted me round the back of the head. The extra money hadn't made her forget about me winding Henry up and she had had work to do, she said – those aprons wouldn't hem themselves.

She had just sat down when there was a knock at the door. 'If it's the constable, come looking for Clarence again,' she shrieked, 'I'll—' But it wasn't, it was a woman, a posh woman with a confused look all over her pretty face.

We cleared off quickly. If a posh woman came to our house it was usually the school-mistress come to find us or a churchy do-gooder, so we waited in the yard for Maudy to send her packing, but she didn't and soon the sewing machine was whirring again and it didn't take us long to forget to be quiet and start screaming and running about the yard. Then Maudy called me in and made me speak to the lady all polite and get her some water. She was pretty and smelled nice and there were no bibles or schoolbooks.

So you think I'm an idiot for not seeing it – that Emma Marks the madwoman from the lido and Emma Marks the grand house visitor were one and the same. But let me tell you that the Mrs Emma Marks that visited us that day was very different from the woman at the lido. She had nice clothes and a pretty face and smelled sweet, like lavender. She had none of that staring-eyed and ice-cream-running-all-over-her-hands-type-madness, not one bit. And the funny thing is that Maudy seemed to like her too. She was all laughter and jokes and chatting like I had never seen her before and once Emma had gone, Maudy even hugged me. The whole thing was very strange, but I knew better than to ask questions. Then Maudy did something that she had never done before – she bunched up her skirts and skipped off singing. And it was then that I realized something was very wrong.

9

Emma

George's decorator fellow, Mr Tuttle, arrived on Wednesday, as promised. He came on an old bicycle, 'Tuttle and Son, Master Decorators of Missensham' stencilled on a rusty plaque which swung from the crossbar. I watched from the doorway as he dismounted shakily, trying to keep hold of a rickety ladder cricked under his arm. He was a thin man, with legs bowed like bananas. He was certainly as old as George, maybe older, but his weather-beaten complexion made it hard to tell.

I had seen the bicycle around Missensham for many years; it was certainly hard to miss when it passed me on the lanes with its squeaking wheels, but it was even harder to miss when it was slung in the hedge by the Red Lion. Still, it was only the rich who hired decorators and, even if Mr Tuttle was not quite a master decorator, I wondered what Audrey would think if she saw the bicycle in my driveway.

Mr Tuttle dropped the ladder to the ground and, one by one, began to take paint pots out of the panniers, each time cursing and grabbing the small of his back.

'Hello, Mrs Marks,' he called. 'How are you these days? Keeping well? And Mr Marks?'

I had never actually met Mr Tuttle before, but answered that my husband and I were both very well and then enquired politely after his own health.

'Mustn't grumble, Mrs Marks,' he said, changing his mind and putting the paint back into the panniers. 'Shall we start in the lounge?'

'The garden gate, Mr. Tuttle, I think that is what George wanted to have fixed first of all.'

'Oh don't you worry, Mrs Marks. I know what I'm doing there – a new hinge. No, Dr Marks was quite clear in his instructions, yes, now what was it? The rooms, yes inside the house, now that's what you'll need to show me.'

I watched in silence as Mr Tuttle paced the lounge, his bowed legs exaggerating his careful steps. He swayed slightly and steadied himself on the mantelpiece. I remembered what George had told me in his briefing the previous evening – to be patient with Mr Tuttle – he was an old man and had a neurological condition that made him unsteady on his feet. This was then followed with a long explanation about the electrical excitability of neurons and how damage from trauma could leave them disconnected and misfiring and I started to imagine thousands of microscopic nerve cells like electric cables with severed ends, the exposed wires spitting lightning bolts as they writhed around in the cranium searching for a connection. Personally, I could smell liquor on the man, but that was George – always looking for the most complicated medical explanation.

Mr Tuttle laid a metre rule along the mantelpiece, marking the end with a shaking finger, and jotted in his notebook with a pencil stub. 'Another lovely day, Mrs Marks.'

I opened my mouth but he continued as if his own agreement was enough.

'So much sunshine. Such a nice ride over here. Dropped in to see my boy on the way, Mr Tuttle Junior, he's nearby you see. Loves this kind of weather.'

'He lives on the Sunningdale Estate?' I said encouraged, if a little surprised. 'Will he be working alongside you at Little Willow?'

'Yes, yes,' he said, nodding. 'Loves this kind of weather, he does.'

I started to realize that I was not needed in the conversation.

Mr Tuttle continued jotting in his notebook. 'So much sunshine, such a nice ride over that I—' He stopped abruptly and looked up. 'What are your plans for this room, Mrs Marks?'

I was surprised by the question. I hadn't thought about it at all, but it was such an obvious question for a decorator to ask, I don't know why I hadn't given it any thought. 'I-I don't know, really,' I said.

Mr Tuttle tucked his pencil behind his ear. 'Well, I must admit I was a bit surprised to be called out to Sunningdale Estate, Mrs Marks, these houses are barely ten years old.'

I nodded, not sure what to say. I knew that I should probably claim that I wanted to keep up with some fad or trend but I didn't have a clue what was in fashion. I imagined Audrey, pacing the room in her yellow pleated hat and waving her arms at the walls and curtains trying to imagine what she would say. In the end I just shrugged. 'You must think us very extravagant, Mr Tuttle.'

'Not at all, Mrs Marks,' he said. 'It's good to get work in a depression, and on the Sunningdale Estate too. Lucky really, you see my son is nearby—'

'Yes, you said so.'

'Though, at the moment, I'm not getting much work of this level. Or at all in fact.'

'Really?' I said wearily.

'I'm mostly clearing blocked drains and sweeping chimneys, this type of thing' – he swept his hand round the room – 'it will be nice to work on the Sunningdale Estate for a change.'

'A change,' I echoed, excitedly. 'That's what Geor—, that's what we want. To have a new start,' I said, remembering George's speech. 'Out with the old and in with the new, that kind of thing.'

'Very good, Mrs Marks.' He hesitated and fiddled with the pencil behind his ear. 'If you don't mind me saying, this room, as it is now is' – his eyes glanced up at me but then darted away as if he didn't have the courage to look me in the eye – 'is perhaps more suited for an older gentleman. Now, I know an old bugger like me don't know much about the latest trends, but Mr Tuttle Junior – he knows about this estate, nearby you see – now he could tell you what's in the fashion. Something new, now what's that fancy word that the youngsters use – *moderne*, well I don't know about all that, but surely a change would mean something bright and cheerful.'

'Yes!' I said, my mood brightening. 'Cheerful, definitely cheerful.'

He nodded, pleased by his own suggestion. 'Well, maybe you can start by telling me how this room is used at the moment?'

I smiled, relieved that he had given me an easier task. I thought hard, looking first at the armchair in the corner. I thought of George, sitting there as he always did, flicking through the newspaper, a glass of sherry on the mantelpiece.

Then there was the wireless on the sideboard, and again there was George, shouting at the disembodied voices: the sham of Baldwin's new government, the idiotic cricket umpires and the bloody French causing problems again. There was the sofa, empty of visitors, the cushions gathering dust. Then there was the seat in the bay of the window, where I would sit, my body twisted towards the glass and my elbows on the sills. I saw an image of myself staring endlessly out across the road, my eyes following each person as their legless torsos sailed past over the privet hedge, a little part of me hoping that each would stop, maybe have a reason to call in – for a voice outside to call my name or for friendly shoes to crunch on the gravel. But that seldom happened and I was left with only the drone of the wireless, the footsteps on the pavement always fading to silence.

'We use it for entertaining,' I said.

*

We did the same for every room in the house – Mr Tuttle asking the same questions and me giving vague answers to each, a string of wishes and lies as I was forced to imagine George and myself fading in and out like ghosts.

There was the dining room where we sat at opposite ends of the table, absent guests marked by empty chairs. We would eat in silence but for George's customary compliment of the meal, the same words no matter what I put in front of him, his jaw working slowly, his eyes never leaving the plate. Always the same remark whether the mutton was tender and the eggs creamy or whether the cabbage was cooked to a pulp or the custard had skin: 'Excellent meal. Good work, darling.'

There was the kitchen, where I would stand, hunched over the gas ring, stirring bubbling pots, hypnotized by the steam until the vegetables boiled dry. The worktop where I would knead dough until my neck ached and my knuckles were sore, tears of self-pity running down my cheeks. And the basin, where I would stand with my hands in soap suds until the water ran cold, staring out of the small window over the garden's large, empty lawn.

There was the unwelcoming hallway, where George would rush on Saturday as soon as he heard the clank of the letterbox, eager for any new distractions that the postman may bring. He would brush past a photograph on the wall – Mr and Mrs George Marks as newly-weds on Brighton Pier – a souvenir framed lovingly but hung somewhere it could be hurried past without even a glance.

There was the bathroom where I would lay in the tub with nothing but my thoughts until the water became cold. The cabinet with no face powder or lipstick, just shelf upon shelf of medicine – chlorodyne, aspirin, surgical spirit – where George would curse as he rummaged through the jumble of packets and bottles, unable to find anything to soothe his wounded back.

There was the guest room that never received guests, the bed made in anticipation. Flat sheets and square corners, towels folded on the back of the chair, but the blankets cold and musty with mildew.

And then there was our bedroom. And it was here that I turned to Mr Tuttle and smiled, a kind of embarrassed smile, not because of what happened in a married lady's bedroom but because of what did not. He looked away quickly and for once I was glad that he never looked me in the eye.

I went to the window and pulled back the curtains. I could just see to the crossroads, with the war memorial in the centre, the tall stone cross throwing a long shadow over the road. On one side was the dirt track to the farms of Evesbridge and to another was the road that led to the old town with the village green, canal and station. Then there was the road to the lido that led all the way to Oxworth and the London suburbs beyond it. It was a view I had gazed idly upon for ten years now.

'A change,' I said again. 'I think we definitely need a change.' Mr Tuttle nodded and I followed him out on to the landing.

'Well the work shouldn't take long, Mrs Marks.' Then he stopped. 'We seem to have forgotten this room, Mrs Marks,' he said, putting his hand on the door handle. 'May I—'

'Oh, I'm afraid we keep that room locked, Mr Tuttle,' I said quickly.

He took his hand away slowly. 'That's a shame, Mrs Marks, it must have a lovely view over the garden.'

'Oh, but it's a very small room, Mr Tuttle,' I said.

He put his hand on the handle again.

'Really, Mr Tuttle, we have no interest in redecorating that room.'

Mr Tuttle's face froze and I realized that I must have shouted. I opened my mouth to apologize, but he just nodded.

'Very well, Mrs. Marks, very well.' Then he stopped at the top of the stairs. 'It's a shame though, Mrs Marks, I expect a room like that was intended as a nursery; a child's bedroom.'

'Oh, I believe it was a nursery at one point, Mr Tuttle,' I said. 'It was decorated for the arrival of a baby. But that was all a very long time ago.'

10

It was a very small room, that much was true, but it was bright. And back in the summer of 1926 it still had the faint odour of paint and sawdust, the glue from the builders' stickers a faint outline on the windowpanes. The walls were a pale yellow, warmed by the low evening sun. Lambs had been painted round the window frame, their legs thin and gangly as they gambolled over grass daubed with red poppies. I remember running my hand over the paintwork, the swirled clots of red- and green-ridged brushstrokes hard under my fingertips. My hands were still swollen back then, my nails polished and my wedding band still bright on my finger.

I opened the top drawer of the sideboard. Inside were squares of white muslin, all folded neatly, and other things – tiny sleeves, hems, buttons, pompoms – which I dared not look at. A rocking horse watched me through glassy eyes. It was a fine one, large with a dapple-grey rump and a flowing mane, the curve of its neck and the spread of its legs frozen in mid gallop, the saddle bare and expectant. Against the far wall stood a cot, empty and stripped, the bare wooden slats casting streaks of shadow.

There were gifts too, dear little items made with care but rushed to be given while there was still a reason to; a knitted rabbit, a rag doll, a lace bonnet and a counterpane embroidered with violets, the fabric puckered where the name had been stitched in haste.

I looked away quickly, glancing out the window and over the empty garden. Things looked so different since I had been rushed to hospital all those weeks ago. The time I spent away seemed just a blur of light and noise, of wet sheets, shiny metal, numb limbs and the dull fog of sedative.

But in those weeks the garden had changed; the firm young shoots of the pansies had now bloomed and wilted away; the daffodils and crocuses had sunk back into the earth; and the grass was now yellow and wispy. The big flowers had taken over, sucking all the life from the lawn, the swollen heads of chrysanthemums and hyacinths drooping onto the lawn, their petals tarnished and rusting.

Before the hospital, I had stood in this room with George, folding the squares of muslin and swaddling into the drawer, placing toys on the shelf, talking, planning and laughing even. But now I stood alone with my thoughts; my belly was now shrunken but the scars were still fresh. I had made it back from the hospital, but *she* had not. I remained in the nursery until the light faded, deaf to the last birdsong of the day, the rumble of cars on the road and the whistle of the lamplighter.

When the clock struck the hour, George arrived home from the hospital. I listened to the drone of the new Austin idling on the driveway, there were a couple of slammed doors and hushed voices, then a final burst of the engine and the click of the latch. George's familiar footsteps were followed by another's and then some muffled words and the creak of the stairs. A woman stood on the landing, watching me through the doorway, a tiny bundle cradled to her chest. It was the midwife, the moon-faced woman who had accompanied me as I sat in the white room with the incubator. She handed the bundle to me but it was cold and lifeless – just the supplies I had taken with me to the hospital; a baby's nightshirt and bonnet and a couple of nappies and towels folded inside a woollen swaddling sheet – as if the baby inside had vanished.

I put the bundle on the bed and unwrapped the layers of swaddling. I folded the nightshirt and tucked it away in the drawer with the towels, bonnet and nappies, finally smoothing the swaddling back over the top. All the time the midwife watched in silence. Although the day was ending, she was still in uniform – the red-lined cape, sash and leather bag – a professional still on call, even though she was no longer needed here.

Then I found something, tucked between the folds of swaddling. It was a small photograph – a grey image of a newborn lying on its back. The face was round, like that of any baby, the scalp haloed by a lace bonnet, the eyes and mouth just furrows in the plump flesh. The head was tilted slightly to show the left cheek – black marks cast on grey skin, four tears, the highest smudged over the cheekbone.

The midwife nodded and put her hand on mine. She did not

say a word but her face now wore the same strange expression that I had seen at the hospital – the raised brow and distant eyes – the expression that I could not quite read. Then she turned her back and was gone, leaving only the creak of the stair behind her.

I stared at the photograph. Was I looking at Violet's last moments? The baby's eyes were closed but the lids were smooth, with no bunching of the skin. The face seemed placid, with no hardness of muscle. Had the image captured sleep or something more sinister? Was I looking at life or death?

I got up wearily and tiptoed onto the landing, the lambs and poppies fading into darkness behind me. Downstairs there were whispers, my name repeated over and over in hushed conversation.

I waited until the dark shape of the midwife had slipped out into the twilight and the door locked behind her, then I crept down the stairs, into the lounge and perched on the window seat.

I could have shown George the photograph then. I don't know why I didn't, but when I saw him coming towards me, I just folded it into my pocket.

George knelt on the carpet and put a hand on my shoulder, patting it lightly. 'Never mind,' he whispered. *Never mind* – that is what he would say when I had broken a plate or burnt the dinner – *Never mind!*

I didn't say anything. The world seemed so different now, like it was spinning without me, and George and the midwife and the motorcars on the road, the singing birds and whistling lamplighters were spinning with it. I alone stayed still, abandoned in time and space. I began to wonder if I had died too.

'Try to look at it this way,' said George after a while. 'Well... we never really did discuss it, did we? It's not something we really wanted.' He forced a little smile and shrugged his shoulders. 'I'm far too old for children... and well, it wouldn't have happened if it weren't for that damn Dutch cap.' He smiled and patted my shoulder again. 'You know that I don't really like children. You do know that, don't you?'

I stared at him. Why was he saying all this? It couldn't be true, could it? That he didn't like children? He had said it before but I had always put it down to his bad moods, when his back was giving him trouble or because he felt frail. I had told myself it was because the noise of boys playing football in the road gave him a headache or because a toddler had splashed him at the lido. But when I had become pregnant I thought things were different – he seemed to have been looking forward to the new arrival, helping me to decorate the new nursery, bringing bags of hand-me-downs from his brother in Oxworth and even getting out the gaudy silver rattle that he had been given when he was a baby – a grand Marks family heirloom placed in my child's humble cot. And then he had seen Violet when she was born. I thought, like me, that he must have loved her instantly but now he was saying this – that he didn't like children. Had Violet meant no more to him than just any another child?

George turned his head slightly. The light caught his hair and I noticed that it was thinning, his eyes seemed to have shrunk behind his spectacles and his voice was deepening with age. Had I married an old man after all? Old men didn't like children, did they? George didn't like children. He sighed and took a large key out of his pocket. Then he left the room and went upstairs. I heard his footsteps above me on the landing and then the rattle of the key in the nursery door. He was locking the room, for the last time, I thought.

He didn't look at me when he came back into the lounge, just sank down in the armchair by the fire. I remember thinking that this was a strange thing for him to do because he'd never sat in that chair before; it had always been for guests. He poured himself a sherry and put the glass on the mantelpiece. Then he took the newspaper from the sideboard and opened it in front of him, holding it high so that the top part of his body became a mass of paper and print. I watched him; the armchair, the newspaper and the legs sticking out underneath – long, spindly legs, crossed at the knee so that his trousers rode up revealing bands of pale skin and a web of blue veins beneath the hem.

That was the first time that he had sat there. I had forgotten that until now. And I sat with him in the same room, childless in a house meant for children, married but alone, together but apart. And from then on, we sat like that every day, George reading his paper and me gazing out the window, just as we did on that day – the first day of my new life.

11

I woke at dawn on Thursday, the dull glow behind the curtains enough to fill me with excitement about what another day at Rose Cottage might bring. By the time George came downstairs I was already perched on the window seat, hat on head and bag in hand. He made no remarks about the fact that my breakfast plate was already in the sink nor that my side of the bed had been empty when he woke, in fact he said very little and soon he was out the door. Once George's car had crawled away past the war memorial, I jumped up and left the house, hurrying over the crossroads and taking the dirt track up to the farms.

When I arrived at the cottage, Maud opened the door in tears: 'I'm so sorry, Mrs Marks, but the garments ain't arrived.'

'What do you mean haven't arrived?' I said.

She snivelled into her sleeve. 'Well it's usually a van that comes you see – my nephew – he delivers them from the factory, along with the wages. He should have come yesterday but we've not seen him. I fear you've had a wasted journey.'

I was about to enquire as to why Maud had not telephoned but then my eye caught the cracked oil lamp on the worktop, the pot-bellied stove with the broken door and the rusted draining board, and I realized that I already knew the answer. 'I'm sorry about that, Mrs Brown,' I said, then, desperate for an excuse to stay, added, 'but they could still arrive today. If your nephew decided to leave this morning, he might only have set off at dawn and it's a long drive from Oxworth. I don't mind waiting, at least until ten.'

'I can't pay you for your time,' Maud said quickly.

'Oh that's quite all right,' I said. I was about to tell her how little I minded, but then I remembered that I was the unfortunate Mrs Marks forced into labour by my husband's terrible gambling debts and instead I added: 'Well, just the hope of earning a bit more makes it worth staying, doesn't it?'

The kitchen seemed much larger with the table clear of linen. And only now, without the din of the sewing machine, did I realize that the house was not just a workshop but a home.

'Are the children at school?' I asked, trying to sound casual.

Maud looked at me blankly. 'It's almost time for the harvest,' she said. 'I need them here to earn.'

'Of course,' I said. I knew little of the school holidays but I had not seen a single book or slate on my last visit.

Maud swept the dust off her basket chair. 'You can sit here while you wait. I can't offer you any—'

'Oh, please don't go to any effort on my account, Mrs Brown,' I said. 'In fact, I thought I might take a stroll outside. It is such a lovely day and I thought that I might see some more of this beautiful place that you live.'

'Beautiful place,' Maud echoed dully. 'Well, I suppose I could show you the yard.'

The kitchen door opened out on to a rough rectangle of well-trodden earth slashed with long tyre tracks. A rickety henhouse leant against the cottage wall, the babble of contented chickens rising behind the slats. There was a rusty pump with a bucket dangling underneath and a skeletal mangle, still digesting a pair of limp long johns. Bed linen was drooping from the clothes line, gusting with freshness as the water caught the air.

A gangly youth lay on a plank bench, eyes closed and snoring gently. His hair was such a deep red and his skin so pale and freckled that I feared he would burn if he stayed in the sun a moment longer.

'Andy,' Maud swiped at him with a dishcloth. 'You fed them chickens?'

Andy lifted his head. 'It ain't my turn!' his voice cracked. 'It's Henry's'. He sat upright, yawned and cricked his neck from side to side.

'He's into communism,' said Maud as if it were an explanation for her son's rudeness. 'He uses it as an excuse to be lazy – says I'm an oppressor.' She swung her dishcloth at him again.

'I didn't know there were any communists in Hertfordshire!' I said, trying to sound friendly.

Andy gave me a withering look then picked up a rusty grain bucket, kicked open a gate to a long, sloping field and threw a handful of grain onto the grass. A loud clucking filled the air and four white chickens fluttered from the henhouse and waddled frantically through the gate, jabbing their beaks into the earth.

Distant laughter came from the field and I saw a small copse of birch and hawthorn at the top of the hill, flashes of movement between the trees.

'Little bleeders!' exclaimed Maud. 'That's our landlord's field – he ain't going to like them running wild up there.' But there was no surprise in her voice and I guessed her displeasure was just for my benefit and that the children were always running wild wherever they pleased. In fact there was a well-worn path between the gate and the copse and several patches of flattened grass.

'Oh, I'm sure the farmer won't mind,' I said. 'The field seems to be in fallow at the moment anyway, so I don't think—'

'Jim-John!' yelled Maud.

A shape appeared from the trees and started moving down the hill towards us. I had thought that I had seen a boy on my last visit to the cottage, but now as the shape got closer, I saw that the boy was in fact two. The two boys then stopped suddenly, at a spot that seemed familiar to them, as if they knew the exact point where Maud could hear but not catch them. I saw that they were almost identical – thin and freckled, but one with hair a shade lighter than his brother as if he were a faded copy on carbon paper.

'Jim-John,' cried Maud. 'Come and be civil to Mrs Marks!'

But the boys just chuckled, the darker one gesturing with two fingers, before they ran off back up the hill.

'Oh dear... but really, it doesn't matter,' I said in response to an apology that never came.

'Where do you think Henry is?' I said and then, trying to sound casual, '...and Ruby?'

'Oh they're around here somewhere,' Maud smiled. 'She's your favourite, ain't she?'

'Ruby?' I said, annoyed that I had been unable to disguise my feelings. 'Oh, I don't know about that.'

'You'd be surprised, it often happens with ladies such as yourself. They take pity on the poor mite.'

'Oh,' I said, surprised. 'Why's that?'

'Well there's always a kind word for her from a vicar's wife or a schoolmistress. Miss Potter in the reception class always took pity on her, gave her humbugs. They feel sorry for her, I suppose.'

'Because of her birthmark you mean?'

'Yes,' she said. 'You see, things will only be harder for her when she grows up. She can't really have any dreams, not with her coming from a place like this and with that face. A farm girl that was bright and pretty might do well for herself, become a shop girl in a town, maybe a waitress or maid. But poor Ruby, with that face, she'll end up doing farm work or sewing just like her mother. They don't want to see the likes of her in town, you see, not with an ugly mug like that.'

I was about to protest at the harshness of her words but there was a sudden creak and a scattering of white feathers and Ruby burst from the henhouse. 'Bitch!' she screamed.

'Mind your language, young lady!' shouted Maud. 'If I'd known you was in with those hens earwigging again, you nosey little…' But she was too late as Ruby was already through the gate and halfway up the field. 'I should have known,' said Maud. 'She's always hiding in there, mollycoddling them chickens, always that mangy Snowflake.'

I stepped through the gate, my eyes following Ruby as she ran. I knew that I had to talk to her, show her that I did not agree with Maud. 'She's upset,' I said. 'Shouldn't we—'

'Oh no, she won't listen to me now, I'll just have to put up with her foul mouth and then she'll get the back of my hand.'

'Maybe I could—'

'You can try, but you won't get nowhere with her. Not when she's like this.'

'But—'

'Oh go on then, if you must, but don't say I didn't warn you. You can't talk about the face, you see, she won't talk about the face to nobody.'

*

I found Ruby lying in the long grass where the edge of the field met a tangle of brambles. She looked me right in the eyes: 'Sod. Off.'

I tried not to react, but I know that she saw the shock in my face and smiled to herself.

'Well?' I said indignantly. 'You are ugly, aren't you; if that's the way you like to talk.'

'Don't matter then, does it?' she said. 'Ugly mouth goes with ugly face.'

'I don't think you are ugly,' I said. 'Not at all.'

'Maybe I want to be,' she said, then smiled mischievously. She hooked her lip with her finger and pulled it down, revealing her teeth and gums. Then she pulled her eyelids down, exposing the mass of red capillaries, and crushed her nose to one side.

'Please stop that,' I said, but she continued, her fingers clawing her flesh until her face became distorted and her skin was crossed with red scratches. 'Stop that!' I shouted. 'Stop that now!'

Ruby jumped as if she had expected me to strike her and her hands fell to her lap, her eyes filling with tears.

'Okay, maybe you are right,' I said more gently. 'It doesn't matter. It doesn't matter at all.'

She twisted her mouth sulkily but would not look at me.

'All right then, will you let me tell you why it's more important how you behave than how you look?'

'You're going to anyway, aren't you,' she muttered. 'I know you grand lady types and your sermons.'

I ignored her and tried to smile. 'No sermons, I promise. Instead let me tell you a story about a girl I once knew. She lived right here and she was Queen of the May – Missensham's May Queen. But because she was a pretty girl she knew that she never had to try for anything, because everything always came to her. She wasn't good at making her own friends because people wanted to be around her anyway and she never learned how to win an argument because she got her own way most of the time. She never had anything to aim for or anything to fight for. The only people who didn't care how she looked were her parents and they made her work hard and she hated them for it. She didn't want to work for things herself, she wanted to be with people who would give her what she wanted without question. So when a rich man wanted to marry her, that was good enough for her, she just went along with it. But the years went by and she wasn't happy and soon she wasn't beautiful anymore and so she had nothing left and people began to realize this and her friends all left when she didn't bother to keep up with them and even her husband found her a bore.'

I drew a deep breath. It was a long time since I had talked for so long. Ruby stared at me thoughtfully. I felt strangely self-conscious under her stare. I had not been so close to her before. Her eyes were an almost hypnotic green, with an explosion of amber from the pupil. Her face was pale, the thread of a thin blue vein in the almost translucent skin at her temple. Even the birthmark now seemed delicate, a gentle feathering at the edges of the red tears. How could something so perfect be considered ugly? Suddenly I wanted to tell her everything and I wanted her to believe it and accept it and I wanted her to walk back to Little Willow with me, hand in hand. I wanted to—

'Did you get to ride a horse?' said Ruby suddenly.

I felt my cheeks warm. 'What do you mean?'

'When you were May Queen? Did you get to ride on a horse?'

'No!' I said sharply, shocked that she had seen through the story, but then I thought that maybe this secret could be the start of our connection. I tried to smile. 'Oh no, I had to walk a very long way and my feet really hurt in the white slippers.' I laughed. 'So you see, being pretty didn't do me any good.'

She laughed too. 'I would like a horse,' she said. 'Not like the farm horses. I saw a grand lady in town once, she was on a dapple grey mare. It was plump and its tail was like silk.' She jumped up and stood with her legs bowed, her hands pulling on imaginary reins as she rode seriously, her face screwed up in concentration. 'I don't care what Maudy says. I just want a grey mare and I will ride it in to town, clip-clop, up to my grand house, which I will have all to myself, just room for me and the mare and Smokey and Snowflake. Nobody else will be invited to stay. They can't live with me. I hate them all!'

'You don't mean that,' I said. 'You surely can't mean that about Maud!'

She stopped riding and the horse vanished from underneath her. Her face became thoughtful, then she said bitterly: 'I don't want to be like her – she leaves us hungry – you know she can't even afford any meat until she does all that sewing.'

'Your mother works hard for you,' I said. 'How would you like to be sewing all the time?'

'Clarence takes all the money and he spends it on beer.'

'And some of it goes back to Maud so she can buy you meat – you just said the sewing buys the meat.'

'Spose so.' Ruby's chin slumped into her hand. 'But my face

is her fault,' she said suddenly. 'I'm ugly because of her!'

'An accident of birth is never the mother's fault,' I said quickly. 'It's nothing more than an act of God. Your face is perfect. so there is nobody to blame.'

She folded her arms and looked at me weirdly, blinking quickly like she didn't understand. I thought that maybe she didn't believe in God. I desperately searched for some words and phrases that a child would understand but none came.

'Whatever you say,' she said, 'but it is her fault.'

'Maud would feel terrible if she could hear you saying that. You don't want to upset her any more, do you?'

She shrugged.

'You called her a nasty word earlier,' I said. I put my arm round her tentatively. 'I've got an idea – why don't you go and pick her some flowers to say sorry?'

She sighed and pulled a face but then she got up and trudged over to the trees and squatted down in the grass, her head bobbing as she worked.

I thought about my young life above the dress shop. I had not known I was poor until I looked back on it, and even then, we always had enough to eat, even if I did work my fingers to the bone to get it. Then there was George: his family's grand house in Oxworth, with the piano in the drawing room; the motorcar bought for a doctor's rounds that barely covered a square mile; and the way that he had become accustomed to dine on a roast chicken whenever he visited his brother. But I had never quite realized just how rich his family had been until I saw the silver rattle he'd inherited for his christening – a silver handle with an ivory teether, with delicate little bells and fine engraving. When his family became mine, the rattle passed to Violet, the daughter of a humble seamstress, yet she was never to use it and it ended up buried with her in her coffin where it was no good to anybody. I wondered what gifts Ruby would have received for her christening, if indeed she had been christened at all.

Ruby returned, her hands behind her back.

'Show me what you've picked,' I said. 'Perhaps we can...'

She opened her fingers to reveal a crushed little posy.

'Violets!' I said, shocked. 'Why did you choose those?'

'Because she says they're unlucky – she says they mean death if they're brought indoors.' She chuckled and suddenly those hypnotic green eyes became narrow and black.

'My mother used to think that too!' I said, trying to sound calm. 'She was an old country woman, like your mother. Only old country woman believe that – I thought you wanted to be a smart Missensham lady, with a grey mare!'

That was enough to convince her and we left the posy of violets behind and walked back to the cottage with Ruby clutching a bunch of wilting primroses and scowling all the way.

'Why are you pulling faces now?' I said.

'I'm hungry. She didn't have money for jam this morning.'

'At least you had the bread and butter, didn't you?' I said, although I couldn't help feeling a little sorry for her. I thought of the silver rattle again and how much bread and jam it could have bought with pawn shop money. Then I had an idea: 'Look, I visited you today, why don't you visit me on Saturday, and I can make you some nice food.'

'Like what?' she said.

'Jam,' I said. 'Strawberry jam – no, what would you like? If you could have anything in the world?'

She frowned. 'Lemonade,' she said, '…and bla-mongsh', she spat the last word out, like it was just syllables she'd heard but not understood and I wondered if she even knew what blancmange was, let alone whether she liked it.

'Yes,' I said. 'Yes, why not?'

I took her hand but she looked right past me and I heard feet thundering behind me as Jim and John ran down the hill: 'Bla-mongsh? Are you having a party, Miss?'

I stood open-mouthed, but they waited expectantly.

'Yes,' I said quietly. 'I suppose I am.'

The boys clapped gleefully.

'Well, I suppose you are invited then.' I said, feeling I didn't have a choice any more. 'Yes, it will be a big party. You can all come.'

Jim and John ran off cheering. I felt my stomach sink. I'm not sure, but I like to think that Ruby looked disappointed too.

I suddenly started to panic. I was having a party! There would be food to buy, and drink too, invitations to write. Wait a minute! Invitations to whom? How could someone with no friends throw a party? And then there would be the matter of telling George… and then making sure Mr Tuttle wouldn't get in the way... and then making something suitable to wear... and then making the house spotless and bunting, and tablecloths and placemats and glasses and napkins and...

...And then Mrs Brown was calling me back indoors because the garments had arrived. Somewhere in the distant country lanes, the factory van grumbled its way back to London but I barely heard it. Maud's cursing and the laughs and shouts of 'bla-mongsh' faded away into the air and I was left alone with my thoughts. There would be no turning back once the Browns had visited Little Willow. They would find out where I lived, bump into my neighbours and meet George and, little by little, I began to realize what I had done.

12

I had last held the rattle on a cold morning in 1926. I remember turning it in my hand – a solid silver bar, with four bells forming a crown round the top and an ivory ring at the bottom. Ornate scrolls were etched into the silver and, in the middle, the letters *VM* were engraved, the initials of George's father, Victor Marks. It was a royal sceptre, a religious relic, hard and cold against my skin – something you would expect to see in the hands of an emperor or a bishop, not next to the soft flesh of a baby.

I tried to imagine the rattle in the hands of a young George, swaddled in lace under the huge black hood of a Victorian pram. But the face I saw in the pram was not that of a baby, it was George's face as I knew it, a face with wrinkles and little round spectacles and I realized that I couldn't imagine George as a baby any more than I could imagine George being a young man.

On that morning frost had come in the middle of May, and at ten o'clock the sky shone red like a sunset and nothing seemed to make sense.

I stood in the lichgate of St Benedict's, upright and rigid in shoes that cut like glass, my temple throbbing with the monotonous clank of an iron bell, the air cold and bitter with the tang of the moss on the tombstones.

This was the church of the old town. It was an ancient construction of jagged flint, tucked away in a triangle between road, canal and railway, and shielded from all by black yew trees. It was a forgotten place, the echo of long-departed trains rattling through the cutting as if phantoms of the modern world.

George stood by my side as a thin trail of mourners wound their way to the church door. They were mostly George's family; his brother from Oxworth and some vague, distant relatives, all afflicted by the Marks's high, hunched shoulders and shuffling gait. They came with stammered condolences and stiff handshakes, the women wiping tears from behind little round spectacles. My own family would have offered condolences too, but they had to make do with just watching, their wishes sent from deep beneath the earth. It was a small number of mourners, but then it was a small church, with a small coffin – a small funeral for a small life.

When the family had passed, George and I were alone, the warble of the organ blunted by the mist rising from the canal. That day was to be the end of it and suddenly I felt that I couldn't bear any more reminders; there had already been too many.

I thrust the rattle into George's hand. 'Please, George, please take it through and get them to put it in the coffin.'

He hesitated and cocked his head, the glass in his spectacles misting over. 'It's too late,' he said. 'Far too late. Everything has been arranged for days, everybody has gone to such a lot of trouble. You can't just—'

'Please,' I said. 'It has to go with her – where it should be.'

He didn't say anything, but I saw all his protests in his face – the loss of his family heirloom, bothering the vicar, the embarrassment of it all. But he swallowed it inside himself. Then he nodded and took the rattle from me, disappearing down into the dark archway. I stood alone for a few minutes, watching my breath as it clouded in the air, and then I followed him into the church.

13

Saturday came with the call of blackbirds at daybreak. By six o'clock the garden looked beautiful. Mr Tuttle had constructed two long plank tables on the lawn and I had covered them with white bedsheets, plates and glasses. There were platters for sandwiches on the tables, jugs for lemonade and flags left over from the King's Jubilee celebrations. A trail of bunting led from the garden to the kitchen, where I worked through the sunrise setting jellies and baking cakes.

George came down at eight. The look on his face and his half-dressed appearance supposedly evidence for the speech that followed about back pain which meant he would be confined to bed all day. He said how terribly sorry he was that he would miss all the 'jollity' but something on his face told me that he was looking forward to a day in bed with a newspaper and a bottle of chlorodyne; time to himself, spent in a fug of narcotics that would blunt the pain of the womanly social engagement. I found that I was disappointed but not surprised.

Audrey was the first to arrive, in a flurry of silk and feathers. She was ten minutes early, because she wanted to help out and lend support, she said, as she cast her eye over the garden, adding: 'There's so little one can do during a depression, isn't there?'

I watched Ethel and Alan chasing round the lawn, their new boots cutting muddy dents into the grass. 'I suppose so,' I said.

Audrey placed two bottles of wine on the kitchen table. 'Chardonnay!' she whispered. 'We mustn't let George know that there is anything French in the house – he would have a fit.' She put a finger to her lips and giggled. 'Silly old man, Forsham would be too exotic for him and there's probably a Huguenot tailor in the high street there too.'

'Oh, I think it's because of the war,' I said. 'He somehow blames the French for—'

'I noticed you are decorating,' said Audrey.

'Yes,' I said, realizing that she must have peeped under the

Union Jack that covered the paint pots in the hallway.

'Who have you got in?'

'Tuttle and Son, Master decor—'

'Oh, dear old Mr. Tuttle.' She laughed. 'I can see why George would want him. Nothing too modern for our George, nothing too expensive. You know, I didn't know old Tuttle was still around until I saw his bicycle up on the green the other day. The sign was almost falling off. Still, a sweet old man.' She smiled. 'A drunk maybe, but a sweet old man.'

I thought about how I had found Mr Tuttle's hammer in the kitchen sink that morning and was inclined to agree, if not admit it. 'George seems to think he's a very upright and amiable fellow,' I said. 'Even says he's seen him leaving flowers on the memorial many a time. He says that Mr Tuttle has a neurological condition, something to do with electrical impulses and neurons misfiring. Like thousands of microscopic electrical cables losing their connections. He says he treated similar conditions during the war. Anyway, Mr Tuttle's son will be joining him to help, so the medical condition won't matter so much—But Audrey was already gazing over my shoulder. 'Mrs Twining!' she shouted. 'Yoo-hoo! Oh, Mrs. Twining, it's been months hasn't it!'

I busied myself in the kitchen while Audrey took it upon herself to greet the guests. Some popped their heads round the back door to say hello, all with the same nods and smiles; the odd insincere offer of help, hopes that the weather would hold and nods of sympathy when I made my apologies for George. Every time I heard new footsteps, I would look up hoping for Ruby and try to stop my smile from fading when I realized that it was not her.

I stood stirring custard over the stove, the tinkle of Audrey's laughter floating in through the window: 'All this work, no, I'm sure it was nothing,' 'Oh no, I must have the credit for bringing the wine.' Then whispering loudly, 'George won't allow anything French in the house!'

Eventually the conversation grew faint as the guests arranged themselves at the tables and I peered round the door to see paper hats bobbing contentedly as people ate. I saw the vicar's wife and the Bridgers from next door, the secretary from George's surgery and her elderly mother in a bath chair. Some people had brought spouses or relatives as there were faces I didn't recognize and then there was a lady in a pink summer dress whose name I didn't know, although we always said hello when we saw each other. But there was still no Ruby, nor any of the Browns and I began to worry that they would not come.

'Emma, Emma, you must stop working and have something to eat.' Audrey stood on the back step, offering me a plate of my own sandwiches, presented gracefully on her open hand as if she had taken hours preparing them.

'Thank you,' I said.

'Come on, take a break.' She pulled me down and we perched on the back step to eat.

Ethel was running over the flower bed and I watched helplessly as the pansies got trampled. Her feet were dangerously close to the one blue bloom I had taken so long to cultivate. I opened my mouth and pointed. But Audrey's eyes were elsewhere.

'Who's that filthy scamp Alan is playing with?'

'Where?' I said.

'Over there, the little kid with the grubby hands and the cap over his eyes. He must have just walked in off the street!'

'Henry?' I said hopefully. 'Oh, that's Henry! He's, um...'

Then Maud appeared, a white collar sewn on to her old brown dress and a rose poking from a knot of hair wound into a Victorian bun. We stood up from the step as she approached.

'Sorry we are late, Mrs. Marks,' she said in voice which sounded like she was doing an impression of the Queen from a wireless broadcast. Then she glanced quickly at Audrey and dropped into a little bob curtsey.

'Audrey,' I said quickly, 'this is Maud Brown, Maud is Henry's mother.'

Audrey's mouth dropped open but she recovered quickly, thrusting her hand forward. 'Delighted, Mrs. Brown, delighted!'

Maud shook her hand warmly then smiled her stubby-toothed grin.

Audrey's eyes widened. 'Really, I am delighted to meet you, Mrs Brown,' she gabbled, 'but Emma has been so terribly naughty and not mentioned you to me.'

'Maud is a friend,' I said quickly. 'She has one of those lovely old farmhouses out by Evesbridge, right in the countryside.'

Audrey's stare had sunk to the handshake and I saw that

Maud's fingers were covered in green dye. Audrey glanced at her own hand and, although it was perfectly clean, withdrew it quickly and wiped the palm on her skirt.

'Oh, it's only fabric dye,' I said, embarrassed. That reminds me, Maud, I have a dress I'd like you to dye for me, if you would be so kind. Grass stains, I'm afraid. If I forget to give it to you before you go, it'll be in the study.' I turned to Audrey. 'She's very good,' I said. 'Good enough to make money from her handicrafts, and working from home allows her to be with her family.'

'Oh, it must be lovely out in Evesbridge this time of year,' said Audrey absent-mindedly. Then she glanced away quickly: 'Alan! Alan! Get off the flower bed.'

Alan sat at a table looking confused and Audrey ran off muttering something about the merits of keeping society and charity separate.

'What a nice lady,' said Maud and then made some comment about hoping that the weather would hold, which was worded in such a way I guessed that she must have been repeating what she had heard among the other guests. I nodded, looking over her shoulder to where the children were running across the garden, the trample of the boys' boots and the billow of Ethel's pinafore.

Then I saw Ruby, alone at a flower bed, bending to grasp a stem. It was a pansy, the blue one, and she seemed drawn to it over all the reds and yellows. She pulled it up at the roots, holding it close to her chest then dropped her chin to smell it, her deep breaths magnified by the rise and fall of her fist. Her nose was buried in the centre of the flower, the petals sucked flat against her nostrils as if she was drinking the scent. I felt my heart thud hard against my chest. The action was somehow familiar but the memory was buried deep in my mind and I could not recall from where it came.

'I'm sorry, Mrs. Marks,' said Maud. 'She's been told not to do that.' Then she cleared her throat with a noise like a motorcar starting in the cold. 'This damn cough has taken the wind right out of me, could you do me a favour and call the little brat over for me?'

I did so, cupping my hand and shouting across the lawn.

Maud looked at me strangely.

'What?' I said. 'What is it?'

'What did you shout just then? Who did you call for?'
'Who?' I said. 'Ruby, of course, like you said.'
'No, no, you called her something else.'
Ruby bounded over breathless. 'Who's Violet?'
'Violet!' echoed Maud. 'That was it!'
'I didn't say that,' I said, feeling my blood warm. 'I didn't.'
Ruby sniggered.
'Yes, she's right, you did!' said Maud. 'That is what you said.' Then she laughed. 'I'd lay off that fancy wine, Emma, maybe you've had a bit much already.'
'I haven't,' I said. 'I haven't had any!'

All around me people were smiling, their eyes fixed on me as if they were waiting for me to explain the joke. I opened my mouth but then shut it again when I realized that I had no idea what I would say. I stumbled back inside, mumbling something about checking on the blancmange and ran into the lounge, collapsing into the window seat.

Maud's head appeared round the door. 'It's nothing to worry about, Emma, I'm always getting their names mixed up.'

I smiled weakly.

'I expect that doctor husband of yours has got you all worried about the smallest slip of the tongue, giving it a fancy name, tongue-tied it is or something.'

'No, you don't understand,' I said but then stopped when I realized that I could not say any more.

'Maybe you should have some of that wine after all.' She handed me a glass tumbler, full to the brim.

I felt the rush of alcohol in my head as soon as the wine hit my tongue and remembered that I had hardly touched any of the sandwiches I had spent all morning preparing.

Maud seemed troubled by the silence so did her best to fill it: 'Once, I got Ruby and the cat mixed up, I was up to my eyes in needlework and calls to Smokey to come and help me. They all heard of course, fell about laughing they did.'

I nodded and tried to smile to show that I was appreciating her efforts but just felt my face crumple.

'Then once I was in the bedroom with Clarence and, in a moment of passion, I calls out the name of my past fella!' She shrieked with laughter and jabbed her elbow into my ribs. 'Well, there was a to-do after that – plates thrown across the kitchen – I had to run and hide in the woods!'

I couldn't help smile at this and realized for the first time that all her talk of lovers was not intended to shock me but rather was an offer of trust and intimacy, something I had never had with Audrey.

'There you go!' she said. 'A smile at last.'

I took another long sip of wine.

'A big family is such a drain,' Maud said softly. 'All those names to muddle up. You're probably better off as you are, with no brats at all. Just more time for you and George to be together. I wish I had that.'

'No you don't,' I said firmly.

'No,' she said. 'You are right of course; I don't want that, not all the time anyway.' Then she patted my hand. 'What I mean is, it would be nice, but just sometimes.' Then she changed the subject: 'How long have you been with George?'

'Eleven years,' I said.

'It's a long time. You must have been a young bride.'

I nodded, thinking maybe too young.

'But a lady such as yourself must have had other admirers?'

I was surprised by the openness of the question, but her talk of her fellas and the warm fog of alcohol in my head had numbed me. 'Yes, one,' I said, then added quickly, 'well, no, none actually, none.' I had been thinking of my past lover my man in the grass, the memory that had been stirred as I sunbathed in the lido, but I couldn't quite manage her honesty. After all, it had been so long ago that it felt like it had been, well before George, almost like another lifetime.

'What do you mean?' she said.

'Nothing,' I said. 'Really, it was nothing.'

I saw the rest of the party through a shimmer of alcohol: Audrey dancing with the vicar under the bunting; the bath chair crashing into one of the tables; Maud singing 'God Save the King' as Jim and John ran round the garden with the Union Jack round their shoulders; the lady in pink clasping her hands in delight at the sight of the blancmange; peals of laughter; empty plates; the chink of wine glasses; jokes, debates and good wishes. But none of this had been my intention – the party had been for Ruby yet I had seen so little of her. Then, before I knew it, the sun had sunk low and people were starting to gather up their coats and bags.

'Wait!' I shouted, running frantically into the house. I had bought new yo-yos for the children and I raced upstairs to find them, rummaging through the bedroom cupboard and stuffing them into my pockets. Then I stopped on the top of the landing by the locked door, my mind racing. I had not been into the nursery for nine years, I had never wanted to until now, but I had always known where George had put the key. I fumbled on the top of the door frame and unlocked the door quietly, trying not to disturb George. Then, very quietly, I went into the nursery. The room was in darkness, the curtains drawn, but I saw what I had come for and took it quickly, locking the door behind me and replacing the key in the hope that George would not notice that the room had been disturbed.

Back downstairs, the Union Jack lay abandoned in the kitchen and I took it, throwing it over Ruby's gift before I carried it outside. Audrey was towing Ethel and Alan towards the house and I heard the growl of Walter's car on the road.

'Wait!' I shouted again. 'I have presents for the children.' Then I looked round and raised my voice hopefully: 'All the children.'

Alan and Ethel took their yo-yos timidly, each saying a quiet thank you.

'You're welcome!' I said cheerfully, feeling giddy inside.

People clustered round and made polite comments: 'That'll give you something for the playground!'; 'What lovely colours!'; 'The other children will be jealous!'

Henry appeared, his eyes round as he thrust his face between the adults' legs.

'Henry, get back!' yelled Maud.

'No, no,' I said. 'There is a gift for him too, there's gifts for all the children.' I handed Henry a yo-yo, and then one each to Jim and John. Henry took his shyly and put it in his pocket, while the other two, span them on the end of their strings, the wood cracking on to the garden path.

'Say thank you to Mrs Marks.'

'Thank you,' they chorused.

Then Henry started playing with his yo-yo – the ball dropped to the end of the string, but the lady in pink showed him how to do it and everybody clapped.

'And now, Ruby,' I said. 'Where are you, Ruby?' People moved out the way as Maud pushed her to the front of the crowd.

'I've got you a special gift,' I said, then I pulled away the Union Jack with a flourish. The crowd gasped. Then there was a cautious smattering of applause. Ruby's eyes were wide.

'Don't you see, Ruby?' I said. 'It's a rocking horse. It's your grey mare.'

She swallowed and nodded, glancing quickly up at Maud.

The horse was magnificent. The dust wiped free by the Union Jack, its flanks gleaming in the last rays of sunlight. It stood proudly, muscles tensed in mid gallop, eyes bright and shining.

'Mrs Marks, you really shouldn't have,' said Maud quickly. 'It really is far too much.' I was shocked to see that she was blushing. She who usually talked so openly was actually blushing. I looked round at the other guests – there were some raised eyebrows and open mouths. A few of the adults shot glances at each other and then at the horse, and most of the children were standing back as if they were scared to touch it.

Suddenly I became aware of the fog of wine in my head. 'You're not too old for a rocking horse, are you Ruby?' I said quietly.

I don't think she heard the question but she had found her voice at last. 'Thank you, Mrs Marks.'

'Good.' I clapped my hands, reassured but disappointed that I didn't see the excitement I had expected. I lifted the rocking horse and handed it to Ruby. It looked massive against her body. She had to twist her shoulder to take hold of it, one of her tiny hands on the belly and another on the neck. Suddenly I felt silly. How would she carry it home?

'Thank you, Mis-sus-Marks,' she said again, almost automatically.

I saw Audrey turn and whisper in the pink lady's ear.

'Of course, it's for all of you really,' I said loudly. 'Henry is just not big enough to ride it yet, so for now it's for Ruby.'

Audrey had still not broken away from the pink lady's ear.

'Oh, no, it's nothing,' I said loudly in response to the muted thanks. Then I felt myself blushing again and said: 'You'd better get moving, Maud, if you want to get home before it gets dark.'

'Yes,' she said quickly, grabbing Henry by the hand, her arm round Jim and John like a protective wing. 'Come along you lot. You heard the lady. Shake a leg!'

I stood in the drive and waved them goodbye. They made a

strange bunch of silhouettes on the road – Mrs Brown walking quickly, almost trotting, my stained dress trailing from her bag, and Jim and John running ahead, swinging round the streetlights. Ruby moved slowly behind them, dragged sideways by the massive gift, moving along the pavement like a big, slow crab. I watched them until they got to the war memorial, all the time not one of them stopping to help Ruby.

Then I turned back to the house, my eye catching a crack of light between the curtains in the bedroom. George's face was in the window, his eyes following Ruby down the road.

14

Ruby

My name is Ruby Brown. But now there is another name on Emma's lips: Violet. And violets bring bad luck.

The morning after Emma's party Maudy had a sore head. She staggered out of bed and slumped in her chair with her head in her hands. She didn't even shout when Jim dragged the rocking horse out of the back room, didn't even stand up or slap him, she just sat all hunched and groaning.

Jim and John climbed all over that horse. They rocked it hard and with each rock it shot forward, the rocker grating on the floor. Jim spied Smokey, the whiskery buffalo, and shot a stick at him with a bow made from bloomer thread. Andy pulled the horse round and round by the tail, Jim and John still riding hard, cheering and whooping like Red Indians. That horse was never going to be my grand grey mare. No, this was always going to be a cowboy steed – shot with arrows, hit, battered and ridden hard. A poor old nag sent to the knackers, worked to death for the glue factory.

The rocking horse was already dead when Maudy stood up and screamed at us. She heaved its poor carcass above our heads and threw it out into the yard, then she bolted the door behind it, locking Jim and John out for good measure. She had work to do, she said. She had to work to feed us because we couldn't always rely on the charity of hoity-toity people who could afford blancmange and wine. Then she let out a little sniff and sucked her mouth in tight until it looked like a dog's bum. Maudy was upset, but this wasn't her usual screaming raging upset, this was something different, like a sickliness she caught from Emma's party and hadn't been able to shake off. So I went all soft and said that I would help her. Maudy beamed brown teeth. I was her special girl again.

Maudy had a problem, you see. When the van had showed

up that week there weren't any aprons inside, just a load of white cotton sheets and a pattern for ladies' gloves. Maudy was no good at gloves. The gloves she made were baggy, with fingers like sausages. She knew that Walker's could never sell those sausage-gloves to fashionable ladies. She'd slaved over them all week, pinning out nice thin little paper fingers and drawing round them with charcoal. But those nice thin little fingers looked like sausages once the gloves were made and Maudy's charcoal had stained the cotton, so the dainty white gloves Maudy wanted were now all fat and baggy and had to be dyed to cover up the charcoal smudges.

Maudy tore open a big packet of red carmine dye and mixed it in a little copper basin. She cursed as some of the carmine spilled onto the draining board, trickles of red oozing from the dark powder. Soon the dye was boiling away on the stove, and the whole house stank like a chicken on fire. When it was ready, she poured the dye into buckets and stirred the gloves in their bloody water, the red soaking into the white. She forgot all about my offer of help and even when I reminded her, she just shook her head as if my help would only knock over the buckets or stop the dye from fixing. She worked for hours, kneeling on the floor until the sun was high in the sky and the day grew hotter and hotter. Then at last she sat back on her heels and wiped the sweat from her forehead.

'This'll be the last of the red,' she said. 'Not enough for another bucket but at least it won't go to waste while I gets my wind back.' She poured a stream of carmine into the bucket and started squeezing the dye through a wodge of material.

'What's that?' I said. 'It's not gloves.'

'It's just some of your old hair ribbons, Ruby, oh, and a dress of Mrs Marks's. She said it had grass stains on. She couldn't get them off. I might as well throw it in with the gloves. Only carmine will be strong enough to cover these stains.'

'Why are you doing that for her? She ain't paying you!' Andy stood in the doorway, pointing to his exercise book as if the dyed dress would upset all his sums. 'Don't you know anything about the Depression? There's people like us in the North that have to take the dole and you're doing this for free!'

'She's a friend,' said Maudy firmly. 'That's what friends do, women friends anyway. I guess it's too much for you men to understand.' She looked at me and winked, just to make sure that I didn't forget – I was a girl, her special girl.

'I want to see.' I sat down on the floor next to her.

Maudy held the wet dress up against her chest, her face peeping over the top. 'She must have been a tiny little thing when she wore this,' she said. 'Still it's a woman's dress, not a child's, you can tell by the tailoring.'

It was a small dress, more like a pinafore with hardly any skirt, and sleeves only just past the shoulders and a low waist. I imagined a little Emma, invisible inside.

'It's a bit old-fashioned now though,' said Maudy. 'Even I know that much – that big bow on the collar and all that scalloping on the hem dates it. I used to see young ladies wearing this sort of thing back in the twenties. She must have had it a while, probably wore it when she was courting.'

'I wonder why she kept it all this time,' I said.

'Oh, I dunno. I doubt she would fit into it now. Not that she's fat, mind, not like your Aunt Sadie, but women of a certain age can't help filling out a bit. Grass stains too! Grass stains on the bum – it's not like a lady to get grass stains.' Maudy drew herself up and twisted her voice like Emma's: 'Not a lady from Sunningdale Estates!' She chuckled and dug her elbow into my ribs. 'Grass stains on the bum, what can she have been doing?'

I ignored her. It didn't feel right to joke about a lady like Emma. I thought to myself that maybe Emma was sad, maybe she wanted to remember some happy times. People keep things for all sorts of reasons, Maudy herself was always saying that.

Maudy ran her hands over the dress, squeezing out the water. 'Still, she must have looked lovely in it when she were younger,' she said. 'No fat flab back then.' She opened up the fabric so she could see the top of the dress again and held it up, a hand on each little sleeve. Then she started to hum to herself, a strange old-fashioned tune, and turned the dress from side to side, making it dance in front of her, the dye tinkling back into the bucket like the most delicate piano notes. Then she stopped suddenly and let out a long sigh. She dipped the dress forward, making it bow to her and dunked it back into the bucket, the invisible Emma swirling around in the red.

'You shouldn't envy her,' said Andy. 'Her kind can afford to look swish. Even back then her husband's money was paying for that dress. You shouldn't be doing this, not people like us, for people like her. It's like you're her slave.'

'I told you,' said Maudy, 'she's a friend.' But this time she didn't sound like she meant it at all.

But Andy wasn't finished: 'It ain't like she can't afford to pay you,' he said. He held up his hand, four shillings between his fingers.

'Where did you get that?' shouted Maudy.

'It's her wages,' he said. 'She must have forgotten to pick them up. Funny – you think she'd need them to afford all that wine and blancmange and--'

'Enough!' Maudy jumped up and slapped the coins from his fingers.

Andy looked stunned. They both stared at each other and neither moved to get the coins. Maudy's mouth tightened. She sat back on her heels and rocked. I looked at the dress in the bucket and saw Emma drowning in blood.

Maudy went all quiet after that. I fancied that she might be a statue if it wasn't for the hollow in her cheek and the pinch of her teeth where she chewed the inside of her mouth. It was something she'd been doing for a week or so. It was a mouth ulcer, she said, it was giving her gyp and our carry-on was only making it worse. Andy made his excuses and left, murmuring something about checking that Jim-John and Henry weren't scrumping. But he took his book with him and the blanket that he lay on when he napped in the barn.

Then it was just Maudy and me and suddenly she had forgotten about her ulcer because I was her special girl. And her special girl had to work hard. Maudy fished the red gloves from the buckets and took them out to the yard. She knelt at the mangle feeding the gloves through the rollers while I turned the handle. When the water had stopped splattering my shoes, she stopped and hung the gloves on the clothes line to dry. It was only when Maudy was sure that all the gloves were drying that she went back to fetch Emma's dress. She forced it hard through the mangle, again and again, then pegged it high on the line, where it hung, limp and dripping with blood.

*

That evening Clarence came home drunk, a bloody sheen on

the flagstones when he kicked a bucket across the kitchen floor.

'What the hell?' He reeled around, looking for someone to blame; the wife, the girl, the cat, the bucket, but with too many culprits to choose from, he just slumped in his chair. 'Can't I come home to a normal house, like any normal man?' he slurred.

For a moment I agreed with him. He wanted a normal home with four windows and a door in the middle and children who went to Sunday school and a wife who kissed him when he came in. But he wasn't normal either – no more than we were, so instead he yelled at Maudy, his arms flailing and spit flying from his mouth. But Maudy was used to it and she carried on working, ringing gloves over the buckets, her back to him as if he wasn't there at all.

'I will move the buckets, Clarence,' she said at last, 'just as soon as I am finished with them.'

I didn't get up to help. I didn't want to risk moving when Clarence was like that. I could smell him over the carmine; a smell like whisky and cigarettes and a wet dog and old muddied boots and rotting leaves, like the back of your mouth when you wake up.

Then his eyes changed and I saw the madness again – the madness I saw when the stove got broken and the Bad Thing happened. 'Ruby—'

I felt my stomach drop but then there was a loud bang and Maudy stood with a bucket at her feet, a pool of red spreading over the floor.

'For God's sake, woman! You're giving me a headache,' he yelled.

'No, Clarence,' she said firmly, 'the whisky did that.'

He turned to me again: 'What are you staring at, Pox-face?'

I looked down and bit my tongue, hard.

'Don't take it out on her, Clarence. What's she ever done to you?'

He answered by calling her a stupid bitch and me a leper, but by then he had no energy to shout, he was just muttering and all the spite was gone.

When I next looked up, his eyes were rolling and his head was nodding forwards. I didn't dare move until I heard his breath slow and the air wheeze from his nose.

'You did the right thing,' whispered Maudy. 'It's best not to rattle his cage.' She sat down next to me like her body weighed the earth. 'You mix with Sunningdale Estate types now, my girl, the blancmange-eating garden-party types. You can't have the likes of Clarence bringing you down.'

'How can you say that!' Andy stood in the doorway, shock all over his face. 'How can you say that about Clarence?'

'Shhh!' Maudy pointed to the sleeping Clarence and Andy came in slowly, followed by Jim-John and Henry, wide-eyed and clutching apples.

'Look, all I'm saying is that we have friends in Missensham now, on the Sunningdale Estates, it might be best for you boys too. Andy, it don't matter how many numbers you write in that book of yours, you won't stand a hope in hell of being a clerk at Walker's if you keep company with—'

'Bitch!' yelled Andy. 'You are trying to tear this family apart. You are always making trouble. I am proud of Clarence. Much prouder than I am of—'

'Listen to your mother,' said the rocking chair. Clarence didn't stir, his eyes stayed shut but he was speaking to us all right, his voice all deep and slurry. 'She's right. You should always ignore me when I'm drunk or you'll be banned from the Red Lion and from all over town, just like I am. Is that what you want for yourselves?'

The boys didn't answer. Andy's face was red like he'd been slapped and his mouth hung open.

Maudy beamed; hands on her hips like a trophy and a little nod towards Andy. He answered by flicking up two fingers but he knew he'd lost that one. Maudy plunged her hands in the bucket of carmine, squeezed the fabric and then brought them out again. Her fingers dripped with blood.

15

Emma

The morning after the party I woke suddenly and wished immediately that I had not. A red hot pain drilled my temple and my stomach fizzed with heat. I peeped through the curtains and screwed my eyes up against the light. The stain of a pale sun hung high in the sky and I realized that it must be nearly midday. The house was deadly silent. Next to me was a dip in the mattress – the indent of an invisible man, as if George had been vaporized. I stood up slowly and shuffled across the landing.

The door of the nursery was ajar and I realized that George must have been inside while I slept. I wondered how much he had seen the previous evening as he peered through the gap in our bedroom curtains. The road had been dark but, if he had not seen the Browns or Ruby's face, he had at least seen the rocking horse leaving and, once in the nursery, he had seen the indents in the carpet where it had once stood. Since finding Ruby, I had thought about going into the nursery a lot but now, in my fragile state, I found that I could not face it, although I walked past the door without shutting it.

I went into the back bedroom, drew back the curtains and looked out of the small window. In the garden one of the table coverings had blown into the fir trees and was snagged on the branches, billowing in the breeze. The other table was still set, plates and glasses half full as if phantom guests were still enjoying the party.

In the kitchen was a note from George. He had gone to visit his brother in Oxworth. The note was a brief one for George, and oddly lacking in complaint. It did not even mention the rocking horse or the nursery, which made me think that he had said all that he needed to by leaving the door open for me to see.

I stared at the plates piled in the sink, the mosaic of servers on the table and the assortment of half-empty glasses clustered on the draining board. The tang of stale wine rose from a bouquet of upended bottles in the bin and I clasped my hand over my mouth as my stomach rose in my chest.

Then I saw George's sherry glass on the counter, the crystal misted by the light from the window. A small posy of flowers wilted over the rim; violets, their blooms already drooping and their stems curled like tendrils. I twisted the glass in my hand. Sticky fingerprints smudged the crystal and I realized that one of the children must have brought the flowers to the party; I immediately thought of Ruby. The violets were in my home – Maud believed that violets indoors brought bad luck but I had told Ruby not to believe her old country superstitions. I did not know what the Violets meant but, I was sure that they were some kind of message from Ruby and that filled me with hope. I held the glass to my chest, and then sat back on the kitchen chair, letting the sun warm my forehead. The violets had brought back memories and I shut my eyes and let my mind wander...

*

It was the summer of 1925; a day of celebration. For months Missensham had been under siege from the railway company. The green fields had been flayed open and iron sleepers driven through the cutting as a tangle of electric cables fizzed and sparked all the way to London. Lorries had rumbled through the lanes of the old town, mud spilling out behind them and throngs of workmen left trails of sandy footprints to the Red Lion. In the middle of a field near the old town, hoardings had been put up, orange mud seeping from under the planks and the din of hammers and saws behind it. Yet on this summer day the noise had stopped, the last lorry rumbled off and the dew cleansed the roads of the footprints and tyre tracks. The hoardings came down and people flocked to the new Metropolitan Line station.

Audrey had bought us special advance tickets for the first train. We spent the morning chatting cheerily in the crammed carriage, whistling past the stations where people stood waiting to get to work in factories or offices. Audrey had planned cocktails at the Savoy – a way to celebrate the railway and what she saw as her return to the 'society' she missed in London, and besides, she said, she wanted to hear all about my honeymoon.

I had worn my new white dress – it had a big bow at the neckline and a scalloped hem that just brushed my kneecaps. I had thought it quite risqué for Missensham but, as Audrey had told me, it would be just the thing for London – and a small white hat with a folded brim.

The journey took two hours. I had to keep a hold of my little hat so I didn't lose it to the subterranean winds in the underground stations and the hem of my white dress became blackened with the grime of London. We arrived at the Savoy smelling of grease and sweat and having missed lunch, the alcohol in our cocktails just adding to the scour in our stomachs. Tired and grimy, we stood glumly in a haze of cigarette smoke, watching the bright young London women posing with champagne bowls and blowing smoke rings in the faces of fresh-faced noblemen. Their bodies were sinuous and tanned, naked but for little dresses which draped from their collarbones, the silk that clung to the jut of their breasts shimmering when they moved. We only had time for one cocktail before the afternoon train.

There was no ceremony on the return journey; the shiny new carriages had suddenly become just another part of the commuter line and the train rattled through the tunnel like all the others that had gone before it. The sight of bunting and the sound of a brass band as we pulled into Missensham lifted our spirits. We had missed the mayor and dignitaries but there was still some cake and champagne left for anyone who could produce a ticket. The champagne refreshed the alcohol already festering in my stomach and my mind melted into a haze of drunkenness.

Walter had turned up at the station to meet Audrey. They embraced excitedly and suddenly Audrey was telling him about all the young lords that had winked at her and how her outfit had been the talk of the Savoy. I tailed behind them, excusing myself when I saw a big bunch of roses on the back seat of their Bentley, and mumbled something about the weather being lovely for a walk on my own. They didn't object.

I stood outside the station alone, stepping back to look at the building. It was long and low, made of wide brick columns, inset with ladders of little glass panes. There were green tiles up to waist height and above them bright posters with scenes of Tower Bridge and the golden beaches of Brighton and Southend, garishly coloured as if by a child. I put a hand on my hat to keep it from falling as I looked up to the flat roof and the halo of the underground sign. Then I heard a noise behind me; a strange 'click-click'.

A man stood on the pavement, shoulders rounded and hands held high as he supported a box camera in front of his face, the lens pointing squarely at me. Then his face emerged from behind the camera, his eyes blinking in the sun and we stared at each other.

'Were you photographing me?' I demanded.

The man shook his head quickly and then his gaze fell to his shoes. 'No, Miss,' he said awkwardly. 'The tiling.'

'The tiling?'

He nodded. 'I tiled the outer wall, you see, I just wanted to keep a record of my work.'

'Oh,' I said.

We both smiled, sharing the embarrassment. He was a tall man, well built and, without the camera covering his face, his features looked large and clumsy.

'Sorry,' he said, his voice was deep and he spoke awkwardly as if his tongue was too large for his mouth.

I wondered what he thought he was apologizing for.

'I'm just a workman at the moment you see, but I need a record of what I have done to start up my own business. Building and a bit of tiling and the like. It's what I want to do. So I need to, well...' he held up the camera by way of explanation.

I smiled. Had I been sober, I would have excused myself and continued home, but the alcohol had made me carefree and instead I said: 'I'm sure the tiles look lovely, but I don't know much about construction.'

'Me neither, Miss,' he said. 'I just did what the foreman told me and put in the hard work.' He shrugged his shoulders – that same awkwardness again, but now he was looking directly at me and smiling. His eyes were a piercing blue and, as a smile grew on his lips, I could no longer be sure how much of his awkwardness was feigned.

'Well, I don't see many of the workmen still around. I

thought you would have all left by now,' I said, 'and you're certainly the only one taking photos.'

'No, the rest of us common navvies are in the Red Lion—' he said, then stopped himself suddenly. 'Forgive my insolence, Miss, I was in there myself a while back but I needed a break.'

I laughed, happy to have a comrade in my drunkenness. I watched in amazement as my hand reached out to him and patted his arm. 'I've had a bit too much myself!' I whispered loudly.

'Really, Miss...' he raised his arm slightly to steady me. 'Well, I suppose a lady doesn't get many chances these days.' He spoke the words carefully as if he was trying to disguise his voice; the flat vowels that were so common just a few stops down the Metropolitan Line, the wrong side of Oxworth. It was how I had spoken in my youth and the smell of his skin reminded me of my father. I smiled up at him as I wobbled on his arm. He glanced down at me; a streak of blue from beneath his lashes.

I stepped back and steadied myself. 'I'm sorry to be trouble,' I said. 'You were just taking photographs of tiles but when I thought you were photographing me, for one moment, I felt like Greta Garbo. But really I'm second to a bit of grouting...' I felt my cheeks warm. It was a silly thing to say. The kind of thing that Audrey would say in the middle of a party and everybody would laugh, but from my own lips it was ridiculous.

But he was smiling. 'Well, Greta, I am sorry to have disappointed you,' he answered quickly, but then looked away again, as if he was somehow embarrassed by the mismatch between his quick wit and his clumsy body.

'I have to go home.' I laughed and then touched his arm again. 'I've had too much to drink.'

I set off down the pavement, my feet stumbling over perfectly flat concrete, his footsteps heavy behind me.

I turned and laughed, waving him away: 'No more photographs!' but his camera was tucked down in his bag. 'Where are you going?' I said. 'First you take my photo and then you follow me.'

'I didn't take your photograph and I'm not following you either,' he said. 'The real celebration is back in the Red Lion.' He pointed down the hedge-lined road in the direction of the green – we were heading in the same direction. 'Will you let me walk with you to there?' he said. 'Think of me as a movie star's bodyguard – if I may be permitted to use the same pavement as a movie star.'

'You have permission all right.' I laughed, surprised to hear the flat vowels returning to my own voice.

He dipped into a bow and tugged his forelock – a comic gesture coming from his huge body.

We walked together, side by side, mumbled apologies as I steadied myself on his shoulder. I glanced up at him but his eyes darted away and he swallowed slowly, the movement deep in his throat. Then I felt the brush of his hand on my hip and my blood warmed. He looked at me again and this time I smiled.

So that's how we began, my man and I. We did not know it then, but further along the pavement was an opening in the hedgerow, where the road bent slightly and ivy clung to an old tree stump. Beyond the opening was a field, a rough triangle edged by woodland, where the earth sloped into the sunlight, where the grasses were long and the hollows pooled with violets. With just a few more paces we would be there, with just a turn of the head and a quick glance over the brambles, our haven would be discovered. We never made it to the Red Lion.

*

A week after I met him an envelope, addressed to me, landed on the doormat. Inside was a photograph of a single figure, a woman dressed in white, her body turned to the side as she put her hand on her hat and tilted her head back, her chin lifted and her eyes gazing skyward. I didn't recognize myself at first. The white dress and the glare of the sun made the woman almost classical, as if she were carved from marble. But there was some abandon about it, the drunken confidence of the pose and the wisps of hair escaping from the hat making it seem alive. The station in the background was blurred, too distant to be recognized, and there was not a tile in sight. The photograph had been of me after all.

I turned it over and read the back: 'My Greta, all my love, P.'

P? I did not even know his name then, but he knew mine. He knew my full name, knew where I lived, and knew that I was married.

A week passed before another envelope arrived. I recognized the writing on the envelope as soon as it stared up at me from the doormat; writing that I had pondered over for seven whole days, wondering what the hooks on the 'g's and the slant of the 't's symbolized in the man who wrote them – the man who dared to address it to Mrs Marks in her marital home. There was no writing inside this time, no message, just a fold of clean white blotting paper enclosing a single pressed violet.

A week later another envelope arrived, enclosing another pressed violet. I put the violets between the pages of my mother's copy of *Mrs Beeton's Guide to Household Management* – the only book on the shelf which George was unlikely to read. Now and then when the housework got monotonous or the days seemed long and lonely I would find an excuse to go into the lounge, to open the book and stare at my violets, touch their frail petals and marvel at how they never lost their colour. Sometimes I would return to the station, retracing the walk along the hedge-lined road, pushing through the brambles on the path and gazing over the triangular field, memories flooding back to me as I smelt the grass underfoot. I would walk the lanes, hoping to meet him again, but hoping not to, scared of his power over me.

The envelopes kept arriving long into August, long after the violets in the field had died, and I realized that this was something that would not fade away. I remembered what my mother had always said about violets, that it was unlucky to bring them into the house, especially a single violet, which could bring death. And that summer did bring death for the yellowing grasses in the fields, the wilting pansies in the garden, the fallen blossoms, the spent mayflies and drowsy wasps. Yet among all this decay, I could not have felt more alive.

I did not see my man again until the fifth envelope arrived. Another pressed violet was inside, but this time the blotting paper was marked with the same slanting hand:

The war memorial, three o'clock on Wednesday.

Six weeks had passed, the days were becoming long and hot, and by that time I was aching for him.

16

Thursday broke with a rumble of thunder, the dull glow of the morning blunting all memories of sunshine, bunting and party frocks. The hedgerows in the Evesbridge Lane gave little protection from the rain, the muddied wheel ruts guiding me as I returned to work, to an aching back and fingers numbed by the press of a needle. Rose Cottage seemed small and dark as I approached, the fat heads of fallen roses dissolving into mud.

I scraped my boots on the iron mat, the swing of the door wafting mustiness out into the rain-soaked air. The kitchen windows were choked with stacks of scarlet linen, pale light struggling through the gaps. Somewhere water seeped through the ceiling with a hollow drip. My special dress was pegged up over the basin, dripping with shiny redness, the sleeves hanging limp like a fox in a snare.

Mrs Brown was sat hunched over the table, coughing into her handkerchief. She did not get up when the door opened, just nodded when she saw me, her mouth puckering into a little blister.

'I've brought some fairy cakes,' I said, squeezing my basket on to the corner of the table. 'There were just so many left over from Saturday and I must have used so much sugar that they are not yet stale!'

She did not answer, just nodded again.

I looked round at all the linen – the heaps on the windowsills and the laden table – and smiled, rolling my eyes dramatically, but still she was silent.

I laughed self-consciously. 'I am sorry if I did anything foolish at the party. I had rather too much to drink. It's not something that I usually do.'

'You left your wages on Thursday,' she said at last. 'They've been sat there on the side all weekend.'

'Oh,' I said. 'It was so good of you to keep them back for me. Thank you.'

She leant forward and grabbed an armful of linen, ramming

it through the Singer, the handle spinning furiously. I opened my mouth but the noise was deafening, so I sat down on my usual chair, taking a frayed napkin onto my lap.

'Where are the children?' I shouted over the noise.

She stopped abruptly. 'Blackberrying.'

'Oh,' I said, glancing at the rain through the window. 'And are they... well?'

She nodded.

'That's good,' I said quietly. I picked up my needle and started to jab at the material. Her silence was not something I had expected. 'And have the children been playing with the rocking horse?' I asked.

'Yes,' she said, then added: 'all of them have, even the boys.'

'That's good,' I said again, trying not to take my eyes off my work. I thought about the horse, how it had stayed locked up in the dark, quiet nursery for all those years. It had been there all alone, its runners denting the carpet, dust gathering on its bare saddle. Suddenly I felt that I needed to see it again, see it somewhere happier – where there were children, somewhere where it could finally be played with and loved. 'Can I see it?' I said.

'See it?' She seemed surprised. 'If you like.'

The rocking horse was in the small back room, squeezed in between a small unmade bed and dresser with bulging drawers. Three colourful yo-yos littered the flagstones and the clothes strewn across the bed smelled of must. The horse's white ears were darkened with dirt and the paint on the saddle was chipped. The neck and rump were bare, the silver hair of the tail and mane lying in a tangle on the floor. It had become a toy, a plaything, just like any other and it was no longer Ruby's dapple grey mare.

'Mrs Brown!' I cried.

She stared at me, her face blank.

I pointed to the horse. 'What happened?'

She blinked quickly and frowned as if not understanding my question.

'It's been less than a week!' I said.

She shrugged. 'They are kids, Mrs Marks.'

I gasped. 'Kids?'

'Yes, Mrs Marks,' she said slowly. 'They are child-ren.'

'No!' I said. 'That's no excuse. No normal child would do—'

'That's exactly what a normal child would do,' she spat. 'Kids is full of life and energy, Mrs Marks, they ain't dolls to dress up in lace and sit all quiet at parties and eat blancmange.'

'I can't believe it!' I whispered.

She gave a little sniff. 'You weren't to know,' she said, tossing her head. 'You don't know about kids.'

She stomped off and I heard the whirr of the Singer from the kitchen. I stood and stared at the rocking horse and then I went back to my seat and sat down heavily. I pulled a pile of linen on to my lap and hunted for my needle, but she had tidied it away, so instead I unpicked a clumsy stitch with an old crochet hook. Gradually the patter of rain on the roof was dimmed by the whirr of the Singer as Maud worked it faster and faster. The clatter of the mechanism began to throb in my head and I was forced to stop. I tried to get her attention but she did not look up. Her hands worked rapidly, feeding the material under the needle. Her face was red, a vein bulging from her temple and her eyebrows knotted and low.

Then the noise stopped suddenly. 'Shit!' she cried, holding up a bloody finger. 'Oh shit!' Then her face seemed to crumple and she put her head in her hands and started wailing.

'Mrs Brown?' I said quietly. 'Mrs Brown... Maud, are you all right?'

'No, I ain't bloody all right,' she sobbed. 'You know what they've been talking about all weekend? Bloody cakes and blancmange. Cakes and blancmange! I can't even give them jam. Let alone cakes and blancmange or a rocking horse!'

I stared at her. Her face was wet from crying but her tears were not accompanied by elegant snivels and lace handkerchiefs like in the movies. Maud was all snot and growling. Her mouth gaped large, crushing her eyes into little black crescents, melting tears onto her cheeks. I put out my hand to touch her arm but she drew it away quickly.

'I'll make some tea,' I said.

I put the kettle on the stove and I stood at the draining board staring out the window on to the yard. The rain was constant, a murmur of thunder somewhere in the distance. Through the slats of the henhouse, the chickens flicked raindrops from their feathers, their dull clucking rising over the rain. The earth in the yard had softened into mud, brown water pooling in the furrows. Ruby would surely catch a chill if she really was out hunting for blackberries. I thought of the nursery at Little Willow; the bright paint on the walls and the thick carpet. Then the stupid extravagance of the rocking horse – given away on a whim, and the silver rattle – buried. I had so much to offer Ruby and, at the moment, she had so little – a run-down cottage, Maud who struggled to make ends meet, and a father - well, a father maybe.

Then I thought of Clarence. Did he even exist? There was no sign of him, only a worn rocking chair that was always empty. I tried to imagine the man who sat in that chair. He was a grafter, Maud had said, did work for the farms and odd jobs, so he would probably be dressed in dungarees or even a smock and be black with dirt. His body would be muscly and built for work, but there was only one other part of his body that Maud had mentioned; his hard oak truncheon. I stopped myself, not wanting to think any more, but only when I imagined his body did I really see the man who sat in that chair – see him, feel his warmth and smell his sweat. He was the coarse labourer, the muscled farmhand. I could imagine him kicking open the door at dusk, demanding his supper and sinking into that rocking chair, with a pitcher of ale in his hand. He would drink and laugh, bark orders at Maud, box the children's ears, spread his legs, rub his crotch. And George, well, George wasn't perfect but he could at least provide security and a regular income and Clarence... well Ruby would surely be better off without him, without any of her family.

My thoughts were broken by a new wail from the basket chair, as if the turmoil Maud was trying to suppress had resurfaced again but then sunk into a fit of sobs and sniffles. Maud was right, of course, she had said that she could never give Ruby cakes and blancmange, but really she had meant stability, education, dreams and a future. Did I want my Violet growing up in a place like this? A place where she had nothing? A place where Maud had to work all hours just to put bread on the table? A place where she had just the ghost of a father? A place where she would feed chickens and milk cows and sew aprons for chambermaids? I was not the only one who thought this – Maud had admitted that much to me not long after we first met – Ruby had no future here, no chance of becoming the grand Missensham lady with the grey mare. But at Little Willow things could be better for her, and I vowed to make them so.

Maud took the tea without a thank you. She had a long sip, the tension falling from her face as if the hot liquid had relaxed every muscle in her body before it hit her throat. She wiped her eyes and smiled at last.

'I'm sorry, I should have brought some wine,' I said, remembering the party and the brimming beaker of wine that she had brought me as a comfort. She caught my eye and smiled weakly. I remembered how close I had felt to her back then. I sat back down and she turned her chair away from the table, stretching her legs out in front of the empty grate. 'You must have had a fair amount to drink that day too,' I said. 'You told me about the time you had called for the cat instead of Ruby,' – I leaned towards her and smiled – 'and then about how you had cried out another man's name when you were in bed with Clarence.'

She nodded. 'Ah, well yes, but you know me.' She winked. 'I would have told you that anyway.'

'I know,' I said, feigning weariness, and we laughed again.

'You raced through that big glass of wine,' she said. 'I never knew a real lady would be such a drunk!'

I laughed.

Then her brow furrowed. 'You were still a lady, though, weren't you? Despite everything.'

'What do you mean?' I said.

'Well, you still wouldn't tell about the other lover you'd had. You came across all bashful, all "yeses" and "nos" and then "don't knows". How much would it take for a lady to give away her little secrets?'

Suddenly I felt ashamed. I knew so much about Maud, yet I had told her so little about myself. She must have already guessed that I had lied about needing money and about George being a gambler, so I felt I owed her something. 'It wouldn't take any alcohol,' I said. 'Just good friendship.'

She smiled.

I thought about her confession again; crying out the wrong name in her passion, the droop in Clarence's truncheon, their fight in the kitchen. And the way she had laughed about it, like she didn't care who knew, as if it meant nothing.

'There was another man,' I said, giggling like a schoolgirl at the memory. 'Shortly after George and I were married. It didn't last long.' I touched her arm but felt her flinch, her face became pinched and she was silent again.

I laughed, nervously this time, patting her knee. 'Oh, come on, you've never met George.'

'I don't need to,' she said. 'After you were married! No man deserves that.'

I opened my mouth in amazement but her face was hard. Then I heard myself laugh again, but my voice was weak. 'Oh come on, Mrs Brown. What does marriage mean to you when you and Clarence never see each other and fight so much? I've never even heard you refer to him as your husband, so I'm assuming that you are not even legally wed. And really, all these children? Henry so fair, but John and Jim so dusky and Andy with his red hair – and well, Andy, at his age he must have been conceived during the war when surely Clarence would have been serving—'

'What do you mean by that?' she snapped, her eyes were wide and staring.

'Oh, don't be so high and mighty,' I said. 'You must know exactly what I mean – some of your children may not be Clarence's, one of them might not even be yours!'

'What!'

'Well, I just thought, what with all your talk of—'

She jumped from her chair, her face red and her body quivering.

'—truncheons,' I whispered.

'Always Clarence's!' she yelled. 'I've only ever talked about Clarence's truncheon. It's all right for you upper classes to sleep around, with your c-c-courtesans and fancy boys, but it's more serious for the likes of us, we stay faithful. These are our kids – mine and Clarence's – we made, and bore every single one of them!'

'You're lying,' I said weakly. 'I know for a fact that Ruby—'

'Ruby? What about Ruby?'

'—with her fair hair… and her face so different from the boys.' I was gasping, my breaths were coming quickly between words. 'And she doesn't even look like you.'

'What do you mean by that?' she shouted.

I opened my mouth, but in all my rage I couldn't bring myself to say it. 'She doesn't even call you "Mother",' I whispered. 'Why doesn't she call you "Mother"? She can't be yours. You must be lying, you must be!'

'How dare you call me a liar!' she screeched. 'When you turn up here from nowhere and sit in my kitchen with your deception?'

'What?'

'Why are you really here, Mrs Marks? A housewife from Sunningdale Estate! Don't tell me it's gambling. Doctors don't gamble and their wives ain't short of money.'

'You don't know—'

'Don't I? I ain't stupid.' She started to cough again. The way she had when I had arrived, burying her face in her handkerchief. 'Ladies what throw parties with wine,' she wheezed, 'and blancmange and give kids rocking horses don't work as seamstresses.'

'I need the money,' I pleaded. 'I do.'

'Then why did you leave it here last week? Any woman in debt would need that money for bread and potatoes, you didn't even know that you'd left it. You didn't even notice!'

'I just forgot,' I said. 'It was an honest mistake, I…'

'Why are you here, Mrs Marks?' she said again wearily. She was staring right at me.

I sat down. It was time to tell her. I searched for the words but I couldn't find them. 'I want my daughter back,' I said at last. 'I want Ruby.'

She opened her mouth, gulping like a frog. 'Your daughter's dead, you said so yourself.'

'Look, I don't know how it happened, Mrs Brown, but she's not. Maybe there was a mix-up at the hospital or something, maybe she was stolen, but somehow my daughter is alive. She is alive and living with you… Ruby is my daughter.'

'Get out!' she screamed. 'Get out of my house!' Suddenly her face was right in front of mine, mouth gaping and eyes wild.

I got up and backed toward the door, tripping over the doorstep, her hand on my back as I stumbled into the lane. Then the door slammed behind me, putting an end to any chance I had of getting Violet back.

17

I had not seen the nursery for nine years. Not properly that is. Of course I had been in there during my drunken plan to get the rocking horse. But then my brain had been numb with wine and I had felt no need to linger.

Now that I stood in the nursery again, I took my time. I felt the softness of the carpet between my toes and opened the curtains, listening to the grate of the heavy rings along the rail. I ran my fingers over the walls, the pale yellow like a captured sunbeam, lambs kicking their feet as they played among the poppies. The curls of their wool were hard under my fingertips, the paint ridged with the stroke of the brush. The counterpane was on the sideboard, folded to show the embroidery on top – 'Violet' – the 'V' was proud and ornate but the other letters were just tacked onto the cotton as if the stitcher had realized that there would be no one to cherish them. Despite everything that had happened, this room was still Violet's. It was this room, and not the white room at the hospital with its cold surfaces and glaring lights, that Violet should have come to – but it was this room that she never saw.

I grasped the rail of the cot, lifting the sheets from the mattress and burying my face in them. They smelt musty now, the newness faded. I opened a drawer and saw the swaddling blanket, just as I had folded it nine years ago when the midwife had passed it to me.

A small piece of card was folded into the wool. It was the photograph of the infant Violet; older and slightly faded but still the image I remembered,

In the end I had shown the photo to George. Not when I first got it, when it was my secret, but some months later. Back then I had told myself that it was my wifely duty to show him, that it was something that should be shared, but deep down there was something that I needed to know – whether the photograph had captured the last moments of life or merely the body that it had left behind.

I remember standing in the lounge, holding the photograph out to him, pushing it gingerly over the top of his open newspaper. He took it, examined it – with glasses both on and off – then looked up at me.

'What a very strange gift!' he had said, his leg quivering the way it did with some trifle or annoyance. Then he had jabbed his finger in the air. 'But I remember her, the midwife, she was a middle-aged woman, wasn't she? Well past her own childbearing years. This kind of thing must have been popular in her youth, some *memento mori*. The Victorians were a superstitious lot – but I suppose in a way it would help them get through the process of mourning.'

He had let out a little chuckle, the kind of coughing laugh he gave when he thought he was about to say something clever. 'Memento mori were usually pretty formal of course, this silly woman seems to have devalued it somewhat by surreptitiously snapping the shot with a Box Brownie'. He rolled his eyes, as if mocking the midwife was more important than the photograph itself. 'Rather morbid, if you ask me.' He turned the photograph over and studied the back, his spectacles folded as he moved the lenses across the paper like a magnifying glass. 'There's a mark here too,' he said. 'Something left by the developer probably, yes a "one" and then a little slash and then I think it must be a "two" after that – one out of two.' Another little cough chuckled in the back of his throat. 'Yes there must have been another copy of it at some point – maybe the midwife kept it for her records or for some superstitious reason. Obstetrics has been in the hands of women for far too long, if you ask me. It's only with proper modern medicine that we will be able to put an end to this kind of mumbo jumbo.'

I had stood in front of my husband, wondering whether it was even worth asking more. Whether my questions would just lead to more rants about the merits of modern photography, memento mori and obstetrics

'And to have the light on that cheek,' George continued, 'the one with the mark, it's not very well positioned!' He touched the photo, his finger skimming the birthmark and he grimaced. 'You know, I do think it would be best if you didn't mention such details to others.'

'Details?' I said.

'Yes – things like the name we gave her and her face;

especially not the face. Talking about such things with other people is far too personal and will only upset you.'

I wanted to tell him that these 'details' that he spoke of were what made Violet special to me but, deep down, I knew that he what he said did not matter – I had never been able to talk openly about Violet and what few friends I had knew only that I'd had a baby who died.

He turned back to his newspaper, muttering to himself and shaking his head.

I took a deep breath and tried to keep my voice steady: 'George, there's no chance she would have been alive when this was taken, is there?'

'Alive?' he said, surprised. He traced his finger over the bonnet. 'No, no not by then. Not by then.'

Not by then, I thought – so final, over.

Then he handed the photograph back to me. 'I'd get rid of it, if I were you.'

'No!' I said quickly. 'How about we just keep it in the nursery instead? After all, it is where she belongs.' He looked at me sharply, so I added: 'It's just that we have so much in there already, and this is just one more tiny thing.'

'Oh, all right then,' he said. 'But I had better do it. We don't want you going in there and upsetting yourself.'

I knew George's ways by now and I knew that he would do as he said and put the photograph back in the nursery. I also knew where he would hide the key to the nursery door. But, as I handed the photograph back to him, I found that part of me wondered whether I would ever see it again.

*

Ten years had passed and now, standing in the warm glow of the nursery, I still had the photograph. I touched the outline of the baby's face; the three tears and the smudge on the cheekbone, just below the eye. Suddenly I was sure. I had not been imagining it – the birthmark in the photograph was identical to Ruby's and, as I stared at the faded picture of the little grey baby, her birthmark bloomed crimson.

18

Without my visits to Rose Cottage, life went back to normal. I became Mrs Marks again, the suburban doctor's wife. But being a wife yet not a mother meant that I could neither work, nor had children to raise. I was too old for the London nightclubs and too young for the Women's Institute, and I could not face volunteering at the Sunday school or Girl Guides, or any of the places that I might have imagined Violet. For the first time in weeks, the days seemed to stretch ahead of me – long and empty. George rejoiced in this and his little notes started to appear again. When I came down in the mornings I would find little bits of paper left around the place, all filled with George's crabbed handwriting. Each note would detail the delivery date of a newly published medical journal, a troublesome bird pat that had landed on the bedroom window or some instruction or complaint to be passed on to Mr Tuttle and, of course, there were arrangements to be made for the Hospital Ball. My days became defined by endless lists of errands and reminders, all so urgent yet all so unimportant. George would sign each note off with 'Your loving husband' and his signature, 'George Marks', ornate with whirls and loops like a royal seal.

One of George's notes was sat on the coffee table as I leafed through my cookery books one afternoon. It was a request for a Madeira cake for George's brother in Oxworth. It was a favourite of his and would be appreciated ('most awfully') on his next visit. One of the books, *Mrs Beeton*, fell open in my lap, the divide in the pages marked by a lifeless flower – a violet pressed between the pages. It doubled over when I took it in my fingers, transparent like tracing paper. I looked at it with fascination; it was ten years since I had hidden it there but it was still the deepest hue.

I did not think of my lover at first, but of Ruby. And of how I had watched her as she stood by the flower beds at the garden party. How she had stooped to pick a pansy, her eyes drawn to the one with the blue petals. How she had held it close to her chest, then dropped her chin to smell it, her deep breaths magnified by the rise and fall of her fist. How she had buried her nose in the centre, the petals sucked flat against her nostrils as if she was drinking the scent – movements so tiny yet somehow triggering an old memory.

It was good weather for violets in the summer of 1935 – just like it had been in 1925, all those long summers ago. Ten years had passed but I remembered that year so well. It had been so hot back then that I would stand at my bedroom window and watch my lover wipe sweat from his brow as he waited at the war memorial, always knowing that the glint of the sun on the glass made me invisible to his gaze. He would shuffle his feet, light a cigarette, check his pocket watch and glance quickly toward the house. Then I would not be able to contain myself any longer and I would go – a quick check in the mirror; hair and lipstick – and run down the stairs not wasting another moment. It was the same routine, every Wednesday, week upon week, and each time with the excitement of the first…

*

'You're late,' he said. 'I wasn't sure you would come.' Then he smiled. He reached out his hand and touched the violet in my buttonhole, the stalk quivering against my breast.

'I was expecting the white dress,' he said.

'No,' I said. 'Grass stains.'

'You are right,' he said. 'You came prepared this time.'

'No,' I said quickly. 'I meant from last time… it's because I couldn't possibly wear a dress with grass stains on it. Someone might notice…' but then I stopped because I was fooling nobody.

'I'm sorry,' he said awkwardly, although I don't think either of us knew what he was apologizing for.

I looked away quickly, feeling the halo of his warmth on my skin. A bus rumbled past, slowing slightly as it passed the war memorial, its windows orange with the glare of the sun. I turned my head quickly, facing the plinth so that I was not recognized by the passengers I imagined.

When the bus had passed, he stooped and kissed me. I felt

the warm fleshiness of his lips on my own and the clamminess of his hand as it gently held my cheek. Then he stopped and glanced towards the house and I followed his gaze instinctively, even though I knew all the rooms were empty.

'Shall we go?' he said.

I nodded quickly.

He took my hand and we started to walk in silence, side by side, towards the centre of town. He walked quickly and I struggled to keep pace with his long strides. As we reached St Cuthbert's, the bells started to strike out the hour, the hollow chime following us down the street.

I untangled my fingers from his. 'Not here!'

I watched our shadows jostling on the pavement, merging into each other and then apart again, and I marvelled at how large he was compared to me. When we reached the edge of the green I saw a lady I knew walking towards us, a forgotten friend from the Missensham Girl Guides, her mother leaning on her arm as she helped her along the pavement. I looked down as they drew closer, sure that somehow this woman also knew Audrey, although I could not think how.

He's a family friend, I said over and over in my head, rehearsing for the meeting, but the woman did not look up until she was very close, and when she finally saw us I just nodded and smiled and, in the corner of my eye, my family friend did the same.

The green was empty but for a few children petting an excited dog and I thanked God for the heat of the midday sun. Outside the tearoom a couple of waitresses sat on the steps, blowing cigarette smoke into the road. They had been at my school but were some years younger, too young to know me well. They watched us carefully as we got closer, too uncouth to look away, their conversation stalling as we passed. I could feel their eyes following my lover taking in every inch of him. I smiled to myself, walking tall and sticking out my chest, allowing my shoulder to rub on his sleeve and noting with pride that he did not look at the girls, that he kept striding forward.

We crossed the canal bridge and headed away from town. Down the long, straight road that led to the station, the road where the tarmac was bordered by high hedges. I looked up at his face, but his eyes were gazing forward, so I turned to look at the road again only to feel him looking at me and I knew that if I turned my head again I would appear foolish if he didn't return the glance. A bicycle whizzed past my ear and I jumped away from him, my face reddening. I began to make an awkward apology but he had stopped walking.

'It was here,' he said, parting the hedge with his hands.

Through the gap, the field shone with the sun and violets.

I stopped and took a step back, suddenly feeling a weight in my stomach. 'I—'

'Come on,' he said. 'It's fine.'

So that was me – Emma Marks, awkward and shy – who entered the field for a second time, and it was me, Emma Marks, who wondered what would happen now there was no alcohol to make her desirable and witty. But it was not Emma Marks who lay down with a stranger in the grass. That was her, and she... well, she was one of those other women: she was Greta Garbo, ten foot tall on the flickering screen, the one who could melt a hundred men with one glance from under those curving eyelashes; she was the model from the cheeky Brighton postcards, the one whose hair cascaded over her proud breasts and whose frozen face laughed at the men who stared and wished; she was the flapper from the Savoy who flaunted her calves and collarbone and blew smoke in the faces of lustful young lords; she was the girl in white who squinted up at the station's tiled facade, the classical goddess with the catalogue pose.

It was those women in the field that day – those women who writhed in the grass and felt the press of their spine against the hard earth. It was those women who gasped and dug their nails into flesh that pulsed with heat, who felt their bodies heave and shudder.

But it was me, Emma Marks, who lay in the field afterwards, my shoulder nestled into the armpit of a stranger. It was my skirt that was hitched up and my body that sank heavily into the grass. It was my thighs, the swell of my buttocks and the small of my back left wet and warm. It was my eyes that saw the violets in the hedgerow and blurred them into blue. And it was me, Emma Marks, who felt that maybe, just maybe, a little part of all those women had stayed with me too.

Above me the clouds swept across the sky, melting into one another and then fading away into little wisps. Somewhere in the distance the wind caught the rattle of carriages on the railway line.

'Those people on the train,' I said, 'I wonder where they are going.'

He opened his eyes, just a slit, enough to shoot me a glance of blue.

'Baker Street,' he said.

I rolled over and punched his arm. 'Baker Street,' I said, 'then a connection to Waterloo and overland to Dover!'

'The boat train?' he said.

'Yes, of course, then a ferry to Calais and then a dirty weekend in Le Touquet. They will bathe in the crystal waters and burn themselves red on the sand.'

'Oh I see,' he said. 'Le Touquet, where Missensham's bank managers, and secretaries can be mermaids and sea nymphs.'

And somewhere down the line the vibration of the train caught on the metal of the track, the echo faded and distant as if it had come from Le Touquet itself.

'I think they are going to Baker Street,' he said.

I laughed.

'Maybe one day we can go to Le Touquet,' I said. 'Or further... further than this field, somewhere with crystal blue waters.'

'You're right,' he said, smiling. 'Maybe one day we can go to the lido.'

I lay my arm across his chest. 'What's your name?'

He hesitated for just a second and turned his head towards me, those blue eyes looking right at me. 'Peter,' he said.

'Peter? Peter who?'

He covered his face with a huge hand and laughed.

'Oh come on, you know who I am, my name, my address, yet you get to be mysterious.'

'Well you can be mysterious too if you like.' He turned his head again. 'So then, mystery woman, what's your name?'

I looked around but the answer was obvious. 'Violet,' I said.

'Violet,' he repeated slowly and then chuckled to himself. He pulled a violet from the grass and held it close to his chest, his breaths magnified by the rise and fall of his fist. Then he buried his nose in the flower, the petals sucked flat against his nostrils, as if he was drinking the scent.

19

Ruby

My name is Ruby Brown but my brothers have their own names for me – Slap-face, Scabby Queen, Domino Pox, Leper. When they tease me, Maudy squeezes me tight; she says that I am too good for Evesbridge and that one day I can leave and find out who I really am. But she is just comforting me, she doesn't know that I will make it true sooner than she thinks. You see, I have been collecting treasure and, now that I have found my final piece, I can leave this place. I can be someone else – the grand Missensham lady with the grey mare that Emma said I could be. I won't have to be Ruby Brown at all.

I found it buried in the yard, just under the mangle. I had wanted the big round stone that covered it but when I took the stone away, I saw the silver glinting at me. The stone was between the legs of the mangle, in the middle – a place easy to remember, as if the treasure had been hidden, not mislaid. But that did not matter because now it was mine.

The treasure was like a silver box, smooth and flat, and as big as a pack of playing cards. When I turned it over, I rubbed mud into the etchings, making the flowers black.

I went into the henhouse and squatted down by Snowflake, reaching under her warm body to the gap in the slats. The rest of my treasure was still there; the four shiny shillings that Emma had never collected. But this new treasure would be my favourite; something I had found that nobody else could know about.

I rubbed the treasure on my sleeve but the wool snagged on a little clasp. The treasure was not solid silver, but hollow, and I fancied that I could keep some chalks inside, and Emma's shillings. My fingers stumbled over the clasp as I tried to prise the two silver halves apart but then the treasure folded open like a butterfly, a bitter smell rising upwards.

The inside of the treasure was not silver but dull and brown. On one side a photograph of a sleeping baby was tucked inside the rim. The picture was battered, like it had been carried around for a long time but also taken out, handled, and then returned over and over again. The corners were curled at the edges as if the photograph had not quite fitted into its home but the owner could not bring themselves to trim it.

I looked into the baby's face. It was peaceful but there was something odd about it, something cold. I stared hard until my eyes blurred. And that was when I saw the baby wriggle.

I felt a jolt deep inside me, like the snap of ice breaking on a frozen pond, then the ice spread through my blood and my fingers throbbed where they touched the silver. But, now that I saw the picture properly again, the baby was still. Something was very wrong with this photograph. I did not want it there. I put my fingernail behind the paper and tried to pull it out but it did not come and I pulled and pulled and then suddenly the photograph flicked out onto the floor and the treasure spun out of my hands, purple exploding all around it and fluttering to the floor.

I looked inside the treasure again. The head of a flower had been pressed flat against the metal, the purple blackening as I watched. There were five petals – the top two pointed like rabbit ears, the other three fanning out underneath – a violet. There had been violets in my treasure and now there were violets around my feet, there were violets still fluttering in the air and there were violets stuck to my fingers. This place was mine, my home, and I had brought violets to it. I had brought them indoors. So many violets, so much bad luck. Suddenly death was all around me.

20

Emma

I hardly saw George in the weeks that followed the party. He would leave for work before I woke, then return home briefly in time for supper. He was on call in the evenings, he said, and every evening at seven, he would drive away in the car, despite the telephone never ringing. He would return at nine, just as the light was fading and wash his hands rigorously until they became hard like chicken claws, the smell of carbolic wafting from the bathroom. Then he would sink into his armchair and I would wake from my trance and scurry around fetching his sherry and newspaper.

I was surprised how little I cared about his behaviour. Some months ago I would have longed for him to distract me but now I welcomed the time alone in my thoughts. Now that I had rediscovered my memories of 1925, I was much more content for my mind to fill with idle recollections than thoughts about housework or little worries about George's funny ways. At least I could console myself with the fact that I had loved and been happy in my life, even if it had been for a short time, and that if I had been Maud I would have spent my years working hard and not have had such treasured memories. If I had been her, I would have spent years tied to one man, a farm hand and a lout, pushing out child after child... four children at least but no, not five, I knew that much.

And then, before I knew it, several weeks had passed in a mist of steam and carbolic and I found myself at the dining room table with George, the Saturday concert crackling from the living room.

We ate supper in silence. The low sun smoked the dining room windows with dull light, bathing the room with a beige sheen. The mutton was cold and flaccid. George's jaw worked monotonously, his face embalmed in the glow of the evening, a dull egg of light reflecting on his forehead. He had put his spectacles back on, I noticed, after hours spent soaking them in bleach.

He cleared his throat. 'I saw that the nursery curtains were open.'

'Yes,' I said not looking up from my plate. 'I was in there a few days ago.'

'Well, good,' he said. 'Maybe this would be a good time for us to clear it out. Get rid of some of the old stuff so that Mr Tuttle can go in.'

I kept quiet, knowing a response either way would not make a difference.

'I'm sure Mr Tuttle understands these things,' George continued. 'I've seen him laying flowers at the memorial many a time. He has had his share of losses too, no doubt.'

'Yes,' I said.

'Well?'

'Maybe.'

A posy of violets sat in the middle of the dining table, their stems furred by the yellowed water in George's sherry glass. I stared at them, wondering where they could have come from. Perhaps George had seen that the ones left after the garden party had finally wilted, and gone to the trouble of replacing them with a fresh bunch – why would he do that? How unlike him!

George positioned his knife carefully on the side of his plate. 'I saw the rocking horse yesterday,' he said casually.

'What?'

'The one that you gave to that tinker family.'

'I know which one!' I said.

He wiped his mouth slowly, his lips unfurling from the edge of his napkin. I waited for him to fold it carefully on to his lap, the way he always did, one of the little rituals he went through before he was about to say anything important. 'I was on call,' he said at last. 'I got sent out to a farm worker's cottage over by Evesbridge. The patient had what looks like tuberculosis, I had to do the tests – tuberculin and so forth.'

'TB?' I said. 'And so near Missensham!'

'I wouldn't worry yourself,' George said. 'There is little chance of it spreading to the Sunningdale Estate. No, this case is most likely isolated and due to the ways of the family – quite unsanitary. These deaths by the thousand that the newspapers like to scare us with are mainly confined to urban areas and the poorer populations. As long as you don't catch a chill or associate too much with these people, you will be quite—'

'Was the patient a little girl?' I said quickly.

'A girl?' George shook his head impatiently. 'No, no – she was a woman, middle-aged, a scrawny-looking thing. I just thought that, as you gave the family the horse, you might know of her.'

'Maud?' I said.

'I wouldn't know. Brown I think the family name was.'

'Yes, Maud Brown,' I said, but he continued, as if not interested in my connection.

'It looks like she's alone, although she swears otherwise. Says there's a husband, no a "partner", how uncouth! But whoever he is, there wasn't much sign of him. No, that poor woman is struggling to look after five children on her own, I'd say. The little vermin were running about everywhere. The place was in a terrible state. Old cat, thin as a rake, and the rocking horse – the one we used to have – with its tail pulled out. A bit worse for wear from what I could see. Piles of needlework all over the place and red workmen's gloves all dried up in buckets. It was like a workshop, yes, like a backstreet sweatshop – hmmph.' He nodded to himself as if pleased with his summation.

'Did you see her?' I said quickly.

'What?'

'Did you see the girl?'

'Girl?'

'Yes, a girl with a birthmark on her cheek.'

'No, I didn't see any girl.' There was a silence and we stared at each other but his expression didn't change. Then he turned back to his meal. 'How about green?'

'Green?'

'For the box room. I don't think it suits those childish pastel colours and we can paint over the sheep.'

'The *box room*?' I said. 'Are you talking about the nursery?'

'Yes, well,' he muttered, 'we can hardly call it that any more, can we? After all, it never really—'

'All right, then.' I nodded wearily.

'I'm sure Mr Tuttle can find a use for the crib – we'll make a gift of it. It will make good money sold on.'

'The woman with TB,' I said. 'Mrs. Brown, What will happen

to her?'

He shrugged. 'Well her fate lies in the tests, although I'm sure they'll be positive. There's not much doubt when you're coughing up blood. An impoverished woman in her situation will probably end up in the public sanatorium at Meadowfield. But there's no issue of quarantine for the moment – she's pretty isolated up there, plenty of fresh air too. Her children don't seem to stray too far and they need her at home. There are new treatments of course, surgical procedures, it was a bit of a speciality of mine when I was on the pulmonary ward at Oxworth General. Quite fascinating actually, involves collapsing the lungs.'

I shuddered.

'The prognosis is bleak though, for someone in her situation. She's probably better off at home actually, the institutions for the very poor aren't up to much. I would be doing her a favour leaving her where she is,' then he added, 'and saving on some paperwork.'

'What about chlorodyne?' I said. 'My mother used to say that it had helped her aunt when she had consumption.'

He laughed. 'Victorian marketing, I'm afraid, just the kind of thing I would expect to fool country people—'

'You use it,' I said.

He tilted his head, so the light from the window reflected in his spectacles. 'Chlorodyne is just a mix of sedative and opiates. It can help for an old wound such as mine, or it can give brief relief, but it is no cure for TB. Some make it through, but the odds aren't good.'

I chewed my food slowly, forcing down each mouthful. George was talking about the Great War now and his time at Amiens. How infections would break out in the field hospitals due to the lack of French hygiene. I nodded and tried to look interested but I saw only the movement of his lips. I remembered how I had suffered when my parents died, but I had been eighteen, a woman, with options and a way out. Ruby was still so young to be left without the woman who had raised her, motherless. There was Clarence, maybe, but this time I found that I could not imagine the farm labourer with the muscled body and the blackened skin, and all that I could picture was the empty rocking chair.

'It will be so hard for the poor lamb,' I said absent-mindedly.

'Mrs Brown?' said George. 'Well you seem to be acquainted with the family, maybe you can offer some support.'

I stared at him in disbelief. Could it be that he had not seen Ruby's face on the day of the garden party? Did he not realize that I had found the girl that I had drawn on the leaflets he confiscated, the one that I had been searching for, our daughter. Maybe the birthmark had not been visible from the window, when he had peeped through the curtains and watched her carry away the rocking horse. And could it be that he hadn't recognized Henry either? That he failed to remember the little boy who had brought my leaflet to the house, the child he had chased from our front door all those weeks ago.

'Mmm' I said, trying to sound non-committal, but thoughts churned in my head.

George turned back to his meal, and to his memories of the war: gruesome stories of infected shrapnel wounds and burns from mustard gas; of men with severed limbs and hospital ships full of maimed Tommies; of feet soaked so long in mud that the flesh peeled away when the boots were removed; of outbreaks of meningitis, rubella, influenza, diphtheria, dysentery, typhoid, trench fever, gangrene, measles and the final indignity of rigor mortis.

'I think I will bake the poor woman a cake,' I said at last.

George looked up. 'A cake? No, I cannot allow it. I won't have you exposed to that unsanitary environment, not with all the filth and disease and—'

'I won't deliver it myself,' I said quickly. 'I promise.'

'Well that's different, then.' I felt his hand, cold on my knee. 'In fact, this is wonderful, darling; parties, redecoration, and now charity – all good ways to speed recovery! I thought I'd lost you there for a while but the prognosis is much better now.' He jabbed his knife in the air. 'Excellent stuff – no more chasing ghosts!'

I nodded and smiled. 'No more ghosts.'

21

I thought it best to wait until Thursday before I returned to Rose Cottage. It was for the best, I thought – that way rain that was forecast for the start of the week would have cleared and Maud would be struggling with her new delivery of needlework, if news of her illness had not already reached her nephew in Oxworth. If Maud was as bad as George had described, then she might even be pleased to see me and be glad of some help with the children. This plan would give me a whole four days to plan a cake for the family – something that Ruby would like but not something that a woman like Maud could easily afford, something that would show Ruby how things should be. I wrote out a list of the finest flour, plumpest fruit, whitest sugar then, struck by inspiration, ran into the dining room as if my idea would evaporate if I waited.

The vase of violets was still on the table. The stems were a little wilted but the petals still broad enough to flatten out and crystallize with sugar syrup and a pastry brush. I knew that Maud would never go to such care as to top a cake with crystallized violets. She would not have the time and, having never seen the grand cakes at the Trocadero or Lyon's Corner House, the idea would never have entered her head. I laughed with glee at my cleverness but the chuckle caught in my throat when I remembered that Maud might be dying and that Ruby would be in turmoil about losing the woman she saw as her mother. It was only then that I realized that any cake, no matter how fancy, would do little to ease her woes.

I could not bear to think of Ruby's sadness. I wanted to hold her and comfort her and make her happy again, just like I had done on the day we sat together on the hill, the day that she had told me her dream of becoming a grand Missensham lady with a grey mare. But that had just been one day and now that day was just a memory. If only memories could be preserved like violets. My memories from the hill were fresh but others would wilt and die. I closed my eyes and tried hard to remember the good times, but I found that even my memories of 1925 were fading; even they could not be preserved...

*

'I love Wednesdays,' said Peter, buttoning his shirt.

Above us, tangles of beech twigs twisted out across the blue. I laughed and wriggled my shoulder into his armpit, resting my head on the hard muscle. He reached into his jacket and took out a cigarette, throwing the case down beside him. A match flared inside his fist. Somewhere, a train rattled down the track. Silver glinted in the grass and I leant over him and picked up the cigarette case.

'Ah, so I'm not your only lady friend!' I said.

'What?'

I turned the case over in my hands. It was a Victorian design, the silver etched with ornate urns and trailing vines. 'I see that your taste is for older ladies!'

A gust of smoke wafted over the sky. He passed the cigarette to me. 'It's my mother's. I borrow it sometimes.'

'Aha!' I said. 'So we know that the mystery man has a mother. He wasn't found in a cabbage patch.'

'I think I can admit to that much,' he said.

I rolled onto my side, pressing the silver case into his chest. 'A man who carries this close to his heart must be close to his mother,' I whispered dramatically.

'Oh, I am,' he said. 'I tell her everything.' His voice was steady, his mouth relaxed with not even the hint of a smile.

'Do you tell her about me?'

'Like I said, everything.'

I punched his shoulder. 'You are such a bastard,' I said. 'I never know when you are telling the truth.'

He looked at me but his eyes were hard.

'All right, I give up,' I said. 'You will always be a mystery.'

He opened his mouth slightly.

'Well?'

'I don't like to talk about my family much. I am close to my mother but the others are a bad lot...' He sighed slowly, his eyes fixed on the sky.

'Go on.'

'All right,' he said. 'You win. I will tell you all about myself, everything.'

I passed the cigarette back to him. 'I'm listening.'

'My name is Peter,' he said, the smile returning at last. 'And I am a businessman. I own my own company of tilers, master craftsmen, who tile waiting rooms and ticket offices.'

'All right,' I laughed. 'I will play along - Are these tilers any good?'

'The best,' he said. 'Take the Orient Express and you can see their handiwork – all the way from the Paris to the Bosporus and the Trans-Siberian Express too, Leningrad to Peking, but their work can also be seen by the common customers of Missensham Station.'

'Fancy!'

'I have a big red motor car and a house in Sunningdale... No, where was that place you wanted to go? The one where you have to get the boat train—'

'Le Touquet?'

'—in Le Touquet. And Charlie Chaplin and Louise Brooks pop round for cocktails. I'm not able to keep them away.'

'Oh really!' I said.

'Well not now maybe, but one day. That's who I will be one day.'

I laughed. 'Not one day soon, I don't think. But maybe when you are really old – maybe when you are thirty!'

'Well maybe then,' he said. 'And what will the divine Miss Violet Garbo be doing when she is thirty?'

I slumped back, letting my head loll on the grass. 'Oh, I don't know.' I watched the sparks circle the cigarette, burning it down into a worm of ash. 'My family's business had to be sold for very little,' I said slowly, 'so I won't have that. Dressmaking was my only skill and no shop or office in town would employ a married lady. My husband spends all his time working at the hospital and has no interest in what I do. I suppose I'll be just like I am now... only fatter and with more wrinkles.'

He glanced at me, a flash of blue under his lashes, but his mouth was grim, his lips puckered round the cigarette. 'Well I suppose you are right, Violet,' he said, his voice suddenly hard. 'You don't have much to aspire to. You already have your house on the Sunningdale Estate and your motorcar and a husband too. Yet all that isn't that enough for you, is it?'

Above me the branches twisted, thinner and thinner into little twigs. I could feel his eyes on me but I didn't reply.

'No,' he said. 'I don't suppose it is. No lady from the Sunningdale Estate who had everything that she wanted would go around fucking a labourer she just met.' He was smoking mechanically, his chest heaving, his lips tight around the stub. Above me the branches shivered and then dissolved into tears, but I sniffed them back.

This was the sixth Wednesday I had spent in the field with Peter; the sixth time we had been together and we had reached it too quickly. One can't be intimate so many times with another person, not if deep down you know you can't possess them, and especially if each time you see them you feel closer. I had felt the tension with Peter growing until this point. Little annoyances at first: suspicions when he was ten minutes late; frustration when he laughed off my invitations to dine together in the city; paranoia that his compliments were fewer than last time. Then came my questions about his life, his family, disguised as jokes to start with but the humour draining when each attempt failed to get a serious response. Then there were my dreams, impossible dreams discussed like serious plans, musings which I would run through while I lay in the grass detailing my hopes of escaping to London or Brighton or Le Touquet while I would monitor his responses for acknowledgment or enthusiasm, listening to his answers and hoping that they contained a 'we' or 'us'.

But I could not go on like this forever, not when the days had become weeks and then months, not when our meetings had become the only way for me to break the tension that had built up over the week, when I could release it with lust and intimacy, only for it to return again once the lonely weekdays dragged on and I returned to a boring and passionless existence.

'Well if you must know, it's not like I'm fucking anyone else,' I said, my voice quivering. 'So I guess that would make me faithful to you. So, as far as you're concerned, I'm not such a bad person.'

He turned his head, his eyebrows raised.

I sighed and wiped my cheeks. 'My husband and I… we don't do it, not generally speaking,' I said. 'I… I mean, we did do it once, in Brighton, but it's not something that we do any more.'

He watched me for a long time, but there was no hardness in his stare. 'I'm sorry,' he said at last. 'I know things aren't working between you and your husband but it doesn't stop me from being jealous. He has you in ways that I don't.' Then he took the cigarette from his mouth and offered it to me.

I waved it away.

'Oh shit, Emma!'

He sank back into the grass and rested his palm on his forehead. His face became still as if he was no longer aware of the sky or the branches or me as I watched him. Then his eyes closed tight, the skin pinched at the corners as if reminded of some lingering pain. I put my hand on his chest but he did not move.

'Peter?' I whispered, but he said nothing. He was not in the field any more. He was in some dark place. I watched my hand rise and fall with his chest then I lay back next to him. Above us the boughs circled gently in a gust of wind and a cloud dissolved into wisps. Violets, smaller now, but still in the hedgerows, watched us like the bright eyes of little creatures. Somewhere, far from us, a train rattled down the track – Missensham, Oxworth, Waterloo, Dover, Calais, Le Touquet: bank clerks, secretaries, travellers, adventurers, bathers, sea nymphs and mermaids.

Then he sat up suddenly. 'What was I thinking?' He flicked the cigarette away. 'I'm sorry, Emma, really I am.' He leant over me and I felt his hand cup my breast. 'Come on, turn over again, we may not have each other all the time but we can still make the most of what he do have.

22

That morning I knew something was different; that change that all creatures can sense when the wind brings the first chill of autumn. The hedgerows on the Evesbridge Lane had faded to grey and the hard furrows underfoot had softened to mud. Autumn seemed to become harsher the further I walked from Little Willow, the air colder and the ground wetter.

I had got up early that morning, the smell of the evening's baking wafting through the house with the morning light. When George caught me rummaging in the cupboard for a basket and an overcoat, he had flown into a panic, forbidding me to enter a quarantine area. I had only managed to leave the house by promising that I would leave the cake on the cottage doorstep and cover my face if I so much as glimpsed a farmhand on the lane.

As I rounded the bend by the old, twisted oak, I saw Rose Cottage for the first time in weeks. It seemed smaller than I had remembered, the thatch heavy with rain and the lime walls, once so bright, now muffled by a haze of drizzle. An old woman was pushing a bicycle out from the yard, the tyres shearing soft furrows into the mud. She was a plump woman with a round face, her bunched skirts and heavy cape making her an ungainly figure as she stepped cautiously over the puddles. I was sure that I recognised her face, although I could not think from where, so I smiled and nodded, but the woman did not acknowledge me and just set her mouth grimly, her eyes fixed in front of her as if concentrating on her balance. I knocked on the door, then covered my face with a handkerchief as I entered.

The kitchen was dark, the windows streaked with rain. As with every Thursday, a large pile of fabric covered the table but, instead of whirring, the Singer lay idle as if stopped mid stitch. Maud was slouched in the basket chair, her body swaddled in an old grey blanket that was tucked under her chin. She lifted her head and stared at me with eyes like broken egg whites and tried to prop herself up on the arm of the chair, her wrist shuddering with the effort.

'Yes?'

I lowered the handkerchief just long enough to show my face.

'Oh, it's you,' she sounded disappointed.

'I heard about... I thought I would come to see if there is anything that I can do to help.'

'Oh, so it was your George was it? The doctor that came to see me? I thought as much, the bald head and the awkward manner and the funny little glasses, just how you described him.'

'I brought a cake,' – I glanced round – 'for the children, they must be hungry.' But seeing nobody else, I added, 'And for you, to keep your strength up.'

'If you've come to see Ruby, she ain't here – they've all gone up over to Evesbridge to play in the barns.'

'No, that's not why I've come,' I said. 'Actually I'm glad we're alone.'

She sighed, then started coughing. The attack lasted several minutes and each time she managed to draw breath the force of each wheezy inhalation triggered another fit. She was doubled over, her chest heaving as if the strain would break her in two. I opened my mouth but then shut it, knowing that I would have to put off what I wanted to say a little longer.

When the fit had calmed I took a bottle of chlorodyne from my bag and pressed it into her hand. 'My mother always said that it was the best thing for TB,' I said. 'It's not a cure, but it might help with...'

She took the bottle from me and, without looking, put it on the windowsill without a word.

I looked at the table with my hands on my hips, shaking my head but she did not look up, so I took an odd-looking pair of gloves from the top of the pile. 'Why are you still taking these in?' I said, waving the gloves in front of her face. 'You can't possibly keep on working, not with a fever.' I tutted disapprovingly and ran my finger over the stitching. 'You won't be able to keep up the quality in your condition, just look at this one, it would fit a giant, and this one is no better and this —' The third glove was perfect, the stitches just tiny humps in the cotton, straight and even. I took another pair from the middle of the pile, then one from the bottom – they were all complete, all perfect. I put the gloves down quickly but Maud's eyes were now on me and her mouth twitched into a little smile.

'Well,' I said. 'You won't always be able to keep up this standard of work, will you? Not this many and not the quality.'

But now her smile was puckered with smugness and I sighed, knowing that she could not be argued with.

I sank into my chair and glanced round the room. Maud may have been able to keep up the work on the gloves but George had been right about the rest of the house – the room was strewn with mess: Buckets of fabric dried hard with carmine; split packets of indigo bleeding onto the draining board; a ragged red stain on the floor where a bucket must have fallen over. There was a trail of mud from the back door, stamped with the soles of muddied boots, plates were piled high in the basin and the kitchen nets were yellowed with fat. There was a mark on the plaster where a naked lamp had burnt the outline of a flame and one of the windowpanes was cracked. There were cobwebs round the door frame, clothes on the floor and soot between the flagstones and all of this steeped in the stale fug of mouse droppings and nebulae of dust and fur. I realized that I had walked in on the backstreet workshop George had described. I could never let Ruby come home to this, so I decided that Maud would have to accept my charity whether she wanted it or not. I recovered the first pairs of gloves I had found and started to unpick the stitches.

'Is Clarence away?' I said.

'No, he's around,' she wheezed. 'He just works long hours during the day.'

I nodded. 'No way he can lend a hand then?'

'No. He's exhausted when he gets in, just wants to relax at the pub away from the kids.'

I looked at the empty rocking chair, I had never seen any of the family go near it, let alone dare to sit in it.

Over by the draining board, the grey cat coughed hoarsely, his body long and flat against the floor, his head snaking back and forth with each wheeze. The poor creature was looking thin and had mange. I put the gloves down, worrying about Ruby again.

'Is there anyone else who can help?' I said. 'There must be someone.'

'Ruby, she's nine now.'

'I meant an adult.'

Maud shook her head.

'Some relative or friend maybe, what about that woman I just saw leaving – an old plump woman pushing a bicycle? I'm sure that I've seen her before somewhere, so she must live locally, couldn't she help?'

'That's the kids' Aunt Sadie, my sister. She can never stay long, she needs all the hours she can work at the hospital, just brings the odd bits of grocery that will fit in the pannier and helps me to get fresh air when I need it.'

'Yes, but you'd think she would want to do more for her sister, especially considering what might—'

'Sadie does enough for us anyway, she always has. It's her son we get the work from, he works at the garment factory, drives the work to me all the way from Oxworth – he don't need to do that, the both of them do us enough favours.'

'It's no favour,' I said. 'It's not right if this nephew of yours still expects you to do all that work in your condition.'

'Sadie will do no more for me,' said Maud curtly, puckering her lips.

I remembered the tight lips of the woman I had seen in the lane, the little grimace she had given in return of my smile – it was the same expression I had seen so often on Maud's face and the one I saw again now. It was obvious to me now that the women were sisters, and they were probably both as stubborn as each other.

I sighed. 'Well at least let me do the washing up while I am here.'

I stood at the sink, whirling the little brush round plates and bowls encrusted with porridge, or at least something that looked like it. The bottoms of the cups were covered with blooms of bacterial growth, like the clinical experiments George talked about so enthusiastically when he read his scientific journals.

I tightened the handkerchief around my face and opened the window, raindrops shuddering down the glass. The cottage walls had not sheltered the yard from the rain, water pooled in muddy tyre tracks and the door to the log store hung open. Sodden gloves hung limply from the clothes line, red dripping from the fingers, and four rusty buckets had been slung into the hedge. Then I felt a chill in the pit of my stomach: Something was different – a silence.

'The chickens!' I cried. The henhouse was shut, the wooden slats wisped with cobwebs.

'Oh Lord!' Maud started to wail into her handkerchief.

I ran outside, mud splattering over my skirt. The door of the henhouse was fused tight with sticky droppings and when I finally managed to heave it open a vile smell wafted from inside. On the floor, lifeless clusters of feathers glowed white in the darkness. The chickens' necks were twisted away from their bodies, as if straining for a final gasp of air, their bodies nothing but feather and bone.

I threw the carcasses over the fence and watched helplessly as their feathers slowly stained with mud. I prayed that a fox would take them before Ruby returned, or that they would sink slowly into the mud. I thought of the plump chicken nestling in Ruby's arms – Snowdrop or Snowflake or whatever it was called. That adored creature had no connection to the scrawny scat of feathers that lay lifeless in the field and nor should it. I took a breath of fresh air and stepped back into the cottage.

'I'm so sorry, Maud,' I said.

She nodded. The wailing had stopped and her eyes had become glazed. I noticed a red stain on the handkerchief she had held to her mouth.

'How—'

'It was the kids' job,' she said. 'They are a forgetful bunch but they'll be devastated, especially Ruby.'

I sat down next to her, drawing the handkerchief firmly over my nose and mouth. 'It's not working is it, Maud? You may be able to keep up your work a little longer but not everything else as well. You say that the children are a help, I understand that, but at the moment they are just more work for you and extra mouths to feed.'

She nodded and wiped her eyes.

'Let me take one from you, one of the children – to live with me on the estate,' I said, then added quickly: 'Just for a month or two, until this is all over.'

Maud stared into the empty grate. She didn't speak for several minutes. At last she said: 'Only if you take that hanky from your face, so that I can see that you mean it, and then promise that you will send my child back to me.'

I made the promise, exactly as she said.

She seemed to relax a little as she heard my words and wiped her eyes. 'At least let me have them all here for a few more days. It would be nice if they were here for me on Sunday. I'd like some time with them all together.'

'Of course,' I said.

Then she seemed to hesitate, her brow furrowed. 'I don't suppose I could get you to take one of the boys?' The words came out with a sigh, not so much a question as a statement.

I didn't answer, just let her stare into the fire.

'No, no,' she whispered. 'We both know that's not what you want.'

23

Ruby

My name is Ruby Brown and I would be lying if I said any different. You see, I don't tell lies, not about the important things. But adults lie to me all the time. Emma lied to me about why she came to work for Maudy and Maudy lied to me about why she fired her. Clarence and Maudy both lied to me about how the stove got broken. You see lies are what I have come to expect from adults – but I did not expect *him* to lie.

His van was parked at the side of the lane, almost hidden by trailing branches, but I could still see the white paintwork and the familiar letters of 'Walker's Fine Garments, Oxworth' winking at me from behind the leaves. It was the day that we were not usually home, the day that Sadie took Maudy out for fresh air, wheeling her along the lanes to Missensham in a Bath chair, and the day that the boys worked with Clarence on the harvests. It was the day that the house was usually empty; but he would have known that.

When I got to the cottage, the front door was open and a rustling noise was coming from inside.

I stood and watched him for some time. He was in the back room, bent over the dresser, his huge shoulders heaving as his hands rummaged through the drawers.

'Fatkins!' I said, but he did not hear.

His shirt was damp and clung to his body, showing the hard bulges in his arms. I got a strange feeling in my stomach, and it wasn't a good one. I felt like I shouldn't be standing there – his presence had turned my home into somewhere strange, somewhere I was not welcome. I turned to go, but that was when he heard me.

'Hello Ruby!' But he did not smile and his words did not seem like a greeting.

Now he stood up straight and looked at me. He was a tall

man, I had always known that, but now that his damp shirt clung to the little humps in his chest, I saw that his belly went in and not out. Just like Maudy had said, he was made of muscle, not fat, and then I realized that the funny feeling in my stomach was fear.

'I'm sorry to disturb…' I whispered.

But it was not me he was interested in and his eyes were already turning back to the dresser, and then his hands did too, and he rummaged around in the drawers for a few more seconds. But then his movements became slower, as if he was starting to realize that he could not carry on with me standing and watching, so he stood up straight again and spoke to me at last, his mouth widening into his usual smile.

'Hello Ruby, how is my favourite niece?'

I said that I was very well, but I did not say any more than that because it sounded silly muttering niceties after we'd already been standing together for all that time and the conversation already felt like it was coming out backwards.

'Sa— my mother was here a while ago, she thinks that she may have left something behind.'

'What?' I said, wondering what could be so important that he would drive all the way from Oxworth for to get it instead of waiting until Thursday's delivery.

'Um – a case of cigarettes.'

'Cigarettes!' Suddenly I realized what my little silver treasure box was and I even fancied that the bitter smell that had wafted out when I opened it had been tobacco, but the word had left my lips too quickly.

'Yes! do you…?'

I opened my mouth but I didn't need to because his pause had merely been to draw breath: 'You poor girl. It must all be such a shock for you finding me here. You must be wondering why I want the cigarettes so badly.' He got down on his knees and held my arms tight against my body, looking hard into my face. 'Well, you see, your Aunt Sadie's ankles are swollen again and she really needs some tobacco to calm them down. She can't get hold of any more until payday, so she has to have the cigarettes that are here, the ones that are in a silver case, with flowers on.' He spoke quickly but I stopped listening, it did not matter what else he said because I knew he was lying – Fatkins and Sadie had fallen out and hadn't spoken for months, so the cigarettes could not be for Sadie. But he knew about my treasure so that, at least, proved that it didn't belong at Rose Cottage.

I didn't know what to say to him. I didn't want to give him my treasure back and I felt bad that there had been no cigarettes left inside. I wanted to tell him this, but I didn't want him to know that I had been nosing inside his treasure either, so I kept quiet.

But he still went on: 'I'm sorry about sneaking in, I didn't want to give you a fright, I hope you weren't scared…' and suddenly he became friendly old Fatkins again, the big softy who spoke to me like I was a posh lady from Missensham and who let Maudy con him with damp aprons and stories about fixing the stove.

'Don't worry,' I said at last. 'I think I have seen it. I will go and get it.' But then I panicked that I would lead him to the rest of my treasure, so I added: 'Wait here!'

There was a big smile on Fatkins' face as he saw the cigarette case in my hand. 'I'm so sorry, Ruby,' he said. 'I hope that you didn't think, well, it's not that Sadie and I don't trust your family to—'

'It's all right,' I said. 'I understand.'

He smiled, and then he bent down and kissed me quickly on the forehead, his hand on the side of my face as he did it. As he pulled away, his fingertips ran quickly over the blotches on my cheek, his eyes on my face but not meeting mine.

I don't like anybody touching my face, so I pulled back and held the cigarettes case out to him.

'Thank you,' he said, smiling and taking it quickly.

'It's all right,' I said again, but I didn't really mean it that time.

Fatkins nodded, then he turned away from me and I heard the click of the clasp opening. When he looked back at me his smile was gone. 'Ruby, there was something inside, where is it?'

'I don't know,' I said, but my face went hot as I thought of the photograph of the baby still hidden in the straw of the henhouse. 'Maybe Clarence has smoked all the cigarettes.'

'Cigarettes?' he said quickly. 'Yes, of course; cigarettes. My poor mother's ankles will have to wait.' Then he stopped and looked right at me. 'Ruby, was there anything else inside?'

'No,' I said quietly. 'I mean, I don't know, I never opened it.'

He was still looking at me, frowning, as if the lies themselves were written on my face. 'Please, Ruby!'

But by then it was too late, I could not go back on what I had said.

I don't know why I didn't want him to have the photograph. Maybe because I thought he was lying to me, but about what I did not know. I wish I had told him. Maybe if I had, things might not have happened the way that they did. What happened was all my fault. And even then I knew it because, as I stood in the doorway and watched Fatkins limp back down the lane, I saw violets shining brightly from the hedgerow, like hundreds of little eyes watching me.

24

Emma

With no more of my 'emotional outbursts' or 'funny turns' as he called them, the only thing to irritate George was Mr Tuttle. The old man had still not finished the decorating and his behaviour was becoming increasingly erratic. He would turn up late, linger in the hallway, or stare at the same light fitting for several minutes, jabbing at it with his finger and then jumping back as if it would bite him. He would talk to himself, sometimes just mutterings of 'silly old Tuttle', but sometimes passionately, as if affronted by his own argument. He seemed to come and go as he pleased, the rattle of his key in the lock at the oddest times of day.

His promises of being joined by Mr Tuttle Junior were starting to seem fanciful too. The old man would always say how he had dropped in on his son on the way to Little Willow, but nothing it seemed could persuade this reluctant master decorator to put in an honest day's work with his father on the Sunningdale Estate. And if Mr Tuttle Senior's behaviour wasn't enough to infuriate George, there was all the unfinished jobs – the old nursery was still gathering dust, the kitchen door had not been painted and, to add insult to injury, the garden gate still hung off its hinges. I dared not tell George that twice I had come home that week to find that the front door had been left unlocked and I dreaded the day that George would return from the surgery to find the house ransacked. Of course, George persisted with his diagnosis of a neurological condition, although his arguments wavered when the smell of whisky filled the hallway.

One Sunday, when Mr Tuttle had left for the evening, George called me in from the garden. 'Have you seen what that man has been doing?' He ushered me into the living room. A stepladder was in front of the fireplace, two feet on the hearth and two feet off, as if it were about to topple over. A pot of paint stood on the bottom step and a brush brittle with blue pigment. The chimney breast was painted a light blue but the other walls were left bare.

'Well,' I said, slightly annoyed at George's fustiness, 'he's not finished, but he's done a good job. I expect he'll come back and finish it tomorrow. He said as much. There are no spots on the skirting or anything like that.'

George screwed up his mouth. 'That's more by luck than by skill,' he said.

I followed him into the dining room. Here the table and chairs were all covered in white sheets, old newspaper lining the skirting boards.

'Well, I don't know,' he said, 'but I would have prepared the living room like this – the room I was actually going to paint. Now, I don't know if this is a nervous condition or alcohol abuse or senility. But I think nobody in their right mind would prepare one room and then paint a completely different one.' He sighed heavily. 'Silly old fool!'

I burst out laughing. There was something about George's face; the grim mouth and the metal-framed eyes that made him look ridiculous, and the more I laughed the harder it was to stop.

George's face softened. 'I've missed those schoolgirl giggles,' he said. 'Come on, we should move these to where they should be.'

I followed George into the living room, dust sheets bunched in my arms. He was listing the other 'little oversights', as he called them: the hammer in the sink, the lamp fitted with a dead bulb and the fence painted two different shades of green. And what about his son? Was that another 'little oversight'? Had he forgotten to bring him along too? And to think that we had trusted this man with a set of our house keys! I couldn't stop laughing, with everything that I had been through, it was somehow comforting to be around someone who still got upset by the things that didn't matter.

Suddenly George realized that I wasn't just laughing at Mr Tuttle but at him as well and he stopped his rant and laughed too. 'Well, it's amazing that the lounge came off unscathed. Oh how do you cope with two old fools in the house?'

I kissed him on the cheek. We had drifted so far apart over

the past weeks that I needed these little moments to remind me that he was a good man at heart.

'I suppose I've already bored you with my lecture about the effects of trauma on neurons and how they can lose their connections and misfire and the analogy of loose electrical cables in the brain?'

I bit my lip and nodded, then started laughing again.

We shook out the dust covers and threw them over the furniture. One had old cobwebs folded inside and they landed on George's head, coating his forehead in dust. He took off his glasses, blinking in the dirt, the skin around his eyes was moist, the wrinkles soft and pink. Without the glasses, his face was naked and vulnerable and I suddenly felt pity for him.

He wiped his eyes. 'I really am your dusty old man now,' he said and for a moment I remembered what it had been like before we were married, the times that we had like this one – the moments that had made me think that being married to him might not be so bad.

'Of course you are,' I said. 'You are my Old Bear, remember?'

We looked at each other and smiled. I wasn't sure what it was that I saw in his eyes, regret maybe, but things had been going wrong for too long. We both knew it was too late.

'Come on,' he said gently. 'I suppose we'd better camp out in the dining room this evening.'

I nodded and followed him through.

'George?' I said.

'What, darling?'

For days I had wanted to tell him about Ruby and how I had arranged for her to stay with us, but I feared his reaction and the right moment had never come. I had rehearsed the argument in my head and imagined myself telling him about how we may never have a perfect marriage but she at least might make us content. About how we could regain some youth – some pleasure in our old age that would see us through our dotage. About how we could watch her grow into a young woman we could be proud of. But now the moment had come, I found myself hesitating again.

'Come on, Old Thing, what is it?' George tilted his head and the light caught his spectacles, glazing them with mist, and the man that I had seen again for just a moment was lost.

'Nothing,' I said. 'I've forgotten what I was going to say. I'm sure it wasn't important.'

George looked at me curiously. 'I don't know!' he said. 'Sometimes I think everybody around me is going mad – your little memory lapses, hammers in the sink, rogue dust covers and your little blue flowers – but maybe it is just me that is going mad.'

'Blue flowers?' I said.

'Yes, your latest fad; glasses of little blue flowers, pansies, no, lilacs maybe.'

'Violets?' I said.

'Yes, violets... Oh I don't know, maybe violets.'

'Those flowers were weeks ago,' I said. 'I remember because they were left at the party.'

'Well yes, there were some after your party and then some more at supper the other week and this morning in the study. You are becoming obsessed with them.'

'There were more violets this morning?' I said. 'Inside the house?'

'Yes, there were more this time. I don't know where you are getting them from. I've not seen them in the garden.'

'It wasn't me,' I said.

He pulled a face, the face he pulled when he thought I was being childish, the face that meant I had ruined our earlier good humour with my infantile behaviour. But I knew better than to argue with him. He wasn't my Old Bear any more.

They were in the study, just as George had said. Five violets in George's little sherry glass, their heads heavy and their stalks resting against the rim. I remembered how happy I had been to see them after the party, when I thought that Ruby had bought them as a gift. But now that the violets were unexplained, I started to think of my mother's superstition about bad luck and death and the flowers that the midwife had lain by the incubator in that cold white room. This time the memories in my head were no longer happy ones.

I took the glass outside and flung the contents onto the patio, the water leaving a dark streak on the flagstones.

'Emma! Don't—'

But the violets lay on the stone, limp and bruised.

*

In my mind it was 1925 again. The violets in the field were dead. The trees were turning from green to brown and the blackberries in the hedgerows had shrunk to husks. In the triangular field the long grass had become dry and yellow and a breeze swept through the copse. But the days were still long and the air still warm. At three o'clock in the afternoon it was warm enough for a man to walk in the open air without a jacket, for that same man to loiter by the war memorial, and rest his back against the hot stone, for him to glance down the road to a house, a house on the edge of a new estate, where the low sun glazed the windows orange.

The man's name was Peter, or that is what he had told me. I knew little else about him – he didn't tell me and by then I knew better than to ask any more. All the same, I delighted in imagining what his life might be by revelling in every little detail of him.

His clothes were not new, but well repaired. He wore work boots, traces of mud staining the leather and the soles re-heeled. He was a labourer, but that I already knew, he had told me as much. . Sometimes bankers' slips fell from his pocket, always deposits – savings to start his business. Bus tickets told me he lived in Oxworth, but as he always carried his camera in a work bag slung on his hip, I guessed that wherever he lived was not a safe place to leave it.

His body told a more complicated story, one I did not understand and one which drew me in further, always wanting to know him more. His skin smelt of ale sometimes, and cigarettes, from the London bars I thought, wild places where the men drank and sang together in a jostle of heat and muscle. But he was always clean-shaven, just for me I hoped, the smell of cologne masking the sweat. His body was big and awkward, but he was aware of that and could not always laugh at his clumsiness. His hands were rough and scarred from heavy work, the fingernails brittle, but capable of tenderness. Sometimes he would go quiet, his thoughts wandering, and I imagined him to be haunted by pain from his past. But that much I could only guess. By now I had found out that questions only soured things between us and I did not want to ruin what was left.

I knew he would be coming that day, this man I knew only as Peter, making his way from the station along the road through town, to the crossroads and the war memorial. I imagined the route he would take, what he would see on his way. I thought to myself of the point he would be on his journey as the time ticked on and by a quarter to three I felt I could feel him, my body warming as I sensed his approach.

George had taken a day off work, but on that Wednesday the day had settled into the comfortable weekend routine of gardening and packing away the keepsakes from our honeymoon and his presence in the house annoyed but did not worry me. I had my best summer dress on, lipstick circling my mouth and a new scent, lavender, dotted inside my underwear where the skin was softest. But I kept up the pretence of potting hydrangeas, my old gardening shoes clomping between shed and kitchen, never stopping long enough for George to notice my smile.

He had sat in the lounge all afternoon, filing the mementos from our Brighton honeymoon; the cheap watercolours of the pier and the esplanade and the photograph we had taken with the donkeys on the beach, the tickets from the tram and the matchbook from the restaurant. He arranged them all in order of date, a clean page for each, his spectacles held in front of his face as he scrutinized the memories.

'Are you finished with those pansies yet, darling?' he called. 'Can you spare ten minutes to help me sort out these postcards?'

I glanced nervously at the kitchen clock. 'No,' I shouted. 'Not just now, can't you leave them in the box?'

'Please!'

I wiped my feet on the kitchen mat and went into the lounge.

He was sitting on the sofa, hunched over the coffee table spread with colourful scraps of paper and card, his spectacles folded in his hand. 'Leave them in the box?' he said. 'Won't you ever want to show people? Audrey perhaps? Sometimes I think it's like you want to forget!'

'No, you silly Old Bear,' I said. 'That's not it at all, I just need to set off on my walk very soon, it's such a nice day, I need to be out by three to make the most of it – the days will be getting even shorter in a few weeks.'

He replaced his glasses and smiled. 'I never knew that I had married such a sporty girl. What a lot of walking!'

I nodded and flexed a bicep in a silly gesture like a bodybuilder.

'Looking after your figure, new clothes and new hair! And you always joked that you'd become a frump once we were married.'

I felt my face redden at the mention of our marriage, so I turned to go.

'Just remember it's the Hospital Ball at the end of the month,' he called. 'You did say to remind you so you had enough time to make a dress.'

'It's not October yet,' I said.

He laughed, his little coughing laugh. 'Yes it is, darling, it's the ninth!'

October! I started to panic.

George was talking about the Hospital Ball. How it wouldn't be too bad, how Walter would be going, so Audrey definitely would be too. There would be food and drink – and of course Walter was ever such a nice chap – he had known him since his service in Amiens – another wounded medical officer – now so highly respected as a psychiatrist in London…

But my mind was racing. How could it be October? I ran upstairs and started counting the days on the calendar. He was right; it was October. The days had come one by one as predicted, but something else hadn't. I thought about the breakfast that I hadn't been able to keep down on Friday; maybe those eggs hadn't been off after all. I had been tired too and my breasts had ached but I had put that down to the exhaustion of a reckless double life.

I asked myself how this could have happened. But the answer was so simple that it could have come from the lips of a schoolgirl – it was carelessness, it was back luck, it was fate, it was basic biology. And not one of those answers had anything to do with George.

I went downstairs slowly and perched opposite George on the chair in the bay. I glanced at the clock – the minute hand taking big bites of time as it clicked forward. I sat still and rigid, the ticks of the clock getting louder until they filled the room. George's breath hissed rhythmically and hooves clattered along the road. My stomach twisted and my palms grew moist, but still I sat, in silence, my heart throbbing in my ears.

When the clock struck three I saw myself jump up from my seat, pick up my cardigan and run out the door, but that was not me, just a faded outline, a ghost. The real me did not do that. I just sat quietly and pictured the date on the calendar – the illustration of red berries that circled the word 'October' – October the ninth.

George raised his head when he heard the chimes. 'Hey, Old Girl, you look so pretty today. You know, it has been such a long time since we were together on our honeymoon. Why don't you forget that walk of yours. Do you fancy going upstairs for a bit instead?'

'Upstairs?' I said.

'Yes, upstairs – upstairs together.'

It wasn't until I looked at his face that I realized what he meant. He had a strange little expression; raised eyebrows and his head tilted in such a way that his spectacles became opaque in the light from the window.

'Oh!' I said. 'You mean like we did in Brighton?'

'Yes,' he said. 'Just like we did in Brighton. Do you still have the Dutch cap I got you from the surgery?'

'Yes,' I said. 'I still have it.'

'Well good.' He stopped to adjust the frame of his vapid glass eyes. 'Well do you want to?'

I thought of the calendar, the berries growing round the October. My mind was still racing but now I questioned not how it had happened but where it would lead – disgrace? Poverty? An uncertain future at least. But here was an answer and George was offering it.

'Yes,' I said. 'I think we better had.'

'What a funny way of putting things!' he said. 'Well then, as you say, I suppose we "better had".'

'Just not right now,' I said quickly. 'I think I would like to have a drink first. I think we both should; maybe some of your sherry. Would you mind—'

He jumped up quickly and headed for the decanter in the study.

I went to the bookshelf and took down *Mrs Beeton*. I sat down again and rested the spine on my knees, leafing through the pages until I found a square of blotting paper with a violet inside, the last one I had received. I pushed the violet aside to read the scribbles of ink: '9th of October – 3pm – usual place'. I touched the violet gently with my finger. It was as my mother had warned: a violet inside brought bad luck – but she had been wrong too – it didn't mean death, it meant life. Already I could feel the baby scouring my insides.

I wanted to go upstairs, into the front bedroom and stand in the bay, to look out over the road towards the war memorial, maybe catch a final glimpse of Peter. I had done it every Wednesday – every Wednesday at three o'clock for three whole months as I waited for him. He would always turn up a few minutes early. Walk up to the cross and rest his back on the stone. Sometimes I would wait a few moments, watching him as he shuffled his feet, put his hands in his pockets and lit a cigarette, cupping his hands over the flame. Then I would run downstairs, only stopping to grab my cardigan on the way out.

I imagined him now, his back against the hard stone and the cigarette burning down to ash. Maybe he would look up the road to the house, take his pocket watch out, turn it over in his fingers, shake it, listen to the mechanism, his large clumsy fingers turning it over in his hands. Maybe he would cup his hand to his ear for the chimes of St Cuthbert's. He would lick his lips, swallow slowly, the bulge in his neck dipping towards his chest. He would wipe the sweat off his face, the sweat that smelled like leather, shuffle his feet awkwardly, self-conscious and alone. Maybe he would nod to people passing by, cast his eyes to the road as traffic passed. How long would he wait? Would he look up to the window? Walk past the house? Oh Peter, my Peter!

George returned with the decanter and two glasses. 'Well, this is unexpected, isn't it? Quite unlike you, darling. It's gone three o'clock, what about your walk?'

'My walk?' I said, the words sticking in my throat. 'No, it's a bit late for that now.'

It was too late. By then I didn't have a choice. Violet was already blooming deep inside me. Peter would know what my absence meant. I had made my decision. It was over.

25

Ruby arrived on the doorstep of Little Willow with her belongings tied in a blanket. She had been walking in the rain and was wet through. I bustled her inside and sat her in the living room, lighting a fire in the grate.

'The chickens!' she said, and burst into tears.

I patted her shoulder, frustrated by her sobbing. It had been a good four days since the chickens had died and I worried if this was the real reason for her outburst. If she felt bad about leaving Rose Cottage, I wanted to show her that she could feel at home here too. I wanted her to feel the softness of a proper bed, to enjoy running in the garden, to feel happy and warm in the nursery, to savour a proper meal eaten at a dining room table, to smell soap and lavender water and to wear proper petticoats. But, most of all, I wanted her to want me.

I put my hand on hers. 'I know what will cheer you up – let me show you your room.'

We went upstairs and I opened the door to the nursery. The sun was beaming through the open window, making the yellow paint glow, and the lambs gambolled happily among the poppies. The room was warm and airy, the furniture glinting with polish, sparkles of dust circling in the sunlight and I breathed in the scent of cut grass from the garden. I thanked God that Mr Tuttle had not yet touched this special place and I smiled at Ruby and squeezed her hand.

'It's a baby's room,' she said. 'I can't stay in here.'

I took her to the back bedroom instead, and flung open the curtains, angry that I had not had time to clean two rooms. I told her to sit on the bed and she slumped down, burying her face in the pillow, her sobs muffled by the down.

'Whatever is the matter now?' I snapped.

She gasped against the pillow: 'Chi-ick-ins!'

I untied her belongings, laying the blanket out to dry over the back of a chair. Then I started to fold her clothes into the drawers, working slowly, all the time willing the crying to stop, but soon all the clothes were put away and her shoulders still shuddered with sobs. I sat next to her and put a hand on her back, but her tears continued, her back warm and damp against my palm, her ribs heaving as she gasped for breath.

'There there,' I said, awkwardly brushing the hair away from the warm curl of her ear. 'There there.'

Then the crying stopped suddenly and a sticky little choking noise came from the pillow. Ruby lifted her head, her damp hair plastered to swollen cheeks. 'There's a nursery here,' she said. 'You had a baby?'

'Yes.'

'Where is it? Where is it now? Is it grown up?'

'Yes,' I said. 'I suppose that she is.'

She looked at me strangely, her eyes starred by clumped lashes.

I smiled. 'Almost grown-up, that is.'

*

Ruby went to bed early, exhausted from her journey. I sat with her until she fell asleep, watching the rise and fall of her chest under the blanket and listening to the gentle gusts of her breath. When I heard George's car on the gravel I closed the door behind me gently and slipped downstairs.

George sat calmly while I explained, his brow furrowed, the way it did when he was studying a particularly challenging crossword.

'Which friend?' was his first question.

'Her name is Mrs Brown,' I said, trying to sound confident.

But then his mouth dropped open. 'Oh God, the tinker woman with TB! The family you gave the rocking horse to. That little brat who I saw carrying it home. It's her, isn't it?'

'Don't shout, George,' I said. 'You'll wake her.'

'Oh God, Emma! I knew you were obsessed with that girl, you must be to give away a valuable rocking horse. But why her? Why that one?'

'Oh George, does it even matter?'

He was silent, his eyes misted out by the little round glasses, a stare of blankness; as if his argument was so obvious that I could not possibly challenge him.

But I was prepared for his objections: 'You said that you were pleased that I was doing more for charity,' I said, resting my hand on his knee. 'And the poor mother can barely cope. There is no money in the family and Ruby's aunt only has space for the boys. I thought that you would be happy about this, and really, how will it make a difference to you, to your life?'

'Well, there is the matter of...' He paused, his expression frozen. 'W-W-Well, there are the wireless broadcasts, I can't have them interrupted. And then there is the matter of noise, I must have my bed rest.'

I laughed. 'George, I'm sure we can manage that. She isn't a monkey.'

His mouth clicked open, but his words were not quick enough.

'She is just a little girl,' I said firmly.

'Oh God,' he said, his hand waving away my arguments as if they were flies. 'Oh God, all right then. But remember, it is only for a short time, until the family get themselves sorted out.'

I nodded.

He took off his glasses and I saw that his eyes were red and weary from his day. 'I will let you have your way this time but please remember that, well – despite everything that happened – we never really wanted children, did we?' He looked at me sternly. 'You know I don't like them.'

George fell asleep after dinner, his head dropping forward as his body slumped in the armchair. I reached over him and turned off the wireless, then I crept upstairs to the back bedroom. Ruby had been too tired to draw the curtains and the moon washed the room with a milky light. I perched on the end of the bed and watched her. The rise and fall of her chest was more pronounced now, her breath sucking noisily, as if she was putting all of her energy into the simple act of sleeping. Her nose was buried in the pillow but her head turned so that her marked cheek was exposed to the moonbeam.

I crept into the nursery and took the photograph from the drawer, returning to Ruby silently and holding the print next to her face in the moonlight. The baby on the card seemed to glow, its pale skin lustrous as if it were about to wriggle and open its eyes. I held the photograph close to my face, squinting at the grey outlines; the bulge of the cheeks, the frilled bonnet and the wisps of hair. Then I touched it gently, running my finger over the marks on the cheek. The marks were the same in number but their size and shape were slightly different. The tears on the photograph were larger on the face and less mottled, and the smudge under the eye reached almost to the ear.

But this was a baby – a baby in a grainy photograph and not the real little girl who lay before me in the bed. People grew, their faces changed, skin stretched. The girl's face was no longer that of a baby, the domed forehead was gone and the button nose. But it was the same girl that I saw in the photo and the same girl that I saw lying on the bed, and then I knew for sure that the girl in the bed was Violet.

26

The photograph was on my bedside table when I woke, the baby framed inside the white border. Its eyes were closed, a little white bonnet haloing the grey forehead. It was just an object, I told myself, an object that had captured light and shadow, but somehow the memories of my brief meeting with the infant Violet had become infused in the ink, and the photo became clear and intense.

But it was not just the baby I was remembering when I looked at the photograph, this time it was the meeting itself; the white, sterile room and the shiny incubator. And the midwife, of course – no longer a vague recollection but her image now pulled into sharp focus; her broad frame draped in a long cape, bag in hand as if ready to leave and her face in front of mine.

I recalled how her lips moved, forming silent words, but it was the expression on her face that I remembered that morning, that expression that I couldn't quite read. A mouth pulled tight and eyebrows raised but her eyes glazed as if staring far beyond me.

I shut my eyes and concentrated on the memory. In my mind the baby in the photograph screwed up its face, the stain on its cheek shrinking into folds of skin. Then I remembered huge fingers encircling the baby's chest, surgical gloves cut at the wrist by the white border of the photograph. The baby opened its tiny mouth in a silent cry. Then it was lifted through the air and cradled against white cotton, a dark sash crossing an ample breast. The midwife looked up and I saw her face. Hers was a face that I had almost forgotten, but it was somehow new in my memory, as if refreshed by the cold light of day and now I knew where I had seen that face again.

I got up and slowly crossed the hall to Ruby's room. 'Time to get up.'

She rubbed her eyes. 'Why? It's early.'

'We are going to visit your Aunt Sadie.'

I had told Ruby that we were going to Aunt Sadie's so that

she could visit her brothers. She had seemed happy with the idea and told me that Aunt Sadie lived at a place called Missensham House. I was somewhat surprised by the grand name, but she sounded so certain that I did not question her further. She didn't know the address of the property but said she could take me there and, not knowing any better, I had to comply.

We left a disgruntled George to tidy the breakfast things and, with Ruby pulling at my hand, we left Little Willow and passed the war memorial, taking the road into the old town centre. We passed the church, then the pub and the village green. All the time I wondered where the grand old house could be – it could not be far if a child could walk there, yet I had lived in Missensham all my life and never heard talk of it.

We continued toward the station, along the long narrow road and past fields that were once hedged with greenery but now were boarded with colourful pictures of bay windows and indoor WCs; advertisements for the houses soon to be built there.

I stood on tiptoes and tried to look over the hoardings. 'I don't think this can be right, sweetheart,' I said. 'I don't know about any country houses in this area and…'

But Ruby was insistent and kept walking.

We continued over the humpback bridge and past the station and out to St Benedict's, the little black church squeezed between the road and railway line. The number 34 bus rattled past and I thought about hailing it or at least stopping it to ask the driver for directions, feeling a growing sense of despair once it shrank into the distance and silence returned. Further along the road, made of the same black stone as the church, was a terrace of five little cottages with arched windows and ornate pitched roofs. 'Missensham House 1658' was inscribed in the lintel of the middle cottage.

I did know Missensham House of course; I had just never known it by that name. I had always known it as the old almshouses, a local landmark in my childhood, though now largely forgotten but for the glimpse from the odd commuter sat on the top deck of a bus or staring through the window of a train carriage.

A low picket fence separated a narrow strip of garden from the road, a wooden sign fastened to the gate:

ESTABLISHED AND MAINTAINED BY THE GENEROSITY OF
THE OXWORTH GENERAL HOSPITAL TRUST

I couldn't help thinking that this generosity was rather lacking now as the cottages stood forlorn, tiles missing from their roofs and cracks in their windows, the lawn unkempt and yellowed.

An old black bicycle was propped up against the wall of the end house and, in the front window, a face appeared. I waved but my hand dropped to my side when the face disappeared just as quickly. I smiled awkwardly at Ruby, but she did not notice and ran up to the door, rattling the knocker violently. I chased after her and pulled her away, chastising her, maybe too severely, for being so impolite.

'Sadie,' I called. 'My name is Emma Marks. I have bought Ruby for a visit. I hope it is not inconvenient.'

Nothing; the window remained black.

'I saw you through the window,' I called, cupping my hand towards the dark glass. 'Please do not worry if you are not presentable. I understand that it is early. We have come such a long way and I have your niece, Ruby, with me. I'm sure that she—'

The door opened a crack, shuddering to a halt against Sadie's foot.

'I'm sorry, Madam,' she said. 'It's not—'

But this was enough of an invitation for Ruby. 'Henry!' she yelled, 'Andy, Jim-John!'

There was a stampede of footsteps and the door was wrenched open.

*

'I didn't know that Maud had a sister,' I said, 'not until I saw you in the lane when you visited her the other day. It is fortunate that I passed you and mentioned that I had seen a lady pushing a bicycle or she would not have told me about you.'

Sadie stared at me blankly. She was an old woman but her face was still plump and round. It was the face I had seen when I had passed her pushing her bicycle outside Rose Cottage – the face that I had recognised but could not place. It was also the face that had come to me that morning when the photograph had refreshed my memories of the baby Violet and now, when I looked at her face, I knew where I had seen Sadie before.

I looked away embarrassed and pretended to glance round the room. I was shocked at how small Sadie's lodgings were. The single room that seemed to occupy the downstairs was no bigger than my kitchen, a stove, a chair and a fold-down bed all jostling for space, and I found it hard to imagine how the explosion of boys that had pushed through the doorway would fit back inside.

Sadie had not offered me a seat, just slumped down in the chair herself, leaving me to perch awkwardly on the bed with its crumpled sheets. The small windows did nothing to relieve the stuffiness from the room and I longed to be outside playing with the children, their muffled shouts making me crave the fresh air.

'You have a lovely place here,' I said. 'Lovely and cosy.'

Silence again.

I looked round self-consciously. The room was sparsely decorated; no pictures or ornaments just a black cape hanging limply from its hook like a dead crow. There were clothes strewn across the floor and a cracked pane in the window. The curtains had been wrenched from their hooks as if the once neat and sombre little house was reeling from a hurricane. I thought about the mess at Maud's house, how I had scolded her for the state of the rocking horse, but it wasn't TB that had hit Sadie and I started to realize that Maud was probably right – this is what it meant to have children.

Sadie jabbed her finger towards a teapot warming on the stove.

'Oh no. I don't want you to go to any trouble on my behalf!'

But she ignored me and poured two cups joylessly.

I took a cup and raised it to her, like a strange little toast, to what I did not know. 'I'm—' I opened my mouth but closed it again when the house rang with the clatter of railway carriages passing in the cutting. 'Such a cosy house,' I repeated once the train had passed, 'and you are so well connected here, what with being so close to...'

But Sadie was staring at the floor intently, her mouth puckered into a grim little kiss, so I gave up on any small talk.

The stuffiness was making me hot and I started to regret the tea. 'I should explain,' I said. 'I'm helping out too actually. Ruby is staying with me, although it seems less of a sacrifice now I see what you've been left with. Do they allow guests here? I thought almshouses were quite strict and had simply loads of rules.'

'They have to be quiet when the warden comes, but they can be quiet enough when they are hidden upstairs,' Sadie said defensively.

'Quiet? I can't imagine!' I laughed, glad for the break in her silence, but she did not smile, her mouth returning to the puckered little kiss.

'Oh, I've probably not made myself very clear,' I said. 'Maud has entrusted Ruby to me because I'm a family friend, a good friend of Maud, perhaps she has mentioned me? Mrs Marks… from the Sunningdale Estate?'

She looked me up and down doubtingly and I wished I had not worn my best dress and hat. 'I'm just helping out while Maud is ill,' I explained again.

'Damn it!' She had spilt tea into her lap, the cup jingling against the saucer and I saw that her hands were shaking.

'Of course I'm terribly sorry about Maud,' I said quickly. 'But you must know the risks of TB.'

The silence returned.

'…Sadie?'

Still nothing.

'Oh well, I'm going to assume that you do,' I said, willing bravery for my next move. 'You see, my husband is a doctor. I've heard him talk about these almshouses. They were founded for retired nurses and widowed hospital staff who lacked the means to rent their own property, so I'm assuming that you have some medical knowledge and a person such as yourself would know the prognosis for a woman suffering from an illness such as TB. Of course I'm assuming that you are a nurse, or at least that you used to be.'

I pointed to the wall where the black cape hung limply and she couldn't help following my gaze. 'Of course, I don't think that's quite right these days, is it?' I stood up and crossed over to the cape, opening it up to show the red lining. 'This looks more like a midwife's uniform. You were wearing it when I saw you in the lane the other day. Maud said you still work at the hospital sometimes.'

'Yes. A midwife,' she croaked and stared into her cup.

'I know,' I said slowly. 'You were there nine years ago when my daughter was born, I'm sure of it. You even tended her in the incubator.'

Sadie said nothing.

I was starting to get frustrated. 'I remember you, Sadie, even though you have changed of course. Your hair was different back then, it is greyer now. You've put on weight. Do you remember me, Sadie?'

She shook her head, quickly but still did not look at me.

'I think you do,' I said, 'and if you don't, you've at least worked out who I am.'

Sadie's jaw flicked open as if she was about to speak but no sound came and she shut it again, her face settling into a blank stare. 'I don't know nothing!' she snapped.

'Well then let me help you remember,' I said. 'It was nine years ago. I had given birth to a baby; a girl with a red birthmark, a port wine stain, on one side of her face. You may remember because I am Doctor Marks's wife – he worked in the pulmonary unit at the hospital back then, but he was seconded to obstetrics sometimes. You would have remembered me. And the baby. You may have remembered her because she was special, although some said disfigured.' I took the photograph from my bag. 'This is her, this is the photo that you gave me back then. It was kind of you. You took the trouble to do this, so I think you must remember, and look – it says one of two – you even made another print. Maybe you kept the other one for your records.' I held the photograph in front of her but she did not look.

'I am sorry for your loss,' she said at last.

'Ruby is the same age as Violet would be now,' I said. 'She has the same mark.'

'You can't say that to Ruby; she don't like to talk about her face—'

'I know,' I said, 'but you and I can talk, can't we, Sadie, as adults.'

She put down her teacup, stirring it slowly, and I wondered if she had heard me at all. Then she looked up sharply. 'Maud is Ruby's mother,' she said. 'You can't try and take Ruby away from her if that's what you're thinking.'

'I'm not,' I said quickly. 'I'm just trying to find out what happened. What happened on that day in the hospital, the day I last saw Violet.'

'You already told me that,' she said. 'Your baby died and I am sorry for—'

'I did not say that she died, only that you gave me a photograph, and besides I never saw her body. They just told me she had died,' I said. 'That doesn't mean that she is dead.'

Sadie shook her head, her brow furrowing as if deep in thought. 'Maud loves her daughter. They are very close.'

'I'm sure they are, but—'

'Ruby nearly died too,' she said suddenly. 'It was a difficult birth. Maud had already been in hospital for several weeks. She was very weak with the infection. They thought that Ruby wouldn't survive because Maud was too weak for the birth. It was a traumatic time for all of us. My sister nearly died herself. And when she finally got better, she was suffering from delirium, did not know that the baby had even been born, and that was the miracle – to wake up from delirium and find out that her baby was born and alive – that was surely a gift from God. You see, neither of them should have made it. And Maud knows that. That's why Ruby is special to her. She spoke with such conviction, like the troubling circumstances themselves were proof of the bond between Ruby and Maud. Her face was hard, unshakable in everything she believed. Her story had shocked me, but I was still not convinced.

'Of course Ruby is special,' I said. 'But don't you think it's funny, Sadie; two baby girls born in the same district around the same time, with the same birthmark. It doesn't add up. It's too much of a coincidence.'

'No!' she said, her voice rising. 'I want no part in this.'

'No part in what, Sadie? All I want to know is the truth. Please believe me when I say that I'm not trying to—'

She shook her head. 'I want no part in it and you can tell Maud that too when you see her. Tell her I want no part in it.'

'It's okay,' I said. 'I won't tell her we spoke. She's got enough to worry about with her illness.'

'She ain't ill,' said Sadie suddenly. 'There's nothing wrong with her.'

'Sadie,' I said. I reached forward and patted her arm gently. 'She's seen a doctor and he said that it was TB. There's been tests and everything. She doesn't like to show it, but I've seen her myself, coughing up blood on her handkerchief.'

'No,' she said. 'Not her. She's had it before and she got through it, she recovered.'

'TB is not like chickenpox,' I said. 'She can have it again.'

'No, that would be bad luck.' She shook her head and her eyes moistened. 'She don't deserve that. It's just too much bad luck.'

'I'm sorry,' I said quietly.

'I'm sorry too,' she said.

And then I saw it again, that curious expression on her face – the one she had all those years ago in the shining white room at the hospital, the expression that I couldn't quite read. Suddenly my head was flooded with sterile metal surfaces and white clinical gowns, with hard metal incubators and the clink of surgical instruments. Somewhere I could smell disinfectant and my stomach churned with the memory of morphine. Sweat trickled between my shoulder blades and the bright orbs of the hospital lights swayed in the almshouse window.

Then Sadie was standing over me again, just how she had done that day.

'Are you all right, Mrs Marks? You seem to have gone pale.'

I opened my mouth to answer but there was a clatter in the hall, a gust of fresh air and giggles.

Ruby stood in the doorway.

27

Ruby

My name is Ruby Brown – that is what they tell me. But why should I believe them when everything else they say is a lie? Clarence tells me that I was born on a Monday, but that is a lie because everybody knows that 'Monday's child is fair of face', and my face isn't at all fair. Maudy tells me she is my mother, but that is a lie because everybody knows you can't have a baby if you aren't married and there is no ring on her finger. Emma tells me that violets indoors don't bring bad luck, but that is a lie because I brought violets into the henhouse and the chickens died. They tell me lots of thing but sometimes the lies hide in what they don't say.

We didn't spend long with Aunt Sadie. One minute I was looking for somewhere to hide for a game of sardines and the next thing I knew Emma was yelling at me to put on my coat and bustling me right out the door again. It was well before lunch and we'd already walked back past the black church and for what seemed like miles down the long hedgy road.

Emma was talking a lot, and fast, like she didn't want me to get a word in. I knew why she was doing it; she thought that if she was always talking then I couldn't question her. She tried to distract me too, wittering on about this and that – the weather that morning, the flowers in the hedgerows, the ruts on the road, the pictures of the posh houses on the billboards, anything at all that she could see – until my head was spinning. She kept on pointing at things and asking questions, then stopping, just long enough to let me nod and then she was off again.

It had all started when I walked in on them, her and Sadie. All I did was open the door and see them both sitting there with faces like stone and right then I knew that I shouldn't be in that room with them, but it was too late, so I just stood there looking stupid. I could hear them talking before I got in, hear their voices from behind the door, but once I was in there, they stopped dead and stared at me like I was a ghost. That's when Emma muttered something about leaving and having to get back in time for something or other and how lovely it had been to meet up and she hoped the weather would continue to be good.

Emma stopped gabbling at last and looked around, all desperate, for something to talk about. She didn't notice that I was dumb anyway. It had shocked me that Emma and Sadie were all tight-lipped like that, and I won't forget the looks on their faces for a long time. I expected this kind of thing from Maudy and Clarence of course, they always had their secrets, but I didn't expect it from Emma. I had thought that I could trust her, but just then I wasn't so sure. So I walked on, lost in my own thoughts, just putting one foot in front of the other.

We walked past the station. Emma looked at the ticket office in a strange way, craning her neck up to look at the roof. She went on and on about how she could remember the station being built and how she was on the first train into London – it made her sound very old. But the building looked even older, with mud splashed on the bricks and posters curling off the walls. Emma squeezed my hand and opened her mouth and she looked like she wanted to say much, much more, but then she just looked sad and we walked on again.

We walked past the village green and there she prattled on about the café where she used to live, as if I cared – I didn't. She squeezed my hand like it was my family who had lived there too, like it should mean something to me. She squatted down right beside me and looked into my eyes, like it was very important for me to know that.

'My parents,' she said all wistful. 'Oh, I wish you could have known them.'

But they were just people who are dead, people who had nothing to do with me.

I didn't care about any of this, of course, but then I started to wonder if she really did either. And suddenly I thought that maybe she was just trying to get me to forget that I had caught her and Sadie plotting and that she was trying to get me to think of something else.

At the doctor's surgery, she pointed to the little white building and said that it was where Dr Marks worked; nothing more. I knew this of course, but here she'd got me because I did start to think about other things – about Dr Marks. And how I didn't want to go back to her house. You see, something had crashed onto the floor as I grabbed my cardigan and ran out door that morning. I didn't touch anything, but the crash did happen the same time as I was running. I felt my stomach go all warm. Whatever it was, Dr Marks would have found it.

I remembered his face as I had come down to breakfast that morning – the look of hate. He kept staring at my face like I was an ugly little horror. I wanted to shout at him, tell him it wasn't scabies, like I did with Emma, but something stopped me. He wasn't the type of man to do that to and, as we looked at each other, something passed between us which Emma didn't see, like we had a pact to hate each other, but Emma was all thrilled to have me there and didn't notice a thing.

That wasn't the first time I had seen Dr Marks, of course; although Emma didn't know that and he didn't either. He had come to Rose Cottage when Maudy first got ill with her mouth ulcer. Jim and John had been running around making a nuisance, but I'm shy of posh-types so I stayed in the yard and peeked through the window.

I thought he was a funny-looking man, and I don't mean in a good way; he was small and thin, with wisps of hair oiled in straight lines over his shiny head. A handkerchief was wound round his face like a comic-book bandit and he had no eyes, just blank little spectacles like cold pebbles.

But it wasn't any of that that made me hate him. It was the way he covered his mouth before he even came through the door, the way he jumped back when anyone spoke to him and the way he would wipe his hands over and over. I fancied that it wasn't the illness he found repulsive, it was us.

It isn't very nice to think like that, I know, but those were the thoughts I had for the rest of the way home.

When we got back, Dr Marks was angry. 'Ruby!' he shouted as we stepped through the door.

'Ruby, go upstairs,' said Emma.

'No, she must stay,' he shouted, chopping the air with his hand. 'She must stay and hear this!'

And so I was stuck wobbling back and forth, one leg stepping to the stairs and the other rooted to the spot until I feared that I would split in two.

He bent down low so that his face was right in front of mine. 'Have you any idea why I am upset?' he shouted. His face was terrible. His glasses were so thick that I couldn't see his eyes, like they had whited themselves out with rage.

'Something broke,' I said. 'I heard it but it wasn't me, it was the wind as I ran out of the door this morning.'

'That!' he shouted. 'Well at least you will admit to breaking something. Have you anything else to tell me while you are at it?'

I tried to think. We had only known each other for one morning and I already knew all the things he didn't like about me – the way I slumped at the breakfast table, took too much butter on my knife and chewed with my mouth open. I didn't think that there could be anything left for him to complain about and I started to wonder if I was drawing breath the wrong way.

I took a guess and pointed at the wireless. 'I'm sorry,' I said. 'I was just playing a game – I didn't know what that knob did.'

He shook his head angrily, as if me merely opening my mouth was a waste of his time. Had I not made my bed? Had I left my shoes in the lounge? I opened my mouth again but he took the breath out of it.

'Theft!' he shouted. 'I'm talking about theft!'

'George!' Emma's hand shot up to her mouth.

'Oh yes, Emma. I warned you about bringing tinkers into the house.'

'You must be mistaken.'

'No, no not this time.'

'Five shillings,' he said. 'Five shillings taken from the pot on the mantelpiece. It was for the milkman – do you not want milk next week, young lady? Because you deserve to go without.'

'Ruby, did you do this?' said Emma. 'Did you take the money?'

I shook my head.

'George, please think! Are you sure the money was there to start with?'

That look came over his face again, the look he had when he examined Maudy, that look of disgust, and this time he was looking at me.

'George, just wait.' Emma's hands were out in front of her,

as if she was holding back an invisible Dr Marks made of air. 'Just because Ruby is poor doesn't mean she is a thief. You are just believing what you want to believe.'

'What do you mean by that?'

'You know exactly what I mean.' She stared at him, her face suddenly all fierce. But his eyes were staring too and I fancied that I could see the line in the air which connected them.

Then suddenly Emma was all smiles. 'Look, George, there must be an explanation – lots of things could have happened.' She was pushing the air again, but this time it was as if she was pushing him back, ever so gently.

'Oh really, I can't think of any other rational—'

'Mr Tuttle!' she shouted all of a sudden. 'He is in and out of this house all the time. Everybody says that he drinks. And he was in the house today and Ruby and I have been out since dawn.'

Dr Marks's mouth was already open, but then he stopped and let out a little gasp. Then there was a loud squeal and his hand shot into the air. I jumped, I thought that he was going to hit me and I ducked from the blow, but it never came. Dr Mark's hand went straight to his back and he doubled over. Then he cried out again and I realized that his raised hand wasn't anything to do with me, just pain – pain from his back.

Emma put her fingers up to her forehead and rubbed the sides in little circles. She told me to go upstairs and get a bottle of medicine from the bedside table. I went up and tried to waste time but the bottle was easy to find and looked just like Emma had described – blue glass with lots of sides like a hole in honeycomb. I took my time coming back and stood outside the door listening.

'George,' Emma, spoke slowly and quietly. 'It's only five shillings.'

He sounded weary. 'It's the principle of the matter and then there are the other misdemeanours too: the sticky fingers on the bookcase, the untuned wireless and the vase.'

'The vase?'

'She broke the vase. She broke it as she was leaving this morning.'

'That was an accident wasn't it, Ruby?'

And then I realized that Emma knew I was hiding and I opened the door and nodded like I meant it. 'The vase on the sideboard was just an accident, Dr Marks.' I said in my poshest voice.

'That big pink egg-shaped thing? George, you always hated it!'

'I know, but it was a wedding present from my aunt and, well, it's just everything; the vase, the wireless – you know the reception has just not been so crisp since I caught her playing around with it this morning.'

Emma took the bottle from me and smiled all knowingly – I wanted him to sleep and she knew this, and soon he would be.

'You know what Ruby's mother told me?'

'What?'

'That I know nothing about children – I see now she was right. I'm sorry, George, I suppose I just didn't know what little troublemakers they are.' She smiled at me and winked.

I wasn't happy being called a troublemaker, but I could be grown-up sometimes and Emma's smile meant that this was one of those times, so I smiled back, all grown-up.

Dr Marks grunted and the liquid poured from the blue bottle.

*

That evening Emma tucked me in to bed.

'Emma?' I said.

'What, darling?'

'About Maudy – about her being ill with this mouth ulcer. How long will it take her to get better? When can I go back home?'

'Mouth ulcer?' She looked shocked and I started to think that a mouth ulcer must be a terrible thing.

'She was chewing her cheek,' I said. 'Does that mean it's bad?'

Emma sat on the end of the bed and wrung her hands, for a long time she didn't say anything. Then her mouth dropped open like she had suddenly thought of something and she smiled. 'Would it be so bad,' she said, 'if you came to stay with me forever?' There was a funny little furrow in her brow and the blacks of her eyes were really big, as if she was trying to look right into the middle of me.

I didn't want to live with Dr Marks so I looked away and pretended to play with the knitted rabbit from the nursery. But then her big eyes went all watery and I felt cruel.

'I suppose it wouldn't be so bad,' I said quietly.

'Good.' And suddenly she looked happier. Then she said: 'It's nice that you are playing with that rabbit. You like animals don't you, Ruby?'

I shrugged.

'I know you do – rabbits, that grey mare you told me about, and those chickens.'

'And Smokey,' I said.

'Well animals don't just come from farms,' she said. 'Would you like to see some animals -- animals from other countries?'

I nodded.

'Well good, we shall go to the zoo at Regent's Park and when we get back we shall talk about the mouth ulcer and what it means.'

I knew very well what it meant – it meant Maudy chewing all day. But I wasn't about to pass up a trip to the zoo that I could brag about to the boys. 'Good,' I said. 'I suppose that will keep me out of trouble for a day, nice and far away from Dr Marks.'

'Oh, darling, I didn't mean it in that way.'

'He doesn't like me.'

'He will come to like you.' Then she added, 'It's not your fault. He doesn't like any children. He's never liked children.'

'How do you know that?' I said.

'He told me that he didn't,' said Emma. 'He decided that he didn't like children a long time ago.' And then she looked sad.

28

Emma

I spent all of the following afternoon repairing the vase. I sat at the kitchen table opposite Ruby, sheets of old newspaper spread between us. I had thought it would be a fun activity for us to do together; to sort through the pieces and match them up like a giant jigsaw puzzle, but I think Ruby saw it as a punishment and just sat quietly, turning the shattered fragments over in her hands.

'I'm sure once this is done he'll be much happier,' I said brightly, trying to make it seem that George could be as easily fixed as the vase, but Ruby remained silent.

When I had finished, I held up the vase to show her. I had made a terrible job of it. The once smooth curves were now jagged triangles of porcelain, webbed with brown seams of gummy glue, which buckled at the press of a finger. It was as if the big pink egg had been hard boiled and smashed with a spoon. Ruby laughed when I held it up and I smiled, encouraged by the first sign of happiness I'd seen all day.

'It's just like humpty-dumpty,' I said. 'Humpty-dumpty sat on a—'

'I'm ten,' said Ruby.

After she had gone to bed, I tidied the lounge; straightening the chairs, replacing the cushions and gathering up the scattered pages from George's newspaper. I wiped the fingermarks from the wireless, then tried to retune the set, nudging the dial ever so gently, but still there was no music, no voices, just the hiss of static. In the end I gave up and turned it off.

I got out my purse and found five shilling coins to replace George's milk money. But on the mantelpiece, next to the housekeeping pot, was something that made me stop and press the coins hard into my palm.

It was a single violet this time, a bright star of petals

drooping over the side of the glass. I felt my heart flutter against my ribs as I remembered the violets that had appeared in the study, followed by George's denial, and then what my mother had said – violets indoors brought bad luck. But odd numbers were worse, and worst of all was a single violet: bad luck, stolen money, broken porcelain... death. The shillings tinkled into the pot. And in my head it was 1926; the end of my youth, the end of the affair. Nothing could be fixed now. Death was on its way.

*

'I think a hospital birth would be wise,' said George.

'Hospital?' I said, surprised.

He stirred his tea thoughtfully. 'Well you know we expect complications. I could even get seconded to obstetrics for a bit while you are there. That kind of experience would put me in a good light with the hospital board. And, all things considered, it would be far more hygienic than a home birth. These new rubber sheets are all well and good but I've seen many a mattress ruined. We don't want that to happen, do we? The stain would be impossible to remove.'

The café on the green was hot and busy. George tried to hail the waitress but the noise from the kitchen was too loud and she turned her back on his raised hand. He rolled his eyes and started to recite a long list of bacteria, with names like Italian opera singers.

I nodded, feeling too weak to argue. I was fed up with seven months of surprises from my body and, now, with my swollen stomach pushing out under the table, I just wanted the suffering to be over with; I did not care how or where.

George had requested the table by the window but, rather than enjoying the view, I had to shade my eyes from the afternoon sun and fan myself with a napkin as my cheeks burned in the heat from the glass.

At last the waitress came over. Her hair was smoothed under her cap and cut short and straight, just a jut of blonde below her ears, making her shoulders and neck look naked. Her dress hung limp from her angular collarbone and suddenly I felt clumsy and bloated next to her. She reeled off a list of cakes and pastries in the clipped accent that the wireless had made so popular in those days and George watched her attentively, his spectacles glinting in the afternoon sun as his head nodded up and down. I recognized the waitress as the sister of an old school friend, but I was relieved when her eyes glazed with the vacant politeness of serving staff. For the first time I realized that I would have been embarrassed to be recognized with George.

I stared out the window, my forehead resting on the glass, trying to remember how life had been when I had lived in the small flat over my parents' dress shop, just a few feet above where I now sat. I could sense the ghost of the old me – a young woman, wrapping herself in a bolt of the finest white lace and posing in front of the mirror with a bouquet of bunched taffeta. Back then I would have been proud to marry a doctor, an older man, but I did not feel any pride right now and suddenly my head felt like lead and my legs went numb, my stomach turning over as acid rose in my throat.

'Just boys,' said George.

'What?'

'Over there on the green.' A group of soldiers were stood smoking outside the Red Lion. 'No idea,' he continued. 'Of course, they'll never go through what we did. They are the lucky ones. There's not much for an infantryman to do these days, just a bit of peace-keeping in benign places; Turkey or Russia, or there's the Rhine Army of course. No, it's nothing like it was before—'

'I don't feel well,' I whispered. 'I need some air.' I stood up, the table shuddering across the floor as my belly rose under it.

'Excuse me, I'm afraid we may have to leave, my wife is feeling unwell,' I heard George say somewhere behind me, but by the time he got any attention I was out the door.

I walked shakily to the bench under the oak tree and lowered myself down.

George appeared from the café. 'Are you all right, darling?'

I nodded, but only because I felt too weak to do much else.

'Tell you what, I'll go and get the car and drive you back home.'

'George, it's only a mile. I just got a bit too hot. I think if I sit here for a bit it will pass.'

'No, no – you wait there.'

I opened my mouth, not wanting to be alone if I passed out, but he was gone, striding off in the direction of St Cuthbert's.

I took a couple of deep breaths and felt better immediately. I closed my eyes and fanned my cheeks with my hand. Hospital might not be such a bad idea if I was going to feel any worse than this. Then I felt cool shade on my face.

'Emma?' He was just a silhouette as he bent over me; an army uniform and a face in shadow, but I knew his voice and, as he sat down next to me, I recognized the broadness of his shoulders and the awkwardness of his movements. 'How are you?' he asked, as if the answer was not obvious to both of us.

'Fine,' I said, swallowing my discomfort, 'and you?'

'Well, things didn't go as planned,' he said, holding out his arms to show his dull green fatigues.

'The army!' I said, starting to worry. 'Surely you don't need to…there must be something else…what about your business, the master tilers?'

'I lost the money I'd saved,' he said. 'My family got into trouble, you see. I said they were a bad lot.'

'I'm sorry.'

He shrugged his shoulders. 'I've still got the camera.'

I thought it was an odd thing to say but then I realized that he was making an effort to mention things that we both knew about and I suddenly felt sad that I had never known him any better.

'That's good,' I said but could not think of anything more.

He smiled and I saw his eyes drop down to the bump under my dress then dart away quickly. I remembered when those eyes had roamed all over my body, when they could not break their gaze, and I realized how I must have changed. This bloated bourgeois housewife was no longer the free spirit who would make love among the violets. I was not his Violet Garbo – she was long gone.

'Oh well, the army is not for ever,' he said, and when I did not smile added: 'just for a very long time.'

'Please,' I said. 'Please just take care, for me and..' but I never finished the sentence. There were things that I could not tell him, things that I was afraid he would ask - how long I had to go, and when I had resumed relations with George- they were questions that I would have struggled to answer. And then he leant forward a little and, for a moment, I thought that he might ask me after all, and then maybe ask me to run away with him, to escape the army and the drudgery of life, to start afresh in Le Touquet, where the waters were crystal blue and nobody cared if we were soldiers, doctor's wives or adulterers.

But his words never came and then I saw our new red Austin pull up at the side of the green. I looked up at Peter and opened my mouth, suddenly remembering all the things that I wanted to ask him; who he was, where he was going, if I would see him again, but the time had passed too quickly.

George jumped out of the car and ran over to me, looking defensively at the soldier.

'George, can I introduce you to a family friend,' I said quickly, reciting the line I had rehearsed for such an occasion all those months ago. 'Our mothers were at school together.'

George stood open-mouthed. 'Well, does your family friend have a name?'

'Wilfred,' I said quickly.

'Dr Marks,' said George, holding out his hand. 'How do you do?'

There was an awkward silence as they shook hands.

'Well, I'd better be off,' said Peter at last.

'Where are you off to, Wilfred?'

'Oxworth way,' he said, quietly. 'I'm on leave.'

'Excellent!' exclaimed George. 'Were you planning to take the train? It would be quicker to take a bus from the lido. My wife and I will give you a lift as far as our house. We are near Missensham Lido. Do you know it?'

'Yes, I know that road well,' he said, his eyes meeting mine.

'Good, Good!'

'No!' I mouthed, but George was already opening the car door and waving Peter inside.

I sat next to George with Peter behind me on the back seat. The engine growled as George wrestled with the gears on the bumpy roads of the old village. Now and then George would make a comment about the state of the highway or the peculiarly warm weather, each time looking over his shoulder so that Peter knew he was being addressed. At St Cuthbert's a horse-drawn wagon pulled out in front of us, making the journey painfully slow.

All the time I could sense Peter behind me, his presence filling the cabin. My back felt warm from his stare and the familiar musk of his skin filled my nostrils. The tension that I had felt in my body since his arrival seemed to have cured my nausea but now I felt heavy inside and my eyes weary, as if I had not slept for days.

'Of course I was an army man myself,' said George. 'A Regimental Medical Officer in the Great War, shrapnel wound almost as soon as I got out there, I'm afraid. Happened in a stationary hospital in Amiens. Wouldn't have happened if those bloody French had got their act together. That was it for me, shipped back to Blighty. Then spent the rest of the war in a hospital bed unfortunately, very disappointed not to have done more, still, I will do anything to help out a fellow soldier.'

I stared at him in amazement. I had never heard George talk like this. He never mentioned what had happened to him in the war, not to anyone but me and even then it was to illustrate case studies of epidemics and treatments always ending in a long list of wounds and infections. And he'd never shown any kind of comradeship with his fellow man, yet somehow he seemed to take a shine to Peter. I felt sorry for him, but not until much later of course – poor George!

'Things aren't as bad as they were in those days, though,' continued George. 'It's all about making peace now, not war. And there's little threat from our foreign cousins.'

'Our unit is to be stationed abroad,' said Peter suddenly. 'We've not been told where.'

I felt myself go cold and I must have gasped because George turned to me. 'All right, old girl. A crumb gone down the wrong way?'

'I'm fine,' I whispered.

I had never intended to contact Peter, yet I'd thought about him constantly, especially on those dull days when I was alone and the housework had become monotonous. Those days when I would wander into the living room, open *Mrs Beeton* and finger the violets pressed between the pages. They had been my reminder, my little bit of hope that maybe, just maybe, we could escape one day, escape to another life together.

George seemed greatly excited, he made the little cough he did before he said something clever and then repeated the list of postings he'd mentioned in the café; Russia, Turkey, the Rhine Army. Oh God! George had dismissed them a few minutes ago – *benign places* he had said, *nothing like it was before*. But now when I heard those words spoken again, they sounded so distant and so final. Then I saw Peter's eyes reflected in the windscreen mirror, the sharp blue piercing through the glass. I looked away quickly, feeling hollow inside.

We dropped Peter off at the war memorial. I turned and watched him as we drove away. He stood at the foot of the cross, not moving, not putting on his jacket nor lighting a cigarette. He just stood watching me as I watched him. He already seemed like a ghost, a man seen only through glass, one of the fallen haunting his name on the stone. I kept my eyes on him until he shrank into the distance. We drove the rest of the street in silence.

At Little Willow George stopped the car. 'Now, why are you crying?' he said.

29

Audrey was wearing the yellow concertina hat again. She ran through the hallway too distracted to remove it as she poked her head into the lounge, the study and then the dining room, letting out little squeals and laughs as she pointed out a newly painted wall or an altered light fitting, the wings of the yellow taffeta flapping with excitement.

'Ooh!' she cried. 'Five places set at the table. We have a mystery guest!'

'I have to see to the pie,' I said quickly. 'I think I can smell it burning.'

Audrey followed me into the kitchen. 'It's not the vicar, is it? Or that dreadful woman from the historical society—'

I turned the oven down. 'No, Audrey.'

She trailed behind me as I walked into the lounge. Walter put a firm hand on her shoulder and extracted the hat from her head.

'—or anybody from last year's Hospital Ball committee, we've got our work cut out this evening, these society events can be such a bugger to organize.'

Supper had been George's idea. He had thought it would be a good way to meet up with friends and finalise the plans for the Hospital Ball. He was on the committee this year - there was still a lot to be done and Audrey had already been such a willing helper. There were place settings to arrange he said, food to orders to confirm, not forgetting drink. Then there was the music, the decorations, the cutlery, the crockery, table settings, napkins, canapés... his list had gone on for so long that I had started to daydream, lost in my own little world as his voice droned on it the background. Then he had stopped suddenly and put his hand on my knee, saying that, most importantly, preparations for the ball would help me take my mind off things.

'I know!' squealed Audrey. 'It's Wallace Simpson, I know for a fact that she loves a bit of shepherd's pie!' She laughed, turning to us one after another like an excited puppy. I blanked her and George looked at his feet.

'Oh, you are keeping us in suspense,' she said but then her laughter trailed off and she stared at the figure in the doorway.

'Come in, Ruby,' I said.

*

Ruby sat bolt upright at dinner, her back straight as if trained by a broom handle. She wore a thin summer smock with bare arms and her hair tied back with a bright carmine ribbon. I marvelled at how fragile she looked. The light from the setting sun made her skin translucent, a vein under the birthmark pulsing red like a wound.

She ate delicately, without pleasure as if the tiny mouthfuls would choke her, a small frown crossing her face when she considered where to place her dirty knife or how to balance peas on the back of her fork.

Audrey stared unapologetically, her eyes wide and her lips forming a perfect red ring. She had been unusually quiet after meeting Ruby and accepted my explanation of the charitable favour without question but also, I noted, without approval. George and Walter discussed work matters between forkfuls of pie, looking up only occasionally to gauge the other's reaction to a point or query as if unaware of the ghost at the table.

Their conversation soon turned to the Oxworth General Fundraising Ball and how important it was this year. The hospital was in desperate need of new equipment – new-fangled sluices and autoclaves as well as more incubators for the maternity unit. The latest technology did not come cheaply of course. And the need for a new operating theatre did not even need to be mentioned. Despite everyone's best efforts, TB was still a persistent problem, there might not be enough money for a separate sanatorium, but a new pulmonary ward could be constructed, away from the main building. More budget was needed for midwives and nursing staff, some were being forced to come out of retirement and work the vacant shifts; it wasn't an ideal situation and they couldn't make-do for ever. And then there were the almshouses on the Oxworth Road which accommodated the retired nurses; the upkeep could not be afforded, they would have to be demolished, but this itself would cost money....

I rolled my eyes at Ruby and waved my hand in front of an imaginary yawn but her head remained down and she did not notice.

At last Walter started to make a rather forced attempt at general conversation, asking if Ruby liked to play backgammon, the names of her brothers, the best buy at the sweet shop when you only had a penny, what she thought of the works of A.A. Milne, whether she had been on the underground. With each question he would look at me, his eyebrows raised, and I would be forced to answer for her. I spoke enthusiastically, but was exhausted by his questions. Ruby was silent but sometimes she nodded and smiled and I put my arm round her proudly.

'Of course, catching the Tube from Missensham doesn't mean you have to stop at London,' said Walter. 'One can get a connection to places such as Brighton also.' He dipped his head to Ruby's level but continued to look at me. 'Did you know, young lady, that Emma and George went to Brighton on honeymoon? And back in those days the journey took nine hours!'

'But there's not just the South East,' I said, 'there are other connections too. You only need to go to Paddington for a connection as far as Cornwall and then there is the East Coast line all the way up to Edinburgh and there's connections to Dover and the boat trains. In a way we are even connected to Calais, or Le Touquet.'

Walter stared at me. 'Le Touquet? Blimey, Emma, that's a bit exotic, have you ever been?'

'No,' I said, unable to hide my blushes as I remembered the visits I had dreamt of with Peter.

Ruby's knife slid onto the tablecloth, a little drop of gravy sinking into the linen. George's eyes became fixed on the spot, his eyebrows low and his jaw twitching.

'Le Touquet, George!' said Walter.

'What?' he snapped.

'You're old lady has plans!'

George looked at him blankly. 'Oh yes,' he said. 'Yes.' His eyes darting back to the spot of gravy and the person who had made it.

'Is that a ruby?'

Everyone stopped and turned their heads. Ruby was pointing at Audrey's neckline. Audrey clasped her hand to her chest in delight. 'Oh, it is!' she said. She held out the necklace in front of Ruby. 'From deepest Burma!' She wafted her hands over her plate. 'And these rings are citrines. And let me tell you about the bracelet, that was my grandmother's and she was a very grand old lady…'

I watched Ruby. She was nodding politely but not sharing Audrey's delight.

Walter leaned in close, his mouth to my ear. 'Who is Ruby's mother?' he said quietly. Then he stared at me, his eyes lingering a bit too long.

'Well,' I said, 'I suppose I am, while she is here anyway.'

'And when she goes back, Emma, who is her mother then?'

I glanced at Ruby but she was running her fingers over Audrey's jewelled knuckles. I lowered my voice. 'There is TB in Ruby's family. She won't be able to return.'

He nodded.

*

After the meal the men retired to the study, throwing open the French window to blow the smoke outside. It was past eight, so Ruby went up to bed, with me making sure that she said goodnight to everyone in turn. Audrey and I went to the sitting room and started to lay the seating plans for the ball out on the carpet.

'Well, well, well!' said Audrey, her eyebrows raised dramatically, 'I had no idea you had this kind of thing in mind. You are a fast worker – a cosy little ready-made family!'

'Oh, do you think so?' I said, pleased.

Audrey stared at me. 'Emma,' she said slowly, 'I was being flippant.'

I blushed.

'So how long have you got the brat?'

'I don't know,' I said trying to rise above the insult.

'You do know that you will have to return her?'

'It might not come to that,' I snapped.

Audrey took a compact from her bag and dabbed her nose

with a film of powder. She examined herself in the glass for a few moments. 'She's not a puppy, you know, people will usually object to you taking away their children.' Her eyes flicked from the mirror and back to me.

'Ruby's got a big family,' I said. 'I'm sure if the worst happens one of them will care for her. Besides, there's everything a girl could want in Evesbridge – she has brothers and a father who is a farmhand and a little cottage. I'm sure she would prefer all that to being with me on Sunningdale Estate.'

Audrey shot me another condescending look and started talking about the preparations for the ball. This year it was to be held at the pavilion in Missensham Lido. This was a much better choice than the stuffy old village hall, she said, and much more modern. I nodded briefly, grim-faced, hoping she would notice that she had offended me. She didn't. Instead she started reeling off a list of names; people I had never heard of and long explanations about who they should be seated with. I gave up and let her drone on, making sure that I nodded at the right moments. I only began to listen again when her talk moved on to the decorations. The theme of the ball was to be the British Empire. Audrey had thought of the idea herself. It was the year of king's silver jubilee after all, and with this bungling Third Ministry of the government, the loss of the colonies, this frightful depression and all the quibbling between fascists and communists, she felt that Missensham needed a bit of national pride. It would be easy enough; everything would be red, white and blue.

At last I stopped her. 'I know someone who dyes cloth,' I said. 'We could dye the tablecloths and napkins from last year, instead of getting those expensive new coloured ones. Then we would have more money to spend on the refreshments, maybe we could even get some champagne!'

Audrey clapped her hands in excitement but looked a bit crestfallen when I explained that the plan would involve working in a cottage in Evesbridge while being instructed by a sickly Maud Brown.

'Wait here,' I told her and ran upstairs, sure that I could convince her when she saw Ruby's beautiful red hair ribbon.

The ribbon had been left on the bathroom sink, the end shivering with the gust from the open window. I tied it round my wrist, but then sat at the top of the stairs breathing in the cool air and wondering how long it would be before I was missed. Paper rustled in the lounge as Audrey rearranged the seating plans and the men's voices droned from the garden. The gentle hiss of Ruby's breath drifted from the back bedroom, sometimes regular, sometimes delayed, as if breathing itself needed thought.

Then a clunk of wood came from downstairs, followed by the snap of a latch. A gust of cigarette smoke wafted up the stairs and the men's voices grew louder.

There was just one word: 'Emma.'

I held my breath, straining to listen.

'I do see what you mean,' it was Walter's voice.

Then silence.

'I thought as much,' George said at last, his voice deep and quiet.

Then Walter said something; such a funny word I wasn't sure if I'd misheard: 'Psychoneurosis.'

And George repeated it.

'I have some old contacts at St Catherine's who know more about these sorts of things,' said Walter. 'But they were pretty sure from what I told them. She still feels guilty about the loss of the child.'

'I have tried to explain it to her, many a time,' said George. 'The problems were down to a placental haemorrhage, there are no obvious causes, there was nothing anyone could have done. Nobody was to blame, especially not—'

'—Yet she clearly does blame herself,' said Walter, 'and guilt can sometimes manifest in this way. The child with the... with the face – well she was just an unfortunate trigger. Have you noticed the marks?'

'She has a birthmark of a kind,' said George. 'But how one could compare it to that of a newborn baby last seen nine years ago is beyond me. I try not to mention it when I am with her, it gets her too excitable.'

Walter sighed. 'And you say she is even trying to force the baby's things on to the girl?'

There was another silence.

Then Walter's voice again: 'I thought you had it sorted, old man.'

'I did,' said George. 'It was sorted a long time ago. You would think that after a funeral and everything—'

'It's a shame they did not let her see the body back then. It's just what was done in those days. Ideas are changing now of course, things are becoming more progressive. I might mention this case in one of my journals, make an argument for facing death...' but his voice tailed off. 'Sorry, old man, how insensitive of me, so sorry.'

There was a long silence and I leant my head on the balustrade, daring not to breathe, willing the rustling of paper from the lounge to stop, for the clock to cease ticking and for the deafening hum of the light bulb to be silenced.

Then Walter spoke again: 'If she believes the girl to be her baby then how exactly does she explain the situation to herself? How does she rationalize it?'

George's answer didn't come immediately. There was a string of stutters and little choking noises before he said: 'Well, I don't know. I just don't know.'

There was a pause and the next voice was Walter's: 'And how have things developed since the girl has been lodging here?'

'I just don't know; they seem two of a kind sometimes, as if they have a bad effect on each other.' George's voice was stronger now. 'Emma seems to be enthralled by her, won't hear a bad word about her, and the girl, well, she has even picked up Emma's little habits. She's taken to sitting on that window seat and staring out towards the memorial for hours and hours, exactly the way Emma—' He stopped suddenly and there was a silence that seemed to intensify with every passing second, the rustling paper, ticking clock and humming light bulb all fading to nothing. Then came a long sigh and I could imagine George stood in the dull light of the study, removing his spectacles to rub his eyes the way he so often did. 'She won't have to go to one of those places, will she? Not somewhere like St Catherine's?'

'No, no, not a doctor's wife of her standing. Look, these things can sometimes sort themselves out, given time.' Walter paused. 'In the meantime these might help.'

There was another silence and I could sense the stillness in the room. Then, after several minutes, Walter said: 'Well, it's up to you, of course, I'll just leave them here. In case you change your mind.'

*

After Walter and Audrey had left, George sat down in his armchair and beckoned for me to do the same. I started to explain about the dirty dishes waiting in the sink but he told me to sit down, saying that he wanted some quiet time with his wife – he should at least be allowed that.

I sat on the window seat, smiling nervously across the room. George seemed distant, his face cast in the shadow of the lampshade. 'I know things have been hard for you, Emma, ever since...' He stopped, as if he was choosing his words carefully. 'Well... sometimes we all need some help, don't we?'

'What do you mean?' I said.

'Well some of your recent behaviour has been a little strange, you have to admit that.'

I said nothing.

He sighed. 'I mean with the girl and everything.'

'The girl?' I said. 'Do you mean Ruby?'

'Yes, yes, I suppose so. It's just that you seem to have developed rather an unhealthy fascination with her.'

'What do you mean?'

'Well...'

'Come on, George!'

He leant forward, the light from the reading lamp clouding the lenses of his spectacles.

'Well, there's the gifts and bringing her to stay here. You seem to have spent rather a lot... and... well when it comes down to it, you have to admit that she is just a little girl, like any other, yet you seem to think she is special somehow.'

'George!' I cried. 'She isn't just any other little girl. Are you blind?'

'Blind?' he scoffed. 'Well I—'

'How can you not see it?'

'See what? What are you talking about?'

'Her face!'

'What? What about—'

'Oh come on, George, don't pretend you can't see it!'

'You mean the birthmark,' he said slowly.

'Yes, yes, of course I do. The mark that you always pretend not to notice. I see when you look at her; you try and look anywhere but her face.'

'That's nonsense!'

'Is it? Look at you – you can't even have a normal

conversation about it!'

'Well it's just a birthmark.'

'No, it's not just a birthmark, it's just like the one that…' I stopped. I couldn't bring myself to say it, to talk about my baby, to say her name.

'Like what?' he said.

'Please don't do this George, you must be able to see that it's the same!'

'No,' he said. 'I don't know what you are talking about.'

I stared at him, searching for some emotion behind those opaque shields of glass, something to suggest understanding, some softness maybe, something to show that he understood how I was feeling, a touch of uncertainty even. But there was nothing.

I felt my body slump, my back resting on the thick curtains, as my eyes stung with tears

'I heard what you said, George, I heard what you were saying with Walter. You said that you had it sorted, that you had it sorted a long time ago. What did you mean by that?'

'Oh Emma, please!'

'He asked you what I thought was happening, how I would explain it. Well what do you think is happening?'

George sat still, his face was blank, not even a twitch of muscle round those frosted eyes.

'When you last saw Violet at the hospital, was she really dead?'

'What?' cried George. 'Of course, of course she was!'

'But I never saw her body; all I ever saw was the coffin.'

George waved his hand in front of his face. He shuffled his feet and started to mutter to himself.

'George, please!'

'Ridiculous, nonsense.' He opened the newspaper and held it high in front of him. I stared at the blur of newsprint, then I got up quietly and left the room.

In the study, a little brown bottle of pills sat on the desk.

30

The sound of the alarm clock drilled inside my head. George swung his arm over the nightstand, sending the clock crashing to the floor. The mattress bucked underneath me as he left for the bathroom and, when he returned, it was only to rummage in the wardrobe for his clothes. Soon after I heard the slam of the front door and the roar of tyres on gravel. Gone were the days where he would hover by my pillow, wondering whether to wake me for the sake of a kiss. The air of the September morning was starting to bite and I shivered as the blankets slid off me, dressing quickly with just a splash of cold water to liven my complexion.

Ruby sat at the dining room table chewing her toast like a cow with cud, her eyes slowly following me round the room as I collected up the mince-smeared dishes. After I had put the dishes in to soak, I found her in the lounge sat on the window seat gazing out towards the war memorial, just the way George had described.

'I know, darling, it's such a sad—'

But she shook my hand from her shoulder and climbed the stairs wearily and soon I heard the ping-ping-ping of the xylophone – a few bars of 'Frère Jacques', then 'London Bridge' and then 'Old MacDonald', as if her mind couldn't settle.

I wandered about, collecting the remnants of the night before: Audrey's wine glass with the red print of her lips; George's plate, spotlessly clean, the knife and fork perfectly aligned in the middle; the tablecloth with the little spot of gravy that Ruby had spilled; and her napkin on the floor by her chair.

In the study were two sherry glasses, amber-stained and sticky. An assortment of cigarette butts remained in the ashtray; Walter's Turkish Camels and George's withered Woodbines. This was where two men had sat and smoked as they watched the light fading over the garden. Two doctors discussing a patient, where the man of the house had diagnosed his wife and, in his mind, committed her to a padded cell.

On the desk the notepad lay open. George had begun to write a letter that morning, but then must have thought better of it. Whatever had been written was torn up into dozens of pieces in the wastepaper basket, the scratch of the nib all that was visible of what could not be said.

*

I was up to my elbows in cold soap suds when the doorbell rang.

'Shit!' I spat, raking my fingers on my skirt and cursing Mr. Tuttle for his impropriety. But it was not the old man on the doorstep. It was an old, plump woman, her bosom almost filling the doorway.

'Sadie!' I said.

She nodded – a curt little nod, not an agreement but an acknowledgement, her lips tightening into one of her poisonous little kisses.

'You wanted your answer,' she said, thrusting forward a piece of paper, 'well, here it is.'

I glanced upstairs quickly but the staircase was empty and the tinkling of the xylophone continued, with no break in the tune. I took the paper, quickly. It was a birth certificate, the birth certificate of a Ruby Brown. 'Oh,' I said suddenly, embarrassed. 'Really, this is quite unnecessary.'

Aunt Sadie jabbed a fat finger at the paper. 'Name of mother,' she said slowly, 'Maud, El-ean-or, Brown.' She looked up at me, her eyes darting over my face as if she was watching for a reaction. 'You have to understand that Ruby is Maud's child.'

'I see,' I snapped. I held the document out to her but she raised her hand to block me.

'No!' she spat. 'You return it to Maud when you see her. Put it in her hands when you apologize... and when you return Ruby. And when you do that you can explain why you have it.'

'Maud is very ill,' I said. 'What about the contagion? I can't return Ruby – she will be at risk if she goes back now.'

'Things have been sorted out,' said Sadie. 'The boys will be going home soon. I've got them trained to behave about the place. They will look after Maud, light the fires and keep her fed. They all know to cover their faces if they get too close.'

'But what about when—'

'Maud will get better, you just wait,' said Sadie firmly, as if stating obvious facts to a child.

'No, Sadie,' I said, putting my hand on her arm. 'Maud may seem better at the moment, but you must know that in the end she may never—' But she shook her arm away from me.

'All right,' I said, 'but I can only ask Maud what she wants to do. It's up to her.'

She nodded again, the same curt little nod. 'But you will respect what she says – respect her wishes.'

'Of course.' I shut the door.

I went inside and sat on the window seat. I watched the people on the street walking past the window, their legless bodies gliding along the privet hedge. I thought how ordinary their lives seemed and then realized that I envied them.

Then I saw the little brown bottle of pills on the mantelpiece. George must have put them there as an encouragement for me to take them. He had been right after all, I must be mad. I held the proof in my hands. It was official – I was holding the birth certificate of Ruby Edna Brown. Ruby was Maud's daughter, she always had been, yet I had mistaken her for Violet, a baby who had died nine years ago. I imagined one of the pills sliding down my throat and everything being erased, everything being happy. But that would be admitting to George that I was wrong and, even if the pills made everything go away, I was still left with the child upstairs. The child I had come to love.

I looked at the document in my hand – the crest of the Missensham registration district adorning the top and a series of boxes, each filled with the slanting handwriting of the registrar. Like Violet, Ruby had been a hospital birth, another baby born at Oxworth General. But where Violet had been born in the labour ward, Ruby's certificate said 'isolation (pulmonary)'. Her mother was Maud Brown, just as Sadie had said, but the father's name was left blank. Somehow I was not surprised. Ruby had been born just a couple of days before Violet on the 5th of May 1926. Ruby did have a lot in common with Violet, this document showed that, but at the same time it proved that she was not her.

But there was another name on the birth certificate; another person had been involved. The informant – the person who had registered the birth – was not Maud and I stared at the entry in disbelief, but there was no mistake. It was one George Arthur Marks, a signature of whorls and loops like a royal seal and an address of Little Willow, Missensham. The only other explanation was written underneath: 'present at birth'.

I shut my eyes, trying to stop my head from spinning. Why would George have been there? At that time he had been well into his secondment in obstetrics. There would have been plenty of doctors to attend a birth on the pulmonary ward. I shut my eyes and saw George bending over me, his face obscured by a surgical mask. Was this my imagination or an echo of memory from Violet's caesarean birth? He had been allowed in the theatre as a doctor and was present there as a father but, for some reason, he had been there for Ruby too, and in my head the two babies, Violet and Ruby, born only days apart, became one again.

I stared at the birth certificate, the little details written in the slanting hand – the dates, the name, the hospital, the mother – and suddenly they did not matter. The only words that meant anything were 'George Arthur Marks'. He was the link, but would I ever know why? All I needed to do was ask him. Asking him should be easy. George was my husband after all. He was the man who had given me security and luxury on the Sunningdale Estate, he was the man who filled the gap after the loss of my parents, the man who had shown me the sea for the first time and paid for a society wedding. But he was also the man who would not let me grieve, the man who psychoanalysed me behind my back, the man who wanted me to take pills so that I would not embarrass him in front of his peers. He was the man that I needed to ask but, deep down, I knew that I could not.

31

Ruby

My name is Ruby Brown but it should be Violet Marks. The girl who lives at Little Willow should be called Violet. There is a room in the house for Violet, a room with little purple flowers embroidered on the linen and the name stitched onto the counterpane in big curly letters. A whole room for Violet would surely bring bad luck. But the death in this house has already happened, I can feel it in every silence and every sigh. I will be glad to get away from here, if only for a little while.

Emma had spent almost a week planning our trip to the zoo but, when the day finally came, she changed her mind and said that I should go back to Rose Cottage and visit Maudy instead.

When I complained, she got all snappy and said that I had to go because Aunt Sadie said so. It was to help Maudy, she said, which sounded oh so grand because it wasn't actually her that was doing the helping and all she did was walk me to the junction with the big stone cross and wave me off. She gave me a basket with a pound cake, which weighed about ten, and a big purple envelope smelling of lavender to give Maudy, which she needn't have bothered with because I completely forgot about it and it never left the basket.

My nightshirt was in the basket too, but Emma didn't say where I would be sleeping, she just said it would be Maudy's decision, so she'd made sure that I was prepared. Well she didn't prepare me that well because she sent me off without an umbrella in the spitting rain.

When I arrived at Rose Cottage Maudy was surprised to see me; surprised but not happy. She was bustling around with armfuls of linen, but when she saw me at the door, she flopped down in her chair and gathered her sick blanket around her, a big dent in her cheek as she chewed the inside.

Home looked different after so long away, smaller and

darker. Aunt Sadie had put some things right – the curtains had been washed and the floor looked swept – but even Sadie hadn't been able to fix the stove; the door was still hanging from only one hinge and it reminded me of the Bad Thing again and suddenly I wasn't happy to be back at all.

Maudy told me that she was too ill to fuss over me; I would have to entertain myself. I reminded her that it was raining but she just shrugged and then I realized that the house felt empty without the boys. I fancied that they would be having loads of fun together at the almshouses, running around and playing tag and British Bulldog. And now I was bored and lonely back home too.

But no matter what I said, Maudy just sat and stared at me as if she wouldn't be happy until she saw me doing something, so I left her and went into the henhouse. You see there was something bothering me, something that I couldn't get out of my head...

'Where did you get that?' snapped Maudy when I came back in. She shuffled in her chair, pulling the blanket over her knees.

'It was in the back room, in one of the drawers,' I said, 'under the order slips from the factory.'

Maudy must have known it was a lie but she didn't stop to catch her breath: 'Well go on, put it back!' She waved me away but I sat down next to her.

'What is it?'

It was obvious; it was the photograph from the cigarette case, the old crumpled photograph of the sleeping baby with the white bonnet and the chubby cheeks. I knew all this, of course, but I could pretend to be stupid when it suited me.

Maudy shook her head like I was a wasp bothering her.

'What's it doing here?' I said. 'Is it me?'

Maudy laughed. She reached out for the photograph but I pulled it away.

'Nah!' I said. 'I'm still looking at it.'

She changed the subject. 'I remember you when you was born,' she said. 'You was such a lovely surprise to me.'

'A surprise?' I said, thinking it a strange thing to say.

Then I got a funny picture in my head of Maudy not realizing that she had got all fat and her mouth going wide like a big 'o' when a baby suddenly popped out from under her skirts.

I started to laugh but her face was serious.

'I didn't expect you to be born alive,' she said. 'I thought you would die.'

'Why?' I said, shocked, she had never said anything like this to me before.

'Well, I was very ill,' said Maudy. 'My lungs were infected and that had weakened me. They said I would be too poorly to give birth, they said that we both might die, you and me.'

'Who said that?'

'The hospital – a doctor at the hospital. You see, I was lying in a hospital bed with my tummy all big and swollen and I didn't know what was going on. All I could see were these bright lights and faces with masks on and I can remember feeling scared, but then everything went black. I thought it was all over, all over for the both of us.'

'What happened?' I said.

'Well then I wakes up. And by then it was a few weeks later and I'm lying in the same hospital bed and I see that I am thin again and then all of a sudden I am sad because I thought I'd lost you.' She looked up at me and her eyes were all wet but then she started laughing. 'Then they bring you to me in a little cot. They don't let me touch you, mind. But they tell me that you made it, we both made it. That is why you are special – because I thought I'd lost you.'

'Oh,' I said, 'I didn't know any of that.'

'I was going to tell you,' she said, 'but I needed to wait until you was old enough to understand, and you're a big girl now.'

'Yes,' I said. 'Almost grown-up.'

Maudy laughed. 'You just remember that you are special.' She winked at me. 'More special than the boys.'

'Why were you ill?' I said.

'I had TB.'

'Tee-bee' I said. 'Emma was talking about that. But that's not what you have now is it, Maudy? Now it's just a mouth ulcer, like you said.'

Maudy looked sad but then she laughed. 'Don't you worry about me,' she said.

I looked at the photograph. The baby looked tired, its eyes were shut and its face looked soft, like it could melt away like butter. I couldn't tell whether its dream was happy or sad. It was dead to the world, as Maudy liked to say.

'Why is the photograph here?' I said. 'Who took it?'

'Sadie did.'

'Sadie had a camera?'

'She did, for a little while, she borrowed it from someone.'

'Why did she take the picture?'

'Sadie took photographs of lots of babies when she worked at the hospital. She liked to give the photographs to the parents. It's something they used to do when she was younger. Lots of people did it back then, in the old days of Victoria.'

Well now I knew that she was lying. If Sadie was always taking pictures of any old baby then why had she never taken them of her own kin? I had never seen a photograph of the boys around the house and I certainly hadn't got a photograph of me. But then I remembered the last time I saw my ugly mug in a mirror and I realized that nobody would want one. I turned the photograph over.

'What's this mark on the back?' I said.

Maudy tried to grab at the photograph again. 'Well I can't tell you if you don't let me see, can I?'

'It looks like the number two and then a slanty line and then another two,' I said. 'What does that mean?'

'Why don't you just shut up?' she said. 'I ain't answering no more of your stupid questions.'

But I knew that once I'd got her going, she wouldn't be able to stop herself. Her answers always came too quick, especially when she was trying to cover up for something.

'Did Sadie take pictures of all the babies?' I said. 'How did she afford all those photographs? There must be hundreds.'

'No-no,' said Maudy quickly. 'She only took them of some of the babies.'

'Which ones?' I said.

'Just the special ones.'

'Why were they special?'

She stopped and frowned. 'Well it was the ones where the parents might never have been able to take another photograph of them. Where Sadie's picture would be the only one.'

I thought hard. 'Because the parents were poor?' I said. 'Because they couldn't afford a camera or to go to a photographer?'

She frowned again. 'Yes,' she said. 'That's right. That is exactly why,' but she said it so firmly that I knew that it was one of those grown-up lies. Then she smiled, one of her big gappy smiles, and held out her hand for the photograph as if our chat was over.

I pulled it away from her. 'There's a photograph like this at Emma's house,' I said. 'I've seen it. I found it in the drawer in that little yellow room with the lambs on the wall. It's just the same as this one, I'm sure of it.'

Then Maudy went quiet.

'Why is this one here?'

The dent in Maudy's cheek got bigger as she worked her jaw but still she said nothing.

I looked at the photograph again. The baby's bonnet had lace round the front, nothing like Maudy could have afforded. The baby must have known that it was born rich because it had an expression on its face of deep peace like an angel in a church painting, the bonnet a little halo. Its mouth was open, just a bit, and its eyelashes were curled like little feathers.

'What's that on its face?' I said.

'Oh, what?' said Maudy.

I held the photograph closer to her and pointed to the baby's cheek. 'It's got some marks,' I said, 'on the side of its face.'

'Oh I don't think it's anything,' she said. 'Probably just a smudge of something on the lens.'

I looked at the photograph and touched my cheek.

*

At dusk Maudy gave me a hug and told me that I had better get a move on if I was going to make it back to Emma's before dark. It was still raining but she didn't seem to care. I didn't tell her about the nightshirt in my bag; I could tell that she didn't want me. I also didn't tell her that the photograph of the baby was leaving too, hidden away in my pocket. I thought that if I wasn't important to her, then at least I would have something that was, and I vowed to keep the photograph close to me, always.

'All right then,' I said, 'bye.' But I was sad. And then I was out in the rain again. I remembered Emma's words – it was Maudy who had to decide whether she wanted me home or not and I realized that Maudy had made her decision clear: she didn't.

32

Emma

Before that summer I had seen a girl with a birthmark like Ruby's on only one occasion. I mentioned this meeting before; the one that happened nine years previously in the spring of 1926, when I met my daughter, Violet.

When I spoke of the meeting before, I probably mentioned how brief it was and how little of it I remembered, then rambled on about the unpleasant smell of carbolic and newfangled incubators and starched uniforms and a big to-do about hospital innovations in the newspapers.

You see, they had told me not to talk about it, said that it would be bad for my nerves if I did. George had told me to be British and not get all silly and sentimental. His generation had been through far worse, he said, and a stiff upper lip was the best way to get through these things. I spoke very little about the meeting before; only said how brief it was and how little I recalled. But the thing is, I have been fooling myself for many years – I do remember the meeting well, more than I cared to admit before. And now I think it is time that I talked about it properly. Despite what George says, it's not always good to be British.

So much time has passed, but my memory is as clear as if I were standing in that sterile room right now, nine years later. The smell of the carbolic has lingered in my nostrils for a decade and the hum of the incubator has been constant in my head all this time. At night I find that I only need to shut my eyes to see the scrubbed walls and the gleaming glass. I can still sense the presences that waited in the white room with me that day. The midwife had little meaning at the time, but now when I revisit that day she feels cold and unwelcome, and there was Violet too, the one who everything centred around, warm and wanted. But I have to mention that there was absence also, the husband and father, usually one and the same, but for me that absence was not one man but two.

So to the midwife first. As I have said before, she was a middle-aged woman with a round face. She had her cape on and was ready to leave, tapping her foot impatiently as she left a posy as a parting gesture. But enough about her; we know who she is now, so let's just call her Sadie.

Then there was Violet. Of course she was just a baby back then. Three days old if you take it from the date she was expected but 35 days old if you take it from the date five weeks beforehand when she was wrenched into this world by the very accident of nature that put her, not in her mother's arms but incarcerated in the metal box. I didn't mention her much before, I blamed a memory lapse and a strong dose of morphine, but the truth is, I just couldn't bring myself to talk about her, so instead I just wittered on about a tiny baby and a dear little domed forehead.

But the birthmark was something I could not forget. It marked the whole of one cheek with bright red tears. They had thought it was blood, tried to clean it off, but it stayed, raw and inflamed like a wound. Some of the nurses had said that Violet was disfigured, others just looked away embarrassed or tutted and shook their heads; 'poor little thing', 'never mind.' But to me these imperfections marked her as mine, not anybody's baby but mine.

And then there was me of course, Emma Marks. But Emma Marks was not the same person she is now. Yes, I was younger then and still a newly-wed, and yes, I was probably too concerned with silliness such as what I was supposed to be doing and thinking, and what the midwife would make of my unkempt appearance. But my body had suffered more than a pale face and dishevelled hair; I was shrouded in a hospital gown and hunched in a wheelchair, my hands supporting the wadding that bound my abdomen. And over the past eight months my life had changed too.

I had already cared for Violet for several months; eaten the right foods, put my feet up, smoked to help me sleep and never dared raise my arms above my head, but now she was a reality, I was helpless.

I had become a mother and suddenly I had a connection to the tiny entity in the incubator – a connection that had not been severed when they removed her from me, the wound on my abdomen a painful reminder of the bond. I could do no more for Violet than watch her as she lay motionless but for the irregular heave of her tiny chest. I held my breath between each flutter of her fragile ribcage until I thought that it was my willpower alone that caused each movement.

Sadie knelt beside me, her bag open on the floor. She rummaged inside frantically as if what she was looking for could not wait. I did not know what she sought at the time, but now I can guess what was hidden among those antiseptics, thermometers and boiling tubes. It was a small box camera and, later that day, she would take a couple of exposures of the baby Violet. Maybe the infant would be alive at the time, maybe she would be dead, but now I know that it does not matter because Violet had been just as close to one as the other. Maybe the photographer herself did not know.

I watched the movements of Sadie's mouth, listened to the drone of her words, but I could not recollect what she said until now.

'You really shouldn't be here for long, Mrs Marks.' Then came a pause as if her statement was a question requiring an answer that did not come. 'It really is late in the day and the matron will be making her rounds soon. I really shouldn't have let you in. It's against hospital policy and...' her words faltered when still no answer came '...it's just, well, I wouldn't have allowed it at all if it weren't for your insistence and Dr Marks's position at the hospital...'

I did not listen to her for long because her face spoke of something deeper. It was a round face, as I have mentioned before, framed by a wisp of hair straying loose from her cap, but the expression on that face is something that has stayed with me for all these years – the raised eyebrows and tight mouth and those eyes so blank and distant. It was an expression that I could not quite read but it is one that I have seen on her face since – and now I understand more about what that expression meant.

'Time to say goodbye to Violet,' she said.
'All right,' I said. 'Goodbye.'

*

So that was my meeting with Violet. Even now I wonder whether this was the only time I met her or if I really did see her again nine years later standing in the lido wearing that little spotted dress.

33

Saturday was beautiful, the air clear and crisp. The leaves in the cutting flashed past the carriage window in waves of amber and gold as the train rattled along the icy track. The grass in Regent's Park was glazed with ice, the cold wind gusting across the zoo's enclosures keeping other visitors away.

We were together but alone as we went from enclosure to enclosure disturbing monkeys huddled on hot water pipes and trying to spot bears hiding in piles of straw. Zebras peered from stables, their breath clouding in the air, and mongooses formed one shivering mass of russet pelts. The penguins, stood rigid by their frozen pool, were the only creatures to face the cold.

We found refuge in the Natural History Museum where the bones of the dinosaurs could not shrink away from the cold and the sandstone monkeys that climbed the columns could not escape from the hundreds of little hands that stroked their backs until they were smooth.

At dusk the lights of Kensington looked magical as we made our way down into the subway and joined the huddle of overcoats that waited in the ticket hall.

It had been difficult to find the right moment to talk about Maud's illness. It had been the reason for the trip after all, but somehow the words failed to come and I could not face ruining what had been a special day. On the station platform was a poster urging people to buy festive stamps to help fight tuberculosis. Relieved, I pointed to it.

'Have you heard of tuberculosis, Ruby?' I said. 'Or of consumption or TB?'

She looked at the poster, screwing up her eyes. 'I can't read very well,' she said.

'No, of course,' I muttered and then mumbled something about the nice Christmas scene on the illustration, thinking that I would have the whole journey back to explain.

At Baker Street the train was crammed full of passengers jostling with bags and coats. I managed to squeeze onto the last free seat and pulled Ruby up next to me, feeling the warm press of her body against my arm. By the door was another poster – a picture of a mother and child at a gravestone with a message about how even kissing could lead to infection. The letters *TB* were printed large and bold and I was sure that even Ruby would be able to read them. Then a man opposite started coughing, a handkerchief pressed over his face and around him others turned away or put hands over their mouths.

'Ruby,' I said. 'About your mother's mouth ulcer…' but then I felt the weight of her head on my lap and saw the slow heave of her chest. She slept all the way to Missensham.

*

As we approached Little Willow, I saw that the curtains were still open, the orange orbs of the streetlights reflected in the black windows. I started to worry – where was George?

My key turned loosely in the lock and I realized that Mr Tuttle must have forgotten to lock up after himself again. The hallway was cold and lit only by a beam of streetlight from the pavement. The hat stand was bare and there was nothing but a dusty little rectangle where George's briefcase usually stood. I fumbled with my gloves and ran into the kitchen to light the burner – the blue light flickering like a will-o'-the-wisp.

George's sherry decanter was on the draining board, the stopper resting against the base and sticky fingerprints on the glass. George must have left Mr Tuttle alone and the old man had helped himself. I took the decanter through to the study, hoping George wouldn't find out. Through the long glass doors, I saw washing still hung on the line, white bed linen billowing like ghosts. I called Ruby to help, watching wearily as she ran out with the basket and grappled with the sheets. Then I noticed a small, white card left on the desk, an invitation written in embossed ink – the hospital ball! It was already the second Saturday in October and I had forgotten about it completely. I had been so preoccupied with Ruby that George had slipped my mind all together. He had not even mentioned the ball that morning and I felt angry that he had just expected me to know. The bells of St Cuthbert's started chiming the hour – eight o'clock – I had already missed the dinner and the speeches. I could try and set off for the lido now, but it was too late; George would already be disgraced.

In the lounge the light switch made a hollow clicking sound in the darkness and I saw a coil of wire and the old bulb and shade piled up against the skirting board – another job Mr Tuttle had left unfinished. I perched on the window seat, under the weak light from the street lamps and remembered how often I had sat alone in this spot over the years. How different things were now! The house seemed accustomed to the silence, but it was the first silence I had heard in weeks.

I got up and switched on the wireless, then flinched, startled by a sudden hiss of static. The noise filled the room and I turned the dial frantically, hearing only faint voices fading in and out of the fog.

Then I saw a glint of metal by the speaker and felt a stab of ice in my stomach. Something else had appeared in the house. I stared at it, my knees starting to buckle beneath me. I touched it cautiously with my fingertips, then picked it up, the skin on the back of my head tightening.

'No!' I gasped, shaking my head. 'No-no-no.' I felt the ivory ring between my fingers, the silver ball cold to the touch and the little bells jangling as I turned it over in my hand. I ran my finger over the inscription – VM.

Then the hands that held the rattle were not my own, they were George's, large hands with slender fingers, the nails bitten to the quick with the stress of loss. It was George in mourning dress, George as he had stood in the churchyard nine years ago. And that George looked at me sadly before nodding his head and carrying the rattle off to the vestry to be placed inside the coffin next to Violet where it would be buried, buried forever.

A floorboard creaked in the hallway and my heart flung against my ribs. A figure stood in the doorway. A little girl in a white smock, one cheek in shadow, the stray hairs rising from her crown catching the light like a halo. I stared at her. Words caught in the dryness of my throat and I held up the rattle with a shaking hand, the silver bells murmuring against the metal.

'Oh,' said Ruby. 'That's mine.'

34

The sky had darkened by the time I reached the lido; the changing block and turnstiles had faded into shadow and the water in the swimming pool had become mere shivers of silver moonlight. In the distance the pavilion blazed with colour, like a flaming galleon floating on a sea of black air.

I walked blind, feeling my way along the railings until the lights grew closer, became flickers and movements and then people – angular dinner jackets and sinuous evening gowns swaying and mingling behind long glass doors. There was a buzz of noise; ripples of laughter and the chink of champagne bowls over the constant babble of voices. From somewhere came the undulating drone of violins being tuned and the rhythmic blasts of a trumpet as it pushed to the top of a scale.

The main door of the food hall was propped open, hot air wafting out on to the tarmac.

'Madame?' A boy in an oversized suit stepped forward, his arms held out in front of him as if to take my stole, but he stepped back quickly, his face reddening, when he saw that I had neither stole nor evening gown and would not wait to be ticked off the guest list.

The food hall was hot, the air thick with the musk of Macassar oil and body heat. The walls were draped with sheets of red, white and blue linen, trails of bunting leading to a stage where the flower of a huge brass tuba blasted over the heads of the band.

Finely dressed people were crammed onto the dance floor, a sea of heads – carefully set curls and oiled partings nodding and swaying while thin trails of cigarette smoke shuddered up to the ceiling.

I pushed into the crowd, leading with my shoulder and parting bodies with my hands. A group of society girls recoiled as I touched them, eyes wide and mouths open in an exaggerated reaction to the disturbance. I passed a group of old ladies decked with jewellery of Victorian lavishness, then an old soldier, the chest of his red jacket fringed with medals. A young man balancing one champagne glass on top of another, the golden liquid slopping on the floor as he was jostled by revellers. The mayor, with his chain of office. A fat man with a monocle and his wife with a sparkling tiara. Harassed waitresses in white caps. Flashes of silk, brushes of feather, glinting jewels, sable furs, waistcoats, handbags, spats – everything blurred by my tears.

Then I saw him, George, trussed in a dinner jacket, his scalp shiny with sweat. His head was nodding quickly and his hand chopped the air as he argued some point with a group of portly gentlemen who clustered around him.

He looked up suddenly. 'Emma!' His hand froze in mid-air and his lips moved silently as he started to stammer: 'Oh-oh-oh my God, what is it? Are you—'

I held out the rattle.

The colour drained from his face. There was some movement around me, people shuffling awkwardly and stepping back, heads bowed and apologies murmured.

'This should be buried, George,' I said slowly. 'Why isn't it buried?'

He laughed self-consciously, pulling me away from the watching faces. 'Good God, woman, what are you talking about?' he rubbed his fingers together but they failed to click. 'Give... give it to me.'

I handed it over.

He turned it slowly in his palm, frowning. He brushed the silver tube with his fingertips, dragging his thumb over the inscription as if it would rub away onto his skin.

'Well?' I said.

'Well what?'

'What!' I shouted. 'I have just given you something that I asked you to bury, to bury in our dead daughter's grave and you have nothing to say to me!'

'Emma!' he hissed, glancing round as heads turned. 'Not here.'

'Where then?' I screamed. 'Where could we possibly go to make your explanation any different?' I realized that the room around us had gone quiet. George's eyes were boring right through me, the pupils little black specks frozen in the glass of his spectacles. Around us the party blurred and flickered but our stare was the only thing that existed, as if space and time has melted away around us and we were all that was left, just us and the silence.

Then a champagne cork popped and people whooped and laughed. The band started playing 'Let's Fall in Love', the pump of the tuba filling the room. There was a hum of conversation and ripples of laughter in the air again. Around us, bodies swayed as people started to dance, hands clasped, cheek to cheek. The air became hot.

'Old man! Old man!' Walter appeared, staggering over to George, his face red and his fist closed round the neck of a champagne bottle. 'I say, old man, have you seen the—' He stopped short. 'Oh my God, Emma!'

George pocketed the rattle quickly, then glanced down. 'Yes, yes.'

But Walter brushed past him. 'So glad you could make it at last – Audrey will be thrilled – Darling! Darling!'

'Emma!' squealed Audrey, the feather in her hair shivering with excitement. 'So good to see you. And to ignore the dress code too – très moderne! We simply must—' She grabbed my arm, pulling me towards the thronging dance floor.

'No,' I said. 'Really Audrey, I'd rather—'

'Oh come on, I can see plenty of spare gentlemen from the committee. And I know that you want to dance with them. Oh yes you do! Oh yes you do!' she nodded excitedly, her ringlets bouncing.

'Audrey,' said George firmly. 'Will you be so good as to take my wife home. She's not feeling well. I'm afraid she's had far too much to drink.'

'What?' I stammered. I stared at George. 'No, I—'

'Oh!' Audrey pulled down the corners of her mouth. 'Oh, so you have, you poor thing. You do look terrible.' She bent her head and made big eyes at me, brushing the hair from my forehead.

'No, I'm fine,' I said slowly, my eyes fixed on George.

'You have had too much haven't you, Emma?' said Walter. 'George should take better care of you. Take her, Audrey, it'll only take a few minutes, you'll be back well within the hour.' He whisked the fur from her shoulders and wrapped it round the bottle. 'Take this for the walk.'

'Where did you get...' she squeaked. 'Oh you glamorous

bastard!' Audrey twisted her silk-covered arm round mine. 'Come on,' she said. 'If I don't polish this off on the way, I'll leave it in the Frigidaire for you tomorrow.'

Audrey yanked my arm and I was pulled backwards through the crowd. My eyes started to sting and, in front of me, George's face quivered and blurred.

'Why?' I mouthed at him. 'Why?' But then the world dissolved in to a blur of light and movement and he was gone.

35

Ruby

My name is Ruby Brown but it did not take Emma long to forget this. One time she called out: 'Vi—' but then shouted 'Ruby' very quickly after it. She labelled my coat with a 'V' and then sighed and added the hook and slant of an 'R'. Once she held me tight, stroked my hair and whispered 'Violet' in my ear. But Violets bring bad luck and death, and if I am Violet, then it must be me that brought bad luck to this house. Maybe death will follow.

That morning Emma slept in late. I lay in bed watching the sun creep higher and higher between the gap in the curtains. I heard the rattle of milk bottles on the doorstep and the plod of the milkman's horse, but there was still not a peep from her. Then came footsteps of people on the road and the rumble of the first bus and at last she stuck her head round the door, eyes all red like she'd been crying.

She sat with me while I ate breakfast, but she didn't touch her triangle of toast, just stared at it until it went cold. Dr Marks was banging about upstairs and she jumped whenever she heard him move. The buttons on her dressing gown were undone and her yellow hair was matted like a bird's nest. Her eyes were red and all runny, but she said it was just ca-junc-shon-itis. She liked to copy Dr Marks's big words, you see, and liked to think that she was frail.

She didn't even blink when I finished eating, so I got down from the table and told her not to worry, and that I would play in my room all morning. She just nodded. So I went upstairs slowly waiting for her to stop me, but she didn't.

Dr Marks's posh black suit was airing on the back of my bedroom door; the trousers fell limp from the jacket like a hanging corpse, the bow tie draped over the collar like a slack noose. The smell of the fabric caught in the back of my throat;

sweat and smoke, just like the evening – bitter and faded.

I fancied that this was my fault. Things like this usually were. It was me Emma was talking to when we got back from London, when she went all shaky and the colour drained from her face. She had left the house as soon as she saw my jingly silver treasure, just charged out into the darkness, with wild eyes and jutting chin. I wish I had tidied it away. I did not know that leaving it out would upset her so much.

It was Clarence that had given it to me. It was on my last visit back to Rose Cottage, after I had shown Maudy the photograph of the baby. I think Maudy must have told him that I had been asking about babies because he said that it had been mine since birth and that he had been keeping it safe until I was old enough. He said that a doctor had given it to me when I was a baby, a special gift made just for me. Well, I knew that the treasure would never have come from my family so maybe the part about this doctor was true but it was never made for me – it had VM scratched into it in big curly letters – my reading had never been good but I did know my letters and VM was surely not me or anyone in my family. I knew that the treasure was not mine or his, but I did think that it might have been Clarence's way to make up for the Bad Thing that he did, so I kept my mouth good and shut. Anyway, I quite liked it. It looked like something that the queen would hold when she wore her crown and sat on the throne and the little bells jingled like Christmas.

It had already lost my other treasures by then - Fatkins had taken the cigarette case back and Jim had stolen Emma's abandoned shillings. The jingly ornament was all I had, so I had taken it to Emma's, where it would be safe. But I did not look after it, I left it lying around. You couldn't be messy at Emma's house. One little thing left lying around could upset her and turn her mad. And now my treasure was with Dr Marks, and that is all that she would say.

I stood on the landing and listened to Dr Marks in his bedroom, his slippers pacing to and fro on the carpet. I tiptoed to the door and peeked through the crack. A suitcase was open on the bed and he was throwing clothes into it; shirts and jackets sailing through the air, gusting mothballs all about the place. He slammed the suitcase shut but then he just stood and stared at it, his hands on his hips. He was breathing quickly, sniffy little breaths, the air going hiss-hiss from his nose. He was the man who shouted, the man who called me a thief, the man who hated me and the man who could not bear to touch Maudy when she was most sick. I hated him. I stared at him, trying to bore into him with my eyes, make him dead, but it did nothing because he just sighed and picked the suitcase up and put it in the back of the wardrobe, as if going away had just been a passing thought and he had changed his mind, for now at least.

I went back to my room and shut the door behind me. I sat on the bed, staring out the window but not seeing anything. Then I got out the xylophone and played a few notes – Emma would be worried if she couldn't hear me. I played 'London Bridge Is Falling Down', but somehow I thought it sounded sad, so I played the other one – Frère Jacques, but then I remembered that Dr Marks didn't like anything French, so I stopped dead, right in the middle of it.

Snuffly little sounds came from downstairs; long sighs and little shrieks and hiccoughs. I listened hard because I didn't know what they meant but then I realized that Emma was crying. I thought of Maudy crying or Henry, Jim, John or Andy. They all cried like big babies, roaring into their hands, all red-faced with strings of dribble and snot, but this crying wasn't like that – this crying was all little whimpers and sobs.

I could see Emma in my head, see her draped over the sofa, the back of her hand across her brow, silver tears rolling into a lace handkerchief like a princess in an oil painting. She was even posh when she cried. Before I met Emma, I had always thought that posh was something that you put on for other people, like when you were on the telephone or ordering something in a shop. But now I know that isn't right. Posh is something that you are born with. Like that baby called VM with that silver rattle in its hand. Posh is blowing your nose silently in a lace handkerchief or not making a sound on your porcelain toilet and not laughing or grinning. Posh is sitting straight-backed, not biting your nails or spilling your food or using a fork round the wrong way to eat peas, and posh is being angry in silence and crying like a mouse.

I lay on the bed and pressed my hands over my ears; it was what I did at home when Clarence and Maudy were fighting. I could see them so clearly in my head, yelling at each other across the kitchen. Maudy's hands were on her hips, her eyes popping with fury, her teeth pointed like fangs. Clarence's face was terrible, his arms flailing like windmills.

It was the day that Fatkins had visited, the day that Maudy had conned money from him for a stove that would never be fixed. It was also the day that the farmer had discovered Clarence stealing eggs, the day that he had been sacked with no wages and came home looking for a fight, the day the Red Lion gave him no credit, the day the rent was overdue and the day that Maudy had money and Clarence didn't.

The next morning Maudy had stood at the sink crying, her eye all puffy and black.

I didn't care. She could wipe her own tears. I stopped caring about her the day she stopped caring about me, the day the stove got broken. She saw what happened on that day; she didn't stop him. It was Clarence that broke the stove. That's all I want to say.

I took my hands off my ears. There were no shouts in this house, no screams no bad-mouthing or curses. Rich people shout with silence.

36

Emma

'It's dead,' said Ruby.

I put the sherry glass with the wilted violet on the windowsill and sat down next to her on the bed. 'I know that,' I said. 'It is now. But it wasn't dead when it was put on the mantelpiece.'

'It's dead now. Now it's dead.'

'Did you pick it, Ruby? Did you put it in the glass on the mantelpiece?'

'No,' she said quickly. I looked at her face, she was blinking quickly like she didn't understand. 'And I never did it. I didn't kill it.'

'Have you ever put any of these flowers in the house?'

'No, I never have.'

'You're sure?'

'Yes, I'm sure. Maudy says they mean death if they're brought inside.'

I sighed. 'You don't still believe that too, do you?

'Yes, but you told me that it was rubbish.' She looked at me for reassurance. 'So it is, isn't it? Rubbish. And I never did it.' She opened her mouth again, then shut it.

'Well?' I put my hands on my hips, waiting for further explanation.

'It's just that…'

I nodded in encouragement.

'It's just that they don't grow in the garden here, not those ones. And there's just a few small ones in the copse by the cottage. But those ones, those ones are all big and purple – there's lots of them in those fields on the way to the station. That's the only place they grow.'

I couldn't help but feel embarrassed – those fields where I had lain with Peter all those years ago mentioned in such innocence. I thought that no one else knew about that place, that it existed only for me.

'Are you hot?' said Ruby.

I couldn't answer her, so I just sat down on the bed and opened the window. 'I'm sorry,' I said. 'I just thought that because the silver rattle was yours, you might have been leaving these flowers too…'

Her face was blank.

'I'm sorry,' I said. 'I'm not making sense.' Then I put my hand out and patted her knee. 'It's all right,' I whispered, lowering my head to hers. 'I believe you.'

I looked out into the garden. Drifts of fallen leaves had gathered in the flower beds and there was a musty smell on the breeze. The pansies had browned and curled and the blooms of the wisteria were creeping with rust. She was right. There were no violets in the garden, no colour or life. I got up and went to the door.

'Emma?'

'What, darling?'

'You were going to tell me something. You said you would tell me it when we got back from the zoo. Something about Maudy's mouth ulcer, about it making her ill and what would happen.' She looked so small sat on the bed, her eyes cast up at me. Small and fragile, the birthmark tracing the pattern of tears I imagined would come.

'Well…' I was about to begin the speech I had been rehearsing, the speech about the chickens, about Snowflake or Snowdrop or whatever it was called, about how they died because they were weak and sick. The speech about how George couldn't always help people, about how some of them never got better. The speech about why I didn't have any parents of my own.

She stared up at me, her face blank.

I opened my mouth but the only noise was a burst from the doorbell. I jumped, then smiled, trying to ignore it. But still it rang, the buzz of the metal echoing up the stairs. Ruby turned away to stroke the ears of the knitted rabbit. I hurried to the doorway, then smiled apologetically and left her.

'Mr Tuttle!' I cried, trying to hide my annoyance. 'I thought you were all finished in the living room. It's really not a good time at the moment.'

'The kitchen, Mrs Marks?' Mr Tuttle scraped his feet on the

doormat, bag in hand, pencil behind ear.

My thoughts turned back to the hammer left in the sink and the fence that was now three different shades of green. I breathed deeply to see if I could smell alcohol – yes, there was the trace of an odour, but he seemed sober enough.

Mr Tuttle placed his feet squarely on the doormat. 'We have an appointment, Mrs Marks?'

Then I remembered a hurried word on his last visit, a handshake with George and a note that I was supposed to write on the calendar. 'Of course we do,' I snapped. 'Come through.'

Mr Tuttle stretched a tape measure over the oven and then rested his elbows on the work surface as he jotted in his notebook. He drummed his foot and shook his head, then drew a line through his calculations and then jotted some more. 'Silly old Tuttle,' he muttered to himself. 'Stupid old bugger.'

The smell of alcohol seemed stronger now. I glanced at the clock – the Red Lion must have already been open for some time. He'd certainly had time to get drunk before he came. The faint chink of the xylophone floated down the stairs, the first bars of 'Frère Jacques' repeated over and over.

'I'm sorry, Mr Tuttle,' I said. 'I know that we had an appointment, but I really don't have time.'

He didn't look up, just kept tapping his foot and scribbling with his pencil. 'Don't worry, Mrs Marks, you can go off and see to your business, just leave me here. I'll be fine.'

'I would rather...' I was about to put a hand on his shoulder but drew my arm back quickly. There was something poking from his breast pocket, something small and fragile and the deepest purple. 'You!' I gasped. 'It's you whose been leaving the violets!'

The back of his neck flushed red. 'I don't know what you mean, Mrs Marks, why this is just—'

I stepped back. 'It was only you all along, Mr Tuttle, only you.' I laughed, relieved. 'Really, they are lovely, but you shouldn't—'

Mr Tuttle turned round slowly, holding his hand aloft as the violet quivered between his fingers. Then his eyes widened as if in surprise to see it. 'Oh you're here as well are you?' He stared at the flower, flicking the petals absent-mindedly with his finger. 'Here again!'

'Mr Tuttle?'

'Oh!' He flinched. 'Mrs Marks, I'm so sorry. It's just that I always take flowers to my son, I usually drop by to see him on my way to your house. But these little purple ones seem to find their way back here with me, always to this house.' He looked at me and smiled, as if he wanted reassurance that such things did not just happen to him and that others too could be absent-minded. 'I don't know if you can understand this, Mrs Marks, but it's as if they follow me, they do.'

'Mr Tuttle, I'm not sure I understand you, there's—'

'To be honest, Mrs Marks, I never remember giving these little purple ones to Mr. Tuttle Junior, but they are always here when I come. I expect he is giving them back to me, he's a kind soul like that. His way of following me after my visit, you see, something to remember him by once I have left the memorial.'

At last, here was the reason for the absence of Mr Tuttle Junior. There was no way he could have painted a fence or lifted a hammer or papered a wall and now I knew that that he never would. 'I'm so sorry,' I whispered.

'Not to worry, Mrs Marks. Terribly bad luck indoors though, these purple ones,' he said, shaking his head. 'Terribly bad luck!'

'Oh no, don't say—'

'You are right, Mrs Marks. I don't expect that he means it that way. It's nice to remember the dead, they are everywhere.' He raised his head, his eyes suddenly clear and his gaze steady, 'And these flowers, well they are rather like the dead, don't you think? Following us where we go, just like they do.'

For the first time ever he looked me right in the eye and I felt a trickle of ice water deep in my stomach. 'That's a nice thought, Mr. Tuttle,' I said, my voice cracking, 'but-'

'They follow you too don't they, Mrs. Marks?'

'What do you mean?' I said, my voice catching.

His speech was more lucid now, as if somewhere deep inside him the thousands of severed neurons that had George had described had found each other and reconnected, and for a brief and random moment, intellect, consciousness and memory were fully restored.

'I've been working in this house a while now, Mrs Marks, got to know it, if you like. Houses speak to you, give away their secrets. And when the nursery was opened and Dr Marks spoke to me about redecorating it, well… I found things in there, old-fashioned, musty things, things for a baby that would now be grown. Her name was Violet, wasn't it? It was stitched on to the counterpane.'

'Yes,' I whispered. 'Violet.'

He turned away and nodded to himself. 'After I had found all that, well, I wasn't sure it would be right to redecorate the room, not rip it all out and start again like Dr Marks had said. That is why I was slow in coming to that particular room. It should stay untouched, I thought, for the memory.'

'Thank you,' I said. 'Thank you for understanding.'

He turned and put a hand on my arm. 'It's quite all right, Mrs Marks, we can all take consolation from the things around us. These tiny purple flowers from the meadows for instance. The flower will die off in the winter but the next summer there will be a new bloom, it will not be the same as the original, but a copy of it, like a memory returning. The new blooms will always remind us of the original, just like memories remind us of the ones we have lost.' He paused for just a moment as if to recover from the effort of his speech. 'It's just that these blooms sometimes follow us.'

I shuddered and just then, as I looked into his eyes, I saw that they had changed again and were brighter still, as if it was not just consciousness that had returned but also his humanity.

'Do you really think that, Mr. Tuttle?' I said. 'That they follow us? You see, recently things have been happening to me, things I don't understand – things with the dead, the one I lost, and always there are these flowers. And these flowers had meaning to the person I lost. I feel like the dead follow me too… you see, these flowers' – I took his hand in mine and raised the violet so it was in front of his face – 'these were *our* flowers, hers and mine, and they are very special to me.'

'Flowers?' Mr. Tuttle cocked his head to one side, his mouth slackened and he frowned as if seeing the violet for the first time. His pupils widened and I realized that the millions of microscopic neurons that George had described had strayed from their pathways once more and the brief moment of lucidity was gone and with it the connection between us.

'Oh, that's a very pretty flower, Mrs Marks,' he said. 'What is it? A snapdragon?'

'A violet, Mr. Tuttle,' I said sadly.

'Oh!' He nodded. 'A violet, of course, violet. Silly old bugger.'

He turned and picked up his tape measure, tucking the pencil back behind his ear. 'Well,' he said brightly, 'I'd better be finishing up here, Mrs Marks, flowers are all well and good, but I will need to be out before the end of the week.'

'It might be a while before you finish, Mr Tuttle.' I sighed. 'There's still the skirting boards and picture rails to be done, even if you don't go into the nursery.'

'Yes,' he said. He was silent for a moment then started speaking slowly, as if he had to concentrate hard to form each word. 'I don't feel that I can finish things here, not the way I would want to.' He waved his hand round the kitchen. 'I can take some measurements, leave some designs but, as for the rest... I'm getting old, my hands are shaky, words don't make sense. I'm not as strong as I was, I get muddled. I thought I could manage one more job but I am just too old and with Mr. Tuttle Junior... with Mr. Tuttle Junior unable to help—'

'I see,' I said. 'I'm sorry.'

He cast his eyes down, adjusted the pencil behind his ear and put his notebook in his pocket. Then he rubbed his head and replaced his cap.

'Why don't you go home early, Mr. Tuttle, put your feet up, go and visit your family. I expect they will be glad of your company. I'm sure we can manage without the measurements for now.'

He nodded. 'Very good, Mrs Marks.'

We went into the hallway and I took his hand and shook it, I lead him to the door and opened it.

'I'm sorry to leave things unfinished. But I'm sure Dr Marks is a strong and upright man. He could surely help...'

I nodded.

Then something strange happened. Afterwards I kept telling myself that it was just a mistake made by a drunk, confused old man. That it didn't mean anything. I could explain it, of course I could. I could see why it happened; how the mistake could have been made, I mean. But inside me I sensed... I don't know, something that gave me the strangest of feelings.

There was a creak of floorboard at the top of the stairs and we turned to see Ruby sitting high on the staircase. Mr Tuttle stopped in the doorway and I looked from one to the other but neither moved nor spoke.

I laughed awkwardly. 'This is Mr Tuttle, darling,' I said.

'He's the… he's the decorator. Say hello to Mr Tuttle.'
'Hello, Mr Tuttle,' she said.'
'Hello, Violet,' he said and shut the door behind him.

37

'Maudy!' cried Ruby. She dropped the sugar cane I had bought her and flung herself at Maud, the basket chair creaking under their weight.

I stood alone, staring at the fragments of colourful sugar on the flagstones. I had become a stranger again – the madwoman from the lido with ice cream melting all over her hands. I opened my mouth to warn about the risk of infection but then saw Maud's face crumpled over Ruby's shoulder, a tear squeezing from her eye.

I shuffled my feet and cleared my throat. Then I opened my bag and took out three more bottles of chlorodyne, the glass clanking noisily on the table, but still they held the embrace and I realized that I had been forgotten. Why didn't Ruby prefer me? I had not left her side for a whole month. I had taught her to write properly and cooked her favourite meals, kept her safe and warm. Yes, things had been a little strange recently and George and I had been arguing and maybe I had been a little short-tempered and quick to scold her, but I had spent such a lot of money on food and gifts and I was sure that this had made Ruby fond of me, made it obvious what Maud could not give her. But now as I watched the pair of them together, I realized how naïve I had been.

At last Ruby wriggled free and I signalled to her to cover her mouth.

She ignored me and turned back to Maud. 'I miss the chickens,' she said breathlessly. And only then did I realize that it wasn't the chickens she had been missing.

Maud sat mummified in an old grey blanket, her legs stretched out in front of a blazing fire. Her cheeks were pale and hollowed but her eyes were still bright.

'I'm sorry,' is all she said to Ruby, 'I'm so sorry.'

The kitchen looked a bit tidier and the boys seemed to be behaving themselves: Andy was bent over the draining board scrubbing plates and cups; Jim, John and Henry were sat quietly in front of the fire, three oily rags and bottle of Brasso resting on the hearth. Even Smokey seemed content, stretched out on the patch of sun from the kitchen window. The perfectly stitched gloves had been removed from the table and the old Singer replaced with a chipped vase of teasel heads. Only one of the rusty buckets remained, a trickle of red dye dried solid where it had escaped over the rim. It was full of cotton handkerchiefs, flecked with brown. I shuddered, thinking that I would throw them on the fire when I got a chance.

'Well, look at you!' said, Maud. She waved her hand in a circle and Ruby twirled round obligingly. Maud looked her up and down. 'A proper little lady,' she said, and then nodded to herself. 'A proper little lady.'

I thought of my conversation with Maud all those weeks ago, the one which Ruby had overhead as she squatted in the henhouse. Maud had said that Ruby's face was a curse in Evesbridge but that she would have more opportunities in Missensham; become a typist or secretary, maybe marry. And here she was now, just as Maud said – a proper little lady.

Ruby crossed her legs, dropping herself onto the floor next to her brothers. Jim and John reached for her new pinafore but she sat up straight pulling it away from their blackened fingers. Only Henry was allowed to stroke her shoes and then very gently. They asked Ruby about Little Willow: How many rooms there were; whether she had one to herself; how long it took to run round the garden; whether hot water came from just flicking a switch; whether she ate blancmange every day. I watched Ruby as she answered, nodding her head and laughing, swinging her arms as she spoke about the monkeys at the zoo.

''Ere!' Maud nudged my elbow. 'I've got something for you.' Then she lowered her voice: 'Don't say anything, mind, not out loud.'

I turned to her, a little reluctant to miss Ruby's stories.

She was holding out a fat brown envelope, bearing the address of Crozier and Hampton, the Green, Missensham. 'I met with Mr Crozier about this matter last week,' she said. 'He is a kindly chap, always ready to help folk like us. He said we would need something in writing, even told Andy which big words to use and checked it all for us after too, said it was legally binding since we'd got it signed and witnessed by someone reputable. I can't read, mind, so he read it to me and showed me how to put my mark by the right bit.'

I opened the envelope but my eyes got no further than the first line of jumbled script. 'Oh, Maud, No!' I said. I thrust it back at her but she would not take it. 'I'm sure it won't come to that. You must have some hope.'

But Maud's face was calm, as if she had some deeper knowledge. 'It's just instructions for when I'm gone,' she said. 'Ruby never had no godparents and with Clarence and me not married I need to make provisions.'

I unfolded the document, my eyes skimming over the blocks of text. Each sentence comprised a mix of clumsy phrases and complicated legal terms and I had to read some of the paragraphs over and over until their meaning sank in. Then I continued until I reached Maud's inky cross. 'Thank you!' I said. 'Thank you!'

'I thought you'd be pleased.' She looked at Ruby. 'After all, you got what you wanted in the end.'

I followed her gaze. Ruby had rescued the remains of the sugar cane from the floor and held a jagged fragment out to Henry, jerking it away whenever he lunged for it. Maud was right, I had got what I wanted but somehow I didn't feel like I had won.

'You understand that it's not an easy thing for me to do.' Maud nodded to herself. 'So please could you leave her here with me tonight and let her stay with me for a week so that I can have some time alone with her - to explain things and say my goodbyes. You can see that the place is cleaner now and I will keep my face covered and—'

'Of course!' I said. My joy had only lasted a few moments for now the true meaning of the document was becoming clear to me – Maud was dying and this was her dying wish.

'You will let her visit her old home, of course and her brothers?'

'Yes,' I said, 'as often as she wants to.' But then I paused. There was something uneasy about the situation and the document did not have all the answers. 'Maud…' I whispered, glancing round to make sure that none of the children were listening. 'What about the others?'

'Clarence will manage, he's a good father when he's around. He'll just need some…' She stopped suddenly her brow furrowed. '…Some support.'

'Support?' I said.

'Yes, support. Do you understand me, Mrs Marks?'

'Yes,' I said, my heart sinking. 'I think I do.'

Maud turned her head slightly and I leaned over so that she had my ear. 'I was thinking a couple of hundred quid would be fair, Mrs Marks.'

'Two hundred pounds!' I hissed. 'What?' I stuffed the document back into the envelope and thrust it back at her. 'You can't sell a child, it's wrong!'

'Oh, I don't like to think of it that way, Mrs Marks.' She patted the fat envelope. 'Can't we call it charity?'

'You always said you were too proud for that!'

'Pride!' she whispered. 'I lost my pride many weeks ago, Mrs Marks, a disease like this robs you of pride. In my last days my own family will have to feed me like a newborn baby. They will watch as I soil myself and sit at my bedside as I drown in my own juices. What is pride anymore? I don't care about pride.'

'No!' I said firmly. 'It's immoral.'

'That's a shame, Mrs Marks, I did think that it was what you had wanted all along.' She stopped and looked me in the eye. 'It is, isn't it?'

I didn't answer.

Henry snatched the splintered sugar cane and ran outside, the others scrambled after him laughing. I watched them through the window. Maud was selling a child – the one who had embraced her so lovingly just moments before, the one who was running past the window, her hair streaming behind her. The one who she told was special. I wondered what kind of mother Maud really was and how she could live with this decision, how she would be judged by God, but then she was not the only one who was shamed, because deep down, part of me was already thinking about the money. It would have taken the family years to save £200 and, if they had it, it would mean that the rent would be paid, the children would be properly schooled and that they always had the meat that Ruby craved. But that was not taking into account all the lemonade and blancmange that would probably be bought instead. Then there was Clarence, Ruby said that he drank; £200 would buy a lot of ale and might mean that he never worked again. It would also be enough for frivolous purchases such as refrigerators, wirelesses, gramophones, even a motorcar! Two hundred pounds was also my life savings. It was what I had managed to squirrel away while George paid the bills, but I did have enough. It was all I had, but it was there if I needed it.

'I don't need to pay you any money,' I said slowly. 'She's mine anyway.'

I had forgotten about the birth certificate in my pocket – the one that Ruby had failed to deliver on her last visit and the one that I had now come to return. But as I reached down and touched it, I wondered what it really showed. It had George's name on it, whatever that meant. He had never wanted a baby, he had made that clear often enough. Could he have taken Violet from the incubator after I had seen her? Could he have been lying to me when he told me that she had died? Could he have given her to Maud? Swapped her for a dying Ruby Brown? I didn't know. Maybe I never would. But what did George's name matter anyway? What did it matter when what could not be disputed was the name of Ruby's mother – Maud Brown. My only hope was a last piece of honesty.

'I had a baby,' I said. 'You know this, Maud, a girl with a birthmark on her face – a mark just like Ruby's. I never saw her body, not after I was forced to leave her. I don't know what happened, but that baby wasn't buried. She's here with you, Maud – you have Violet.'

Maud's face didn't change, maybe even the flicker of a smile crossed her lips as her beady eyes watched me intently. 'Can you prove it?' she said.

I fingered the birth certificate in my pocket again but there it stayed.

'Can you prove it?' Maud repeated slowly.

I knew that I could not.

38

I had left Rose Cottage without Ruby. Maud and I had agreed that Ruby would not return to me until a week on Sunday. It was not really an arrangement that I was happy with, but I consoled myself with the fact that I had left Rose Cottage with something much more important – a document that said that Ruby would soon be mine forever. All I had to do was keep to my side of the bargain.

The bank in the High Street had demanded a week's notice for the withdrawal of two hundred pounds. When I dropped in to request it, the pinstriped manager remarked that it was a substantial sum, considering the weight of the Depression. He hoped I was going to spend it wisely. I nodded and said that I surely would and, unperturbed by his stern manner, I couldn't help smiling to myself like a schoolgirl as he signed the forms.

It had been agreed that Sadie would meet me at Little Willow to collect the money. Ruby was sharp and it would not do for her to see anything changing hands between me and Maud. Ruby would stay with her brothers in the almshouse for the night – this would make the departure seem less final and avoid things being held up by any tearful goodbyes from Maud. Then Sadie would prepare her for the move during the day and bring her round to me at Little Willow in the evening. Ruby would be told that she was visiting again. It was a little unfair but I didn't want anything to suggest that her farewells would be final or reveal the inevitability of her mother's death. Still, I thought, once she had settled in, had a warm bath, proper food and a comfortable rest, she would soon forget Maud and when I finally had to tell her, the blow would not be so hard.

The next Saturday Sadie called round early. I had the money ready in a large purple envelope and handed it over. In return she gave a little nod but could not manage a smile.

'It's just the milkman,' I called to George playfully. Then I gave her a little wink and shut the door.

I busied myself arranging the back bedroom, locking myself

away from George but, as the day drew on, I knew that I had to tell him. After all, it seemed respectable enough – a friend, a dying woman, had made me the guardian of a little girl. It was her last wish and it was all I could do to help. After all, we had, long ago, nearly had a child of our own.

George tilted his head, the light from the window washing over his spectacles. 'Forever?' he said slowly. 'Stay with us forever?'

'Yes!' I smiled.

'After all her trouble?'

'She's no trouble, George, you know that. Mr Tuttle took that money – we shouldn't have left it out to tempt him.'

He shook his head. 'I don't just mean that, there's the matter of… well there's…well there's everything else too.'

'Oh George, can't you just see it as giving a needy child a home? Think of all the charity work you do for the hospital, and they do say that charity begins in the home, don't they? Think how it would look to the hospital board if we did this.'

'Well, I suppose that is true and usually I would do, but…' He paused.

'What, George? What?'

He made a little cough while gathering his thoughts. 'Well it's just this child in particular – she does seem to have an unhealthy effect on your mental state, Emma.'

'You mean her face, George – the mark. It's that mark that means she's mine.'

George opened his mouth but then shut it again. He took off his spectacles and rubbed his eyes, as he did when he was studying one of his medical texts.

'You never wanted a child before,' he said. 'Yes, there was that little mistake – we should have been more careful about that, and it's natural that there was a lot of expectation there. But you never wanted us to try again, never wanted to adopt. It doesn't make sense.'

'It makes perfect sense, George; it's only natural that she comes here.' I knelt beside him and patted his knee. 'Can't you see, she's been mine all along? She's not some tinker girl, as you put it, and she's not really Maud's baby, she never has been, she's my Violet. Can't you see she's Violet?'

He stared at me for some time, then said firmly: 'Violet is dead.'

'No George.' I laughed. 'Violet's coming home!'

*

The next morning I found a note from George on the breakfast table. He was going to stay with his brother in Oxworth for a while – needed some space to clear his head. I was surprised at how little I cared and I actually felt relief; George had complicated things. All those accusations and refusing to make the effort, deliberately not understanding, making things difficult and, besides, George's absence would give me the time that I needed together with my daughter. She had lived as Ruby for so long, but now that time was over and it would be as Violet that she came home to me. From now on, things would be simple – Little Willow would just be for the two of us; me and my daughter. Violet and I.

I removed the rest of George's things from the bedroom, locking them away in a cupboard. Then, full of energy, took the Tube all the way to Regent Street and to Hamleys, where I flitted through the aisles, filling bag upon bag with dolls and teddies. The bags hardly weighed me down on the way back home and I swung them happily by my sides. The payment of the two hundred pounds had made me frivolous, and I felt heady as I skipped along the pavement, like I imagined an American movie star would feel; Peter's Greta Garbo all over again, the fortune I had spent on toys suddenly feeling small to me.

I hurried back to Little Willow, half expecting to find Violet waiting on the doorstep, but no, she wasn't there; it was still far too early.

I sat in the lounge, arranging the bags around me and glanced nervously at the clock on the mantelpiece; both hands were pointing to the twelve, the big neatly obscuring the small. Suddenly I realized that I was in silence but for the tick of the clock. There was no wireless and not even the rustle of George's newspaper.

After a while I noticed that the minute hand had moved a whole half hour while I had been sat with my thoughts. I went into the kitchen and made a cup of tea, standing in the hallway while the kettle boiled so I did not miss the sound of the doorbell.

Then I went to the window seat and sat there until my untouched tea was as cold as the rain that fell on the glass. I mused that maybe Sadie and Violet would be arriving by bus and I rested my head on the windowpane to listen for the vibration of engines. But buses meant problems too; the old 34 often broke down and there would be nobody to help the driver in the lane. And now the rain would bring plenty of mud for the wheels to get stuck in.

As the hands of the clock clicked on to 5 p.m. I cursed myself for not agreeing a time. At the cottage, the excitement had been too much and I had been carefree, not worrying about details and being generous with what I agreed to. I kicked myself for my lack of foresight. I didn't want our first evening together to be spoiled by last minute rushing around.

I went up to the back bedroom and arranged the new toys on the bed – Violet wouldn't have any time to play with them now, but they would be nice for when she woke. I took out the baby photo and looked at it, thinking about how much the little girl had grown, and I started to daydream. Sometime later I started to plan supper; shepherd's pie, Violet's favourite. I had been keeping the ingredients since the weekend.

But I ate my supper cold, putting hers in the larder, the mashed potato hardening under the baking parchment. I went back into the lounge and sat in the window seat, checking the clock against my wristwatch; only three minutes behind. The front garden was still empty and, through the glass, the sky was almost black.

I started to get a sinking feeling in my stomach. What if Violet didn't want to come? What if she was being difficult? What if she didn't want to leave after all? Maybe they'd had to tell her that Maud was dying? Was there a problem at Missensham House? Maybe she had been unable to find her clothes among all the boy's clutter – yes, those kinds of thing would all take some time.

I wrote a note for Sadie and pinned it to the front door. Then I grabbed my coat and hat and set out for Missensham House. I hurried past the war memorial, lifting my skirts to quicken my pace once I had passed the village green. The dark clouds of night chased me along my way, but I seemed to be moving in slow motion while the hands on my wristwatch whirled round. I could not be gone from Little Willow when Violet arrived home, not after all these years had passed, and I quickened my pace until I was running, my boot's echoing past the builder's hoardings and the dark station.

At last I reached St Benedict's, where a dull reflection of stained glass shimmered in the puddles and the rain pattered loudly on the tiles of the lichgate. The almshouses were in darkness, the only light coming from streaks of moonlight reflected in the windows.

'Hello?' I called, my voice tiny in the darkness. 'Sadie?'

But there was nothing but the distant quake of rails from a train far down the line. Fence posts jutted from the lawn, barbed wire pulled taut between them. I grabbed the wire and pushed it down, scrambling onto the entrance path, not caring when the fabric of my skirt shredded on the barbs. The door to number five was boarded over as well as the doors to numbers one, two, three and four. There was not a soul in sight. I put my face up to the window of Sadie's lounge and saw nothing but the grey outline of an empty room, the air echoing hollow as I rapped my knuckles on the glass.

I hurried back into the road, my heart racing. 'Sadie? Vi... Ruby?'

A sign flapped loose on the wire and I tore it free, holding it close to my face. It was printed large and bold but my eyes struggled to make it out in the shadow of the building. Then the crack of electricity on steel sounded from deep in the cutting and the railway came to life with the hiss of the approaching train. I waited for it to pass, the clatter of wheels getting closer until the engine sped by. But I barely noticed the train – as I stared at the sign in my hands, the strobe of carriage lamps flashed through the trees lighting the air around me. The sign flickered out of the darkness, a triangle of bright red and one single word: 'CONDEMNED'.

*

The road was in darkness, the distant wobble of an approaching bicycle lamp the only marker of the carriageway. My boots fell heavily on the mud but I continued homewards, barely noticing that my hair had unravelled down my back and my stockings were swollen with rainwater.

The flat clank of St Benedict's bell tolled nine – indisputably night-time. The evening I had so long anticipated was over and I could never get it back. The agreed handover had not happened and Violet and I remained apart.

At Missensham station, the ticket hall stood empty, the platform lost in darkness, as if it ceased to exist after the departure of the last train. Somewhere a drip of water echoed in the night air, then a gust of wind from far down the line. I folded my arms to my chest and continued down the road, the rhythmic trudge of my boots the only reminder that I was moving at all.

In front of me the hazy outlines of neat bay-fronted houses faded slowly out of the darkness; eerily tidy gardens, perfect fences and grinning cardboard housewives. This was the site of the new housing estate – no longer hedge-lined fields but a bulldozed pit caged by advertising boards. Then the neat brickwork and privet hedges flashed with colour and I looked up the road to see the quivering filament of a cyclist's lamp tracing circles of light across the hoardings.

The bicycle I thought would pass me was stationary and stood upended on its handlebars, the wobble of the lamp not caused by a journey over rough tarmac but by the rider, a dark figure crouched low in the road, winding the bicycle pedals and wrestling with a broken chain.

Now, closer to the light, I saw that the rider was a woman, plump and full-skirted, her voice familiar as she cursed the broken machine.

'Sadie?'

She looked round quickly but then squatted back down by the bicycle, frantically turning the pedals with her hands until mud spat from the wheels. 'Damn-Damn-Damn!'

'Sadie!'

A bundle of belongings slipped from the pannier; petticoats and drawers, all wrapped in the scarlet lining of a midwife's cape. She grabbed at the underwear frantically, stuffing it back into the pannier, then threw the cape around her shoulders, buckling it at her throat like armour. She wrestled with the pedals again.

'Stop!' I cried. 'Stop right there.'

'Looks like I don't have a choice,' she said, standing up

wearily and lifting the bicycle onto its wheels.

'Are you trying to get to Ruby? Where is she?'

'I don't know,' she muttered.

'You don't know!' I yelled. 'You were supposed to bring her round to mine.'

She stopped, her fingers tensing round the handlebars. 'That's the first I've heard of it,' she said. 'All I know is that they've gone. Maud's not told me where or why.'

'Gone! But my daughter—'

'She's not yours, you know that.' She turned to face me. 'You must know that really.'

'Of course she's mine. Her real name is Violet Margaret Marks, she was born on 7th May 1926, nine years old, she has a birthmark on the side of her face—'

Sadie shut her eyes as if troubled by some lingering pain, but then her features hardened. 'Ruby is the girl's name and she is with her mother, where she belongs.'

'I am her mother,' I said. 'All Maud has done is take her in for a few years, but that time is coming to an end, now it is my turn to have her back. Soon Maud won't even be able to lift a finger to help her children. She is dying...' but my speech slowed when Sadie shook her head slowly.

'I told you before,' she said, 'there is nothing wrong with Maud.'

'You can't deny it, Sadie. I've seen her coughing blood on her handkerchief. I've seen how weak she is, she can hardly get out of that basket chair, she—'

'A well woman has no need for these!' She rummaged in her pocket, blue glass enclosed in her fist. 'She gave them to me, for my ankles. Would an invalid give away chlorodyne?'

'No but—'

She swung her arm at the ground, a bottle smashing into blue shards.

I let out a shriek and she threw another down, the glass shattering on the toe of my boot.

'Maud has no need for medicine, not her, strong as an ox she is. But she knew how to fool people, oh yes, she'd had TB before, back when she was pregnant and on the pulmonary ward. She knows what TB looks like. She's not dying any more than you are Ruby's mother.'

'But I am her mother,' I said. 'I am.'

'Then you will be able to prove it.'

'I don't have to—'

'Prove it!' she repeated.

Proof: It was the answer I had been unable to give Maud. It was the scientific evidence that George craved. It was the rational explanation demanded by Walter and it was the common sense argument that Audrey knew I could not make.

'Well there's the matter of...' I began, but suddenly my head was flooded with thoughts: there were the similarities on the birth certificates – the dates, the hospital and the presence of George; there was Ruby who was an oddity in her family yet shared my fair hair and eyes; there was the birthmark – the one in Violet's photograph identical to the one on Ruby's cheek; there was... But as I said each thought over in my head, I realized that they were proof to me alone and that, even together, they would convince no one. And there were other thoughts too, thoughts which I dared not speak out loud: the way both father and daughter would bury their nose in petals to smell a bloom; the silver rattle that had returned from the grave; and the violets that appeared indoors to accompany the dead as they came back to the living. No, these were such fanciful things – I could not say these things out loud!

'I can't prove it,' I said at last, 'but I do have this.' I fumbled in my pocket for the legal document Maud had given me, the one which granted me guardianship of Ruby. I held it out to her, but she did not take it. 'The law is on my side, Sadie, you will find that Mr Crozier will be brought into this matter and —'

'Mr Crozier?'

'Maud has signed Ruby over to me,' I said firmly. 'She belongs to me in the eyes of the law.'

'It don't sound like Maud to trust a solicitor, she couldn't afford Mr Crozier anyway.'

'Of course Maud couldn't afford the fees for Crozier's to prepare the document,' I said, 'but Mr Crozier is a kindly man who made time to advise her on how to draft such a thing. It is a legally binding document, signed by Maud and a reputable witness.'

'I doubt Mr Crozier's ever set eyes on that.'

'Of course he has, put it under your bicycle lamp. Read it!' I thrust the document at her, angling the lamp over the paper. 'It says that I will become Ruby's guardian as soon as Maud becomes too ill...' then I stopped myself, not knowing what I could say next. What did these bits of paper mean if Sadie was right and Maud was not ill? 'Please take it, Sadie,' I said at last, but she did not take it or even attempt to read it.

Instead she looked right at me. 'So Mr Crozier has signed this, has he?'

'No, but—'

'The contract will have his stamp though?'

'No, it doesn't but—'

'And you know how to get hold of this witness who saw Maud sign it? This Mister...'

'No, but I could look for—'

'So you still think these bits of paper prove anything?'

'Yes...' I said. I tried to hand the document to her again, but she still did not take it and now I knew that I had no hope of persuading her. 'No,' I said my voice cracking. I felt my arm weaken and the document quivered in my fingertips. 'Oh God!' I breathed.

'I suppose it was money that was in that envelope I collected from you then?'

'You didn't know?' I said weakly.

'No, I suspected but I try to keep out of Maud's business as much as she will let me. I should have known better. I knew about Maud and her ways.'

At last Sadie took the document from my hands but she did not read it, just folded it carefully and returned it to my pocket. 'I never wanted to help Maud with this,' she said. 'I told you as much. But Maud said that, if I helped her, it would be the last time that she asked anything of me.'

'You still could have refused her,' I said.

'Yes,' she said, 'and I wish that I had. I did not know about Maud's plan or what she intended in the end, but I suspected that she was up to no good. I did try to put you off – I told you that Maud was not ill, I told you that you were not Ruby's mother and I hoped that you would believe me, but no words from my mouth would prove it to you – I suppose you had to find it out for yourself.' Then her face softened. 'You had some hope for a little while, that's all. That's the best way to remember this. When you think about all this nasty business, just remember how good it felt to have that little bit of hope.' She drew a long breath and her voice sounded weary. 'She was my little girl too, you know, she was my granddaughter – the little girl with the birthmark.'

'You're not making sense, Sadie,' I said. She had not said *niece*, she had said *granddaughter* and she had said *was*. I started to realize that the girl she was talking about no longer existed; she was talking about someone who was dead. She wasn't talking about Ruby but a baby who had died nine years ago, she was talking about Violet.

'Violet had no grandparents,' I said slowly. 'My parents have been dead for years and George's mother…'

But then my voice faltered and I drew a sharp breath. Sadie's face was angled downwards, the way the elderly do when they speak of the dead, but under her eyelids I saw a flash of bright blue.

'Peter!' I said. 'You're Peter's mother?'

'He told me you were pregnant,' she said gently. 'I saw your name down in the register at the hospital. I found out what had happened and I changed some of my shifts. I never thought that it would mean much to me; the bastard offspring of my son's affair with a married woman, I mean. So I visited Violet out of curiosity at first. But then after I had seen my own flesh and blood, my grandchild…' Her lip wobbled slightly but then she tightened her mouth and continued, her voice still strong. 'Many think an illegitimate birth shameful but not him – we barely talk these days but back then things were different; he told me everything, we were close back then.'

'I know,' I said. 'He told me that once.' I thought again of Peter and our flirtation. How he had carried a silver cigarette case close to his heart, the one that belonged to his mother. Peter had told Sadie about Violet, he had guessed that she was his child and he had found out what had become of her, perhaps he had cared about her too and now I not only mourned Violet but the life that I might have had with him.

'What happened to him, Sadie?' I said. 'Where is Peter now?'

'It's too late for all that, Emma,' she said. 'None of that matters anymore.' Then she added; 'I'm sorry,' but the words were more of a lament than an apology.

So here she was, sister to Maud but also grandmother to Violet and mother to Peter, the woman he had spoken about, the woman whose cigarette case he carried and the woman he told everything to. She was the midwife who had attended the birth, tended Violet in the incubator and the one who had photographed her in the hospital and given the print to me. Violet was gone and Peter too and now Sadie, the last link to the life I had wanted was leaving me. Sadie kicked away the stand and started to push the bicycle along the road.

'No, you don't!' I said, wedging my boot in front of the tyre.

'Let go of me!' she growled.

'You still have to return my money or I will call the constable.'

'And tell him what? How is buying a child going to look for a respectable woman from the Sunningdale Estate?'

'I was not buying any child, I was buying *my* child—' I stopped suddenly. *My child* – I had said the phrase so often in my head that it had started to sound natural, but now the words sounded strange and, after everything Sadie had said, I felt embarrassed to say them. 'My child,' I repeated weakly.

'Oh, Emma, really?' She pushed the bicycle over my foot and I grabbed at her hands, squeezing her knuckles hard over the break levers.

'No!' she shouted and we became locked together our faces inches apart as we wrestled across the cold metal. Her whole face was drawn into a frown, her eyebrows bunched low and her jaw thrusting forward but she kept shoving the bicycle hard against my thighs, as if nothing else mattered – not the mud on the road nor the broken chain, nor the bone in my hips nor the headlights approaching on the road nor the rumble of the evening bus which drowned out her curses.

Then came a screech of breaks and the bus was alongside us. The driver popped his window and peered out from under his cap. 'Excuse me, Madam. Is this woman bothering you?'

'Oh, thank God!' I panted. 'Yes she is. Please could you—'

'Not you, lady, I was talking to the matron.'

Keeping her eyes on me, Sadie turned her head slightly and gave the driver a little nod.

I opened my mouth to protest but the driver's eyes were moving slowly up and down my body and, in the light from the cabin, I saw the same woman that he did: the straggle of my loose hair hanging over my breast; the mud on my blouse; the ripped skirt; and my hands gripped tight around Sadie's.

My arms dropped to my sides. Sadie's eyes met mine again

– it was just a glance but it was enough to tell me that this was farewell. She wrenched the pannier from the crossbar and kicked the bicycle into the hedge, the light from the lamp fading away into darkness. She mounted the bus and disappeared behind the dark windows. Then the door closed and the bell rang out as the bus pulled away into the night. I was left standing alone.

39

Ruby

My name is Ruby Brown, but Emma told me that it is not our names that make us who we are; it is our memories. She began to tell me that she had memories of a precious baby, but then she stopped like she wanted to tell me more but couldn't bring herself to speak the words. She asked me about my memories too – where I lived before I came to Rose Cottage, how old I was in my first memory of Maudy. She would ask me these things over and over until I could not answer because my head swirled like carmine in a bucket. But there is one memory that I cannot shake, one that I must play in my head over and over again. If I don't, I will start to believe their lies.

'I know I didn't break the stove,' I said. 'I don't care what you say because I do remember what happened that day and I know it wasn't my fault.'

Maudy didn't look up. She stayed on the floor, her body bent double as she reached her hands into a bucket and squeezed carmine through a wodge of fabric. I watched her rock back and forth on her heels as she kneaded the cloth, but she didn't say anything, the squelch of the water as it rushed red round her hands the only sound in the room.

'Why did you let him do that to me?' I said. 'Why?'

She stopped moving, her body still like a statue, then she gave her head a little shake as if there was something bothering her, like the water had gone cold or the dye wasn't fixing and she let out a big sigh. 'You might think you remember what happened, Ruby, but you don't, not really.' She wiped her hands on her apron and sat back on her heels. 'We just gave you a tot of gin to clear up that flu you had, you remember you'd had that cough since spring, you remember how you were coughing, don't you? And you know we couldn't afford a doctor.'

'I was getting better,' I said. 'It was just a cold.'

'All that happ—' but a cough took the word away and then she kept coughing until she had to take out her handkerchief and wipe it round her lips. I felt bad for her but the doctor had told her to rest and she hadn't listened. I still wanted my answers, so I just sat and waited for them.

'All that happened is that we gave you a little too much by mistake,' she said at last. ' You got tipsy, that's all.' She gave me a funny twisted smile and a wink and plunged her hands back into the water. 'No wonder things are getting all muddled up in your head.'

'I didn't do it,' I said again. 'I didn't break the stove.' I held my arms out wide like a scarecrow, I knew that they looked all thin that way. 'Look at me, I'm not strong enough. How could I?'

Still Maudy didn't look. 'You fell, I told you. You took a nasty knock there. That must have muddled things in your head. Not that you ever had much brains to start with.' She smiled again, a bigger one this time, trying to turn things into a joke, but I wasn't about to let her.

'I didn't do it,' I said.

She shook her head all weary. 'Well it's just like I said, you don't remember, do you?'

'It isn't that I don't remember, I do, I just remember something else, something different from what you're telling me.'

'Well you remember what you want to then,' she snapped. 'It don't make no difference to me.' She started to knead the cloth again, but this time she put all her strength into it, her hands got faster and faster and the water sloshed over the sides of the bucket. She was chewing her cheek frantically, her forehead was squeezed into lots of little lines and her breaths were fast and wheezy, then her eyes went round and she stopped dead and just stared into the pool of red. 'This thing that you think you remember,' she said, suddenly all quiet, 'well, no matter whether you think it's the truth or not, you can't go around telling it to people.'

'Why not?' I said.

'Well, how would it look? You remember it one way and Clarence and me remember something else, and so you would look foolish wouldn't you. Like a liar, nobody would believe you, so it's best not to tell.'

'I might tell someone,' I said. 'Someone who would believe me. I might tell Emma.'

'No!' she shouted and suddenly she was standing up, water gushing down from her hands. 'Someone like her is the very worst person to tell.' She started jabbing her fingers at me, her knuckles red. 'Mrs Fancy-Pants of all people! Can't you see what she would do? She would call the constable, get all hot under the collar. Then what do you think would happen? You want to make it look like you come from a bad home? You want to get taken away from me and end up in the children's home? Because that is where you would end up if you told someone like her.'

Then I started to get scared. I didn't want to go into a children's home, so I didn't push it. 'I won't say a thing,' I said. 'Not to Emma, not to anyone.'

Maudy knelt back down again but this time she moved as if she was carrying a big weight on her back. 'All right,' she said, 'but you must promise.'

'I do,' I said. 'Cross my heart.'

She put her hands back into the bucket but her movements were slower and the bites into her cheek became harder and more deliberate until she was licking blood round her lips. 'Good girl,' she said. 'Special girl.'

I watched her rocking back and forth, the triangles of her shoulder blades squeezing together under her dress. All I could hear was the sounds from the bucket; the slap of cloth each time she pounded into it, then a squelch and gurgle of water as the dye raced round her hands. I stared into the back of her head, trying to bore into it with my eyes, using all my energy as I tried to hear her thoughts, but there was nothing, and I just got a blank feeling.

'I just want to know why you did it,' I said at last.

'I told you, it was to help get rid of your cough.'

'I don't mean the gin.'

She stopped working and sat back on her heels again. Then she pulled her hands from the bucket and gathered the material onto her lap. She had forgotten that it was soaking wet and the red bled across her apron, but she didn't notice and just sat cradling it like a baby while dye trickled onto the floor. Then she sighed. 'Look that's the end of it. I don't want to hear no more about it. We gave you a little too much gin, you tottered around and then you fell on the stove. Hit your head on the door and that's what broke the hinge. It's your own fault. That stove ain't never been the same since. I have to keep a candle underneath it now in case a draught gets in and it blows out. That's why Clarence is mad. I keep nagging him for a new one but you're the one who broke it in the first place, you broke it when you fell.'

'No,' I said firmly. 'That's not what I remember.'

She stared into her lap.

'It's something to do with this—' I took out the photograph from my pocket, the one of the baby in the bonnet. 'Isn't it?'

Her face went all red and her eyes went big and shaky. 'Jesus!' she screamed. She jumped up and flung the soggy material at me but she missed and it made a loud bang as it hit the wall. Then it slid down, leaving a red stain on the plaster.

The sound jolted cold all through me and my blood must have been ice because for a moment I couldn't move. I tried to say something but no sound came out, no words anyway.

'Shut up, you little bitch!' screamed Maudy. 'Shut up, shut up, shut up!' Then she was gone, the door banging behind her.

I got up slowly, my legs shaking. I looked at the photograph again. The baby was still but it was not peaceful and nor was I. I tore the baby in half, separating the pretty half from the ugly one. Then I threw both halves into the grate.

I walked over to the stove. The door was still hanging by one hinge, taunting me. I pulled at it with all my might. Then I summoned all my strength and kicked it, trying to break the hinge, then I dropped to my knees and bashed it with my shoulder as if I was falling. I could not break it, it was hard.

40

Emma

Rose Cottage was just a hazy outline against the purple sky as I rushed down the lane, panting and sweating after the long walk from Old Missensham. As I rounded the bend by the twisted oak, I saw that the cottage windows were black and lifeless and when I tried the door it was unlocked and opened easily, sweeping a draught across my feet. I felt my way into the front room, guided by the hollow strike of my heels on the flagstones. The only light came from a square of pale moonlight cast on the floor by the kitchen window and the faint glow of dying embers in the grate.

I stumbled to the hearth and felt for the wood box but it was gone, just an old log wedged under the grate. I threw it on the embers, cinders spiralling up the chimney as the bark crackled to life.

In the light of the flames the emptiness of the room was revealed to me. It seemed unnaturally large without the jumble of furniture or the bustle of children. The table was gone and the old basket chair. The Singer, Clarence's rocker and even the iron doormat were gone, now just outlines etched in dust and memory.

The back room was empty too, the night gusting in through the open window and the rail hanging loose as if the curtain had been wrenched off in a hurry. The rocking horse was gone too, just stripes on the floorboards where the rockers had once stood. Only the bedstead remained, stripped of its mattress, and the dresser, pulled away from the wall as if an attempt to move it had been abandoned in haste.

I ran to the dresser and wrenched open the drawers. Maybe the family had left a letter for me, I thought, something from Maud excusing herself for some unfortunate misunderstanding, but the drawers were light and empty. I chastised myself for the foolish thought, and I realized that not only were the family missing, they did not want to be found.

I attacked the dresser, wrenching the drawers from their runners and flinging them onto the floor. Then I hurried back into the kitchen, stopping suddenly when I realized that I had nowhere to run – there was nowhere I could go now and nothing I could do.

I sank down in front of the fire and stared into the flames. There was a creak at the kitchen door and Smokey melted out of the darkness, rubbing his head against my knee. I picked him up and squeezed his warm body against my face, smelling the cold night on his fur. His purr was wheezy, the vibration strong enough to rattle through his whole body. The poor little thing, was abandoned, left all on his own, just as I was. Then I started to cry.

All I had left was Maud's broken promises and meaningless words typed on office paper yet signed only with a cross and the unintelligible scribble of a witness who probably didn't exist. How could Maud do this to me? Maud who was a friend but now an enemy. Maud who was fatigued yet took on work, her stitching still as perfect as the day we met. Maud who needed medicine but did not take it. Maud who was too ill to be moved, yet now she was certainly gone.

Sadie's words played again and again in my head: 'She ain't ill – there's nothing wrong with her!' But I had not listened. She had delivered Ruby's birth certificate into my hands, but I had refused to believe what I saw.

And there was Ruby; the little girl was always insisting that Maud just had a mouth ulcer. Maybe she had suspected that Maud wasn't ill and had been trying to tell me. She was just a child, but was she part of Maud's plan all along? Had she known... she couldn't have, could she?

I bit my lip to control the sobs, burying my face into Smokey's soft coat. Pieces of what had happened flashed into my mind but never lingered long enough to make sense: there was little Henry who had picked up my leaflet yet could not read; there was Ruby stood waiting by the railings at the lido, but who was she waiting for; there was the midwife in the white room with the strange expression on her face; the seamstress coughing blood into her handkerchief, fed-up of sewing uniforms for hotels she could never afford; the grieving grandmother; the birth certificate with George's name on; broken rocking horses; locked nurseries; the toll of St Cuthbert's; pills for the insane; silver rattles; the smell of carbolic; violets indoors; tiny coffins; bad luck; death.

Then the tears stopped, the long draw of my breath filling the room. Around me the walls had melted into blackness and the dull square of light at the window had dissolved into the night. The fire in the grate had taken hold like it was draining the light from the room, sucking the darkness in closer and closer. My hands grew cold and the air around me chilled. It was the kind of stillness you only get at night. Like nothing existed outside this little room, not even time.

It was then that I saw it. It was lying in the grate, wedged between the slats, just inches from the flame. It was a photograph, ripped in half, the two pieces shivering in the draught from the chimney. I leant into the grate and rescued it, matching the pieces together. It was a small photograph – a grey image of a newborn lying on its back. The face was round, like that of any baby, the scalp haloed by a lace bonnet. The head was tilted slightly to show the left cheek – black marks cast on grey skin. Four tears, the highest smudged over the cheekbone.

The paper pulsed with my breath. It was my baby.

I turned the pieces over in my hands. There was a printer's mark in one corner, '2/2'. This was my baby, there was no doubt, but this was not my photograph. Just as George has remarked all those years ago, there had been another copy all along. But the second copy had not been for the midwife's official records. Sadie had intended it as a morbid keepsake of her granddaughter – a baby that had only ever drawn a few breaths. And somehow the photograph had made its way into this house.

So this is how the Browns had found out about Violet and my connection to her – through Sadie and the photograph. They had known all about me all along, my name and where I lived, and once Maud had befriended me they found out about my past life and my loves and losses. But despite Maud's constant chatter and lewd confessions and Ruby living under my roof, the Browns had made sure that I did not know them.

I threw the photograph into the fire. The paper curled in the flames, the two halves cleaving apart, splitting the image into two once more. I stared at the baby again – the flickering outline the face, the lowered eyelids and slack cheeks that had once suggested slumber – but this time I knew that Violet was dead.

41

Ruby

My name is Ruby Brown and I am not Emma's daughter.

I watched Rose Cottage from the back of the van as we drove off down the lane. The white walls, looked bright in the evening light but they were getting smaller and smaller, as if they would shrink away forever. I looked as long as I could because I was certain that it was the last time that I would see the cottage and all of a sudden I felt very sad.

They didn't care, of course. No, they didn't give a toss. Not Maudy, not Andy, not Henry, not Jim-John. They all sat squeezed tight together on the van's hard wooden benches, the last rays of the sun lighting up their faces, and those faces were happy.

But it wasn't just us Browns in the back of the van, oh no, there was all the Brown's worldly goods too, packed so snugly among us that we could barely wiggle or dare to let out a fart. There was Maudy's sewing machine and Clarence's rocking chair, there was the upended table and the bed sheets, pillows and linen. Old apple crates crammed with pots and pans and cups and plates, clothes and packets of flour and suet. There were metal buckets, basins, chamber pots and washboards and parcels of carmine and indigo. There was everything but the dresser and the old bed frame - the only things that Clarence could not drag over the floor or wrench from the walls.

My face was pressed against the back window, the rocker of Clarence's chair digging into my shoulder. When I complained all Maudy did was wedge her sick blanket between me and the metal but my arm was stuck flat against my chest and I could barely draw breath. Maudy kept one hand on me and the other on the roof, her back braced against the wall to stop us sliding all over each other.

'Many more hours to go,' she said but she was grinning like

a lunatic.

Clarence sat up front in the passenger seat, barking orders to poor Fatkins who did his best to avoid the wheel ruts and steer though the fading light. I felt bad for Fatkins. Earlier that day he had been called into the factory by a stone-faced Mr Walker, office telephone in hand. He was told about a family emergency, so he set off right away and lost all his delivery money. He drove all the way to Evesbridge to find the Browns and all their belongings sitting on the doorstep with a dodgy story about a threatening landlord and rent they couldn't pay.

So he came and he helped, not complaining as usual. Just like he didn't when Maudy gave him damp aprons or passed-off her sausage-fingered gloves as fine tailoring. I couldn't see his face, just those massive hunched shoulders and big hands on the steering wheel and sometimes his eyes checking the road in the little mirror above the windscreen.

Maudy leant forwards and tapped Fatkins' back. 'This is ever so kind of you, nephew,' she shouted over the din of the engine, 'and I do hope your leg won't suffer too much what with all this extra driving. Promise me you will look after it when you get back and put it up on the couch...' I stopped listening and I suppose that he did too. His eyes flashed in the mirror - they were hard, like blue ice, darting over the road but never looking at her.

But Maudy saw none of this and she just kept on going on and it was only after some good long minutes that she realised that she wasn't getting anything from him so she turned on me: 'You need to look after yourself too, my special girl.' She pulled her sick blanket tighter against my shoulder, then higher up so it is rested on my cheek. It wasn't grey any more, not like it was when she was pretending to be sick; now it was bright red, freshly dyed and all bright and lively just like she was. The smell of carmine was strong in my nose.

The van slowed all of a sudden, a crunching noise from deep beneath us as Fatkins wrestled with the gears. The pots rattled and Andy's face grew grim as his forehead tapped against the metal. Twigs squeaked across the windscreen.

'Can't we turn round and go through Missensham?' Andy whined. 'We ain't even gone half a mile yet and there's miles of these dirt tracks before we get to Evesbridge.'

'We can't go that way,' hissed Maudy, 'in case we are met.'

'Met?' I said. 'Met by who?'

But nobody answered.

I saw Fatkins's eyes in the mirror again. Suddenly they flicked up towards me and I fancied that they were looking right at me. His hands tightened on the steering wheel.

Clarence rested a hand on his arm. 'Calm down, Old Fellow. We got money, is all,' he said, 'from a grand lady in town.' He patted his chest pocket, which crinkled under his hand. 'Got a little sympathy gift for our sorry predicament – a dying mother and a disfigured daughter. Best to make a quiet exit.' He chuckled to himself.

Maudy's stared at him. She had already sold Fatkins the story about the threatening landlord and now Clarence was ruining it. She wanted to shush him but all she could do was bore her eyes into the back of his head.

In the mirror, Fatkins's eyes flicked back to me. But now I didn't care if he was looking at me or not. I looked away and out the window, feeling sad and watching the blotchy rainclouds and the pale light winking through the trees. I started to think about earlier that day when me and the boys were sent out to get milk for Maudy and about how everything was different when we got back to Rose Cottage. And I got to thinking about how they had tricked me yet again...

*

'Surprise!' cried Maudy, flinging open the door.

We stopped dead on the step; she had never opened the front door to us kids before and she was panting with excitement, her grin so big it could swallow her whole face.

'Guess what I've been up to since you've been gone – my big handsome boys and my special girl – come inside. I bet you ain't expecting this!' She opened the door up wide. Henry, Jim-John and me all turned round to look at Andy but he just shrugged his shoulders, so we did as she said and we went inside.

In the front room the doormat was propped against the wall, the floor was bare and all the pots and pans were piled high on the draining board. In the back room the dresser was away from the wall and the drawers were empty. In the corner was a pile of old wooden apple crates stuffed with clothes and bed sheets.

'What the bloody hell?' yelled Andy. 'What have you done to our things?'

'Are you blind as well as stupid?' said Maudy, pointing to the crates. 'That daft wooden horse had to go though – but then it was a big ugly thing after all and there ain't going to be room for everything in the van. Here, Andy, you're a big, strong man now, help me shift the dresser. I'm worried we may have to leave it if--'

'What are you talking about, you silly bitch?' yelled Andy.

'We are moving house!' she cried, and clapped her hands together with a big gappy grin like a baby with wind. I thought that there was something different about her then I realised that she was looking well, almost healthy, the sweaty patches had gone from her armpits and the coughing has stopped, in fact her cheeks were rosy from the exercise.

'No we ain't,' said Andy. 'Moving house takes weeks, you have to have somewhere to go!'

'We do,' she said, all excited. 'We are going to Birmingham. Now come along and help me, my kindly nephew is coming with the van and we don't want to miss our lift.'

'This is madness,' said Andy. 'I ain't helping nobody.'

'Don't then-' she threw the broom at him '-just sodding help or sit out the way-' she pointed at the pile of crates '-sit over there!'

She stormed into the back room, cursing all the way. She rammed her shoulder into the dresser but it wasn't going to help her either and didn't move an inch. Her chin was stuck out the way it was when she was in a proper mood but there was a twinkle in her eye that I hadn't seen for weeks.

'What about the job I was going to get at the garment factory?' shouted Andy. 'Or all that sewing work Fatkins brings you. Now we won't have no money.'

'There will be work in the factories, me and Clarence can both work,' she said, abandoning the dresser. 'Andy, you, my big grown-up man, can get any job in any factory or any accounts department you want. We'll have enough money to live in a boarding house while we get settled. We can make motorcars in the factories and we can buy a house of our own.'

'Are you mad?' said Andy. 'We'll never have enough money for our own house, I've been looking at your accounts, remember, we...'

But Maudy was grinning madly, she took an envelope from her pocket. It was big and purple just like the envelope I forgot to give to her when Emma sent me visiting with the pound cake. She waved it in the air, a big grin on her silly face.

Andy snatched it from her. He peered inside, rummaging his hand between the folds. Then his face turned white. 'What have you done?' he said.

'Just trust us,' said Maudy. She wouldn't say anything more.

We sat down quietly on the apple crates. Maudy was acting all busy bundling up linen but Andy looked thoughtful. I wanted to ask him what was in the envelope but I got a feeling that then wasn't the right time. I stared at it in his hands but the paper was thick and I couldn't even guess what was inside. It smelled of lavender and I started to feel like something bad was about to happen.

'Where's Smokey?' I said.

'Clarence caught him,' said Maudy, wiping her hands on her apron. 'He left him with Sadie, she will bring him to Birmingham for us.'

I knew it wasn't true. Smokey had been spending all day at the rabbit warrens. He would have never come back. He hated Clarence and never went near him. Clarence would never have caught him. I tried to think of a plan.

'Oh no,' I said. 'I've left some things at Emma's house – she gave me a xylophone and a knitted rabbit and a book about animals from the zoo. I was going to pick them up when I went back. I can still run over and get them.'

'No,' said Maudy. 'Clarence will be back soon and my nephew will be coming with the van. We have to leave as soon as he gets here.'

'No!' I said. 'I've got time if I run. We can even sell the xylophone when we get to Birmingham. We can't come back for it once we're there, can we? I will be quick.' I was about to stand up but she was on me in a flash, her hands tight round my wrists.

'Sit down!' she yelled.

And I did. I stared at her. Everybody stared at her.

Maudy sighed. She knew that she had to tell us everything: 'Back in January,' she said, 'Sadie came round. She'd been helping me in the yard with some dying, but while she was out the back, Clarence decided he wanted a fag and went rummaging in her bag. He didn't find one. There weren't nothing in her cigarette case but a photograph, a very old one. He didn't think of his plan right then, he ain't that smart, but over the next few days he had got everything planned out in his head.'

'A photograph of what?' said Jim.

I stopped listening, I already knew, and I hated Clarence even more.

42

Emma

I walked back in the darkness, feeling my way along the path but not caring if I stumbled or fell. I cradled Smokey under my coat, the gentle swell of his purr the only reminder that I was alive.

My heart leapt when I passed the war memorial and saw that the light was on in the house, the curtains glowing with warmth. When I got to the front door I found it unlocked and my note torn down from the paintwork. I pushed the door and flung open my coat, letting Smokey run into the hallway. I called out, rushing into the lounge but there was no laughter to greet me and no child running towards me. The room was still and quiet.

George was sat in his old armchair with his head in his hands and I suddenly thought that the past weeks had all been a strange dream and that Ruby had never existed. I perched on the window seat and bit my lip. George raised his head slowly as if in a daze, his face weary.

'The bank telephoned me last week,' he said, 'while I was at the surgery.'

'Oh,' I said, kicking the floor.

'Mr Arbuthnot thought it only courteous to call me.' He paused and rubbed his eyes. 'Two hundred pounds, Emma!'

I stared at the floor. 'You didn't stop him.'

'Stop him? Well I didn't believe you would go ahead with it, not until Mr Arbuthnot telephoned again today. You know there has been some concern about you recently. Audrey hasn't helped matters; your affairs seem to be known all across Missensham.'

'You didn't stop him, but you didn't stop *me* either,' I said.

'Stop you from withdrawing your life savings? What would be the point? I've been trying everything to make you happy. If I thought that this one last thing could help—'

'Oh, George! I—'

'I know things haven't been perfect between us but I have tried the best I can: given up my place at the hospital so we could spend more time together; built up my business at the surgery; provided you with a motorcar and a warm, modern house and paid for its redecoration. When I've given you all this, why would I stop you from withdrawing your own money?'

'You did all that for me?' I said.

'I thought you wanted to live on the Sunningdale Estate,' he said quietly. 'It was you that chose to live here, with the central heating and electric lighting and the Frigidaire. I was never bothered by any of those things but, with your childhood home sold and your parents gone, I thought a nice house and garden would be important to you.' He looked at me, his face had a kind of childish blankness to it and suddenly I saw past the medical jargon and the political rants. At heart he was a simple man, he had not wanted the detached house, the red Austin car, or the refrigerator. All that he'd ever wanted had been simple things and I had not been able to give them to him.

'I thought that living here would help things,' he said. 'I know I'm not an ideal husband. I know that you didn't love me when we married, maybe you never did. I could accept that but I thought that I could at least make you… content.'

'I'm sorry,' I said.

'Will you let me know what you want this time? What was the money for? You at least owe me that.'

'I thought I could buy a child,' I said. 'I thought I could buy our baby back, I thought I could buy Violet, but I was wrong.'

He sighed and wiped his eyes. 'You are talking about Ruby Brown. Well, that child is none of our concern. She is better off with her mother.'

'Her mother?' I said.

'Yes, her real mother. The tuberculin tests came back negative; Maud Brown doesn't have tuberculosis after all. So it's all for the best in the end – the child has a home and it is not with us.'

I thought of the unopened chlorodyne bottles that Sadie had smashed at my feet, the piles of perfectly finished gloves, the protests from Ruby and Sadie. Maud did not have TB. Her coughing and wheezing had all been to fool me and make me believe that she was just a caring mother forced to part with her child.

'It doesn't matter what I say, anyway,' I said. 'The family are gone. I don't have that choice to make any more.'

George's face showed no surprise and I realized that, to him, Ruby had always been just an inconvenient visitor and never someone who he could imagine spending the rest of his life with. 'Why did it mean so much to you?' he said. 'We could have adopted any child, yet you never showed any interest in that. You flung yourself into gardening. I thought you were happy with that. But I'm just a doctor of the body. I cannot read your mind.' He paused, tilting his head so that the lenses of his spectacles shielded his eyes. 'Was it because the baby wasn't mine? Was it because it was *his*? Is that why it meant so much?'

'George!'

'Please don't treat me like a fool. I was happy to turn a blind eye to it at the time, but please have the respect not to treat me like a fool.'

'You knew?' I whispered. 'You knew all along?'

'No, I didn't know about the affair to start with, I had my suspicions but I wasn't sure, not until you became pregnant. Then I knew.' He sighed. 'Well I don't suppose it matters now, we've both had our secrets.'

'What do you mean by that?' I said.

For a long time he did not say anything, just sat in his old chair. The clock on the mantelpiece ticked steadily and started to whirr as the minute hand clicked onto the hour. He waited for the last chime to finish, then put his head in his hands.

'I was in Amiens during the war,' he said quietly, 'working at the field hospital.'

'I know,' I said. 'That is where you were—'

'Where I became hospitalized myself? Yes. I have told you that much before. I have a shrapnel wound in my back, which you know about, but I always let you believe it was that which got me sent home.' He hesitated, the hiss of his breath rising over the ticking clock. 'The thing is, I wasn't in that hospital for my back; I had complications from an infection.' He stopped suddenly and made his little coughing sound but there was no arrogance to it this time and he smiled weakly. 'So no great battle deeds for heroic George, no venereal diseases from the wild women, just a simple infection. It was mumps, just like any schoolboy would get. I caught it from a troop of French soldiers brought in from the battlefield. I was only a junior medic but I was the only one on duty that night and I had to tend to a tent full of them, their faces swollen like toads. They were filthy creatures, crawling with disease. Their trench had been disorganized, with no sanitation, and the smell...' He drew a sharp breath as if the stench was still in the air. 'The bloody French.' He sighed. 'The bloody French.'

'Oh, George!'

'You always wondered why I hate the French and not the Germans,' he said. 'Well, the French gave me more than a shrapnel wound. The treatment should have been so simple – some bed rest, isolation and a course of cold compresses and saltwater gargles. But I was one of the unlucky ones, I was exhausted and weakened by the infection, there were no proper facilities and the medicines had been held up at Dover for two weeks. I suffered complications and I was left damaged. The medical term is orchitis. It hurt like hell. Then, when the swelling had gone down, they said I could not father a child. When I take a little bit too much chlorodyne, it is not because of the pain,' he said. 'I take it for the shame.'

He took off his spectacles. The skin underneath was tender and moist as if never exposed to the air. He rubbed his small, blinky eyes as if seeing daylight for the first time. I wanted to reach out to him, put my arms around him but I could not. He was already a memory to me, something that would fade if I tried to touch it.

'I wanted to tell you so many times, but you seemed happy with what we had back then. I suspected that you were having an affair but, when you told me that you were pregnant, I knew that under the circumstances you would be forced to stay with me and so I accepted your little secret. I knew about your lies, how could I not? But if I said nothing, then my own lies would not matter so much anymore.'

'Oh George, I'm sorry!' I started to cry. The more he had loved me, the more I had hated him. He had concealed his lie, but all the time he'd had to confront mine – every day that my belly grew larger. And when the lie was born it was weak and disfigured but could no longer be ignored. The one special secret I had from him had been shared between us all along.

'Did you take my baby, George?' I said. 'Did you take my

baby away from me and tell me that it was dead? Did you do that because you knew that the baby wasn't yours?'

'How could you say that?' he whispered.

'You were in the hospital that day, George. You were at my baby's birth but you had been working on the pulmonary ward and there was a woman on that ward, a woman whose baby was very sick, I know this much, you can't deny it.' It was what I had wanted to say to him for so long. The only explanation that had made sense, but my voice was faltering with every word. 'You had plenty of opportunities to take my baby away and give it to Maud Brown – a woman whose baby was about to die, a woman who was so sick that she would not know any different.'

'Emma!'

He got up and knelt in front of me and his face alone was enough to answer my questions.

'The rattle then?' I said quietly. 'Why didn't you bury it like you said you had?'

'I thought there might have been another child,' he said. 'When Violet died I didn't know what you would do. I suppose I thought that you might go off cavorting again. You were still young after all – I didn't expect you to give up. I never expected that you would spend so much time in mourning, but then the weeks became months and the months became years. You never said anything about it to me but I could see the change in you; the time you spent around the house, the gardening. This…' he waved his hand round the room. It was the room we sat in every day, but just for that moment I saw it exactly as he did – the emptiness, the silence measured by the tick of the clock. 'You wanted to stay here with the memories,' he said. 'And memories are everywhere in this house.'

'Oh, George, I—'

'I put the rattle away for the day that another child would come,' he said. 'The day that all this would end. I buried it deep, just not with Violet. I buried it within the house instead of in the soil and buried it in my memory. I never expected it to be found. That girl must have meddled…' He frowned as if making a conscious effort to correct himself. 'Or Mr. Tuttle.'

'I'm sorry,' I said. 'I'm so sorry.'

He rubbed his eyes. 'I took our baby and rubbed her flesh, pounded her heart, breathed into her mouth for half an hour. Walter tried to stop me. He could see that Violet was premature, small, and weak. And in the end he could not watch anymore and I was left alone; just me and a tiny body.'

It was true. I had known it all along. Why had I ever doubted this poor wounded man? I felt numb, like I had cried all my tears and had nothing left. 'Why didn't you say so, George? Why have we never talked about it? I've been blaming you all this time!'

'Well maybe that's something,' he said sharply. 'It's easier when there's someone to blame.' He cleared his throat and stood up as if the conversation was over and the matter resolved. Then he put on his spectacles and returned to his armchair, crossing his legs as he sat down, the newspaper rustling as his face disappeared behind the pages of print.

I parted the curtains and stared out the window. The road was in darkness but I watched the still night air for minutes on end. It was the way I had always looked out on to the road, day in, day out for the last ten years, always waiting for something to happen for something that would give me a little bit of hope and show me that my life would change. But now when I looked out onto the road I could feel more years racing past and my gaze stretching into my dotage. After all, why should anything be different for me? I did not deserve anything more than the silence.

The lounge door creaked and wavered gently. A hooked tail sailed behind the arm of the sofa, the soft pad of paws on the carpet.

George looked up. 'What's that?'

'Just a cat,' I said.

'Oh good,' he said. 'I like cats.'

43

Ruby

My name is Ruby and rubies are red. But there are lots of things that are red that aren't so precious or pretty, and that red is all around me: red are the berries of the poisonous yew that grows in the churchyard; red is the coal that glows inside the stove with the broken door; red drips from the fingers of gloves that point their fat, accusing fingers at me; red is the swell of blood on the consumptive's handkerchief; red is a warning sign strung on barbed wire; a red face of shame; a cheek gnawed raw; fire; blood; rage and hate.

But then all was dark.

Everything that was Ruby was in that darkness. My whole world, my family and everything we owned from the smallest thimble to the treasured sewing machine and we were all together in one tiny space. You might think that some terrible fate had befallen us, but there was no justice for my family, no lessons to be learnt. It was the darkness that hid us and the walls of the van that kept us safe as we made our escape along the back roads and country lanes.

I saw only what the van saw with its shining eyes, two circles of light skimming over the pits and ruts of the Evesbridge Road. Sometimes moonlight would burst through a gap in the hedges, like the flash from a photographer's gun and for a second I would see the photograph of us as we were then: the metal sides of the van, wooden apple crates bursting with pots and pans, upended tables and chairs and the stony face of a brother or mother.

Clarence was barking at Fatkins; ordering him to speed up, to mind the potholes, to let out the choke. But Fatkins didn't say a word, he didn't even turn to face Clarence, I could see the shape of his face, a dark shadow in the windscreen mirror and I got a cold feeling that he was looking at me.

Then Maudy's face was right up against mine, her old sick blanket wafting bitter carmine into my nose. 'Here, Ruby, you awake?'

I grunted, but it wasn't enough to silence her.

'I'm sorry about moving,' she said, 'and about Smokey and Emma and the xylophone, but things will be so much better for us in Birmingham.'

I grunted again.

'Remember, you are special.' She had said it before so many times, but it seemed that I was extra special that day. She had said it over and over as we were sat on those apple crates: 'You are special, Ruby'. But, so happens, lots was special to Maudy that day and she started to mouth off again, going on about special-big houses and special-fast motorcars in a special-big city until I started to think that maybe she was right. I was special, without me there would have been none of those dreams.

Maudy only shut up when the hedges stopped and there were moonlit fields all around. Now I could see them all, looking pale and sickly in the moonbeams as they slept – Jim-John and Henry with ghostly white faces, the moon washing the freckles from Andy's cheeks. Maudy grinned at me, her mouth wide like a skull.

In the front of the van Clarence was patting the big purple envelope in his breast-pocket: pat-pat-pat. Fatkins glanced over at him but then I saw his eyes flick back in the mirror – he wasn't looking at the road and I started to think that he was looking at me again. I started thinking that he blamed me for driving his cousins to Birmingham, blamed me for keeping him from his bed in the middle of the night, blamed me for the boys staying with his mother in her little house and for all the money we had scabbed off him for damp aprons and stoves that would never be fixed. I looked away quickly. And then I started to remember what had happened earlier that day in the empty cottage. In my head Clarence and Fatkins and the envelope and everything else in the van just faded away and all I could see was our kitchen again, and it looked empty, with the floor bare and piles of apple crates against the wall. I started to think about what Maudy had said again. Of course I was special; without me, we would have never been in this mess…

*

'So it all started when Clarence finds the photograph,' Maudy said as she sat down on an apple crate. 'We could tell from Sadie's face what the photograph meant to her and then she broke down and told us all about this granddaughter that never was.' Maudy smiled gleefully. 'The thing is, once Sadie has started talking, she couldn't stop. She told us all about the affair and the pregnancy and the birth, even the posy of violets left on the incubator. You see her son had told her everything, even Emma's name, and where she lived, and even what she didn't tell us weren't hard to figure out.'

We all sat on our crates in the empty cottage and we listened to her as she told us the story, her voice all earnest. We sat and listened till our bums were sore, our ears were ringing, but at last Maudy was talking, and talking so fast that I fancied she didn't have time to think up lies. Then all of a sudden she slowed right down and got all serious.

'Then Sadie says something that gets me thinking,' she said. 'She goes on about how whenever she sees you, Ruby, she thinks of Violet. You see, there was things about Violet and you that was just too similar.' Then she started prattling on about how Violet would have looked at my age, how our birthdays were only days apart, how we were born in the same hospital and even how Dr Marks was there for both our births. She knew from Sadie's stories that they never let mothers see their sickly babies after they had faded. Maudy seemed delighted – clapping her hands all excited – like having such a convenient daughter was a gift from God.

But then she stopped for breath and suddenly looked all thoughtful. 'Once we'd realized this, Ruby, well we thought that if Sadie could see Violet in you, then why shouldn't Emma? We thought that maybe, just maybe, you could become Violet; if not a switch at the hospital, then a ghost risen from the grave.'

I felt a trickle of cold down my back. Maudy's plan had worked of course. I had stayed at Violet's house, worn the clothes she would have worn and eaten the same food. I had played with expensive toys and been on day trips to the zoo and the museum and I had been like a daughter to Emma and I had let her love me. I had become Violet to Emma and, if Maudy had wanted me to be Violet too, then what had happened to Ruby? Could nobody see Ruby anymore? Just then I felt that I couldn't see her either and I felt all empty inside like I had swallowed a ghost.

'But it weren't enough,' said Maudy suddenly. 'Emma could just think it chance that you and Violet was alike and we didn't know what to do about that so I wanted to forget the whole thing. But once Clarence had a snifter of money the idea wouldn't leave his head and neither could Emma.'

This was when Clarence took to lazing in the orchard, Maudy explained. He could hide from the farmer there and he could doze, that was true, but he could also think and he could look across the road to Emma's house. So he sat in the shade of a tree, peering through the hedge at Little Willow, the house with its four windows and the door in the middle and the neat hedge and the red car with the big owl eyes.

He sat there day in day out, hoping to find out where Emma went and which friends she saw, but no friends came and Emma hardly left Little Willow. One day that Emma did go out, Clarence had tried to sneak inside the house, but people on the Sunningdale Estate are untrusting and the garden gate was bolted so tightly that he broke it as he tried to force it open.

'I got other ideas,' said Maudy. 'I thought it was time for Emma to meet her Violet.'

But things weren't that simple for Maudy; she had never clapped eyes on Emma but she did know where Emma's house was and that she just sat at the window all day and didn't ever leave. So she got me lingering in Willow Street across from this smart house with the red motorcar as she scrambled up the bank and stole apples one day. She hoped that Emma might glance out of her window and see me, notice my patchy face. But the lady of the grand house was not at the window that day and instead the door banged open and two little kids were running all over the place. Then came a pram and two ladies talking behind it, one was tall and hefty but Maudy didn't care about her because she could tell straight away that the other lady was Emma, all prim and pretty, just how Sadie had described her. So now Maudy had her eyes on Emma, all she needed to do was follow her into the lido.

I blew it for her, of course. She never expected me to run. But I did. And all of a sudden she saw her plan falling apart. But

Maudy's luck changed when she found a leaflet on the green, a leaflet drawn by Emma, with her address on it. She sent Henry to bring Emma to us. She knew he wouldn't say anything; he was born an idiot, how could he?

And so we were brought together, Emma and me. But as usual I wasn't making things easy for Maudy. I wasn't the little lady that Violet would have been and every time Emma came to the cottage I was there with dirty fingernails and a bird's nest on my head, cursing and cuddling dirty chickens. Maudy realized that Emma would never think that I was Violet unless they did something more.

'You had to become Violet,' Maudy said. 'So violets are what we gave Emma.'

There had been a decorator working at Emma's house, Maudy said, an old man. He was an absent-minded bugger, always muddling his words, leaving jobs half done and leaving the front door unlocked. And that is how Clarence got inside Little Willow. He would wait until Mr Tuttle had gone and steal the violets that the old man had left at the war memorial. Then he would slip inside and leave them all around. It was only little posies, mind, but Clarence knew that violets were the gift of Emma's lover, the name of her daughter and the posy on her incubator, Sadie had said as much. Emma wouldn't know where they had come from, so maybe she would take them as a sign of Violet's return. Maudy chuckled to herself when she said this, but I could only think about the time when the old man saw me, the way he had looked right through me like I was a ghost and then called me Violet.

When I had moved in with Emma, the house became emptier than ever. There were days out in the city, visits to Rose Cottage and to Missensham House. There were trips to buy toys and books and fittings for clothes in the London stores and all of this gave Clarence the chances that he had hoped for – time to let himself into Little Willow and mess with the wireless dial, steal sixpence from the mantelpiece, drink Dr Marks's sherry and move the old man's tools around. He found a baby's rattle buried deep in a gentleman's suitcase and gave it to me when I visited Rose Cottage, telling me that it was precious and knowing that it would find its way back to Emma's house with me when I returned. And little by little, I did not know it but, the ghost took over and I became Violet.

I sat on my apple crate, squirming as she talked. She chatted away, like a gossiping neighbour, chuckling all the time like none of it mattered. She clapped her hands together and slowed down at the important bits, just to make sure that we all shared in her pride.

'But it still weren't enough,' Maudy said excitedly. She told us how no decent trustworthy family would part with their daughter for money, and how no respectable lady from the Sunningdale Estate would want to buy a child. There had to be one last reason for the money to change hands – Maudy had to be dying.

In the darkness of the van Maudy hugged me so hard my arms went numb. Her breath smelled like dogs' meat and I fancied that she must have gnawed her cheek to a pulp. She'd only done it to get blood to spit in to a handkerchief, she said, and she'd had TB before, so it hadn't been hard for her to fake it. She was even laughing to herself. She was far from dead, not a doctor nor a sickbed for her now, not a blanket, not a handkerchief or a cough, not even a snivel. I wished she did have TB, I wished she was dead.

I wriggled free from her, but I caught Fatkins' eyes in the mirror and I was sure that he was watching me again.

'Spose we'll be learning a thing or two about vans like this in Birmingham, eh nephew?' Clarence chuckled to himself. 'There's jobs for mechanics and panel beaters in them factories. No, wait! We could buy one of these little vans for ourselves. We got the cash, we'd just need to hand it over, how's about that then?' His face was turned to Fatkins waiting for an answer but Fatkins didn't give one and his eyes didn't move from that mirror. 'What do you think, Ruby? Wouldn't you like to be driven about in a little van?'

I said nothing.

Maudy gave Fatkins a sly little glance. I wondered if she'd seen him watching me and she gave a nervous little laugh.

I started thinking again. I thought of the weird old man with the haunted eyes, calling me dead names. Two little photographs, like faded memories, the babies in them sleeping so deep that they might be dead. A little yellow room and a cot never slept in. I shook my head and tried to chase the thoughts away but they kept coming; broken vases, a rattle in a dead baby's hand, Emma's eyes turning all glassy. I thought of gloves hanging limp from the line, their fat fingers pointing and accusing me, and Emma's dress drowning in a bucket of blood. I closed my eyes and tried to think of a big house in a place called Birmingham, money and motorcars, but all I could see was blood spots on handkerchiefs and violets bringing bad luck and death. The van rattled metal through my head and the bitter carmine scoured my nose, my cheek started to throb as cruel memories returned. I could not be happy. Something wasn't right.

'Maudy,' I said. 'There's something I don't understand.'

'What's that, my special girl?' She looked at me, drawing her head closer so that she could hear over the engine noise.

'You remember you told me that Sadie would send the dead baby photographs to the parents, well why were there two photographs of Emma's baby and why was one of them in Aunt Sadie's cigarette case?'

Maudy made a little shushing noise and glanced quickly over her shoulder, then she opened her mouth. But suddenly her eyes grew large and she grabbed at the sideboard. There was a screech of metal. A bang.

The seat bucked under me and I flew across Maudy's lap, cracking my forehead on the sewing machine. Henry and Andy became a blur of arms and legs. Jim and John flopped about in their seats like rag dolls. The sideboard lurched, packets of carmine exploding from the drawers.

Then everything was still.

44

Emma

I met Violet on one occasion only. It was the meeting that I mentioned before, the one that had happened in the spring of 1926. That was the one and only time; I have not seen her since.

They had told me not to talk about the meeting, said that it would be bad for my nerves if I did. And of course George had lectured me about the evils of sentimentality and its effect on women and how such silliness could be overcome by a stiff upper lip and a good dose of Britishness. But how can I not talk about it when this memory is all I have? I have endured ghostly violets and silver rattles fresh from the grave and the apparition of a little girl with the mark of a long-mourned baby on her face. My nerves were shot to pieces long ago, so what does it matter now? Fuck not talking about it. Fuck sentimentality, fuck being British, fuck George. I've been silent for long enough.

I do remember the meeting. Of course I do, I remember everything – Every. Single. Thing. I remember the ward, the globes of light reflected in glass, the gleam of the scrubbed walls, the scour of the carbolic in my nostrils and the electrical hum of the incubator – that steel sarcophagus. I can feel the presence of the midwife and the baby. And I can feel the absences of the husband and the father, but these are all just details, there is more to tell, so much more.

Ten years may have passed but, in my mind, time has stood still and any careless daydream or little lapse of concentration can send me back to the hospital. I can be scrubbing the kitchen sink when a gust of carbolic in my nostrils will return me to that room with its scrubbed surfaces and shiny medical implements. The hum of electricity when I flick a light switch becomes the hum of the incubator and suddenly I am beside it again, hunched in a wheelchair, watching, waiting. If I walk at night the headlights of a car reflected in a shop window startle me and when I close my eyes I can see the purple ghosts of the ward lights. I still go back to that room. I go back often. Nothing is faded.

So to the midwife for a final time – Sadie, the missing piece. The one that binds the triangle together; mother, father and child. To me she was the stranger, the faceless woman in a uniform, but to her I was more than the patient in the wheelchair; I was her son's lover and the mother of his child, the one she blamed for his enlistment and deployment far away overseas. Some might have said that I was her daughter-in-law, but Sadie must have known that this could never be, not in the eyes of the law or God. She was a grandmother though, if only for a fleeting moment, and nobody could take that away from her.

She had her cape on, as if she had not wanted to remain but had been compelled to by circumstance. And she was tapping her foot, with impatience I had thought at the time, but now I can sense her anxiety. She felt for the baby more than I knew but could not show it. She placed a posy in the incubator, violets of course, but I do not know if they were from her or a sentiment from the absent father, the son who I had forced to leave her.

Then there was Violet – just a baby back then, and a baby she would stay forever. A baby that never had the chance to grow, a baby denied existence. The doctors had talked about the birthmark, that was true, but they had only mentioned it in passing as they peered into the incubator; small talk to avoid commenting on the real horror of what lay inside. Of course she was just a curiosity to them, a medical subject, and when they looked at her they would only see a tangle of slack flesh the colour of a bruise, a pathetic specimen, no more than a jumble of meat in a butcher's window. Their trained eyes would know that the subject was merely a semblance of life, with nothing flowing or connected, empty lungs and a still heart, nothing to support it in this hostile world. They did not have a mother's eyes, the eyes that would see a baby, a little girl, a name – Violet, my Violet, and they would not see that it was the birthmark, the final abomination, that marked her as mine.

And then there was me, Emma Marks. It does not matter who I had been up to that point; young, middle-aged, newlywed or adulterer. And all the little details that had concerned me so much at the time – those little worries such as the state of my hair, the midwife's impatience or the doctor's whispers – they do not matter either. What matters was what could not been seen, because over the past eight months I had changed, I had become a mother. The bond I had with Violet was severed when they wrenched her from my body, but such things do not happen without leaving wounds.

So I watched her. It was all I could do to focus on those tiny faltering breaths – the effort for each gasp of air, the shuddering ribcage, the gape of the mouth. In out, in out… my own breath held in anticipation… because I feared each breath to be the last.

Sadie knelt down next to me, her bag open beside her. She rummaged inside frantically, as if what she was looking for could not wait. I did not know what she sought back then, but now I know about the old Box Brownie that was hidden among the thermometers and boiling tubes. It was a camera that was to produce two photographs – one for each parent. But Sadie knew more than the words that were recorded on the birth certificate and she was to keep one photograph, not for George, but for her son. She must have thought it an innocent keepsake, but it was an image that would haunt so many people.

So, more about Sadie; the midwife, the professional, the starched uniform and the bedside manner. She spoke of the matron's rounds and Dr Marks's senior position, but her words were just diversions as her face spoke of something deeper. It was the expression that I could not quite read. But now I see the professional holding back her own tears – the attempt at a smile of reassurance and the tensed muscles and distant eyes masking worry and concern.

I did not know that she had seen the doctors' notes and the nurses' charts nor the death certificate prepared and waiting. I did not know that Violet was already dead to her, she had already moved on and now her look of concern was for me.

'Time to say goodbye to Violet,' she said.

'All right…' I said, this and only this because I did not know that would be the last time that I ever saw her.

'…Goodbye.'

45

Ruby

My name is Ruby Brown, but it should be Ruby Red – red like the glow of the broken stove. Red like a hot poker. Red like the burning of flesh and the scar left behind. Red like a broken heart.

There is one thing missing, of course, one thing that doesn't make sense. I know you are not stupid; you must be thinking it already. Well, you know I said that there was a Bad Thing that happened? The part of the story that I didn't want to talk about? That part you didn't want to know? Well this is that part…

My hand shook as I gave the mug back to Maudy, fire sliding down my throat.

Maudy's face swayed. 'A bit more, my chicken. Like I told you, gin is good for the flu. You need it to get rid of that cough.'

'I don't like it,' I said. 'It burns.'

'Yes it burns a bit, but it won't work unless you have more. You can do this – remember you are nine years old today, so show me you can be a big girl!'

'I can't,' I said. 'I feel funny. I want to go to bed.'

She leant forward and stroked my hair. 'Not yet,' she said and poured more into the mug.

Clarence sat in the chair by the stove. He was drinking too, half of the gin bottle already sloshing around in his tankard. He lifted it earnestly to his mouth, as if getting drunk was a solemn duty. Trails of smoke came up from his pipe. His legs were outstretched, warming on the stove that glowed and spat in the corner.

'I will put up with the coughing,' I said. 'It isn't so bad.'

Maudy gave Clarence a quick look, her eyes all wet like puddles. He stared back at her, raising the tankard slowly, as if thinking hard. Then something passed between them. It was that look that adults have when they know something;

something they won't share, that only they can understand. Then Maudy looked away quickly and stared into the fire, the embers shining in her eyes.

Clarence jumped up like he'd been stung. He slammed the mug on the table in front of me, and Maudy jumped in her skin.

'Drink it!' he screamed. His face was huge and his eyes wild. 'Don't stare at me, girl. Drink!'

I picked up the mug and swallowed the gin quickly, it slid down the corners of my mouth and burned a hot river inside me.

'Good girl,' he said. Then he went to sit back down, but he didn't. I heard the creak of his chair but he just slid away into darkness. I looked at the candle on the table, but the flame was circling, tracing snakes of light and the windowpanes were ghosting squares of purple.

'I'm going to bed,' but I didn't hear myself say it, just a noise, a grunt from swollen lips. I stood up, but my legs weren't there and I fell through the air, landing back on the chair. I held my head up with my hand. It was heavy, as if it would topple from my shoulders.

Maudy folded the blanket and put it behind my head. She was looking right through me, as if I was not there. She raised her hand and waved it slowly in front of my face. 'Gone!' she said.

Clarence came over, his body dark and blurred, but his hand was big next to my face. He put something on the table next to me. It was a copper basin, the one Maudy used to mix the dye. But there was no water inside. It was red – a mound of red carmine powder.

'I told you,' he said. 'I told you we'd need the whole mug.' His voice was hard like a thimble on a washboard. He took something from his pocket, something white and clean against his dark overalls. It was paper, a photograph. A grey print of a baby's head, a baby with a patchy face.

'Like this,' he said and they both stared at the photograph. 'It's important that we get it right. The pattern must match exactly. Three long marks and a longer one under the eye.'

The lamps flickered. Maudy breathed heavily. 'I ain't sure about this,' she said, but he glared at her and she lowered her head.

'What is it now?' he barked.

'She won't never believe us,' she said quietly. 'She won't never believe she fell.'

'She won't remember, will she? She'll have to believe us.'

Maudy was looking up at him, a ripple across her eyes.

Clarence strode across the room and kicked the stove door. It clattered as it fell away and sparks circled, smoke and soot filling the room.

Maudy screamed.

'There!' he shouted. 'That's what she did. That's where she fell. That's where the brat fell, you get a nasty burn from these things if you go running into them.' He came back over, his face was black with soot, making his eyes seem white and huge. 'Just hold her in case she wakes.'

She nodded, but she didn't move, just wrung her hands.

'That poker ready?'

She glanced at the fire but just mumbled.

'Well, go on then!' he shouted.

Then she was gone and I felt her hands pressing on my shoulders.

Clarence wrapped a rag round his hand and took the poker from the fire. I saw the end circling in the darkness. It clanked into the basin of carmine and the smell of burning filled the room. The powder in the bowl started to crawl like ants and Clarence lifted the poker in front of his face. He stared at the hot tip, twisting it in front of his eyes, like it was magical to him. Then he blew on it gently, and it glowed white, the light fading with his breaths.

I felt Maudy's hands start to tremble.

'No!' But the scream was inside my head and I heard only the click of my mouth opening.

Then the white metal was by my face, ghosting purple insight my head. I twisted against the chair, but Maudy's hands pressed hard on my forehead, pushing me down.

Then white heat. The smell of fire. Metal pressed hard into my cheek, then the ache of bone and teeth. Then there was only silence and all was black.

Like I told you, there are some things I don't like to talk about. This was the bit you didn't want to know.

46

Emma

Late that evening George left me for the last time. All he took with him was a small suitcase that he had packed several days ago and hidden in the back of the wardrobe. He did not take anything else; not his armchair, the wireless or his crystal decanter. These things, he said, had been bought for a house on the Sunningdale Estate and that is where they should stay. After all, they held too many memories. He did take Smokey though, bundling him into and old cardboard box and tying it carefully with string. He had never cared for children, but he liked cats.

I felt numb as I watched his car pull out of the driveway, the clatter of the engine deafening in the still air. Next door the bedroom light came on, the curtains twitching as the neighbours peered after the car that had woken them so rudely.

I went upstairs and tidied the back bedroom, putting the crumpled sheets and pillowcases into the washing basket. Ruby had left a small knitted rabbit on the windowsill and I took it into the nursery, placing it in the empty cot. I took the silver rattle and the old baby photograph of Violet from the sideboard and buried them deep in a drawer. Then I covered the cot and the furniture with sheets and drew the curtains across the dark windowpane. I stood on the landing and turned the key in the nursery door; the room sealed for good with the clunk of the lock.

In the lounge, the light switch clicked on and off in the darkness, the coil of wire and domed glass fitting still piled against the skirting board. I walked through the darkness and sat in the bay of the window, pulling my shawl tight around my shoulders as the chill of the night wafted under the curtains. The timbers of the house groaned and clicked and somewhere a pipe shuddered deep in the skirting.

Some hours later pale moonlight glowed through the crack

in the curtains, an owl calling out as if to encourage it. A narrow beam of cold light struck the mantelpiece and I saw both hands of the clock pointing to the twelve – it was the start of a new day.

Around me the walls and furniture emerged from the fog of darkness. The chairs were empty, a small indent in the sofa cushion where Ruby had once sat. On the mantelpiece was the jagged outline of the repaired vase; reminders everywhere, just as George had said.

Then the doorbell rang.

'Who's there?' I called.

47

Ruby

My name is Ruby Brown. It has always been Ruby Brown and never Violet Marks. There was a Violet, of course, a lone violet, the worst, the type that bring death. But this Violet never made it indoors, to her home at Little Willow, and the death she brought was her own. But when a violet dies, another can replace it. The new bloom will not be the same as the original, but a copy of it, like a memory returning.

'Why were there two photographs of Emma's baby and why was one of them in Aunt Sadie's cigarette case?'

It was just a question, I had not meant anything by it but, as soon as it left my lips, the van had stopped suddenly. We were flung against each other, furniture tumbling as if it was made of matchsticks and packing crates crashing onto the floor. For ages there was nothing but darkness and silence, and I sat up slowly, the screech of metal still ringing in my ears. Then, at last, came a long sigh, like everyone breathing together from one big lung.

'What the hell—' yelled Clarence. He raised a fist to Fatkins' face but the big man didn't even turn his head. He just sat dead still, his huge shoulders hunched over the wheel.

Clarence's fist fell back into his lap and he turned to look out the windscreen. The road was empty, the light from the headlights showing only two bright circles of nothingness. Somewhere next to me Maudy shuffled awkwardly.

Then I saw the windscreen mirror. And I saw those eyes again. Fatkins was watching me, his eyes frozen in the glass, all bright and blue and they were looking right at me.

I opened my mouth, but closed it again quickly. It was all my fault again; I wasn't sure why, but I knew that it was. Then the driver door flung open so hard that it slammed into the side of the van. Fatkins jumped out and crossed through the light beams. He wrenched open the passenger door and his face was right up close to Clarence's and I thought that he was going to punch him, but he didn't. He grabbed at the front of Clarence's overalls and pulled the purple envelope from his pocket.

'That's my money!' yelled Clarence. 'Where do you think you're going with it?'

'Where do you think? To give it back to this "grand lady" of yours. It's only thanks to Ruby's little remark that I know who she is now. This money isn't yours.'

'No, you can't do that to us!'

But what Clarence said didn't matter to Fatkins. He slammed the door shut and punched his fist into the side of the van, so hard that everything shook.

'I looked at that photograph every day that I was on duty,' he shouted. 'The other soldiers had wedding rings and pictures of their sweethearts but I just had my mother's cigarette case and a photograph of a dead baby. But it was more than that to me – it was a photograph of a family that I could have started, part of a life that I could have lived.'

'Darling, I am so sorry,' said Maudy quietly.

'You say that you're sorry? Oh yes, you're sorry for scabbing the odd shilling off me or for passing me shoddy tailoring or for making me drive you to Birmingham and for losing me a day's pay, but sorry isn't really enough now, is it?'

'We was going to give you some of the money,' said Clarence suddenly. 'We still can give you a good share of it, how's about that then? As for the baby, well, how was we to know that you cared so much? That ain't our fault. It was Sadie who had the photograph not you.'

'I gave the photograph back to my mother when I was sent home wounded,' shouted Fatkins. 'I was returning to a place with so many memories that I felt I didn't need any more reminders, so I gave the cigarette case back to her, and the photograph with it.'

'Shut up, Clarence,' hissed Maudy before he could even open his mouth. 'For once in your life just shut up.'

'Then years later I thought I saw the infant in the photograph again,' Fatkins wasn't shouting any more but he was talking all loud and slow. 'But then she wasn't a baby of course, she was a grown girl but the birthmark was still the same. But the girl I saw wasn't a ghost; she was Ruby, dear old Ruby, just the same as I had always known her, but now her cheek was marked. You all said that she had fallen but she wasn't going to talk about it with me – she had a secret she wasn't going to tell. At first I thought my memories were playing tricks on me. But then my mother told me that you had got hold of the photograph. I wanted it back; I didn't trust you but I still had no idea what you were planning. Now I see how it all happened. And I have to find it out from an innocent child!'

Then he was gone from the window and I heard his footsteps at the back of the van. He flung open the doors and apple crates and dining chairs crashed onto the road. He peered inside the van, but it was dark and he struggled to see me. 'Where are you, Ruby? Are you really so innocent in all this? Or are you as dishonest as the rest of your family?

He was right, my family were all liars. They had lied to me about what happened the day the stove got broken and they had lied to me about Maudy's illness. They had lied about who Emma was and why I was sent to stay with her. But Emma had lied too – she had wanted me to be Violet so badly that she had lied to herself about who she really was. But none of those lies would have happened without me. Through Maudy's cunning and Emma's longing, I had been the one forced into a life that should have belonged to another child, and that life had been a lie. I had not known it at the time, but I had become the liar.

'Nothing to say, Ruby!' Fatkins stared into the darkness. 'Come on! Someone must be able to tell me. How did you mark her to look like Violet? Did she really fall or do you paint the mark back on every morning? Come here, Ruby, so I can rub it off!'

I opened my mouth but the words stuck in my throat. I felt tears slide down my cheeks and my own sobs were all I could hear for the next few minutes. I felt Maudy's hand on my shoulder but I shook it away. 'It won't rub off,' I whispered at last. 'They burnt it on and it hurt me. It still hurts me.'

Maudy sucked in a quick little breath but she did not say anything, nobody said anything for what felt like ages. I suppose there was nothing more for anyone to say. Then at last, Fatkins said: 'I'm sorry, Ruby,' but his voice sounded all funny as if he was only saying the words because nobody else would, like he knew that I wouldn't hear them from Clarence or Maudy. Then his fist slammed into the side of the van. There was a loud bang and a ring of metal, the seats rocked and crockery tinkled beneath us. Then he hit out with another fist and then another and another until he was pounding the metal so hard that the seats quaked underneath us and thunder rang in my ears.

'Sadie, your devoted sister, was the baby's grandmother,' he yelled. 'But that meant nothing to you – you still went and did this! You stole the picture from her cigarette case so you could copy the baby's birthmark and even brand your own daughter for your little scam.'

'But—' began Clarence.

'You really didn't care, did you? All of that didn't mean a thing to you. All you wanted was money. You didn't care about Sadie or me or Emma or Ruby.'

'Look, just stop this for a moment,' said Clarence at last. 'Please get back in the van and listen,' but his voice wasn't like I had ever heard it before; it was all quiet and shaky.

'Yes, calm down, please,' said Maudy. 'Please calm down.'

'We can come to an arrangement,' whispered Clarence. 'Please remember I have children to provide for…'

I stopped listening. I thought of the photograph, remembering when I had first seen it tucked inside the cigarette case. I smelled the carmine wafting from the blanket against my face and my stomach started to churn. I touched the side of my cheek and it stung with heat. I closed my eyes but under my lids there was nothing but red. I felt the press of the poker on my face once more; the scour of the flesh and the ache of the bone. Then came the cold sweats of restless agony, the heat of the swelling and the blistering of the skin, the cracking of the scabs and the itch of the scars. I didn't want to talk about it, I didn't want to remember, but the memory was throbbing inside me – my skin my blood, my flesh, my bone – they burned me and they did not care. *They burned me.*

'Wait!' I shouted. 'Please wait!' I scrambled over the Singer and the rocking chair. There were hands pulling at my legs but I kicked myself free. And then I was standing on the road, next to Fatkins. 'I'm coming with you,' I said and the voice that said it wasn't one that I recognized but somehow it seemed like my own.

Fatkins stared at me, his mouth open and he just stood there a while like he couldn't decide what to do. But I stood with him and I was not going to move.

'You can't take it all from us,' said Clarence. 'Ruby and the money was both sides of the deal.'

And at that moment I saw the whole story like someone else was telling it and everything suddenly seemed clear: I saw Maudy, wheezing, her face swollen, coughing blood into a handkerchief; I saw Clarence's eyes staring at the tip of the white-hot poker; I saw Emma's face large over mine, her eyes all big and watery asking if I wanted to stay with her forever. I realized now what she was asking me. She had looked happy because she had believed it really could happen –she believed that she could have me forever and that was all that she had ever wanted.

'You burned your child!' shouted Fatkins. 'You burned her and then you sold her!'

There wasn't even a whisper from Maudy and I started to think that even she couldn't face the truth when she heard it like that.

But the truth meant nothing to Clarence. 'Without that money we can't make it to Birmingham,' he said. 'We would have to stay round here forever, begging favours from Sadie and you know she ain't never going to turn us down. All you have to do is give us back the money and we are gone. You won't have nothing to do with us ever again. Just give it back and we won't be no trouble to you no more.'

I didn't know what two hundred pounds bought but I knew that it was more money than I had ever heard of and more numbers than I could count. For a moment Fatkins held onto the envelope and suddenly I saw all us Browns walking back along the road in the darkness and opening the door of the cold empty cottage, unpacking all those apple crates and waking up the next morning to Clarence's swearing and the sound of Maudy's sewing machine like this day had never happened.

I looked up at Fatkins and then, ever so quickly, I thought that he glanced down at me, but he didn't look long enough to catch my eye. He flung the envelope back into Clarence's lap and slammed the door.

Maudy made a pitiful little cry like she had pricked her finger, but Fatkins didn't care, he just walked off, back past the van, glowing all red in the backlights for just a second, and then away into the darkness and he was gone.

I stood by the back of the van for what seemed like hours, just staring through the open doors but I didn't see my mother or brothers any more, just shapes in the darkness.

'Ruby!' It was only the sound of Clarence's voice that woke me and then I ran as fast as I could.

Somewhere behind me the van started up but then it shuddered and stopped like the engine didn't want to drive anywhere and all I could hear was the squelch of my feet as I flew over the mud.

Then I saw Fatkins in front of me, a shadow, moving along the hedge. I tried to catch up but my shoes cut into the back of my ankles and my lungs burned. 'Stop!' but it was just a whisper as if there was nothing left in my lungs.

I heard the van again, the engine failing over and over, but I didn't think of the people inside, for now they were just memories, and even the sound of the moaning engine was starting to fade as I ran further and further into the night.

But soon my breaths became long and heavy and my legs felt as if they would buckle and I had to slow down and walk. I started to cry again. I could still see Fatkins some way ahead of me but the lane around me was sunk into darkness with only a dull glow from behind the clouds to show where the moon was hidden, and I feared that I would be swallowed up into the night. I felt like I had walked further than I ever had walked before but I knew that I had to keep moving and, after what felt like forever, the road became lined with high hedges and I started to recognise the curves of the track and the shape of the hills.

It wasn't until we reached the bend in the lane with the twisted tree that Fatkins stopped. But he didn't go inside Rose Cottage, he didn't even look at it. He just stopped, like he was listening out for something, and then I knew that he was making sure that I could follow him. But he didn't stop for long and after a few seconds he started walking again, his bad leg dragging heavily in the mud.

'Fatkins,' I called. 'Please... Fat—, Mister Atkins.'

'It's Peter,' he shouted. 'My name is Peter.'

When the road opened up at the Missensham crossroads he stood and waited in the trees looking out over the road towards the war memorial. He still didn't look behind him, but now, at last, he waited for me to catch him.

Then he stepped out into the road. He rested his back on the memorial, crossing his legs and peering round the stone, like he didn't want to be seen. His chest was heaving and his hands were shaking. He looked at his pocket watch, but it was too dark to see the face or hands, but he did it anyway, like it was something that he did every day. I waited with him in silence.

Then the clouds shrank away and the moon glowed big and bright. Now I could see Emma's house but it was smaller and greyer than I remembered. The car with the owl eyes was not there and the drive looked empty without it. But the house was not asleep – there was a crack in the curtains, as if a tiny part of it had stayed awake to wait for the morning.

Then an owl called out into the night.

Peter waited for it to finish. Then he took a deep breath, he gathered himself up and he walked up to the house and I followed him. He rang the doorbell.

'Who's there?' said a voice.

Peter looked worried and for a few moments he just stood there like he didn't know what he should do. He opened his mouth, the big knot in his throat drawing low like he was going to say something, but he just wiped his hands on his trousers and shut his mouth again. He shook his head slowly and then he looked at me. I looked up at him but he just smiled and nodded his head.

'It's Violet,' I said. 'Violet Marks.'

We hope you enjoyed this book!

The next novel from Jennifer Wells will be released in winter 2017

More addictive fiction from Aria:

Find out more
http://headofzeus.com/books/isbn/IS9781784977146BN

Find out more
http://headofzeus.com/books/isbn/9781784977177

Find out more
http://headofzeus.com/books/isbn/9781786690814

Acknowledgements

I would like to thank the strangers who inspired me – The chatty office cleaner who told me that violets brought bad luck indoors, and the builder who said that the draughty vents in my 1930s house had been put there to prevent the spread of tuberculosis.

I would also like to mention the place that inspired me – Missensham – in reality not one town but many; the area where I was raised on the outer reaches of the Metropolitan line where the blackened London tube trains rattle through meadows and trees.

I would also like to thank my partner, James, and Alison Bonomi at LBA for reading the early drafts of my work and for the people at LBA and Aria who made it possible to share this story.

About Jennifer Wells

JENNIFER WELLS works in Market Research when not writing. She lives in Devon with her young family and cat. *The Liar* is her first novel, she is busily working on her next…

Find me on Twitter
https://twitter.com/jenwellswriter

Become an Aria Addict

Aria is the new digital-first fiction imprint from Head of Zeus.

It's Aria's ambition to discover and publish tomorrow's superstars, targeting fiction addicts and readers keen to discover new and exciting authors.

Aria will publish a variety of genres under the commercial fiction umbrella such as women's fiction, crime, thrillers, historical fiction, saga and erotica.

So, whether you're a budding writer looking for a publisher or an avid reader looking for something to escape with – Aria will have something for you.

Get in touch: aria@headofzeus.com

Become an Aria Addict
http://www.ariafiction.com

Find us on Twitter
https://twitter.com/Aria_Fiction

Find us on Facebook
http://www.facebook.com/ariafiction

Find us on BookGrail
http://www.bookgrail.com/store/aria/

Addictive Fiction

First published in the UK in 2016 by Aria, an imprint of Head of Zeus Ltd

Copyright © Jennifer Wells, 2016

The moral right of Jennifer Wells to be identified as the author of this work has been asserted in accordance with the Copyright, Designs and Patents Act of 1988.

All rights reserved. No part of this publication may be reproduced, stored in a retrieval system, or transmitted, in any form or by any means, electronic, mechanical, photocopying, recording, or otherwise, without the prior permission of both the copyright owner and the above publisher of this book.

This is a work of fiction. All characters, organizations, and events portrayed in this novel are either products of the author's imagination or are used fictitiously.

9 7 5 3 1 2 4 6 8

A CIP catalogue record for this book is available from the British Library.

ISBN (E) 9781786691071

Aria
Clerkenwell House
45-47 Clerkenwell Green
London EC1R 0HT

www.ariafiction.com

Printed in Great Britain
by Amazon